C000145313

STAR FIGHTER CHARLIE

THE DRAGON MAGE BOOK 5

SCOTT BARON

Copyright © 2019 by Scott Baron

All rights reserved.

Print Edition ISBN 978-1-945996-27-6

No part of this book may be reproduced in any form or by any electronic or mechanical means, including information storage and retrieval systems, without written permission from the author, except for the use of brief quotations in a book review.

A NOTE ABOUT SERIES OVERLAP

Dear Readers,

A friendly note regarding spoilers.

The Dragon Mage series will begin featuring more crossovers with the Clockwork Chimera series characters from here on out. If you've read that series, no worries, you're all good.

If not, just be forewarned that some unavoidable spoilers will be popping up in future books in Charlie's series. Having read Daisy's series is **not** needed to continue on Charlie's journey, but I felt it only fair to warn readers of potential spoilers.

"We are gods in the chrysalis."
– Dale Carnegie

CHAPTER ONE

"What do you mean we're under attack?" the confused AI repeated for the third time.

Dukaan clenched his teeth as he worked. "I mean something is attacking us, Kip," his Chithiid pilot replied, all four arms quickly operating the controls beneath his dexterous hands. "It seems rather obvious, I would think."

The ship rocked yet again from an invisible impact, though no visible attacker was to be seen. The poor AI finally had to admit that it was not merely a faulty sensor reading or two. *Something* was definitely trying to blast them from the sky, and whatever type of stealth tech it was using, they simply had no means of scanning it.

"Right, well, that's not cool at all," Kip said, spinning one hundred eighty degrees and loosing a spray of small pulse fire in his wake.

They were far enough out in the space between Earth and the sun that the blazing rounds would not accidentally strike their home on Dark Side moon base or any of the other ships in the very sparsely populated fleet. Most were still far, *far* away, anyway, surveying distant systems and hoping for first contact with new intelligent species.

Dukaan happened to *be* of one of the alien species that came from far out in a distant solar system. A Chithiid, to be precise. Former enemies of the human race, in a manner of speaking, who were now their close allies. It hadn't been an easy transition for the towering, four-armed, four-eyed aliens, but they were now a fully integrated part of Earth society, and that included operations in and around the formerly secret moon base.

"Sid, we're under attack and can't seem to shake whoever's dogging us," the ship called out over comms to the distant lunar facility.

It would take several seconds for the message to reach its intended recipient at this range, and he spent that time engaged in very evasive maneuvers. Finally Sid, the powerful military AI mind in control of Dark Side Base, crackled over his comms.

"I've received your message and have dispatched three ships to assist you," Sid replied. "They will launch and be at your position in two minutes."

"Great. We could really use some heavy firepower covering our butt. I hope you sent the big guns," Kip transmitted.

A long silence hung in the cockpit as the message made its way to the AI on the moon. It continued to stretch out as they awaited a reply.

"Negative," Sid's voice finally said. "Heavy cruisers are still out of system. We're pulling the training fleet from drills and sending them to you."

"They're what?" Kip said as his hull shook with another blast of the strange energy.

"He said they're sending the training--"

"I heard what he said, Dookie. But those kids haven't got a clue how to fly in real combat."

"You began the same way, if I recall correctly," the Chithiid said. "Pushed into service after a hasty transplant into a small ship."

"Shut up. I know where I came from. But this is different."

"You were a toaster, Kip. An artificially intelligent toaster."

"Hey, I've been greatly upgraded since then. And that's not the point--"

Smoke wafted in the air as a relay overloaded from another barrage, the force trying its best to tear the ship asunder.

"Okay, we don't have time to wait for the FNGs to get here," Kip said.

"The what?"

"I'll tell ya later," the ship replied. "Gird your loins, or whatever you have. This is gonna suck," Kip blurted mid-dive as he diverted even more power to the rear shield generators.

"You're going to get us killed!" Dukaan grunted as his AI friend abruptly changed course yet again, twisting into a corkscrew spin before performing a flat one-eighty once more, spraying pulse fire all around at their invisible attacker as he hit the gas.

"Well, I don't have much of a choice, do I?" Kip grumbled. "That is, unless your four eyes are better than my scanners."

"That is not fair. You know two of them are situated toward the rear of my head. That is not a tactical advantage whilst riding within a spaceship."

"It was a joke, Dookie."

"I do wish you would stop calling me that."

"It's a nickname. You know those are a sign of friendship and endearment on Earth, right?" the quirky ship replied as it was shaken by yet another invisible assault.

"Perhaps," Dukaan replied. "But I asked the others why they were laughing every time you spoke my name. They informed me of the meaning of this moniker."

Kip let out a little chuckle despite the strain of his evasive maneuvers.

"Well, not all terms of endearment are sugar and spice, ya know. Hang on."

"What does this have to do with foodstuffs?" the Chithiid asked before abruptly passing out from the smashing g-forces that assailed his body as Kip banked hard, tumbling with the impact of whatever the hell it was that hit him yet again, despite his very evasive maneuvers.

He had been lucky so far, and whatever it was that had been targeting him seemed to either have very underpowered weapons, or was simply unable to pierce his state-of-the-art phasing shield array, courtesy of the greatest military minds on Dark Side's shipyards. Whatever the case, however, the upgraded AI ship knew better than to keep swinging wildly in a fight against someone he couldn't see.

Eventually, that's how you get knocked the fuck out.

"Hang on, Dookie. I'm getting us out of here."

Kip quickly powered up his warp drive and plotted the most perfunctory of courses to the far edge of the system. He didn't really care where, he just needed to get away. Anywhere was better than here at the moment.

"Sid, I'm performing an emergency warp. I'll contact you on the other side," Kip said.

The AI ship shuddered and shook as more of whatever his attackers were throwing at him struck home, but then, in a crackling blue flash, he was gone.

Standing on the bridge of his shimmer-cloaked ship, Captain Jimtee stared out of the magically sealed windows of his attack ship with an interested look in his eye.

"It has vanished," his lead pilot said, relaying the information calmly despite the surprising nature of the event.

"Yes, Ulus, it appears to have done precisely that," Captain Jimtee said. "And with no trace of magic, it would seem." The green-skinned man stroked his chin a moment as he pondered their situation.

"Shall we attempt to track them, sir?" Ulus asked.

"No," the captain replied. "We have gained much in the way of knowledge this day. And that was but a small taste of a much larger meal." Captain Jimtee walked to the magically sealed doorway leading from the command area of his ship. "I will be in my chambers," he said. "There is much to study of our new adversaries. Skree over to Captain Fratt's ship. Tell them I wish to have a face-to-face discussion with their captain as soon as they've completed their survey."

"It shall be done immediately, Captain," Ulus replied.

"Good. We have many strange new enemies in this realm, and we are drastically outnumbered. But we shall do our duty. We shall find their weaknesses and win the day no matter the odds."

CHAPTER TWO

Charlie and his dragon friend were lounging comfortably on the shores of Malibu when the call came in. But Charlie wasn't home, and he'd left his comms unit on the kitchen counter.

They'd just saved the planet a few days prior--quite literally--having thrown a magical portal-creating device into the heart of the sun in a daring, last-minute effort to protect Earth. As such, Charlie thought they deserved a little break.

While their young friend Ripley was excitedly showing off her newly acquired magical skills to her parents--courtesy of a neuro-stim upload in a time of dire need--the others were also taking a decidedly more low-key approach to their recovery time.

Bawb and Hunze had been inseparable since she was unfrozen from the spell that had subjugated the entire population, people and animals alike. For the deadly assassin known as the Geist, it had been unbearable seeing her like that. Frozen in stasis, not moving, not aging, just locked in time, touchable, but entirely out of reach.

He had been beside himself with anxiety and a plethora of other emotions, ranging from rage to depression. For the master assassin, that meant his frown would sometimes deepen, or perhaps you might even see the slight hint of a vein throbbing on his temple.

Bawb the Wampeh assassin was not one to show his cards, though his friends had finally learned some of his tells, hard as they were to see.

Hunze, on the other hand, was an open book, and the looks the golden-haired Ootaki gave her man made it clear that her feelings had only grown stronger since she gifted him half of her magic-storing hair out of love, an act that had amplified its magical potential exponentially. Having been a slave to the Council of Twenty her whole life, living with the man she adored in peace and freedom was more than she'd ever dared hope for.

As for the other woman previously enslaved and mistreated by a member of the Council, Rika had at long last begun to shed the burden of the experience.

The thing helping her slip back into her old self and finally feel truly free of the horror inflicted on her by those who wiped her mind in that distant galaxy, was the fact that she now had a ship of her own to fly. The cockpit was her happy place, and she was indeed happy.

In a world where so many craft were guided by AIs, having the artificial minds who oversaw the planet gift her so fine a vessel was kind of a big deal. But, like the others, being a savior of the planet afforded you certain perks. In the case of the former pilot turned magic caster turned world saver, it was one of the fastest, most maneuverable craft they'd turned out since the end of the Great War against Earth's alien invaders all those years prior.

Rika had used a far lesser ship to help steer the deadly portal-carrying shell of her former craft into the sun. After her performance with that one, even rivaling the abilities of some lesser AIs, the big brains had decided to upgrade her.

She named her ship *Fujin*, after the Japanese god of wind, and given the speed and maneuverability of her new toy, the name was quite apt. And with Rika Gaspari at the controls, the *Fujin* was already performing aeronautical and extra-atmospheric feats the AI pilots simply would never have thought to attempt.

A kid in a candy store, some might say.

"Charlie! Cal's trying to reach you!" Leila called down to the beach, where her king was lazing in the sun with his Zomoki friend.

"Tell him I'll call back later," he called back up to his olive-skinned queen. "We deserve a little break, and it's a really nice day."

"It is at that," Ara agreed. "And the fish are plentiful," she added, her belly full from her recent meal.

"Why don't you come down and join us?" Charlie asked. "The sun feels awesome."

"Charlie, I'm serious. Cal wouldn't be calling if it wasn't important," she persisted.

Unfortunately, he knew she was right. The massive AI controlling all aspects of life in the Los Angeles area would have been perfectly happy to leave them to their own devices for a bit, especially given what they'd so recently been through. For him to be interrupting their downtime, it must be something important.

With a little grumble, Charlie rose to his feet, dusting the fine sand from his body.

"Okay, okay. I'll be up in a minute. Tell him I'll call him right back."

Leila nodded and walked back to their house, which was a rather impressive estate on the bluffs of Malibu. One of the perks of settling down in a place where the population had been eradicated but the buildings were left unscathed.

He tried not to think about that part of the Great War. They benefited from it, after all. But every once in a while, the thought of an alien race nearly succeeding in wiping out humanity gave him a sudden flash of unease.

"You coming?" he asked his dragon friend as she lay basking in the sun, soaking up the rays that fueled the magic naturally flowing through her kind.

"No, I believe I will stay here a bit longer, if you don't mind. The sun is quite strong today, and it really does feel wonderful. But if you need me, I'm here for you."

"Thanks, Ara," he said silently, his mind speaking to hers through their silent connection.

"Of course," she replied with a warm grin and a cheerful crinkling around her massive, golden eyes.

Charlie gathered his things, took one final look at the clear skies and glistening blue waters of the Pacific, then turned for the little trail leading back up the bluffs to his home.

Whatever it is, I hope Cal and the other AIs can handle it this time. But if they're calling us, that's probably not the case, he mused. *But at least it can't be another magical attack.*

CHAPTER THREE

"It appears to be a magical attack," Cal said when Charlie came on the line.

"Goddamn it, Cal. For real?"

"I'm afraid so," the AI said.

"Well, that's just great. I mean, we just fended off a freakin' alien takeover attempt, took out not one, not two, but *three* Tslavar scout ships, as well as their mercenary crews, and then, oh yeah, we shot their booby-trapped portal-generating Trojan Horse into the sun. You'd think we'd get maybe at least a week without the shit hitting the fan, yet again."

Leila began to gently rub his tense shoulders. Her touch reminded him of what he still had to be thankful for, and in her own way, she defused his anger and stress far better than the local shrink ever could.

"Sorry, Cal. I don't mean to go off on you. I was just kind of enjoying some downtime, ya know?" he apologized.

"I understand your frustration, Charlie. Believe me, none of us expected another attack so soon. Given that the portal generator is now safely resting in the sun, the odds were slim, to say the least."

"And yet, here we are," Charlie replied, pinching the bridge of his nose. It was looking like a headache kind of a day.

"Ara, you'd better come up here," he sent to his friend down on the beach.

"Is there a problem?"

"Oh, you could say that," he silently replied. *"Looks like we didn't get all of those bastards last week. I've got Cal on the line now. He's giving us a rundown."*

"I'll be right there," she said, smoothly rolling to her feet, then leaping into the air, the wind blowing away Charlie's footprints as she flapped her enormous wings.

It was just a quick hop up to Charlie and Leila's place, and when she touched down on the sprawling yard overlooking the ocean, her friend had already routed Cal's comms to the outside vid screen set up for just such occasions.

"Hello, Cal," the Zomoki said.

"Hello, Ara. It is nice to hear your voice, though I am sorry to have disturbed your leisure time."

"If the Tslavars are back, there is certainly nothing to apologize for," she replied. "Now, tell me, what happened? Did we miss a ship hiding out somewhere? I thought we had devised a means to track them via bioluminescence in the sea, and temperature and water vapor fluctuations in the air."

"And those methods should work," Cal replied. ***"However, this was not a terrestrial attack that caught our attention, but rather an encounter by one of our recently returned AI ships and his Chithiid pilot."***

"The ones who have been scouting other systems?" Charlie asked.

"Indeed. This ship—Kip is his name—just returned the other day."

"But why was he attacked? Didn't other vessels return in recent days as well?" Leila asked.

"A few. But over ninety-five percent of the exploratory fleet are still away doing their surveys," Cal noted.

"Are we sure it was a magical attack? I mean, if he was the only one to have issues, it seems kind of strange, don't you think?"

"Normally I would agree, Charlie, but in this case, the description and recordings of the incident gel with what we have seen in the past. A magical attack by an unseen enemy."

"Were they badly damaged?" Leila asked.

"No. Kip is installed in a very robust craft. He was one of the original AIs involved in the retaking of Earth all those years ago, and as such, he has been afforded frequent upgrades."

"Earned it," Charlie noted.

"I agree one hundred percent," Cal said. *"And his highly advanced phase shielding seems to have easily deflected the main force of the attack. But he was tossed around something fierce, and had the attack persisted, there is little doubt he would have eventually suffered structural damage despite his shielding."*

"But why him, Cal?"

"It would appear the only reason Kip was targeted was because of his proximity to the sun," the AI replied. *"Upon his return to Dark Side Base, he was fascinated to learn what had transpired in his absence. Being a rather 'unusual' intelligence, he decided to go see for himself, though I told him repeatedly there was nothing to see but the burning mass of the sun."*

"But he went anyway," Ara stated. "And that was how he drew the attention of the hostile craft. But what can you tell us about them? The vessels we encountered recently were not highly maneuverable attack craft. This sounds as if it was something different."

"Yes, Ara, I believe it was. And backtracking all traces of energy in that area for the week leading up to the incident, it seems clear that this ship came from the portal."

That caught Charlie's attention. "Cal, we dropped that thing into the freaking sun. There's no shielding powerful enough to withstand that. Not in our galaxy, and sure as hell not in theirs."

"I agree with that assessment," Cal said. ***"However, there was an unusual surge of energy just before you dropped the*** **Asbrú*****, and the portal it was generating, into the sun."***

Charlie knew what Cal was going to say. He remembered it clearly.

"The bright flash, Ara. Remember? Right when the portal spell kicked in. So bright we had to look away."

"I recall," the Zomoki said. "But if that is true, then we are undoubtedly dealing with the frontmost craft in the assault fleet that was waiting on the other side."

"And they wouldn't send slow, weak ships through first," Charlie realized. "So whatever came through, it's gonna be fast, powerful, and dangerous."

"Precisely."

"Just our luck," he griped. "All right, let's brainstorm this, then. Is there any way to know what came through? I mean, it's obviously a shimmer ship of some sort, based on Kip's report. And for a shimmer to be that effective in space, it must be a huge power draw."

"But a shimmer that powerful would also mask the power being used to feed it," Ara noted.

Leila was studying the replay Cal had brought up of the engagement on the small screen off to the side when something dawned on her. "Cal? You said this ship came through just before the portal fell into the sun, correct?"

"That is correct."

"Then it had to come into direct contact with a massive amount of the sun's energy, and no matter how powerful the shimmer is, that should provide us some sort of marker we can trace, right?"

"But, Leila, we're in a system full of that power," Charlie noted.

"I know, but this is different. Because it won't be radiating like normal sun rays."

"A good point. The solar power's rate of decay should be constant as you travel from the sun, but if a ship is moving about at different speeds and in different directions—" Cal noted.

"Oh, shit! That's brilliant!" Charlie blurted. "Then you could trace that anomaly even within our own solar system. Leila, you're amazing!" he said, kissing her joyfully. He turned to his giant friend. "Ara, do you think you could––"

"I'll be ready to go long before you get your space suit on," she replied. "Though I think, given our last run-in with these Tslavars, it would be wise to bring along backup."

"Bob and the others wouldn't forgive us if we didn't," Charlie replied with a laugh. "I'll get them on the horn. Let's gear up and go hunting."

CHAPTER FOUR

"Oh, you've got to be kidding me," Rika groaned, immediately regretting answering her comms.

"Sorry, Rika, but it's for real," Charlie apologized.

Rika was not amused. Not only was she finally getting some downtime to tinker with her new ship, but she and Joanne, the cyborg mechanic Cal had sent to help, had finally achieved something of a comfortable rapport despite their bumpy start.

And while Jo might have been artificially created, the cyborg was, much to Rika's surprise, proving to be a much-needed ear for the woman who found herself still healing from the mental trauma she'd endured at the hands of alien captors.

But now that was looking like it was about to change.

"Seriously, Charlie? We just saved the goddamn world. I think we deserve a rest."

"Couldn't agree with you more. Hell, Ara and I were just enjoying a nice bit of sunbathing on the beach when the call came in."

"How does a forty-ton dragon sunbathe?"

"Same as anyone else. Though in her case we skip the sunblock."

"Since she absorbs the rays like an energy-hungry sponge, I suppose that makes sense," Rika noted. "But seriously, Charlie. Can't the AIs handle this one? I deserve a freaking rest. You deserve a rest. We all do."

"I know, but from what Cal says--"

"No, this is bullshit! I need time. You always tell me to take care of myself. Well I'm trying."

"Really? You listened to me? That's a first," he joked.

"Seriously. I've been trying to smooth out the rough spots in my head from hastily loading up more spells from the neuro-stim files Bawb and Ara made. It's a lot of magic, Charlie, and my brain was royally fucked with."

"I know. Malalia did a number on you."

"And the Tslavars before her. But now that we're safe--or *were* safe--I was hoping to get my noggin back to normal."

"Understandable."

"Yeah. But it seems like eighty percent of those spells are hitting some kind of residual block from Malalia's mindfuck. Or maybe the Tslavars' messy damage. Or both, who the hell knows? But the resulting mess is not pleasant, to say the least."

"Damn. That sucks."

"Yeah, it does. And the headaches have been a killer. It's like those traces of her meddling are still fouling my fuel lines, so to speak."

"Have you asked Cal about it?"

"Of course. But he just says it's some kind of systemic interference that their technology can't do anything about. So some spells I can tap into just fine--"

"Like the force tunnel one you and Rip used to rescue me and Leila from that sub."

"Exactly. But others--even seemingly simple ones--they're bugging the hell out of me, but they just won't flow. Like, I have all of that knowledge there, but something keeps stirring the pot and muddying them, no matter how hard I try to let it be. It's frustrating as hell, Charlie."

"I can imagine," he commiserated. And he honestly could imagine. Being a human himself and having to learn to use magic in a distant galaxy under less than hospitable circumstances had been one hell of a challenge. One that, at first, he didn't know if he'd even survive.

But Charlie was nothing if not stubborn, and eventually the magic stuck. His blood bond with a Zomoki might have helped in that regard, but the basics of it all, the learning of the spells in the first place, had been all him.

"In any case," he said, "we've got a problem, and it looks like we're going to need all magic-using hands on deck. So, much as I'm sorry to say it, you need to gear up and meet us in orbit. That is, if your ship is in shape to make the run."

"Hey, Jo. Is the *Fujin* ready for space flight?" she called out to her mechanic.

"She's been ready all day. I'm just installing the new warp coupling Cal sent over. It's pretty cool, too. Usually, he's kinda stingy with the top-notch tech."

"Well, we did just save the solar system," Rika noted.

"Yeah, I guess that may have greased his wheels a little," Jo replied with a chuckle.

Rika turned her attentions back to her comms.

"Yeah, we're good to go."

"Excellent. Then gear up. We'll meet you up top."

Not far from Charlie's ocean-view home, Bawb and his golden-haired mate were engaged in a meditative exchange of a different type.

Neuro-stim bands were resting on each of their heads as the couple lay side by side, fingers intertwined as the gentle exchange of magical knowledge transferred from the deadliest man in thirty systems to his sweet and demure love.

Being in a galaxy so far from the one in which he had once sworn a blood oath to never reveal the secrets of his order, the assassin known as the Geist reasoned those rules simply didn't apply here. And even if they did, this was Hunze he was talking about. The Ootaki he had rescued from slavery. For this one woman, he'd have broken them willingly, regardless of which galaxy he inhabited.

Having so nearly lost her during the Tslavar attack that had frozen all of the population, Bawb was determined to do all he could to ensure she was properly prepared to defend herself if he was not present.

The ironic thing was Hunze, being an Ootaki, was a natural-born creator of enormous magical power, which she stored in her golden hair. And that hair had been growing since birth, a massive length braided and wrapped around her body, decades of power stored and ready for anyone but her to use.

For Ootaki could not wield the magic they held. It was one of nature's little jokes. The most powerful of beings were wholly unable to utilize so much as a drop of the magic potential they carried. And even though she'd gifted half of her hair to Bawb, an act of pure love that tied the power to him and him alone, Hunze still possessed an incredible reservoir of magic growing from her head.

She had been quickly learning the spells Bawb was teaching her, the neuro-stim playing a key role in her rapid absorption of the arcane knowledge. In short order, she possessed a treasure trove of magic, both benign and deadly. Sadly, however, even with one of Bawb's finest magically charged konuses, she was woefully bad at casting spells.

Leila had posited it might be a residual effect of her natural-born inability to use her own magic bleeding over to the use of external power sources as well. Much as he hated to admit it, Bawb gave credence to that assessment.

Nevertheless, the couple spent several hours every day, slowly adding to her stockpile of knowledge in hopes that perhaps, if they got lucky, she would be able to at least protect herself should they come under attack once more.

"Bob, why aren't you picking up?" Charlie said over the comms. "We're under attack again. Come on, man, answer!"

The Wampeh slowly pulled himself from the neuro-stim link with Hunze and padded over to the table where his comms lay.

"What is it, Charlie? I am rather preoccupied at the moment."

"Looks like they're back," his friend replied. "We're not sure exactly who, what, or how many, but there's definitely a magic source out in space. One of our ships was getting its ass kicked by it and had to do an emergency warp out of here, but not before relaying what was going on."

Bawb furrowed his brow.

"This is bad, Charlie. We disposed of the portal. No one can fly through it while it is deep within the sun. There should be no other vessels from my galaxy."

"I know. But something's up. Leila's gonna ride with Ripley and Eddie, and Rika's already heading to orbit. Grab your suit. I'll have Ara swing by in a few minutes."

Reluctantly, Bawb roused Hunze from her neuro-stim-powered nap. "Charlie just messaged us. There appears to be some form of magical vessel in the system."

"But you destroyed them all," she said.

"So we thought," he replied, sliding a powerful konus onto her wrist. "In any case, we are to fly out to engage whatever this is."

"Bawb, you know I'm no good at casting," she replied, looking at the konus.

"Perhaps. But I feel better if you wear it. And I shall have Ripley and Eddie pick you up as well. Leila will be flying with her, and the Magus stone she possesses should protect you if something happens."

He just hoped it wouldn't come to that.

CHAPTER FIVE

After what had so recently transpired with shimmer-cloaked Tslavar vessels and a booby-trapped Trojan Horse ship damn near succeeding in overthrowing the planet--and opening a portal to another galaxy in the process--what might otherwise have seemed like a bit of over preparation actually made perfect sense.

The team's weapons stockpiles had been topped off and greatly added to after their recent victory. All of their magical items had received a full charge of energy, courtesy of Bawb, channeling magic from the incredibly powerful hair gifted to him by Hunze, and Ara, imbuing them with hefty doses of her uniquely Zomoki-flavored magic.

Of course, there were conventional weapons galore as well, ranging from bladed ones, to projectile shooters, all the way to pulse rifles, and even a few plasma guns. They'd only just begun working on portable rail gun tech, but the larger-scale one already mounted on Eddie the AI's ship was being replicated at great speed, the first of the modified new units put into service affixed to Rika's new ship along with her pulse cannons.

And now they were about to fly off into space, once again

putting themselves in harm's way to defend the planet. It seemed this was becoming a habit.

"You guys load up on extra ammo and pulse charge packs?" Charlie asked Ripley as Hunze and Leila lugged their gear aboard her ship.

"Dude, really?" the teen snarked back at him.

"Yes, really. Only a fool doesn't triple-check every last thing before a mission. Remember the saying, 'Proper prior planning prevents piss-poor performance.'"

"You just make that up?"

"I wish," he replied. "Had that little tidbit drilled into my head way back in Basic Training many moons ago, and it's still as relevant today as ever."

"Yeah, well, fine. To answer your question, yes, I stocked up on extra ammo. And a shit-ton of sabots for Eddie's rail gun. Isn't that right, buddy?"

"It's awesome!" the AI ship practically squealed. "We finally got to get in some proper practice time at the targeting range, and holy crap, this thing is so much fun! Zero recoil, and it's stupid accurate, and in space, the range is amazing!"

The fact that what was essentially a teenage AI was in possession of such a ferocious weapon of destruction would normally have put Charlie more than a little on edge. But given his exemplary performance when the fate of the world was on the line, and the fact that he'd been instrumental in preventing their alien attackers from opening the portal to their home galaxy on schedule, Charlie found himself entirely okay with it.

"Glad to hear it, Eddie. Now, I expect you to take good care of the ladies, okay?"

"Of course. They'll be perfectly safe."

"That's the right answer," Charlie said, turning to his friends as they carried duffle bags of weapons and supplies into the ship. "You guys doing okay?"

"We're fine," Leila said, hefting a load of magical devices aboard. "What about you guys?"

Charlie turned to Ara and Bawb. The dragon was sporting a new tactical harness built for her by Cal's fabrication facilities. It was light, non-restrictive, and allowed Charlie and Bawb to strap in far more securely for both atmospheric and space flight.

Additionally, it afforded a much easier carrying of extra supplies, such as their new armored guidance and comms package that allowed them to communicate with Cal and the other AIs from greater distances than their suit comms normally allowed.

After the recent events on Earth, they all figured it would be a wise choice if the most powerful members of their team didn't have to rely on relaying messages through a nearby ship.

"Okay," Charlie said as he looked over the nearly ready team. "Rika should be up in orbit waiting for us. Let's get the last of this stuff loaded and get a move on. No telling what kind of trouble we'll find out there."

"We're not ready," Jo said, tightening a bolt with her ratchet.

"Jo, we have to go. Now," Rika insisted, stowing the last of her supplies in one of the *Fujin*'s storage lockers. "Look, just take your tools and stuff and get clear. There'll be plenty of time to do all of this when I get back."

The cybernetic mechanic gave her one hell of a side-eye for a machine. "Oh, really now? Let you go flying off in this bucket with its warp system still not online? I think not."

"I'm serious, Jo."

"So am I," she shot back.

"But we're not even leaving the system. I don't even need the warp to work right now."

"I thought you didn't want to deal with any more magic for a while. You said no matter how cool it may seem, magic ruined your life. Stole your past. And now you're raring to jump back into a magical fight?"

Rika was silent a moment. It was true, she had confided in her new friend her deepest feelings about magic. It was a neat party trick and a useful tool, obviously, but every time she used her skills--magical talents forced into her brain against her will--it reminded her of who she had been, and what she had lost.

She had a new life now, and was making new memories with her friends, but that didn't change the fact that a violence had been done to her, and she'd never be the same because of it. She had been very much looking forward to settling into a non-magical life and getting busy with the business of healing. But not today. Today, she was needed.

"I don't have a choice, Jo. Like it or not, I have skills the others may need. Now grab your stuff and get clear. I've got stuff to do."

Jo assessed the tough woman standing before her a moment, arms crossed, thinking.

"Look, Rika," she finally said, "you're the pilot, and you want to get out there and do that pilot thing. I get it, really, I do. But I'm your wrench, and I can't just let you go flying off with this ship in a state of disrepair."

"It's not in a state of disrepair. It flies just fine. And from what I can tell, it's only the warp that's not online."

"Well, yeah. The warp, which is a crucial part of any advanced ship's propulsion systems, I would remind you. And further, I would also remind you that I am a cybernetic organism, meaning I can handle the g's you pull with ease, while still doing my work."

Rika had gotten to know her cyborg mechanic pretty well over the past several days together working on her new ship, and despite their somewhat frequent headbutting over how best to do things, she couldn't help but like the woman.

And knowing her as she did now, she was also pretty sure there was no way she'd be able to talk the stubborn AI into leaving the ship.

"You're seriously going to do this? You're going to make me take you with, on a potential combat flight, just so you can keep tinkering with that thing?"

"Yep," Jo replied with a grin. "That about sums it up."

Rika knew when she was beaten. Or at least, when it simply made more sense to give in than to continue fighting.

"Fine. But you'd better stow your gear tight. No telling what we're going to run into up there, and I don't want your shit rattling around and breaking stuff."

Jo cracked a wry grin. "Already loaded and secured."

"What? When?"

"About fifteen minutes ago, while you were in the crapper."

"Sonofa––"

"Hey, language."

"You're lucky that's all I'm saying," Rika shot back, but there was amusement in her voice and a slight crinkling around her eyes. "Well, we'd best get to it, then. Don't want to miss the party."

CHAPTER SIX

Rika still managed to beat the others into orbit--barely--and it was from that meeting point that the team set out on their recon mission toward the sun.

Not too much time had passed since the AI ship named Kip had called in his distress call and emergency warped away, so whatever magic-using craft it had encountered was pretty likely to still be out there in the same general area. The only question was where.

"Okay, everyone. Stay sharp and keep all sensors wide open. We don't know what exactly we're dealing with, but we do know it's using magic and already attacked one of our ships," Charlie said. "We'll take the lead with Ara. Hopefully she'll be able to sniff them out long before they become a problem."

"And if not?" Rika asked.

"If not, then you'd best have your best flying shoes on, because you'll need 'em," Charlie replied.

It was unlikely they would wind up in a deadly engagement. There were three of them, after all. Two state-of-the-art ships--one powered by an AI, no less--and an actual magical space dragon. More than most opponents would wish to face head-on.

And they had another trick or two up their sleeves.

"Ripley, why don't you try to help Eddie with that shimmer spell?" Bawb said over their comms. "It may provide you a slight advantage in our approach if you are somewhat hidden from view."

"I thought you said we'd be invisible," she griped.

"If you were a truly talented caster with a massive amount of power at your control, then perhaps. But as it stands, we are in space, and shimmers typically do not work terribly well in the void. However, with Ara and Rika's ship approaching, the distraction might be enough for you to remain unobserved."

Ripley laughed. "Yeah, space dragons can have that effect."

"Precisely," the Wampeh agreed.

"All right. We'll give it a go. But don't laugh if we mess it up," Ripley said. "You ready to try this, Eddie?"

"As ready as I'm gonna be," the AI ship replied.

Together, Eddie and Ripley began casting, Ripley pulling from the konus she wore on her wrist, Eddie from the konus Bawb had welded into his framework as an experiment.

The spell was clear in both of their minds, thanks to the neuro-stim implant they'd been provided. It wasn't the most in-depth, high-end of spells, but it would hopefully suffice to at least shield them from most casual observation.

Eddie's form began to blur and, well, *shimmer* against the starry sky.

"Hey, guys, look. It's working," Rika said. "Well, kinda, anyway."

What she was referring to were the multiple spots of ship clearly visible through the weaker portions of the spell. Apparently, the konuses used by Ripley and her friend weren't powerful enough to do the spell justice. Still, it was better than nothing.

"Can we help at all?" Leila asked.

"Nah, you and Hunze just sit tight and enjoy the ride,"

Ripley said. "Me and Eddie have things under control."

"We don't, though. You do realize that, right?" Eddie said. "The spell is only partially functional."

"Shut up. It'll work for what we need," she hissed back.

The comms were still open, but Charlie and the others, miraculously, refrained from sarcastic comments.

"Okay, we should be close pretty soon. We should slow our speed down and start a proper scan of the area," Charlie said. "Rip, you watch our six. Ara will fly point, and Rika will follow on our back. Keep your sensors open for any anomalies. They *should* be calibrated to pick up magical disturbances. It won't keep you from getting attacked, but it may give you a second or two heads-up."

"Gee, that's reassuring," Rika cracked.

"Is he always this positive?" Jo asked as she worked on the warp drive.

"Oh, even more so," Rika replied with a laugh as she took up her position to the rear of the mighty dragon and her two passengers.

Ara was using her powerful senses to sniff out traces of magic that might be lingering in the area, while Charlie and Bawb continuously cast layers of defensive spells around her so she could properly focus on that one task.

It wasn't too long before she latched onto something.

"There's magic here," she said silently.

Bawb was still able to communicate with her in this manner, as Charlie could. Whatever sharing of power had occurred in the battle to save Earth, he, Ara, and Charlie were now linked, and it appeared to be permanent.

"Can you tell what type, Wise One?" Bawb asked. *"And how close is our prey?"*

Ara focused her attention, sniffing out the details in the magical signature left hanging in space.

"Shit."

"Did she just say shit?" Charlie asked.

"Yes, I believe she did," Bawb replied.

"Oh, that is not good. Ara only swears when things are really *bad."*

"And they are, Charlie," the dragon replied.

"Go ahead. Rip the Band-Aid off and tell us."

"There is magic here, as we anticipated," she said.

"Guys, Ara senses magic here. Heads on a swivel and weapons hot," Charlie called out over comms.

Immediately, Rika powered up her weapons and shifted her phase settings in her shielding to the most likely of ranges to be able to diminish a magical assault. Eddie did the same from his semi-hidden position far to the rear.

"It's more than just magic, though," the mighty Zomoki added.

"What do you mean, Ara?" Bawb asked.

"I mean there are two *distinct trails, Bawb,"* she replied. *"We have company, all right. Shimmer ships, and more than one of them."*

"Shit," Charlie blurted. *"Oh, this is so not good."*

"No, it is not," Ara agreed.

"And let me guess. They're heading straight toward Earth, right?"

"In that assessment, I believe you are actually mistaken," Ara said.

"Well, that's some good news, at least."

"You didn't let me finish. What I was going to say is they're not heading toward Earth. But rather, it appears they are heading straight for the moon."

The moon. Home to Dark Side base and staging point for most of Earth's off-world forces.

"Guys, we have a problem," Charlie called out to the team. "There are *two* ships."

"Aww, sonofabitch," Rika grumbled. "Well, where are they, so we can blow them out of the sky?"

"That's the other problem," he said. "They're on their way to the moon."

CHAPTER SEVEN

No sooner had Ripley heard Charlie's words than she jumped on her comms to call the AI running Dark Side moon base. Being a child of free Earth, she'd grown up with the massive intelligence serving as part of her extended family, and she'd be damned if she was going to let anything happen to him.

"Uncle Sid, you've gotta get your defenses on high-alert!" she blurted into the comms.

"Yes, Ripley, I am aware of the situation. Cal and I have been monitoring your channel. I am grateful for your concern, though."

"So you're okay?"

"Of course. All of the ships we had available are in orbit and scanning as we speak."

"But this thing has a shimmer cloak, Uncle Sid. And there are *two* of them."

Another voice joined the conversation as Bawb interjected his observations.

"Hello, Sid. I am sorry to be speaking to you under these circumstances," the Wampeh said.

"Good to hear your voice, Bawb. And I am truly sorry you

and your friends were unable to have a proper vacation. I believe you more than earned it."

"Thank you, Sid."

"So, what have you observed, Bawb?" the AI asked. "Cal is listening in on the line, by the way."

"Yes, I heard. And greetings to you as well, Cal."

"Bawb."

"It would appear that these vessels must have been the vanguard of the enemy forces that were preparing to invade this system," the Wampeh said. "As such, they would have been at the very front of the fleet, and if they were close enough to the portal when it engaged, it is entirely possible they came through the instant the portal opened. It was being supercharged by its proximity to the sun's power, you see."

"You're saying they've been here for days?" Sid asked.

"Likely. And they were probably attempting to retrieve the portal to bring the rest of the fleet through when that one ship stumbled upon them."

"Which set this whole thing into motion," Charlie noted.

"Ah, hello, Charlie," Sid said.

"Hey, Sid. We've been talking amongst ourselves about this a bit, and the best we can guess, these ships came through when the portal first opened."

"But how is it you did not notice them at that time?" Cal asked.

"If I may," Ara said, enjoying the novelty of using Earth-tech comms. "You see, there was a massive flash of light and power when the portal burst into activity. Far more than our protective spells were prepared to dampen, and as a result, we were all forced to shield our eyes. It is entirely possible that in that instant, those first ships were pulled through and spat out into this galaxy."

"And with their being cloaked, we would not have seen them but for that first, blinding instant of transition," Bawb added.

"So, what do we know, then?" Sid asked.

"Know? We are uncertain," Bawb replied. "However, it is most likely that these ships were reconnaissance craft. As such, there will almost certainly be no top-tier power user on board. They will fly with plenty of weaponry, mind you, and undoubtedly with a fair contingent of skilled combat troops, but there should be no highest-level natural power-wielding beings aboard either vessel."

"But there are two of them," Ripley said. "And you guys remember what happened the last time there were multiple invisible alien ships running around."

"Yes, Ripley. We do find it rather disconcerting hearing that aspect of the situation," Sid replied. "However, I concur with Bawb's assessment that these ships from his galaxy are likely lead vessels, designed for scouting and recon, and perhaps skirmish engagements, not for full-scale attacks."

"But they use magic."

"Yes. And we use a variety of weaponry that they seem to have a lag in adjusting their defenses for, so I think that makes us even, more or less."

"But what about the rest of our ships? Kip came back, but where are the others?"

"You know how warp tech works, Ripley. The rest of the ships are one, if not more warp jumps away, and our comms cannot travel that distance. Unless a craft is in proximity to our system, it is simply impossible to reach them without sending a messenger ship to relay whatever we wish to say."

"So send them out. Tell them we need them back here to defend Earth."

"We have already sent several, but those survey craft have been gone for months now and will most certainly not be at their original destinations. That's the whole nature of this search for life, Ripley. They keep moving until they find something of note, at which point they will warp back to relay the information and procure additional resources. But if they do not make contact, they simply continue searching until their scheduled return."

"Which is over a month away," Cal added. ***"So, it seems we are left with our original circumstance."***

Charlie knew all of this, as he'd asked a rather similar question of the great AI minds when they'd first encountered the previous alien attackers. It wasn't an ideal situation, but this time, without a powerful spell disabling lesser craft and freezing organic life, they--for once--had the home field advantage.

"How many armed ships do you have in orbit around your base, Sid?"

"After the last incident, I retrofitted any who could carry any sort of weapon."

"So?"

"So, that would make forty-six craft in orbit. That's twelve larger ships and a few dozen smaller ones, though only nine of those were able to be upgraded with the more powerful, modified pulse cannons. The rest have far more basic models, but they can still fight, if need be."

"If they can see their adversary," Bawb noted.

"Yeah, and that's the big issue," Charlie added. "Hang on, Sid, and keep on your toes."

"I do not have toes, Charlie. I am an AI."

"My God, do you all share the same literalist sense of humor?" Charlie replied with a chuckle.

"Yes, we do," Cal chimed in with an amused laugh.

"Great. Well, stay *sharp*, then, in lieu of toes," Charlie said. "We'll be there as fast as we can to sniff those bastards out. You ready, Ara?"

"Always."

CHAPTER EIGHT

Moving at great speed through the easy vacuum of space, the great red dragon led her friends toward the distant moon, powered by her considerable magic, which was all the stronger so close to the sun.

On her tail, the two ships were following single-file. Rika and Jo scanned their instruments for any signs of alien craft, while Eddie flew farther in the rear, his shimmer semi-functional as it sort of masked them from view.

"What are you doing?" Rika blurted as the *Fujin*'s rail gun abruptly spun on its gimbal.

"Just getting a feel for the controls," Jo replied with a cheerful grin. "If we're going in hot, I thought I'd better make myself useful."

"So the warp coupling?"

"Oh, I finished that ages ago."

"Ages ago, as in, before we actually took off?" Rika asked.

"Well..."

"Goddamn it, Jo. You tricked your way into combat?"

"You wouldn't have taken me along otherwise. And besides,

if you get banged up, you know you'll need someone to patch up the *Fujin*."

"We are not going to damage my ship," Rika stated.

"Well, we *hope* not. But you know how these things sometimes go. One minute it's all puppies and rainbows, then the next, you're fighting for your life, ripping your enemy's entrails from their chest cavity."

Rika fell silent a moment as she looked at her mechanic. For all the chipper demeanor and bright-eyed appearance, she had to remind herself that Jo was a cyborg survivor of the Great War. She'd seen a *lot*, and who knew what she'd been forced to do to survive.

"Yeah, about that," Rika said. "Let's just focus on keeping the ship in the air for the time being, okay? I'd rather we avoided any hand-to-hand encounters with these green bastards if we can. If Bawb thinks they're commandos, then they're sure to be ten times tougher than the ones we recently faced."

Jo paused, wondering if maybe she'd shared a bit too much of a glimpse into her darker side.

"Uh, yeah. Sure," she said. "That sounds like a good plan. We'll just stick to the flying and shooting. Yeah."

The cyborg then fell rather silent in her seat.

Rika noted the cyborg's shift in tone. She hadn't meant to bring her down. Jo had been doing a great job, after all, and she really was becoming a friend of sorts. Rika looked back at her controls and abruptly rolled the *Fujin* in a tight corkscrew.

"Hey! What are you doing?"

"Just having a little fun," Rika replied. "You know what fun is, don't you?"

"Obviously."

"And this is fun, right?"

"Well..."

"Cool," she said before rolling the ship the other way a few times, tossing her cybernetic sidekick to and fro a little.

Jo, she noticed, was smiling once more.

Far behind them, another ship followed, and its passengers were a bit confused by what they saw ahead of them.

"What is she doing?" Hunze asked. "Is this a normal thing for a pilot to do?"

"Nope," Ripley said. "And even Eddie, here, got the spinny zoom-zooms out of his system in his early check-out flights. Ain't that right, Ed?"

"Hey, the ship was new to me. Can you blame me for wanting to see what it could do?"

"Of course not, buddy. Just sayin', is all."

"Do you think Rika is in some sort of distress, then?" Hunze asked.

"Nah, I bet she's just getting a feel for the controls. You know, in case we actually do wind up in combat again. Gotta shake out those cobwebs, after all."

"So long as she doesn't fly right into a cloaked Tslavar ship," Leila said. "That would be pretty unfortunate."

Far ahead of the bantering shipmates, Charlie and Bawb could feel Ara tense up beneath them, both physically, as well as through their mental connection. Something wasn't right.

Again.

"What is it?" Charlie asked. *"We're almost at the moon's perimeter defense satellites."*

"Give me a moment," she replied, changing course and flying a large loop of the area.

"Ara, is everything all right?"

"No, Charlie. It is not all right."

"But you've got the scent, right? You're able to track it?"

"Of course. This close it is not hard."

"Then everything should be—"

"The ships split ways," she said.

At that bit of news, Bawb chimed in. *"This does not bode well."*

"No, it does not, for, as Charlie had originally posited, while one of

the ships is still headed toward the moon, the other appears to have diverted directly toward Earth."

"Shit," Charlie growled. "Hey, guys, it looks like they split up," he called out over open comms. "One is now heading toward Earth. Cal, Sid, you guys see any signs of a ship entering atmosphere? Contrails or heat signatures?"

"Nothing from here," Sid replied.

"And I, too, have not detected any anomalies. I'm having the global network placed on high alert and all instruments set to maximum sensitivity."

"That's about all we can do, then."

Eddie chimed in. "Hey, guys. If we can catch them before they enter the atmosphere, we might have a real chance at stopping them from doing any damage down below. What do you think?"

"I think you're spot-on, Eddie," Charlie replied. "Sid, Cal, you two agree?"

"I speak for both of us, Charlie. Yes, it is a wise plan of action," Cal said.

"Okay, then. Eddie, Rika, you two break off and run parallel scans. Ara will give you the likeliest course to follow. If the two of you can lock on, then a crossfire should make it shift in a way that should give you a better fix on it despite its shimmer."

"And Eddie," Bawb added, "the shimmer spell you and Ripley are casting, it should function far better should you descend into the atmosphere. I fear you may not have enough power to maintain it much longer, though. Never before has an artificial mind cast magic."

"To be fair, I am doing it with Ripley's help," Eddie said.

"Yes, of course. But in any case, use your reduced signature to your advantage, but do not forget your enemy likely has much experience combating cloaked vessels. You will need to work as a team with Rika."

"Got it," Ripley said. "You good with that, Rika?"

"You bet, Rip."

"You will lack my nose," Ara said, "but you should be able to follow their trail if you search for unusual decay in your sun's energy. It will be faint, but if you get close enough, you should be able to detect them. The sun's natural rays travel at a fixed rate and power loss. The cloaked ship will appear different from that."

"On it," Eddie said. "Cal, Sid, you guys mind helping me out here?"

"I have already linked the network, Eddie. We will have a tracking algorithm momentarily."

True to his word, Cal sent a scanning protocol to both Eddie and Rika moments later.

"Damn, this dude is good," Jo said as she looked over the code.

"With a team of the greatest AI minds in the system, I'd hope he'd be good," Rika replied. "Now, dial that in to the ship and get scanning. We don't have the luxury of an AI to do it for us."

"But I *am* an AI," Jo said.

"Obviously. But I mean one built into the ship like Eddie. Now stop jibber-jabbering and get to work."

"Already on it, Rika. We'll have full scanning parameters integrated in twelve seconds."

Rika had gotten so used to Jo's human presence, that she had forgotten that the woman seated beside her was actually a powerful AI computer inside her flesh exterior.

"Loaded," the cyborg called out *exactly* twelve seconds later.

"Okay, then. Here we go."

The *Fujin* pulled away from Ara, changing course to pursue the faint trail of their alien quarry. Jo activated the rail gun and sat ready for action.

Hot on their heels, Eddie stuck to Rika's tail, also ready to fire at a moment's notice should they encounter the alien ship.

At the speed they were traveling, he couldn't help but wonder if they'd catch them before hitting the atmosphere.

In the distance, a pair of bright explosions filled the darkness above the moon, then quickly extinguished as the ignited fuel and oxygen succumbed to the void of space.

"Shit. Looks like they're attacking Dark Side," Charlie said over his comms.

"It does seem that way," Sid said. "But I have no sign of them on my scanners, even with the modified algorithm."

"Hang on, Sid. We're coming. Ara's nose is far better than any program you guys have. Just do your best. We're almost there."

"You guys ready for this?" Charlie asked.

"Indeed," Bawb replied.

"Yes, Charlie," Ara said. *"Now, let us hurry into the fray. Our friends need us."*

And with that, the giant red Zomoki dove toward the most recent explosion, ready to engage their invisible enemy.

CHAPTER NINE

"I can't see anything," Charlie called out, his voice clear through the space suit's comms.

"Why are you using that device?" Ara asked.

"Because I want Sid to be able to keep track of the action," he replied.

"That is a logical course of action," the dragon said over comms. "I am sensing a lot of their magic here. Far more than I should be able to, actually. It is disconcerting, to say the least."

"You hear that, Sid? It looks like something bigger than we expected is going on up here."

"I heard, Charlie. And we have lost four ships now, though their attacker has been unseen in each instance."

"Yeah, well, that's a shimmer for ya."

"Apparently. I am redirecting additional ships to your location. You should have reinforcements in under two minutes."

"Thanks, Sid. Have you tried updating their shielding with the new phase spectrum Cal came up with?"

"I have, but these are mostly smaller ships, and their shield arrays are simply not cut out for a large-scale attack. But they are brave, and I assure you, they will do their best."

As if to punctuate the statement, another small ship burst apart in the distance before its flash of flames was snuffed out by the vacuum. Other ships swarmed the location and arranged themselves in a semi-spherical formation, ensuring their weapons were not lined up with any other ship in their cluster.

They then began systematically firing test shots through the inner circle formed between them, hoping to land a shot on their hidden attacker to give them something to target and properly lock onto.

Farther away, another ship erupted in a ball of destructive plasma before reducing itself to atoms.

"What the hell was that?" Charlie blurted. "I've never seen magic do that before."

"That was our tech, actually," Sid informed him. "Whatever just happened to that ship, its warp core was compromised in the process, causing an unstable reaction that vaporized the entire vessel."

"You're saying our ships' drive systems are freakin' bombs?"

"No, Charlie, that's not what I'm saying at all," Sid replied. "To be precise, they are warp engines whose potential destructive energy is *similar* to that of a bomb."

"Oh, that makes it *much* better," Charlie snarked. "This is getting out of hand, Ara. Have you been able to get a fix?"

"Still no," she said. "The traces are all over the place, and the power within them is far more complex than I'd expect of a scout ship. There's something else at play here."

Reinforcing her statement, a powerful magic blast abruptly threw them aside. Only Charlie and Bawb's combined defensive spells managed to prevent any harm to their friend and ride.

"That was a direct hit," Bawb growled. "They are close."

"Yeah, but where?" Charlie said. "With that damn shimmer, we can't see them to properly engage. I mean, don't they have to lower their shimmer shield or something in order to launch an attack?"

"Why would they need to do that?" Ara asked.

"Because, I don't know. Because it would make things easier for us," Charlie replied. "All I'm saying is, we have to have some way of locking in on their location, right?"

"One would think," Ara noted. "However, in this instance, that is most apparently not the case."

Off in the distance, another ship erupted.

"Okay, now how the hell did they get all the way over there so fast? Ara, you're sure there were only two ships?"

"Positive," she replied. "And the only magic I can sense here still bears the scent of the one craft that remained in space. The one heading toward Earth has not returned to the fray that I can sense."

"Then there's something else afoot," Bawb observed. "There is simply no way a lone ship could be attacking all of these vessels on its own."

"I know what you mean, Bob. It's like, this thing is *too* good, ya know? Like, how is it jumping around so easily without us even seeing it? There have to be other craft of some sort. Maybe they were aboard the main ship and launched as smaller away ships or something."

"Oh, that's not what I meant," Bawb said. "What I meant was it seems highly unlikely that we are facing the spell-casters of a single ship."

"Meaning?"

"Meaning we are likely not facing any ships at all."

"This would be bad, Bawb."

"I know, Wise One. But can you think of any other explanation?"

Ara paused a long moment. *"Sadly, no, I cannot,"* she said, flaring her nostrils as she took another loop of the battleground, flying in close to the locations of the downed ships. What she discovered was not at all what she expected.

"Sid, Cal, this is not a normal casting that has taken out your ships," she said, a tinge of shock in her voice.

"So, this is some new form of weapon in our enemy's possession?" Cal asked.

"That's just the thing," she replied. "This isn't a normal weapon at all." Ara smelled the magic one more time, untangling the mess around them from the one moving steadily away. "This isn't a battlefield, Sid. This is a *minefield*."

"Wait, are you saying there's no ship?"

"Oh, there most definitely is a ship, Charlie. But that vessel is heading straight for the moon. All of this up here? These are booby traps designed to keep us occupied."

"Oh, shit. Sid, you hear that?"

"I did, and am recalling all of my remaining ships at once."

"We're coming, Sid," Charlie replied. "Just hold on."

"Get us down there, Ara," he sent to his friend. *"They're going to attack Dark Side Base itself."*

"I know," she replied, rushing toward the moon. *"All of this is just a distraction."*

CHAPTER TEN

London fell under attack first.

"We've received reports from Vic. Apparently, there have been what appear to be magical attacks on the population of London and surrounding areas," Cal transmitted to the rapidly approaching craft.

"So they've already made landfall," Rika growled. "Damn it, Cal, I thought you guys could track them when they entered the atmosphere."

"As did we. But apparently, whatever form of shielding they are utilizing is capable of negating their heat signature as well as obscuring them from visual contact."

"Well, that's just great," the pilot grumbled. "You hear that, Jo? We're going needle hunting in a pile of needles."

Her cyborg co-pilot quickly adjusted the magic-sniffing settings on their forward scanner array. "I don't know if this'll do it, but hopefully we should be able to get some idea which of these incidents is the most recent and can maybe make some kind of pursuit from there."

"Sounds like as good a plan as any until the big brains come up with something better," Rika said. "You guys hear that?"

"Yeah, we're on the line," Ripley replied. "How are we looking, by the way?"

Rika and Jo checked their rear imaging units. There was a mostly invisible ship flying a fair distance behind them. Bits were visible where the spell wasn't quite strong enough to fully envelop the craft, but if nothing else, it broke up the shape of the ship to the naked eye.

"Looking pretty good," Rika said. "At least from a distance. The bits still showing almost look like they could be birds or something. At least from here. But up close I don't know if it'll cut it, so be ready to fight. They very well may still see you coming."

"If we find them, that is. Gotta make contact, first."

"Rip, you know how sneaky these guys are. Eddie'll need to keep his eyes peeled in all directions."

"Not a problem," the ship replied. "I am a state-of-the-art AI, after all. And with my current upgrades--"

"Yeah, we know, we know," Rika said with a sigh. "You're super bad. Got it. Just stay sharp, Mr. Confident, okay? I don't want to have to go searching for your semi-invisible wreckage."

They came in hot, swooping low over portions of London where the human and Chithiid population had fallen to the alien attack. From what they could see, not only had buildings and infrastructure been targeted by damaging magic, but maiming spells had also been utilized against the panicked populace. Limbs were rent from bodies, and it appeared very likely a lot of people were going to be sporting mechanical replacements before the hostilities were done.

They circled, rising higher into the sky to once again take in the big picture. There had to be a pattern, but so far as they could see, there was none. Even the AIs with their brilliant minds were unable to discern a method to the madness.

"We do not see a definitive pattern to these attacks," Cal said, a note of uncertainty in his voice. ***"This makes no sense. In the past,***

the invaders had a target, be it the destruction of a particular facility, or the snatching of civilians to experiment on. But this? This appears as arbitrary a series of events as any of my random number generators would produce."

He was right. There was no logic at play. But for Rika, having been in the military, and knowing her history firsthand rather than from records loaded into files hundreds of years after the fact, this was looking disturbingly familiar.

"It's terrorism," she said with an acid flatness to her tone.

"What, like in the history books?" Ripley asked over comms.

"Yeah, Rip, just like that," she replied. "Back in my day-- before the whole time travel mess, and long before AIs had been perfected--the world was a far more violent place. And extremists would sometimes make their points through horrible acts against the least protected of the population."

"Your people were this cruel?" Hunze asked from her seat aboard Eddie. "From what I have observed so far, the human race has been nothing but kind and wise."

Rika couldn't help but chuckle, and it was not one of joy. "Yeah, we kind of have a history of being right bastards at times. Mankind has always been violent. It's just the post-war version you've seen that's so enlightened. We've had it all on this planet," she noted. "Even slavery."

The golden-haired woman fell silent at the thought.

"I am inclined to agree with Rika's assessment," Cal said. ***"This appears to be an attempt to sow chaos and disrupt the population's daily life, putting fear in the hearts of the citizens. You will notice, these have not been lethal attacks. At least, not for the most part."***

The team circling above realized he was right. As they reviewed the reports and imagery from the attack sights, it became clear that this was a scattershot attempt at injuring as many as possible, while leaving them alive.

A classic way to not only spread resources thin, but also to ensure the fear and anguish they caused that day would continue well into the future, both in the form of physical injuries that needed to heal, as well as the mental ones that could often take far longer.

"I can't help but think there still has to be some reason for all of this," Leila said. "They aren't just wild beasts. I've had plenty of experience with those, and let me tell you, if these attackers are Tslavars again, they are anything but random in their actions."

"She's right," Hunze said, looking at her friend as their ship bounced in the wind above the UK. "I've spent my entire life a slave in that world, and it's true, Tslavars, or any Council servants, for that matter, do not act on a whim."

"So there actually *is* a plan. We just don't know what it is," Eddie noted. "And these are almost definitely military ships, from what Bawb said."

"Meaning they are piloted by disciplined crews and are almost certainly acting out a set series of commands," Ripley added.

"Except we appear to have separated them from their fleet," Cal added. ***"So it is entirely possible they are engaging in some protocol for such instances. But I do not know enough about their culture and tactics to even begin to hypothesize what that may be."***

"None of us know that stuff," Ripley said. "Uncle Cal, I think we're gonna need some help up here. How many ships are available to join the fight?"

"We have a few dozen capable of some degree of combat, but most flew up to assist Sid defend Dark Side. Others are still being retrofitted, but, as you know, since the previous attack by the invaders, we have been spread rather thin, as once the population was freed from stasis, those craft were required for their normal duties once more."

"Got something," Jo said, staring intently at one of her displays. "A slightly stronger power signature lingering at a rural attack site near the Welsh countryside."

"Wales again?" Rika groaned. "All right, then. Cal, you need to have your buddies pull as many of those ships out of civilian service as they can, immediately, and get working on weapons and shielding upgrades," Rika said. "Because it looks like we're going hunting."

CHAPTER ELEVEN

Ara was pulling some serious gs as she dove into the moon's low gravity on her rapid descent to Dark Side Base. Charlie and Bawb both found themselves grateful for Cal having the foresight to fabricate a far sturdier harness for their dragon friend.

Sure, it made carrying additional equipment, like their comms and scanning tech easier, but, at this moment, far more important was that it kept the two from being tossed from her back as she dodged and wove her way around the magical booby traps left in the alien ship's wake.

Once she dialed in the scent from the first of the landmines--or *space*mines, to be precise--it was then just a matter of flying clear of the myriad destructive spells left hanging in the moon's orbit.

Unfortunately, for the smaller ships attempting to assist, they were not so well versed at sniffing out magic. In fact, they weren't versed in it at all.

"I do not understand. There are no weapons signatures," one modified AI transport craft said just before being torn to bits.

It was a scene being repeated in orbit around the moon as

the unprepared vessels attempted to handle a completely novel form of attack. Fortunately, most seemed more than happy to heed Sid's command that they slow their movements while he attempted to modify scans to map out the new, hidden hazards apparently hanging silently in space, like enormous, invisible jellyfish just waiting to snare another victim.

"Sid, have you locked down your airspace?" Charlie called out as his winged friend dove toward the base.

"I've been somewhat successful in altering the firing solutions for the defensive cannons, but my scanners are still not showing any--Hang on. I think I may be seeing--"

A fierce blast of magical power erupted across the surface of the moon, wiping out several surface transports as well as some repair equipment, but leaving the base itself unscathed. Another followed in its wake a little farther away, targeting the auto-cannon that had begun firing in the area of the previous attack.

"Looks like they've got a bead on the ship," Charlie said. *"Get us into the thick of it, Ara."*

"I am already one step ahead of you. I can sense their path now, and our course should take us slightly ahead of them, if my estimates are correct."

"Excellent," Charlie said as the Zomoki spun into a steep dive.

"You may want to prepare yourselves," she said to her passengers. *"I believe we are about to engage the enemy."*

But her warning was followed by nothing, and the lack of enemy contact was more than a little disconcerting.

"Uh, Ara? What's going on?"

"I don't know, Charlie. They should be here."

Charlie surveyed the area, looking for any signs of the shimmer-camouflaged ship, but, with it being invisible, he saw none.

"Sid, we're drawing a blank up here. You see anything?"

"Not yet. I showed some unusual readings for a moment, but then they were gone."

"Unusual? Like how unusual?"

"Surface contact near Hangar Two. But I tasked a team to do an EVA and check the area, and there are no signs of the alien ship."

Charlie was perplexed. It simply didn't make sense for the alien craft to go to such great lengths setting up a false presence and laying so many booby traps for them to simply fly away. Something was up, but he simply didn't know what.

"Have you seen any changes in—" A small explosion on the surface caught his eye. "Sid, what was that?"

"The airlock on Pod Seven was targeted, Charlie," the AI replied.

"Shit! They're targeting the base. We need to get down there, now! Ara, go, go, go!"

The dragon didn't hesitate, abruptly shifting her course, making a beeline toward the open airlock. She was nearly there when a flurry of magical attacks burst against the layers of shielding Charlie and Bawb were casting on top of her own defensive measures.

"It appears we have found the invading ship," Bawb noted with his usual calm.

"No shit, Bob. Ara, can you get us down there?"

"Not at the moment," she replied, spinning away from another round of vicious spells. *"This is not a booby trap. We are, in fact, facing what appears to be a very well-armed vessel."*

"Yeah, we noticed."

"But as the ship is presently casting these attacks at us, I cannot safely break away to reach the surface incident," she replied, increasing her evasive maneuvers.

"Sid, are your weapons able to track and fire this far above the base?" Charlie asked over their comms.

"Yes, they have a fairly long reach, though I've been utilizing the smaller craft as a defensive shield of sorts in lieu of using the bigger guns."

"Well, I think it's time to break out the big toys. Ara, can you land a shot on them to help paint the target?"

"I may be able to get close enough to land a flame burst, but I will require you and Bawb to increase your defensive spells, lest their attacks fly true."

"We shall do so immediately," Bawb replied, focusing his considerable power on defense, foregoing offense entirely.

He was wearing his thick braid of Ootaki hair, gifted to him by Hunze. The power-storing locks were fully charged and brimming with magical potential, just waiting for him to tap into them, and as he loosed that magic around his Zomoki friend, the rumbling impacts of the magical attacks were suddenly diminished.

Charlie, likewise, was pouring all of his energy into protecting his bonded friend. His internal power had grown exponentially since he and Ara had merged their power in the defense of the planet. And the fact that some of her blood had now flowed in his veins for several years, increasing its potency the entire time, only served to make him more powerful. In fact, Charlie was essentially as strong as many native-born magic users. And that power was only growing.

"I am ready," Ara said.

"Stand by, Sid. You've already got Ara's magic signature in your systems from her work with the AIs, so once she lights up that ship, you should have no trouble targeting it."

"I am ready," the AI replied. "And several of the support ships appear to have made it clear of the minefield left by our attackers."

"Excellent. The more guns the merrier," Charlie said. "Okay, Ara. We're ready when you are."

The powerful Zomoki nodded once, then spun into a tight roll, flipping in mid-flight and reversing course directly toward the pursuing ship rather than evasively fleeing it. The vessel was not visible, per se, but Ara could smell it clearly at this range.

Her jaws opened, and a blaze of magical fire spewed forth, the flames burning bright even in the vacuum of space. The stream impacted the invisible craft with a splash of red-orange light, briefly providing a glimpse of the ship's actual form before flickering out.

"I have them target locked," Sid immediately called out. "Get clear. Opening fire in ten seconds."

"Screw that," Charlie replied. "Fire *now!* Don't worry about us."

Sid, by this point in their relationship, had learned the capabilities of these unusual people, and did not question or hesitate upon hearing the command. Instead, he opened fire with everything he had.

Surface cannons lit up the sky with a trail of pulse fire, while the circling ships above likewise spewed forth a stream of smaller rounds, all zeroing in on the coordinates sent to them by the brainy AI. The ship's shielding spells lit up with dozens of impacts, several of which appeared to penetrate to some degree, though the pulse cannon fire was somewhat diminished against a target at such a long range.

Nevertheless, the defenders' ability to accurately target their ship seemed to have caught the attackers off guard, and with a panicked series of abrupt course changes, they abandoned the moon entirely, streaking off into space.

"We have images," Sid called out. "Did you see it?"

"Yeah, we saw it," Charlie replied. "Bob? You're way more versed in that sort of thing than I am. What's your take on it?"

The Wampeh was silent a moment as he replayed the captured images on the small visual display they had installed on Ara's harness.

"Good-sized," he said. "Sleek. Well-armed. Dangerous."

"So more than just a scout ship?"

"I cannot say for certain. The design is hundreds of years newer than any I would be familiar with."

"Yeah, the pitfalls of time travel."

"Precisely. But so far as I can tell, this is indeed an advance craft, but it appears to be one of significantly greater power than I'd originally anticipated."

"But we drove it away with only minimal damage to a small section of the base," Sid said triumphantly. "So at least there's that."

"It would appear so," Bawb replied. "Though I do feel we should reposition your ships in a defensive pattern, while Ara, Charlie, and I disarm the spells that still float above."

"Good idea," Charlie agreed. "And then we can get to work tracking those bastards down. Okay, Ara, let's clear some mines."

The mighty Zomoki altered course, carefully bringing them close to the invisible spells lingering in wait, until, one by one, the trio could defuse the power, saving any further damage to hapless ships.

Charlie felt good about the overall success of their efforts. They'd engaged the enemy and come out on top. It was a nice change from their previous run-ins, for sure.

But the situation was not as rosy as it seemed, and, unbeknownst to them all, invisible footsteps were now softly ringing out inside the walls of Dark Side Base.

CHAPTER TWELVE

It only took a few minutes for the first of Sid's internal defense protocols to register that something was amiss within his walls. Fortunately, it was not in a crucial section of his facility. Nevertheless, like a ship in hostile seas, it appeared Dark Side Base had been boarded.

He immediately went into emergency defense protocol and slammed all doors and hatches shut, locking them down so tight that neither tech-savvy invaders nor magic-wielding attackers could force them open.

"It appears I have an infestation problem," Sid called out over his comm link. "I'm sending in one of my combat teams to flush them out but wanted you to be aware. Keep an eye out for their ship. I would posit they are lingering nearby to collect their men when their mischief is done."

"Shit, we missed some?" Charlie said.

"Easy to do, given our recent situation," Sid replied. "But my teams should make quick work of these intruders. This is our turf, after all."

"Do not underestimate the abilities of highly trained

mercenaries from my realm, Sid. They possess a degree of skill that is not to be trifled with," the assassin noted.

"I understand, Bawb. But my people are well armed and... Oh."

"Oh? Oh, what?"

"A massive firefight has just erupted within the corridors surrounding Pod Seven."

"So you have them pinned down? Excellent," Charlie said. "Kick their asses, Sid!"

"I'm afraid it's not so simple," the AI replied. "It would seem the enemy is invisible. My men are taking heavy losses."

"They have individual shimmer spells," Bawb said. *"This is just like the invaders we faced on Earth so recently."*

"I know. And we don't have any way to disrupt the shimmer spells from out here. Ara, you have any ideas?"

"Unfortunately, none that will not result in the demise of the men and women fighting on our side," she replied.

"Yeah, I didn't think so," Charlie said.

This was a decidedly unpleasant development, and one they simply had no easy answer for.

"Sid, there's not much we can do from out here," Charlie said. "But these guys are new to this galaxy, and this is their first run-in with our tech, besides that one ship, so they really haven't had a chance to learn any of the technical systems that this world functions by. That should hopefully stymie them for a while."

"I've already noticed their futile attempts at disrupting some of my systems and countermeasures, Charlie. And the progress of their forces, while invisible to my ground troops, is something I *can* track by heat fluctuations within compartments, as well as variations in oxygen-consumption rates."

"Good thinking, Sid."

"It's imperfect at best, and a method that requires more observation time than I would like to be of use, but at least within these closed walls there is a means to track them that would otherwise not be at our disposal in the open."

"Better that than nothing," Charlie agreed. "Okay, keep tracking them, Sid. We're gonna pow-wow a minute."

With that, he turned his attention to his two magic-wielding friends.

"So, what do you guys think? I mean, we can drop in and lend a hand. I'm sure some magical assistance would be a welcome bit of help, but that would leave Ara on her own to defend and attack if the ship returns."

"Which is not acceptable, in my opinion," Bawb said. *"The Wise One is far too valuable an asset to leave in a vulnerable position. And she is our friend. In this situation, I opt to stay by her side."*

"Thank you, Bawb," Ara said. *"The concern is appreciated, my friend."*

"I agree with him on this. These guys are far too tricky to lower our guard to go chasing after some foot soldiers, even if they are in Dark Side's walls. We just have to hope Sid and his men are able to flush them out before they do any real damage."

From what they had seen so far, the invaders lacked the ability to gain further access into the base and were opting instead to cause as much damage as possible to the facilities they did have the ability to reach. It was a mess, and would require a lot of cleanup, but compared to the deadly ship hiding out somewhere just beyond their sensors, it was a far smaller concern.

Or it should have been.

"I sense something," Ara said over open comms. "Something within the base."

Charlie immediately took note of her concerned tone. "Sid, are you detecting any fluctuations in your readings?"

"There's a little spike in one of the scanners, but nothing I can make heads or tails out of."

"No. Something is definitely building down there," Ara

persisted. "We need to fly lower, so I can get a better sense of what it is."

"Then let's get to it," Charlie agreed.

Ara left her minesweeping and made a quick redirect straight for the section containing the fighting. The close quarters combat was still raging fierce inside, and even through the base's thick walls, all of the magic users could sense the spells being cast inside.

Expertly cast, it seemed. These were no ordinary mercenaries. These were well-trained soldiers.

"There it is again. Bawb, can you sense it?" Ara asked.

"Yes," he said, straining his senses, which were enhanced greatly by the Ootaki hair he wore. "There is a compounding of power. It feels like a––oh no."

"Oh no, what, Bob?"

"I know this spell."

"As do I," Ara said. "I have seen this before. It is an explosive spell of great destructive power."

"A bomb? Oh, shit. How do we disarm it?" Charlie asked.

"Without access to the individuals casting it, I'm afraid we don't," Bawb replied. "And if I am sensing this right, it would be ready to detonate long before we could land, penetrate the facility, and reach the magic users."

"Sid, you hear that?"

"I did, Charlie. But what is the destructive range of this bomb-thing you're talking about?"

Ara sniffed deeply, the magic apparent to her even in the near vacuum of the moon's surface. "This is a powerful iteration, Sid. I am afraid if this is detonated within your walls, it may very well compromise over fifty percent of your facilities."

A long silence hung in the air.

"If the people casting this spell are taken out before it is completed, will it still detonate, or will it be defused?" the Base's AI asked.

"The magic will dissipate if the final layering has not been cast in place," Ara said.

"Then you need to get out of there," Sid replied.

"Why? What are you going to do?" Charlie asked.

"What has to be done," he said. "Attention, all ships in the immediate area. You are to target the coordinates I am now sending you at once, then fire on my command."

Bawb and Charlie watched the readout mounted on Ara's harness flash out a stream of coordinates.

"Sid, this is targeting your own base," Charlie noted with concern.

"Yes, it is. But one section we can rebuild. Half of the base? The amount of lives lost would be catastrophic, and reconstruction could take years, if not more."

"Yeah, but you've still got people down there fighting the intruders."

"Believe me, I am very well aware, and this is a decision I hoped to never have to make. But the survival of the base is at stake, and the good of the many outweighs the good of the few."

The AI then cut his comms as he sent a quick message to his team in the fated compartments. They deserved to know. And their sacrifice would not be forgotten.

"Fire."

The nearby ships did as they were told and unleashed a barrage on the pinpoint target that had been provided to them. Sid had lowered the shielding in that section, and their pulse rounds soon tore through the layers of ceramisteel, igniting the oxygen-rich atmosphere inside in a violent explosion that tore through the compartments.

Moments later, the vacuum of space extinguished the flames, and the destroyed section fell silent. All of the comms chatter that had previously been flitting between the ships was conspicuous in its absence as the weight of their dead friends was felt by one and all.

Debris slowly wafted from the hole rent in the thick walls. Equipment, metal and stone fragments, and some limbs of the recently deceased. Bawb and Ara immediately recognized a few of the avulsed body parts, leaking green blood.

"Tslavars," Bawb said. "We might have guessed."

Other limbs floated free as well. Those of humans and Chithiid, and even a few cyborgs who had been party to the fight. Those who had given it all in defense of the base. Dark Side would stand, but it was a high price to pay.

Sid's normally calm voice had an edge to it when he finally came back online.

"Can you still sniff out that ship?" he asked, an uncharacteristic anger clearly audible.

"I believe I can," Ara replied.

"Then, please. Kill those sons of bitches for me."

CHAPTER THIRTEEN

"Have you got them?" Charlie asked as the Zomoki flew high above Dark Side Base.

"Yes, I think so," Ara replied. *"They appear to have drastically altered course after what happened on the surface of the moon."*

"Yeah, we kicked their buddies' asses," Charlie said.

"Obviously, though at great cost. But be that as it may, the shimmer cloaking is still making them difficult to track, while they are moving at high speed. I think I have a decent lock on them for the moment, as my own magic is now melded to their ship. But we will have to move fast."

"Then we must act. Now," Bawb said. *"There can be no indecision."*

"I agree with Bawb," Ara replied. *"Charlie? Are you on board with this?"*

"I am. But what about the others?"

"We shall call them as we pursue," Bawb said. *"It seems to be the most logical way."*

"I agree. And they are needed here to help combat the ship on Earth, anyway. Splitting up is the logical path."

"I know you're right, but I don't feel good about dividing our

forces," Charlie said. *"Aww, shit. All right, get after them, Ara. I'll pull Sid and Cal on the line as we move."*

He quickly fired up the comms line and connected to their AI friends.

"Hey, you guys. Ara's still got a fix on the ship up here, but it looks like it's peeling off and making a run for it."

"Is it heading toward Earth?" Cal asked.

"No. It looks to be on a course away from it, out into the far reaches of the system," Charlie replied. "Hence the need for speed. But how are you doing tracking the ship on Earth? Were you able to adjust your machines to follow the fluctuations in the sun's power stuck to the other ship?"

"It seems to be working," Cal said. ***"But they're wreaking havoc down here. Attacking civilians, causing massive injuries and destruction on a grand scale, but without a seeming plan or defined target. It is most vexing."***

"Yes, a terror-style attack to disrupt the enemy and put the populace on edge," Bawb said. "A distasteful, yet frightfully common, and effective, tactic."

"Indeed, so it would seem. Rika had posited the same opinion when the attacks began."

"And how are they doing?" Charlie asked. "Have our guys managed to track them down yet?"

"They are working on it, and my AI network and I are retrofitting ships as fast as we are able, to help them in the pursuit. This particular craft, while invisible, does not appear to have the submarine capabilities we saw with the previous invaders."

"Good thing. Those suckers were damn near impossible to deal with," Charlie said, briefly flashing back to his near-death experience at the bottom of the sea.

He shook himself out of the thought. That was in the past, and they'd survived. But the what-if of the whole thing still haunted him.

"But you've got the new scanner parameters set up, right? I

mean, you have a basic idea where they are?" he said, getting his head back into the game.

"Yes. And the others are already hunting them as we speak. Rika and Jo are taking point, with Eddie following in the rear. The shimmer cloaking he is utilizing, while not perfect by any stretch of the imagination, does at least provide him a modicum of the element of surprise."

"I am glad to hear it is working better now that they are in atmosphere," Bawb said. "I feel we are fortunate that whoever is piloting these ships has no idea what befell their associates who came through before them. With any luck, they will make mistakes due to that shortcoming. Mistakes our people can capitalize on."

From what they could tell, this duo of ships, while certainly deadly in their own way, were not quite the same sort of threat the previous attackers had been. These, unlike the others, were never intended to function on their own for any length of time. Advance assault ships meant to be followed by the bulk of the fleet.

And now they were entirely cut off from them.

"You guys think they know what happened yet?" Charlie asked. "I mean, they obviously know the portal was dropped into the sun. That much is pretty plain to see. But about their buddies we wiped out? Once they realize they're stuck here on their own and there are no reinforcements coming, I can't help but wonder what they might resort to next."

"More terror, to start," Bawb said. "But I do see where you are coming from. Once they realize that not only is their mission a bust, but that there is no way home, they will undoubtedly modify their actions accordingly."

"Meaning?"

"I honestly do not know, Charlie. But I can tell you what my instincts tell me."

"I trust your instincts more than most other people's facts, so hit me with it."

"Very well," the Wampeh replied. "It seems they have already attempted a disruption of the status quo on Earth and realized it will not be as simple as they'd hoped. So their next step, logically, would be to attempt to find an energy source powerful enough to either allow them to return home, or, if they are truly lucky, to let them retrieve the portal and bring the rest of their fleet through."

Charlie thought back to the moment they dropped the portal into the sun just as it opened. Ara had agreed with his assessment of the spell, and it was very likely that whoever was waiting on the other side of that portal was incinerated instantly. But these ships, fleeing the scene to regroup, would likely not be aware of that.

"Their fleet is toast, but they don't know," he said.

"It would be a reasonable assumption."

"But you say they would look for energy sources to open a new portal," Cal said. ***"There is no magic in this galaxy. They're stuck here."***

"Ah, but that is where you are mistaken," Ara noted. "As we have already seen from your system's sun, there is, indeed, powerful magical energy in this realm. However, it seems the residents of this galaxy have not yet evolved into a magic-using culture, relying, rather, on your technology to make advancements."

"You're saying we're less evolved because we have tech?" Charlie asked.

"Not exactly," she replied. "But think of it like this; in my galaxy, clean, simple magic powers our conveyances, be they small ones used to carry goods, or large ones used to traverse air and space."

"And here, up until a few hundred years ago, we burned the decomposed remains of dinosaurs to push our vehicles."

"Precisely," she agreed. "Rather inelegant, from a magic user's perspective."

"I suppose I see your point," Charlie said.

Suddenly, a disturbance in the power they were pursuing tickled all of their senses, but none so keenly as Ara.

"They have just jumped," she said, a sharp note of concern in her voice. "I think I can follow their path, but we must go *now*."

"Guys, let the others know we'll be back as soon as we're able," Charlie said. "Okay, Ara. Hit it."

Without delay, she summoned her magical powers and jumped them through the reaches of space in pursuit of the alien ship. Their destination, some distant solar system, but where, they wouldn't know until they arrived.

"Uh, guys?" Sid said. "Hello?"

"They're gone," Cal said. ***"I will inform the others."***

CHAPTER FOURTEEN

"What do you mean they jumped?" Rika said over the comms as Jo silently pointed, directing her to make a sharp right turn in pursuit of their invisible quarry.

"I mean exactly that," Cal replied. *"The alien craft they were in pursuit of suddenly performed some sort of spatial warp—"*

"We call it a jump," Leila interjected from her seat aboard Eddie's craft. "Usually it's a team of powerful Drooks who cast the spell, but since Ara is an old and powerful Zomoki, she's able to do it on her own pretty easily, though she does need a bit of recoup time afterward. But you say they jumped a few minutes ago?"

"So they just left us here?" Rika grumbled. "I mean, what the hell? We're a team, right?"

"Yes, you are. However, sometimes a team finds it needs to split its resources to best complete a task. As is the case at the moment. They were already working on a different engagement than you were. Now they are simply doing so in a distant part of the galaxy. Regardless of distance, you are still working in tandem on a two-pronged problem," the powerful AI said.

Rika hated to admit it, but she knew Cal had a very good

point. "Yeah, I guess," she muttered. "But they still could have at least called us on comms before they jumped."

"To be fair, they likely didn't have time if they were in close pursuit of a Drook-powered craft," Hunze pointed out. "Once the ship jumped, there would be a relatively short window in which Ara would be able to track the residual magic if she hoped to keep them close, even through a jump."

It was annoying, but the golden-haired Ootaki was right. The logical thing to do was to stick with them as best they could and try to keep track of them, hopefully preventing any further incidents. Given their luck so far, however, they all had their doubts.

"I hate to interrupt," a new female voice said, breaking into the conversation, ***"but there is something of a battle underway at the launching facility in Gibraltar."***

Cal stepped in, quickly making introductions. ***"Everyone, this is Eva. She is the AI overseeing all of Spain at the moment, as well as the island of Gibraltar."***

"Wow. A whole country? Uncle Cal, I thought you said you guys only cover one major city apiece," Ripley said.

"Normally, yes. But we had to take the others off the grid while major repairs were being made to their power and data transfer infrastructures. Eva volunteered to be the last to be upgraded, which left her covering far more than her usual home city of Valencia and the surrounding area. But, Eva, you said there's a battle?"

"Sí, the Chithiid landing site on the island of Gibraltar is under attack."

"Eddie, change course for Spain!"

"Already on it, Rip."

"We'll hop ahead," Rika added. "I'll steer the *Fujin* to the north, while you guys swing in from the south. Hopefully our coming in hot will catch their attention and buy you some time."

"How long until we're there?" Leila asked, sliding her

konuses onto her wrists and her pair of slaaps into position on her gear harness along with her blades and pulse rifle.

"Should be there in ten minutes," Rika replied. "Too close to make an orbital hop worthwhile. The UK isn't all that far, you know." She turned her attention to her mechanic, gunner, and co-pilot. "Jo, I'm thinking we do a very controlled strafing run to see if we can hit that invisible fucker. You good with that?"

"Of course I am. But what about civilians?"

"Cal? Eva? What's the sitrep on the ground?"

"The last I heard, a substantial force had wiped out the few Chithiid who were present at the facility. It's not a terribly important location, but a few of our AI ships are currently parked there awaiting minor repairs," Eva said.

Rika hit the throttle, upping their speed to supersonic.

"Then let's hope they give those mercenaries a hard time and can hold out until we get there."

CHAPTER FIFTEEN

The shimmer-cloaked invaders had slipped into the relatively empty facility in broad daylight, their shock troops easily overwhelming the limited number of Chithiid pilots and crew in a short, but bloody fight. Several ships attempted to flee, but were shot from the sky with brutal force.

The remaining ships turned their shields to full and fired back, at least as best they could with their limited weapons, but in short order they found themselves restrained by some form of strange power device. Later, the surviving AIs would learn it was actually magic that held them fast. But in the moment, it didn't matter what was holding them, only that whatever it was, it had rendered them incapable of flight.

The largest of the AI ships was scheduled to have his shields and weapons upgraded that very afternoon over in the much larger shipworks in London, but it seemed it would be too little too late.

With a terrible shriek of rent metal, the AI ship's rear hatch was forced open by some unseen power. His scanners were all working perfectly well, but for all of his efforts, the poor ship couldn't see anyone.

But someone had come on board, of that he was certain, as his limited Chithiid crew were soon dead or dying on the deck. Finally, a chattering gibberish became audible within his walls as over a dozen green men with pointed ears seemed to appear out of thin air.

Magical beings would have known this was simply the shedding of shimmer cloaks now that they had taken the facility and commandeered the most valuable ship, but the poor AI hadn't been briefed on any of that, so it was all new––and most surprising––to him.

"What are you doing?" he demanded over his internal comms system, while simultaneously attempting to force his way past whatever blocks they had thrown over the facility in hopes of making contact with his AI brethren for help.

The green men––Tslavars, he would have known if he was from the distant, magic-powered galaxy––ignored the voice coming from the walls at first, instead tearing through the ship, looking for Lord knew what.

Finally, frustrated at their futile attempts, they turned to their leader, who muttered some guttural words and waved his hand. To the ship's surprise, a moment later he was able to understand what they were saying.

"Whoever you are, you aren't going to get away with this. Others are coming, and they'll make you pay," the scared AI blurted.

"Oh, is that a fact?" the boarding party's leader replied to the air. "Why don't you come out and show yourself, coward. Face me like a man. Then we shall see who will make who pay."

The ship was confused, and rightly so. Did this strange invader just ask him to show himself?

"You do realize that I cannot do that, right?" he said. "I mean, I'm an AI, not a cyborg."

"What are these strange terms you speak?" the Tslavar demanded. "The translation spell is unable to do its work with them. Are they enchanted? Are you attempting a counter spell?"

"A counter *what*? What are you talking about?"

"It is of no matter. We will commandeer this vessel and begin rebuilding our fleet to a mighty fighting force, starting here, today."

At that the ship regained some of his confidence. His laugh, ringing out from speakers throughout the ship, caught the Tslavar invaders off guard.

"Oh, that's funny. You think you're going to fly this ship? *My* ship?"

"Yes, we will. We shall take it by force. Something you have already seen our prowess at."

"You're from that other world, aren't you? The other galaxy?"

"So, you do know of us. Then you should also know to fear our might."

"Fear you? Like your buddies who were here not so long ago?"

"Yes. A deadly fighting team we shall merge our forces with, expanding our reach as we subjugate this world and its pathetic population."

Again, the AI laughed. "Oh, you don't know, do you?"

"Know what?"

"That your friends are all dead."

"Lies. We have seen your defenses, and they are sadly lacking."

"So you saw the dragon, then? And her friends? Because, from what I heard, they torched your buddies to a crisp, then blew them to pieces before dropping what was left of your gear into the sun."

One of the crew turned to their leader.

"This would explain why the portal was situated so far from its intended location," he said. "What if this man tells the truth?"

The Tslavar leader rubbed his hands together menacingly.

"If that is the case, we will torture him until he dies a slow and painful demise. But only once he has given us control of this vessel will we allow him the mercy of death."

Realizing these strange invaders didn't understand what was going on, the AI tried to simplify things for them.

"I'm not able to be tortured," he said. "You're not from around here, so I guess this is all rather new to you. But, you see, I'm not a person. Not in the traditional sense of the word, anyway."

"What trickery is this? What sort of magic?"

"None of that," the AI said. "I'm just trying to tell you that you can't take the ship from me because I *am* the ship. I'm an artificial intelligence, and this ship is my body. So, you see, you can't have one without the other."

"And you will not give us control?"

"Of course not. You're bad guys."

"So you will not submit to our rule?"

"Nope. Not a chance."

The Tslavar leader looked at his men. "Everyone clear out."

The troops immediately hurried for the exit, leaving just the commander aboard.

"Smart move, leaving like that. I mean, all of this is just so far over your head."

A slight smile tickled the corner of the green man's mouth. "Perhaps you are correct," he said. "And perhaps there truly is no way to operate this craft without your assistance."

"Like I said."

"But if we cannot fly it," he said, slipping a heavy slaap onto his hand. "Then no one can."

"Wait, what are you--?"

The Tslavar barked out a guttural spell. A killing spell.

Nothing happened.

"Uh, what was that?" the ship asked, perplexed.

"That should have ended you," the man replied, rather

disconcerted. That spell always worked. *Always*. "What sort of magic is this?"

"Like I said. I'm not a flesh-and-blood person, I'm afraid. So that stuff won't work on me. You really should go now. I'm sure my friends will be here any minute."

The green man pondered a moment.

"You *are* the ship?" he said. "An integral part of this vessel's structure? So it will not function without you?"

"Again, like I said."

"Very well, then," the Tslavar replied as he walked to the exit and stepped outside. He turned around, once more facing the ship, and raised his hand, his slaap pointing into the open door.

"If a killing spell will not serve its purpose, then I shall settle for a far more blunt instrument."

With that he cast a violent and powerful destruction spell, the surge of energy and ruinous force racing through the interior of the ship.

Normally, the shields and thick skin of the hull would have taken the brunt of the power and come out relatively unscathed, but the unprotected interior of the craft was another thing entirely.

Magic fried wires and connections in the walls instantly, the spell rushing all the way to the artificial mind tucked safely away in its heavily reinforced cradle. But it was not reinforced against magic, and especially not a direct attack of this nature.

The AI didn't even have a chance to scream before its life was snuffed out in a violent flash as its processors and relays were turned to ash.

"Come," the Tslavar said to his waiting men as he turned toward his cloaked ship. "There is nothing for us here."

CHAPTER SIXTEEN

The carnage was appalling. Chithiid workers lay strewn about, either dead by magic or hacked to pieces by bladed weapons, many missing more than one of their four arms, lost as they futilely tried to defend themselves.

Bodies lay where they had fallen, slowly swelling in the sun. There were no signs of their killers, save for the occasional bloody bootprint.

The ships that had not been torn to shreds by powerful magic sat in their moorings, struggling against an invisible restraint, unable to move or fire their weapons. And in the middle of all of this chaos sat the remains of their largest ship. An AI craft that had been working with the Chithiid for a number of years.

Now he was simply a smoldering husk of metal, all of the electronics inside crushed and reduced to bubbling slag.

"What happened here, Cal?" Leila asked over their comms as she stepped from the safety of Eddie's hull, pulse rifle in hand.

"Whoa," Ripley gasped in agreement, the teen going uncharacteristically silent at the sight of the dead Chithiid.

"C'mere Rip. You don't need to see this," Rika said, quickly walking over from her ship to join them, with Jo close on her heels, packing not one but two pulse rifles, as well as a bandolier of spare pulse charges.

"No, I'm okay," Ripley said. "I'm good."

The slight green tint now coloring her face told a different story, but she was nearly an adult, and if she wanted to be a part of war, then this would not be the first horrific sight she would see.

She'd been in battle before, and had handled herself fantastically, killing several of their adversaries from within her ship. But that was different. This was wholesale slaughter of innocents. And it was up close and personal.

"Just a little too late," Cal said, assessing the site as the team walked among the dead. ***"The attackers departed just a few minutes ago. One of the lesser facility AIs is still able to speak with me."***

"What about these other ships? What's up with them?" Rika asked.

"I am unsure. Eva lost contact with them when the attack began, and neither of us can get a word out of any of them. It is most unusual."

"This is magic," Hunze said, holding her hand up to the nearest ship. She could feel it slightly vibrating with the strain of its efforts to move. "They've been enchanted."

"They what, now?" Rika asked, putting her hand to the hull and feeling the same low vibration. "That's weird. It feels like their engines are firing up, but there's no movement. I'm pretty well versed in magic, but this is new to me."

"It would be to me as well," Hunze replied. "But Bawb has been imparting his knowledge to me since the... event," she said, going silent a moment at the thought of being frozen in stasis, helpless, unable to do a thing while her love fought for her freedom.

She shook her head, clearing the unpleasantness from her mind.

"This is a rarely used Tslavar slave trader restraint spell. One which cripples all but the mind. But for an AI, I would think it a far less effective restraint. For that reason, it seems they have somehow left these craft on the verge of movement, trapped between action and silence."

"That sounds horrible," Jo said. "So they're trapped in there, mid-motion?"

"Yes," Hunze replied.

Rika scanned the area once more, calling upon her konus to reach out magically in addition to her sharp eyes, looking for any sign of danger. But none was sensed, and none was to be found. They were, indeed, alone.

"If this is a Tslavar spell, then we know what sort of people we're up against," Rika said, releasing her magical draw on her konus. "Always the Tslavars, it seems. Their love of money and battle seems to make them everyone's favorite mercenaries."

Jo, being an AI herself, was particularly horrified at what was being done to her electronic brethren. She was even more so when she walked into the smoking wreck in their midst, its AI mind snuffed out in a violent flash of magic.

"Cal? Eva?" she said, pulling her electronic emotions under control, silently cursing the programming that gave them to her in the first place, in this instance. "This ship was much stronger than the others. What did they do to it?"

"I have reviewed the lone surveillance camera that was not destroyed in the hostilities. It is some distance from the hot zone, and thus escaped the violence. The image required some reconstruction to enhance, but I will transmit the footage to you now."

A tickle in the back of Jo's head notified her that an incoming packet was being sent. She, like nearly all cyborgs, functioned like their human counterparts--favoring manual and voice devices rather than their internal electronics. It was just a thing they adopted, a way to fit in better with their fellow citizens.

But the underlying technology allowing them to link with other AIs was still present, just waiting to be utilized. She unlocked her firewall and accepted the trusted file. A second later, her powerful mind had processed the images in their entirety.

"They used some sort of power from their ship to pry the outer door free," she said, running her hand along the doorframe. The buckling now held different meaning than before. It wasn't the heat of a flash fire that did this, it was a magical infiltration.

"What else?" Rika asked, joining her sidekick at the craft.

"They were tall. Green. Over a dozen of them," Jo replied. "They just appeared out of nowhere."

"That would be them removing their shimmer cloaks," Hunze noted.

"I see. Well, they stepped into this ship and were gone for several minutes. Then the men all filed out of the ship, more than I saw enter––cloaked on entry, I assume––followed by what I assume is their leader a minute later," she said, replaying the scene in her mind's eye. "He stepped outside of the ship and said something with his hand pointed at the open door. Smoke and flames blasted out immediately, then extinguished a few moments later."

Rika knew what had happened. A destructive spell intended to kill the mind living within the ship itself. That meant this enemy understood how AIs worked. That they were vulnerable inside their protective shells. And his actions were precisely what she would have done, were she still under the sway of her former mind control.

Rika shuddered at the thought. She still had nightmares about the time spent under Malalia Maktan's control, and the terrible things she had done. She knew, rationally, that it was not her fault, but that didn't make it much easier to swallow.

She had killed emotionlessly. Used as a tool. She was determined that would never happen again.

"These Tslavars are different," she said, putting her head back into the game. "They obviously figured out that they can't crack an AI mind from the outside, so they tried it from within."

"And *inside* his hull, this poor AI was relatively defenseless," Jo said softly. "All of his armor and shielding was on the outside. Designed to stop attackers without, not within."

"Eddie, I need you and Rika to fly to the shipworks in San Diego," Cal said out of the blue.

"Why? These bastards are still close. We can catch them," Rika said.

"Because the situation has apparently changed, and I want to do all I can to ensure you are as prepared as possible to handle it."

"What did you have in mind?" Eddie asked.

"A hasty upgrade for you, Eddie. It's not normal for a ship so young to receive this level of equipment, but given the situation, I believe it is warranted. And Rika, I will also have the **Fujin** ***outfitted with upgrades as well. You will both possess the most formidable shielding array we possess for craft of your size. It is still in testing, but the AI network has been working round the clock to devise a means to adjust the phase spectrum of the shielding arrays to shift instantaneously upon attack to best deflect or at least reduce the effect of magic-powered attacks. It is not perfect by any means, but it will provide you a much more powerful layer of protection when you face these attackers."***

Rika was already walking to her ship. "Come on, Jo. The sooner we get this done, the sooner we go hunting. *Proper* hunting."

Her AI mechanic wasn't normally a violent being, but seeing what had been done here flushed her electronic synapses with an unfamiliar feeling. Anger. And with it, the desire for revenge.

"Coming," she replied, trotting after her friend. "The rest of you had better saddle up and get moving," she called out to the others. "As soon as we level up, we're getting even."

CHAPTER SEVENTEEN

Ara dropped out of her jump in a new solar system quite some distance from Earth. Despite the usual stresses of performing such a feat, she felt fantastic, not drained at all. Soaking in the restorative power of the Earth's sun for so long had built her reserves of power to massive levels.

And it was a good thing, because, so far as she could tell, they might need them again, and sooner than later, if the Tslavars caught wind of their Zomoki stalker and her deadly passengers.

"I smell something," she said as they gained their bearings.

Charlie was already fast at work with his tech devices, getting a fix on their location as best he could, matching it with star charts loaded into the portable system by Cal when he had it installed.

So far as he could tell, they were in a previously mapped and somewhat desolate system with no habitable planets. Most were too far from the weak brown dwarf sun to support life, but others were so close as to render them an inhospitable blast furnace for any who might try to land on them.

"How close, Wise One?" Bawb asked.

"I cannot say with certainty. But there are definite traces of them, of that I am sure. And they have not jumped again. Not yet. That leaves a much different residual energy."

"So they're still here," Charlie said. *"Now we just have to track them down. Bawb, do you think they'll keep their shimmer active now that they're away from Earth?"*

"It is likely," he replied. *"They fled in a state of panic, having been successfully targeted and attacked. It would be tactically sound to remain shimmer cloaked as long as possible until they are certain of their safety, even if it has a higher power cost."*

"Then we'll have to do this the magic way. You guys smell which way they went?"

Ara cocked her head, taking in the traces of magic swirling around the system. Bawb also focused his energies, the Ootaki hair he wore boosting his senses.

"There is something there," the Wampeh said. *"Ara, can you feel that?"*

"Yes, I can," she replied. *"The faintest hint of something. Some energy that is not from our quarry."*

"Energy? What energy? My scans aren't showing anything," Charlie said, adjusting the settings on the array mounted to Ara's harness.

"I can't say for sure, but there's some strange magic here," Ara said. *"At least, I believe it is magic."*

"Is it the sun?"

"No, this sun does not possess more than the tiniest bit of magical potential. But there is a trace of something out there."

She adjusted her course, moving toward the outer planets to begin a survey of the area. It was a tactic they'd briefly discussed while figuring out how to follow a ship that could surprise them at any moment, popping into the visible spectrum and launching an attack.

"We come at them from the dark," Charlie said. "Kind of the

opposite of old fighter pilots back when they flew airplanes on Earth."

"I do not know what you are talking about, Charlie," his Zomoki friend chided. "Please, remember I am not of your world."

"Right. So it was an old-timey combat tactic I learned about in basic training. Essentially, a pilot would fly behind their target while keeping the sun behind them. That way the other pilot wouldn't be able to see them."

"But they would be pinpointed against the sun's glow," Ara said.

"Well, for you, yeah. But these guys didn't possess spells to protect their eyes from bright light. If they looked at the sun, they'd go blind, so flying in with the sun at your back was the perfect way to remain unseen until it was too late."

"I do not see how this helps us, Charlie," Bawb said. "The spell to negate the harmful effects of the sun is incredibly simple, and common. No one would be taken by surprise by your tactic."

"No, you don't get it," Charlie replied. "I'm not saying we come from the sun. We come from the *dark*. It's the opposite, see? We aren't a self-illuminating ship. No windows or running lights. So we'll be just a tiny, dark blip in the middle of the blackness of space."

"Until we are illuminated by the sun's glow," Bawb noted.

"Well, obviously. But until that happens, we can position ourselves to be shaded by planets or moons while we search. We'll be able to sense their magic as it grows stronger, but they won't be able to see us. It's not a shimmer spell, but it's pretty good, if you ask me."

Ultimately, they agreed with him, though the encounters thus far hadn't provided them opportunity to test his theory. But now, in this distant system, test it they would. Charlie just hoped he was right.

Ara dropped into the shadow of the farthest celestial body in the system of eight worlds, then gradually flew closer to the thin atmospheric boundary of the planet. She passed through it easily and proceeded to make a wide loop of the area, taking in the smells of the system, filtering as she searched for the hidden ship.

"It is not here," she said. *"The scent is nearly gone. We must move to the next closest planet."*

"You do what you need to do," Charlie said. *"I'll keep scanning back here. And Bob'll help you sniff them out as best he can."*

"As I am already doing," the assassin said. *"As of yet, however, I concur with Ara. They would appear to be closer to the system's sun."*

"Then we head that way. Do you think we should skip a few planets?"

"No," Ara said. *"That would be unwise. The unusual trace of that strange power is disconcerting and is making it slightly difficult to accurately track their scent. Cautious and methodical will be the best choice."*

Ara spent the next several hours slowly moving in from the outermost worlds to those nearer the small sun, but they hadn't found the ship yet. They had, however, picked up a much stronger trail.

"I think they are most likely orbiting the next planet," Ara said. *"Prepare yourselves in case we—"*

"What is it, Ara?"

She sniffed the magic in the void and abruptly turned. Charlie and Bawb could feel the magic building in their friend.

"They jumped again," she said. *"The surge of their magic gave me a clearer fix on them. I was mistaken, they were two worlds away. But now I know where they went. Hold on."*

Without further delay, the mighty Zomoki unleashed her magic and jumped in pursuit, once more flinging them to an even more distant system.

CHAPTER EIGHTEEN

It had been nearly a half dozen jumps since the Tslavars had been forced to flee the surprisingly robust defenders of the base orbiting the Earth. Not only had the weapons of the planet's forces managed to land hits on their ship--despite their shimmer shielding--they also had a powerful ally. A very surprising one, at that.

They had a Zomoki.

When Captain Jimtee had been assigned the honor of being the first ship through the portal, he was briefed on the invasion plans. The sun in the new system they were going to was potent, but none of the discussions had mentioned any magic users on the other side, and certainly nothing about what appeared to be a particularly strong Zomoki.

The other defenses he was fairly confident they could overcome, even shorthanded as they were. But *that* enormous red beast? Blasting magical flames in space, no less? It was obviously a far different adversary they were facing than planned.

And on top of that, the portal was gone, buried deep in the burning mass of the system's sun. It was still active, so far as they could ascertain, but there was no way to retrieve it without a massive amount of power. Power they simply did not have.

So it was that they went in search of magical sources to help their cause. Surely somewhere in this galaxy they would find some, and with them they could finally retrieve the portal from its fiery resting place. But the question in the back of all of their minds was, exactly how long would it take?

"Captain, that's our fifth jump in short succession," Ulus informed his superior.

"I am aware of this, Ulus," the captain replied.

"Ah, yes, sir. But I fear our Drooks will need to rest if we keep up at this pace. This many jumps so close together is draining their magic too quickly for them to properly replenish between them."

Captain Jimtee was not thrilled with the news. He was well aware that he was pushing his crew hard and would have to ease up in his search for a new source of magic, but hearing someone else say it aloud drove it home in a rather uncomfortable way. He was being a bit obsessive, and his men were noticing. That was never a good thing.

"Of course, you are right," he said to his second-in-command with a casual grin. "Take us to the nearest habitable planet. There appears to be some slight power emitted by this system's sun. Perhaps we may find means to harness some of it while the Drooks replenish themselves."

"I shall carry out your command at once," Ulus said, then hurried off to make it so.

Jimtee couldn't help but wonder what they might find on this new planet. If it was anything like the last one, he would not be impressed.

"Save your magic," Ulus called after the hunting party as they headed out to slay some of the native creatures they had seen when the invisible ship was coming in to land.

The men nodded and slid into their shimmer cloaks. With those on their backs, their prey would never know what hit them. Soon, there would be fresh meat on the table, which would do wonders for the exhausted crew.

He sent another group out to survey the area and magically scan local vegetation for both anything edible, as well as anything that might contain magical properties. He knew it was a long shot, but even in a system with a weak sun, it was still a possibility.

In his many years serving beneath Captain Jimtee, Ulus had seen the captain find resources in places no one would have ever thought to look. It was how he had climbed the ranks so quickly. While others went by the book, Captain Jimtee tended to color outside the lines, and more often than not, to the benefit of his mission.

And so it was Ulus once again sent their men out on that familiar reconnaissance mission. He doubted they'd find anything with magical properties––at least, not enough to even have the slightest hope of helping them retrieve the portal back to their waiting fleet that was currently trapped within the Earth's sun. Nevertheless, he was sure his men were thorough in their duties.

A short while later the hunting party returned carrying a pair of rather large quadrupedal animals with violet-hued skin beneath their thin blue fur. The creatures possessed strong haunches and appeared as if they could even stand upright if they desired. Ulus posited it might be a means for them to gather food from higher branches on the low trees that dotted the landscape.

Their front paws were more like hands in that they possessed opposable thumbs, though they were a bit short to be of use for any fine motor skills. He pried open one of the dead animals' mouths.

"They are herbivores," he noted, seeing the decidedly non-pointed teeth. These were plant eaters, and as such, their flesh would likely be far less gamey than that of carnivorous beasts. It would be a good meal, and one that would undoubtedly raise the spirits of the crew.

Being trapped, for all intents and purposes, in a distant galaxy with no way home--at least, not yet--had cast a gray mood over the men. They still performed their duties with precision and efficiency, but gone were the laughs and casual banter in their quarters. All could not help but wonder what the captain was going to do about their situation.

And Ulus knew that the captain was well aware of the issue and was doing his best. He had a plan. He always did. But he didn't want to get his crew's hopes up. Not yet. But if they could somehow gather enough of the weak magic found sporadically in this galaxy's systems, he thought there might be a chance to use it to their advantage. To return to join Captain Fratt back in Earth's system and recover the portal from the sun's flames.

But for now they would search and gather samples, preparing for the day when, hopefully, they would be joined by the rest of their fleet and hailed as heroes.

CHAPTER NINETEEN

Not too far away in what was yet another new system, Ara flew through the empty space between the dozen planets that orbited this new, more powerful sun. She knew the shimmer ship they sought had to be somewhere close--there were only so many planets in this system--but her energy was finally flagging.

"I must rest," she informed them, altering course for the nearest planet with a habitable atmosphere.

There were four such planets, though the outer and innermost would have been uncomfortably cold or hot, respectively. Ara selected one of the two in between. With the new sun's unusually strong energy, the smell of their quarry was a bit muddled. They were near, but she was simply in no state to confront them at this time.

Fortunately, she selected the world the Tslavars were not occupying. Of course, stumbling into a single shimmer-cloaked ship on an entire planet would have been a feat to stun any oddsmaker, but her selection of worlds on which to recuperate provided them that extra bit of safety, whether they realized it or not.

"Yeah, I think we all could use a break," Charlie said. *"I know my*

ass is numb from all of this flying around out here. Even in zero-gs, sitting gets kinda old. How 'bout you, Bob?"

"I have endured worse," the stoic Wampeh said. *"However, I believe the Wise One will benefit greatly from a respite. She has performed many jumps in a very short time."*

"I'm with ya on that," Charlie replied. *"Ara, you see a spot where you might find yourself a little something to eat?"*

She dropped down into the atmosphere of the planet, her golden eyes scanning the terrain below.

"Yes, I see what appear to be herds of some sort of beast in the distance. I also see a water source, though I'm unsure of its purity. I will land there and leave you to ascertain its potability as I hunt. Obviously, what is readily ingested by a Zomoki might cause distress to one or both of you."

"No worries. We've got plenty of clean water packed, but with a few well-placed spells we should be able to purify it to make it safe enough to refill our stores."

"Very well," she said. *"I will bring you back one of the beasts, should they prove palatable."*

With that, Ara circled a flat clearing on a small rise above a slow-moving stream, settling in for a soft landing.

Charlie and Bawb quickly dismounted, taking the supplies they'd need to set up a campsite from her harness, then stepping clear.

"Happy hunting," Charlie said.

"May fortune smile upon you," Bawb added with a warm smile.

Even exhausted from their flight, the Wampeh was exhibiting a level of peace and calm that seemed almost outside of his usual level demeanor. It was largely due to the connection with Ara that had remained intact ever since they shared power not so long ago.

He was a man of violence and death. An assassin of the highest order. Yet, now that he was bonded in a manner with this mighty, noble creature, Bawb, it seemed, had begun to mellow a bit. Almost as if their connection was a chrysalis, and what was emerging was a new man. One with the skills of the deadliest Wampeh Ghalian, but the tranquility of one completely at ease with himself and the universe.

Charlie had noted the change, as had Ara, but as it was a shift in a positive direction, neither felt the need to say anything about it. Bawb was their friend, no matter what, and now he was evolving yet again. Hunze had started the shift, but Ara had given it an additional nudge.

"I sense magic here," Ara said. *"But it is of this world, and does not appear to be controlled or cast in any meaningful way. You should both be safe up here, and the water source is just below."*

"We've got it, Ara. We're fine. Go get something to eat and get yourself some rest, okay?"

Ara chuckled. *"Of course, Charlie. I forget the others are not with us on this excursion. I have the utmost confidence you both will be fine. I'll be back shortly."*

She flapped her mighty wings and took to the air, sniffing deeply to lock in the scent of her new prey, then flying off toward a distant plain to fill her belly with some new and exotic beasts.

"You think she's holding up all right?" Charlie asked his friend.

Bawb sat on a rock and looked out over the verdant, multi-colored landscape of the alien world. "Yes, I do," he replied. "Sharing our link, as we do, I am still somewhat able to sense her power."

"Ah, right. You've got your Ootaki hair pumping your magic," Charlie said. "I've gotten so used to seeing you in it, I almost forgot."

"Yes, Hunze's gift is providing me the strength needed for this task," Bawb said, a slight shadow passing over his face at the mention of his golden-haired love.

"Hey, man. She's fine. The others will look after her."

Bawb shook off the gloom. "Yes, of course. I know this,

Charlie, it's just that I have been utilizing Cal's neuro-stim technology to attempt to give her as much of my magical knowledge as possible. I can never repay her for this," he said, running his fingers over the thick braid of magical hair, "but I hoped to at least provide her a means to protect herself in the future."

"And she'll be able to," Charlie said. "Just give it a little time."

Bawb smiled wistfully. "I hope so, my friend. But it seems that her Ootaki nature is at odds with her casting spells. Even wielding my most powerful konus, she is still struggling to make even the most basic of spells work."

"You think because Ootaki are genetically used as power storage devices that they've got some sort of built-in block to using magic?"

"It seems that way," Bawb replied. "I shall continue, regardless, of course. But I worry she may always be vulnerable when I am not present to protect her."

Charlie could understand the concern. He felt the same way about Leila, though she was a far more skilled fighter than most, and a fast learner. With a bit more training, he was pretty confident she would wield magic as well as any. Plus, she wore her Magus stone pretty much constantly, which would keep her safe of its own accord.

It was frustrating to her that she could not consciously tap into the stone left to her by her mother, especially now that they all suspected it might very well be one of the most powerful Magus stones on record. But, it seemed, her half-breed blood made it difficult to connect to her mother's side. The side that could control it.

That said, it did seem to automatically recognize danger, and had saved not only Leila, but all of them by extension, on more than one occasion.

"I hear ya, Bob," he said, patting his friend on the shoulder. "That whole giving-you-her-hair-out-of-love thing must've been a bit of a head trip for you. I mean, who knew that it would make it *that* much more powerful? Or that it would be bonded to you alone for life? But I guess that's an Ootaki thing no one ever thought about. They're just not expected to cut off their hair and give it to you, ya know?"

A strange look flashed briefly across the Wampeh's face, quickly replaced by one of intense thought and curiosity.

"Uh, Bob? You look like you just ate a fly. What's going on in there?"

"What? Oh, I was just thinking a moment. Your words, they made me ponder the nature of my connection with Hunze."

"In a good way, though, right?"

"Always," Bawb replied, rising back to his feet and stretching wide, filling his lungs with fresh air as he once more looked out over the tranquil world. "Now come, let us make camp and replenish our water supplies. This system's sun should help the Wise One recover a bit faster than the previous worlds, but it is nowhere near the same variety of magic of your system's star."

"Why can't I feel that?" Charlie asked. "I have Ara's blood in my veins, but I still can't really sense that stuff."

"She is enormously powerful, Charlie. And while your own powers are growing--faster and greater than I believe you are aware--you are still nowhere near her level of magical potency."

"Great. Magical impotence. Way to make a guy self-conscious, dude."

Bawb laughed merrily. "Oh, my friend, you are far from impotent. Never fear, you will mature into your power soon enough, the pieces merely need to slide into place. But come, we have work to do. We will be here for at least a day, so long as our prey does not bolt again--though by my calculations, unless they are carrying an unusually robust contingent of Drooks, they will need to replenish their energy as well. In any case, we would be wise to make the most of this time."

Charlie agreed with his friend, and once the two had set up a basic camp, protected by a few spells, courtesy of Bawb's wand, they headed down to the shore to collect water and see if there might be some sort of native fish they could catch.

And sitting on the bank of the stream, smelling the fresh water wafting in the breeze, Charlie thought it almost felt like those fishing trips in his youth. And the alien man at his side had become as much a brother to him as he'd ever had.

CHAPTER TWENTY

The fabrications facilities controlled by the greatest AI minds on Earth were designing, testing, retooling, and retesting their creations at lightning speed. Time was of the essence, something they were acutely aware of given the incident with the previous invasion such a short while ago.

All of the available munitions experts were pulled into the discussion, and even some of the original designers of the rail gun system now gracing Eddie's ship were tracked down. It was something of a coup, finding such highly specialized minds given what had happened to most military AIs in the Great War. But a few had survived and were now gladly sharing their expertise and knowledge.

The plan Cal and the others had come up with was a novel one never before attempted. Given the nature of the invaders' shielding, it seemed unlikely they would get more than one chance at penetrating it before their enemy modified their defenses. What had worked with the previous hostile forces would likely not fare nearly so well against what appeared to be a far greater shielded ship.

But they had an idea.

Building a specialized sabot for Eddie's rail gun was the easy part. The mechanism would fire the hypersonic projectile at blistering speed, defeating the enemy's defenses and penetrating their hull. The hard part was figuring out how to embed a tracking device that would allow them to pursue the ship no matter where it went.

Ultimately, it was Eddie himself who came up with a novel idea.

"Why don't we embed a minor AI in it?" he asked the others. "It seems like it would make sense, having a smart tracker rather than one that just blasts out noise and would probably be discovered because of it."

The AI conglomerate discussed the idea, which, given no human minds were involved, took mere seconds at their incredible processing speeds. A decision had been made. They would not sacrifice a properly matured AI mind for the purpose, but if they could retask one of the lesser models with barely any sentience, it just might do the job.

The coding took some doing, reworking the central drive of what had formerly been a coffeemaker or a vacuum, but as the test rounds were being shot off in a controlled setting, they were able to recover the units and make adjustments rather than starting from scratch each and every time.

In the meantime, a modification was installed in Eddie's firing system. The rail gun would fire as it normally did, but if they got a fix on the alien ship, he could immediately drop an AI round into the firing chamber from a separate feed. Given the experimental nature of the device, and the possibility he might miss, it was decided to make as many of the highly specialized rounds as possible in the short window available to them.

After round-the-clock-testing, and hundreds of rounds fired, stripped, rechambered, and fired again, they finally had a working design.

The AIs within them had been reduced to what Cal had called a breadcrumb.

"It is now set to continuously send tracking signals on a randomized interval," he said. ***"This serves a twofold purpose. One, it will prevent detection by the hostiles, and two, it will reduce energy consumption, as sending these signals takes significant power to have any semblance of inter-system reach, in the event they flee our solar system as the other ship previously did."***

"But I thought we couldn't communicate that way," Rika said when she heard the plan. "You said all of the ships out there were out of touch until they came back, and that no comms could travel that far."

"That is true, but only to a point," Cal replied. ***"By sending only one tiny pulse signal with massive power, it is the equivalent of a glowing breadcrumb beaming its location across great distance far faster than any actual communications could. Putting it in communications terms, this signal is tiny, and a ship's AI is not. It is the difference between a crumb, and a loaf of bread."***

"So this superpowered breadcrumb will help lead us to wherever they go, even if they run off-world."

"Exactly."

"But how do we find them?" Ripley asked. "They keep popping up all over the place."

"It seems they are attempting to commandeer additional craft, likely to strengthen their fighting force. That will help us narrow the list of potential targets, given their path so far. In fact, after the attack in Gibraltar, and given the general easterly trend of their flight, I would think the former base in Sicily would be a tempting target."

"Seems as good a bet as any," Rika said. "But even with Eddie's new tracking rounds, we're still not equipped to deal with them. They're invisible, and all we're tracking is the faintest of solar power variations. Not the most pinpoint accurate system, if you catch my drift."

Ripley started bouncing on the balls of her feet. "Ooh, I have an idea!"

"Yes, Ripley?"

"What if we have Eddie fly us out there first. *Before* they even get there. With the shimmer cloak we've been using, they might not see us."

"So you'll be lying in wait for them," Rika said. "Damn, Rip, that's a good idea. But that shimmer isn't terribly effective."

"Doesn't have to be. By the time they're close enough to see us, hopefully it'll be too late for them."

"*Hopefully*," Rika said.

"It seems the best option we have, given our resources," Cal said. ***"I will alert the individuals stationed there to stay well clear until any action is over."***

"Great! Then it's settled. Come on, guys, let's get moving!" Ripley chirped, rushing to board her ship. Hunze and Leila followed close behind, while Rika and Jo headed off to the *Fujin.*

"We all loaded and good to go?" Rika asked her gunner.

"Green across the board," Jo replied. "Let's get airborne and punch it. There's no telling how much time we'll have to spare if we want to get there before the Tslavars do."

"*If* that's where they're going," Rika added.

"Yeah, it's a big if, but what else do we have?"

"Not much," Rika replied. "They're probably moving at a very low speed to avoid sensors, so it'll likely be a while before they actually get there. But better safe than sorry. Hang on, Jo. I'm gonna burn hard."

With that, the *Fujin* blasted into the air and took off like a bat out of hell on a course for the base on the island of Sicily.

CHAPTER TWENTY-ONE

Eddie arrived well ahead of the *Fujin*, having the benefit of not only a head start, but also the lack of need to take much of a roundabout course in case enemy eyes might be looking. Sure, his shimmer was spotty, but unless they were really looking, he was pretty confident the Tslavars wouldn't be able to see him.

At least, he hoped that was the case.

When they arrived in Sicily, he did a quick loop over the airfield before selecting the best spot to touch down and wait to take his shot.

"Whaddya think, Rip? Over there, between those two freighters?" he asked.

"I don't know, Eddie. I mean, yeah, they probably won't try to commandeer those clunky things, but I would worry about being stuck between them in case they manage to get the drop on us and we have to bail in a hurry," she replied.

"Yeah, I guess you're right. If this shimmer thing was stronger we wouldn't really have to worry so much about that. But we work with what we've got, right?"

"You said it, Eddie," Ripley agreed. "So how about you tuck in over by the tool shed area? It's got a clear line of fire to just about the entire facility, and, *bonus*, the building is low enough that we can easily hop up and over if we have to do an emergency egress."

"Copy that," the AI ship said, flying over to the designated area and settling in for the wait.

"Excuse me," Hunze said. "I was wondering, this shimmer spell you are casting, you say it is actually being cast by *both* of you?"

"Yeah. Me and Eddie are layering up the spell."

"But he is a machine. How can he cast with you?"

"Well, I've got several konuses to work with," Ripley said. "And Eddie now has one installed into his infrastructure, courtesy of Bawb. It's not a perfect system by any means, but it's a pretty cool idea, and it actually does let Eddie cast."

"Thanks to the neuro-stim data, of course," he added. "I'd never have gotten the whole 'intent versus words' part of it without the visceral understanding from a stim transfer."

"I know, right? It's really cool," Ripley agreed.

Hunze knew full well what they spoke of, though her experience with the device had been less than fruitful. "Will you show me this konus Bawb gave to you both?"

"Sure," Ripley said. "Eddie, shout if it looks like we have company, okay?"

"You got it, Rip."

"And load a tracker sabot so it's ready, just in case."

"One step ahead of you," the ship said. "And I can back-feed the system to remove it in under a second if we need to switch back to regular rounds."

"Sweet. Then hang tight and shout out if ya see anything. Rika's gonna be circling high above, waiting for our signal to make her diversionary attack."

"So long as this shimmer holds out, they should never know what hit them," Eddie said with a chipper tone.

Ripley walked to the door leading to Eddie's inner workings. "C'mon, Hunze, it's this way. You wanna check it out too, Leila?"

The olive-skinned woman rose from her seat. "I don't see why not. Lead the way."

The teen guided them down a series of short corridors with heavily reinforced walls and shock-dampening fittings, all protecting the vital core of the ship. Eddie's processing core. His mind.

"There it is," she said, pointing to the thick golden band fused into the metal of Eddie's central housing itself.

Bawb had been masterful in his use of the welding magic, managing to smoothly attach the device without compromising the stability of the original housing. Hunze knew the konus on sight. One of his most powerful ones, now given to their friends in time of need.

It must have been odd, parting with it after so many years of use, but there was much at stake, and he had obviously wanted to do all he could to help his young friend survive.

"Impressive," Leila said, running her fingers over the embedded metal. "He fused it directly to Eddie's equivalent of a skull, I suppose. And all without damaging the metal. He really is quite skilled in ways I never expected."

"That he is," Hunze agreed as she stepped closer to the konus.

With one fluid motion, she plucked a single strand of hair from the top of her head and began wrapping it around the magical device.

"What are you doing?" Ripley asked.

"I am giving you a gift," she replied, tightly winding the lengthy strand in place.

Leila was taken aback by the action. "Hunze, you don't have to do that," she said. "You aren't just someone's power-making tool anymore. You're a free woman."

"I know, Leila, and I have you all to thank for that. You are all my friends. My family, really. And this world is my home now. I know I am terrible at casting, no matter what Bawb tries, but this, at least, I can do."

She finished tying the hair in place and stepped back. "Freely given," she said warmly. "That should help your shimmer spell, I would think."

Indeed it did, and Eddie and Ripley both could immediately feel the massive surge in power now fueling their magical spell. Instantly, the shimmer spell was operating at maximum potential. The gaps in their invisibility vanished, leaving the entire ship completely invisible.

"Hey, what happened down there?" Rika said over the comms. "I saw where you parked, and it was a good spot, but you guys just suddenly went entirely invisible."

"You can't see any breaks in the shimmer anymore?" Ripley asked.

"Nope. You guys are ghosts."

"Awesome," the teen chirped. "Thank you!" she blurted, wrapping Hunze in a warm embrace. "You're the best. You know that?"

The Ootaki smiled, happy to have been able to contribute in some way.

"Wow, those guys are going to be so surprised," Ripley said with a happy chuckle as they walked back to their seats in command. "They are so screwed!"

"I believe you're right," Leila agreed. "At least, I certainly hope so. Now all we can do is wait."

CHAPTER TWENTY-TWO

"They were here," Ara said, sniffing the air.

Charlie looked at the charred remains of what appeared to be two animals, slaughtered and eaten by the people they were pursuing. "Yeah, I can see that," he replied, nudging the bones with his boot.

There had been a feast here, and there were so many bootprints that even Bawb was unable to determine the group's numbers. More likely than not, he thought, their captain had eased off the gas for a moment to allow some morale-boosting surface time for his men. Charlie couldn't help but appreciate a leader who was cognizant of his people's needs.

Nevertheless, they were the enemy, and no amount of consideration toward his crew would change that.

"But why would they burn the carcasses like this?" Charlie asked, examining the blackened pile. "It was obviously a magical flame that did this. Even I can tell that much. No burnt wood, no ashes or embers. But they still took the time to reduce the remains to just bones."

Bawb walked over and looked at the pile. "I think this confirms Ara's assessment of our quarry based on what we saw of their remains at Dark Side," he said. "Tslavars, if I am correct. Do you concur, Wise One?"

Ara didn't even need to try to smell the thick traces of Tslavar sweat that lingered in the air like a pungent musk. "Indeed, Bawb. Tslavars, and Drooks, as well."

"I would assume as much," the assassin replied. "Though it is surprising they would allow them off the ship in an unsecured environment."

"Not like they've got anywhere to run," Charlie noted.

"Oh, it's not about running. But there are things out there that might make a quick meal of a defenseless Drook. And *that* would leave their ship with that much less power."

"Valid point," Charlie said.

"And to your question about the remains," Bawb continued. "It is a Tslavar habit to never leave anything behind an enemy might find use from. They always destroy foodstuffs left behind."

"But they don't even know we're following them. At least, I don't think they do. Ara?"

"No, they have not fled the planet yet, so I think not. From what I can tell, they have flown toward the rising sun. Perhaps five hours ago."

A slight rustle from the bushes made Charlie jump back and spin, a disabling spell already on the tip of his tongue, drawing from his internal power rather than the konus on his wrist. His tapping into that replenishing source was becoming second nature at this point.

Bawb was suddenly nowhere to be seen.

"Ara, what do you smell?"

"It appears to be some sort of local creature. I noticed them when we arrived. Medium-sized, quadrupedal." She sniffed the air again. *"And I believe this is the same type of creature the Tslavars feasted on last night."*

"Dangerous?"

"Doubtful."

Charlie felt the tension in his shoulders ease, but he kept his spell ready anyway, just in case. A moment later, the violet-skinned creature came rushing from the brush, but it was, Charlie noted, actually tumbling rather than running.

"Bawb, that you?"

The Wampeh removed his shimmer cloak, slipping back into visibility. "Of course it is," he said with a grin. "I thought we might have a word with our friend, here."

"A word?" Charlie said, confused.

"Oh, yes. I have extended our translation spells to those around us, if you recall. And I heard this one muttering in the bushes."

"I sorry," the creature babbled, its eyes wide at the sight of the massive dragon staring at it calmly with its enormous golden eyes. "I no bad. I only look for Dima and Poona."

The poor creature was obviously terrified. Charlie relaxed his grip on his magic, letting the spells at his disposal retreat back into his mind. "Who are Dima and Poona?" he asked. "And why were you hiding in the bushes? We're not going to hurt you."

The four-legged creature seemed to relax, but only slightly.

"The green men come. Take Dima. Take Poona. Come from nowhere. Come like *he* do," it said, nodding its head toward Bawb.

"They were using shimmer cloaks for a hunt," the Wampeh said. "And I assume the two this one speaks of..."

He didn't need to say any more. Whoever they were to the cowering animal, Dima and Poona had obviously been killed and eaten by the invading force.

"Ara, why is it we can speak with this one?" Charlie asked silently. *"We can't talk to animals with translation spells. I know, I tried when Leila was showing me around Visla Maktan's holding pens."*

The Zomoki assessed the creature with her golden eyes. *"Because it only works with higher intellects, Charlie. Despite this creature's appearance, it may very well be one of the top intelligences on this planet."*

"So they killed and ate talking, conversing creatures? That's horrific, even for Tslavars."

"To be fair, they likely did not even attempt to provide a translation spell to a creature that so greatly resembled one of their usual food sources," Bawb interjected. *"But I agree, it would be extremely traumatic for a creature capable of higher brain function and reasoning to suffer their fate, though given the typical Tslavar hunting tactics, I doubt they ever felt a thing."*

"Not like that'll make our new friend here feel any better," Charlie said.

"It is commonplace, this underestimating of creatures that look different," Ara commented. *"Believe me, it is something with which I have great familiarity."*

Charlie turned to the creature. "Hey, buddy. What's your name?"

"Orta," the creature replied.

"Okay, Orta, why don't you and I go take a look around and see if we can find your friends, okay?"

"What are you doing?" Bawb asked in his head.

"Getting him out of here long enough for you to bury those bones."

"It would be easier to just tell him," the Wampeh noted.

"Yeah, well, I think a bit of misdirection won't hurt in this instance. It's our first contact with intelligent life in my galaxy, and I'd rather not start by telling the fella his friends were just killed and eaten."

"Fine. Go for a walk. I shall cleanse the site," Bawb said with a shrug.

Charlie and his temporary companion headed off into the nearby tree line, leaving Bawb to do what needed to be done. By the time they returned a half hour later, there was no trace of the carcasses.

"Well, I guess they must have gone somewhere else," Charlie said. "Or maybe they decided to travel with those green men you saw."

"But why they leave me?"

"I can't say. But you're a big fella. You can take care of yourself, right?"

"Yes, I suppose," he replied.

"Good. Now you head on to your family and let them know not to be afraid of us. We're friends, okay? Like we talked about on our walk."

"Friends, yes," he said, then abruptly turned and trotted off through the trees.

"That went better than expected," Charlie said when Orta was out of earshot. "Thanks for cleaning that up."

"Happy to be of help, Charlie. But we have pressing matters. While you were gone, the Wise One sensed movement from the enemy craft."

"Yes, it seems to have headed off-world to the planet we just came from," she said.

"But it didn't jump?" Charlie confirmed.

"No. And it is moving at a surprisingly slow pace. I believe the Drooks powering that ship must be tiring."

"I agree with that assessment," Bawb added. "But they're also more methodical in this system. Have you noticed? Like they're looking for something."

"Yeah, some kind of magic they can use," Charlie said. "But Ara's far more sensitive to that stuff than they are, and there's not much they'd find of use here."

"I agree with that assess—"

The comms array on Ara's harness interrupted her, a faint bleep rising from the machine. Charlie rushed to her and quickly climbed into his seat, keying the device. The volume had been turned down low, but now that he had it fully powered, the signal was clear.

"It's a distress call," he said. "On *our* comms network."

"A trap?" Bawb asked.

"No, the Tslavars don't have this kind of tech, and even if they had stolen one, there's no way they'd have figured out how to work it this fast."

"So what is it, then?" the Wampeh mused.

Charlie had already hopped off of Ara and was packing up his gear. "We'll find out soon enough."

CHAPTER TWENTY-THREE

Ara took a circuitous route to the location of the faint distress beacon, and Charlie was perfectly fine with that. There was no way any of the survey crews were in this system. The odds of simply stumbling upon one of them were infinitesimally small. In addition to that, bumping into a cluster of well-armed and very experienced AI ships, all ready for a rumble, if necessary, would have likely sent the lone Tslavar vessel running.

The Tslavars, it seemed, had missed this signal entirely, relying on magical means of communication rather than technology-based ones. But even so, Charlie and his friends were wary of the distress call. But it checked out all the way down to its transmission frequency. If it actually was a trap, it was one hell of a good one.

Ara had said she'd noted the strange smell she had been picking up for a few systems now once again, but also a new smell. Something different. And it grew stronger as they neared the mysterious signal.

"You ready to jump if we have to?" Charlie asked.

"At a moment's notice," Ara replied. *"I am well rested and ready."*

"Good," he said. *"Let's just hope that doesn't become necessary."*

They circled the hot zone where the call was coming from. The tree line seemed to have been toppled in a linear manner.

"Look like a crashing ship's path to you?" Charlie asked.

"Indeed, it does," Bawb said.

"And it seemed to have come in under at least some power," Ara noted. *"Shall I descend?"*

"No time like the present, I suppose," Charlie thought with a sigh. *"Take us in, Ara."*

The massive dragon rapidly approached the ground, her senses on high alert as she swooped in closer and closer to the site of the crash landing. Finally, with a mighty flap of her wings, she touched down in a rather breathtaking manner.

Right beside what seemed to be an Earth ship.

A Chithiid who had been resting in the shade of the craft scrambled to his feet, trying to pull his pulse rifle free from the rest of his gear, nearly tripping over himself in his haste.

"Pulse rifle! Defensive spells!" Charlie called out.

In seconds, he and his friends were fully protected by the specialized spells they had designed to use against Earth weaponry. They had figured that someday, perhaps an enemy might gain control over some of their firepower. If that was the case, it would be wise to have some sort of countermeasure spell in place.

But this was the first time they'd ever actually used it.

The Chithiid popped off a series of shots at Ara, then tracked his rifle on Bawb, again firing a volley of pulse rounds. Fortunately, both the dragon and Wampeh easily blocked the incoming attack.

"Hey, hold your fire!" Charlie called out, pulling his helmet from his head, as Bawb had already done.

At the sight of what seemed to be a human, the Chithiid ceased fire, but did not lower his weapon.

"I recognize you as human," he called out. "But I do not know this other species. This, *pale* being."

"He's called a Wampeh," Charlie informed him. "And this is Ara. She's a dragon."

"Another creature I have never before seen."

"Actually, I've heard of this one," a voice called out.

"Hang on, is that an AI ship you've got there?"

"Yes indeedly-doo, I'm an AI. Kip's the name," the ship said. "Stand down, Dookie, that's the creature the AI network was all abuzz about when we got back from our scout."

"The one from the past?"

"Yep," Kip said. "And I'm willing to bet these two fellas are her friends. The human and the space killer guy, am I right?"

"I am a Wampeh Ghalian. The most elite of assassins," Bawb said. "But yes, your basic assessment is correct."

"Oh, man, that's some good news," the relieved ship gushed. "I tell ya, there've been some seriously weird things going on around here in the last couple of days, and it's really good to see friendly faces."

Charlie walked over to the ship. It appeared to have landed just fine, although it scuffed its paint while taking out a few treetops on the way in. But other than that, it seemed unharmed.

"So, what the hell happened to you guys?" he asked. "I mean, obviously you're in a tight spot in a distant system, but how'd you get here?"

"Funny you should ask," the ship replied.

"It is not funny at all, Kip," his Chithiid pilot said.

"It's a figure of speech, Dookie."

"I do wish you would stop calling me that."

"Fine. It's a figure of speech, *Dukaan.* There, happy?"

"No, not at all. We are stranded on a planet a vast distance from our home," the Chithiid griped. "But at least you have finally said my name correctly."

"Always look on the bright side of li—"

"Hey, guys, can we skip the banter for a minute?" Charlie

interrupted. "We're kind of on a clock here. No telling when we'll have to jump."

"Jump?" Kip said with a curious tone.

"It's like a warp."

"Oh, gotcha."

"So why are you here?" Charlie continued.

"Well, we were out near the sun--we'd just come back from our deep survey run, you see--when we came under some ridiculous kind of energy fire the likes of which we've never experienced before."

"Kip is correct in his assessment," Dukaan said. "It was unlike anything I have ever seen. An invisible attacker with firepower of vast potential, but which we could not read on our sensors until it was too late."

"Yeah, we were getting our butts kicked," Kip added. "So, basically, it was the choice of either being blown to bits, or doing an emergency escape warp without even plotting a course. We just crossed our fingers and hoped we didn't warp into a sun or something."

Judging by the look of the ship, they'd actually taken very little damage from the Tslavar attack. In that, at least, they had been fortunate.

"So why the distress call?" Charlie asked. "Why not just wait it out a few days, then turn around and warp back home?"

"Because something they did to us made our drive systems short out mid-warp."

"That would be magic," Bawb noted. "I can sense the residual force still lingering on your ship, though it is incredibly faint."

"Magic? Like hocus-pocus magic?" Kip asked.

"Actually, yeah. You know the stuff you heard about when you got back in touch with the other AIs? The stuff beyond Ara here being a dragon? Well, that was real. The magic, the time travel, all of it."

"Great. So a magician shorted out my systems. The guys are never going to let me live that down. If we ever get back, that is," Kip griped.

"Pop your doors and let me take a look. Maybe I can help," Charlie offered.

"A man from a few thousand years in the past?" Kip replied sarcastically. "Yeah, good luck with that."

"Hey, I designed and built the *Asbrú*, so I'd hope I could figure out a tiny little ship like you. Now quit your whining and give me your specs so I can get to work. There's no telling how long the aliens we're tracking will stay in this system."

That got Dukaan's attention. "The beings who did this to Kip are in this system?"

"Yeah, and we're tracking them. Trying to get a fix before they attack anyone else."

"You say that as though they'd already gone after more people," Kip said, uneasy. "What have they done?"

Charlie looked at Bawb. The Wampeh merely gave him the slightest of nods. Might as well bring the somewhat odd AI up to speed, regardless if he would become an asset in the fight or not.

"They attacked Dark Side," Charlie said. "Managed to knock out several ships before inserting a strike team into the base itself."

"Dark Side has fallen?" Dukaan said, a slight panic in his voice.

"No, the base did not fall, friend," Bawb said. "Sid called in a strike on his own facilities to stop their progress. It worked, but at the cost of many innocent lives."

Dukaan and Kip both went from merely upset to utterly livid at that news. They had many friends on Dark Side, and any one of them might have been a victim. It was something they could only wonder about until they were finally able to make it back home.

After a long silence, Kip finally spoke again.

"You say you can track them?"

Ara turned toward the ship. "Yes, I can. Even through warp, if we jump close enough behind them."

"Then get me working," Kip said with determination adding a sharp edge to his voice. "Get me working, and I'll gladly come with you. Payback is a bitch."

"We'll talk about it," Charlie said, not sure if the odd ship would be up for the task. "For now, let me see what I can do."

CHAPTER TWENTY-FOUR

The technology was far more complex than anything Charlie had worked with in the past, but his engineer's mind was still able to quickly grasp the essential elements of the design. Once that was accomplished, the rest was just a matter of time.

Unfortunately, time was one thing they really didn't have much of.

"There has still been no sign of a jump," Ara told him when he came out to get a few more tools from his emergency kit.

Charlie selected the instruments he needed to finish his tinkering in Kip's inner workings, then pulled a moderately powered konus from their stash. Bawb raised a lone eyebrow but said nothing.

In a perfect world, they would simply repeat the process Bawb had performed upon Eddie for all of the ships that might encounter their Tslavar enemies.

But this was not that world. Not that galaxy, for that matter. And their supply of magical devices, while substantial, was not limitless. If they continued to give them to others, they might actually run low in short order.

This instance, however, left them no choice. To send Kip out without any magical upgrading was essentially leaving him wide open to any attacks the hostiles might throw at him. But with a konus melded to his structure, Charlie could cast a broad-spectrum defensive spell that would be only a trickle drain on the device when inactive.

But should Kip fall under attack, the konus would roar into action, dispersing as much of the magic directed at the poor ship as possible. It was an imperfect solution at best, but it was better than nothing. And at the very least, it would hopefully give the AI and his Chithiid pilot enough of a window to jump to safety.

With the sun still relatively high in the sky and the day becoming almost uncomfortably hot, Charlie climbed back aboard the AI ship and made his way back to the damaged drive systems to affect his repairs and tie the konus to the odd little ship's frame.

It had taken many hours, and the sun was low in the sky when he finally emerged at the end of a long work day, but Charlie actually seemed energized rather than drained when he stepped out into the fresh air.

The effort of going through the problem-solving routine had brought him back to his former life as an engineer, and, much as he was happy with who he had become, the familiar routine of testing and repairing had been an almost meditative act for him.

"Okay, that should do it," he said, brushing off his hands out of habit, though there was not a speck of grime or dirt to be found within Kip's pristine vessel. "Go on and fire up your drive systems. But *slowly*--I'm still new to your design, and I think I might have overpowered the energy relays a little bit."

Kip heeded the warning and gradually increased the power flowing through his drive systems until everything was humming nicely. "Heya! Seems okie dokie fine to me!" the abnormally chipper ship said.

"This one truly is odd," Bawb noted.

"Tell me about it," Charlie silently replied. *"And you didn't have to listen to him rambling all day while you dug around in his systems."*

"I'm gonna do a quick check-out flight, you guys. Everyone step clear," Kip said, silently lifting into the air. "Okay, back in a jiff!"

With that, the ship moved a safe distance from the others, then accelerated away in a flash.

"Yeah. Definitely overpowered the energy relays," Charlie said with a low chuckle.

The Chithiid pilot walked over to him and grasped the human by the shoulder with one of his four hands, while warmly shaking Charlie's hand with another.

"We appreciate all you have done for us, Charlie. I am a pilot, not a mechanic, and I fear we might have been stranded here a very long time had you not come along."

"Glad to be able to help, Dukaan. Also, just so you know, I installed a device from Ara and Bawb's galaxy while I was at it."

"Oh? To what end? I would think the technology would be incompatible with ours."

"Yeah, about that. It's not *tech*, exactly. More like magic, in fact."

"Magic? You gave Kip magic?" The Chithiid shook his head like an exhausted parent. "Oh, I fear this will not end well."

Charlie laughed. "Don't worry, it's nothing he can control himself. Just a little safety system I whipped up to help you guys out if you come under magical attack again. Kind of like your shields, only not, because, you know, *magic*."

"Ah. That is a relief. While Kip is a very capable ship, he does possess some personality quirks that occasionally prove a bit worrisome. Him in possession of magical abilities? The very thought is quite disturbing."

"I can only imagine," Charlie commiserated.

Bawb walked over to the two and offered an electrolyte pouch to them both.

"Drink. This is a particularly hot world. The breeze can be deceptive."

Charlie downed it in a few gulps. "Thanks, Bob. I kinda got in the zone while I was working in there and totally forgot to drink. Wouldn't want to be passing out now, would I?"

"Obviously not."

"It was a rhetorical, dude."

"Yes, I know," Bawb said with a hint of a grin.

"Ara, is it just me, or is Bob's sarcasm getting stronger the longer he's on Earth?"

"Technically, we are not on Earth. But your point is accurate," she replied.

Charlie thought his Zomoki friend was looking particularly rested, despite the heat. Of course, being a fire-breathing space dragon, she had an entirely different spectrum for her comfort zone when it came to a whole lot of things.

"You good, Ara?"

"Quite. This sun, while not nearly as strong as your Earth's, is nevertheless a welcome source of power," she said, breathing the air deep into her lungs and letting out a contented sigh. "It is an amazing thing, you know. How the suns of your galaxy cast off such a different form of power than those in mine."

"Helpful when you need a quick pick-me-up, right?"

"Yes, it is a wonderful discovery indeed. And this means we are ready to jump whenever needed, though I am of the assumption that the Tslavars will not yet leave this system."

"You think they found something they want?"

"Not so much that as they are flying under Drook power, and Drooks do not absorb energy in the manner of Zomoki, or even Ootaki."

It was a bit of welcome news for Charlie. Finally, they had an edge, no matter how slight. The trick now would be turning that little advantage into a major one.

Kip came roaring back across the horizon in a flash, executing a one-hundred-eighty-degree spin and settling down softly exactly where he'd taken off from.

"Damn, he really *is* good at that," Charlie mused. "So, I take it everything checks out okay?"

"Better than okay!" Kip chirped. "I've got a fifteen percent higher energy to drive ratio now, and my warp core is purring like a kitten."

"Fifteen percent? Shit, I guess I really overdid it in there. You need me to dial that down a bit? Wouldn't want you blowing yourself up, after all."

"Nah, I'm good. I adjusted my own internal limiters, so don't worry about me," Kip replied. "Anyway, my meal fabricators are pretty minimal, so I can't offer you much in the way of a thank you, but would anyone like any toast?"

"Kip, please," Dukaan sighed.

"Hey, people like toast."

The Chithiid turned to their new friends. "My apologies. He sometimes gets a little fixated on bread products. Before he was repurposed in the Great War, he had been an artificially intelligent toaster."

"Classist," Kip snarked.

"Merely relaying a fact," Dukaan replied.

Charlie chuckled at the odd couple. "It's all good, guys. But listen, it's been a long day, so what do you say we focus on scouring up some edible stuff and having a proper meal? Ara, can you take a sniff and see if there's anything that won't kill us growing around here?"

"Certainly, Charlie," she said. "I shall return momentarily."

The dragon surged into the sky to make a short loop of their general area as she scouted the vegetation.

"You choose not to hunt?" Dukaan asked.

Charlie and Bawb shared a glance. “Nah. After our last run-in with some local wildlife, I think I’m sticking with veggies for the time being.”

A few hours later, with bellies full of surprisingly tasty indigenous fruits and vegetables, the unlikely group settled in for what would be a welcome slumber.

CHAPTER TWENTY-FIVE

Eddie could feel the strange new Ootaki power gently bolstering the magic he was casting along with Ripley flowing through his very framework. It was something completely novel to him. And equally new was what he had so recently become.

The first AI magic-wielder.

Cal had posited that the ability would likely not be able to be taught to an AI. Their neural pathways were simply too different, and once matured, locked into their ways of perception and thought just enough to make successful casting unlikely, perhaps with the exception of Ripley's aunt's highly unusual AI.

Eddie, however, was a very young ship still possessing that flexibility. So young, in fact, that not only was his ability to cast intact, it was actually more robust than Cal had expected it could be. Further, because of his already present link with Ripley from their early days of her helping him pass his flight basics, he possessed a solid neural handshake with the first Earth girl to use magic.

The result was that their teamwork, along with Hunze's lone strand of supercharged Ootaki hair, had managed to not only cast, but also sustain a fully functional shimmer over his entire form. They were silent. Invisible. Stealthy.

"Just like ninjas," Ripley had said, "only minus the black clothes and swords."

Her aunt Daisy actually had a sword--the most amazing weapon she'd ever seen, in fact--but she was still off-world, so a swordless ninja Rip would remain, unless her alien friends wanted to share.

"Hey, I feel some vibrations," Eddie said to the women patiently waiting in his command pod.

"I don't see anything on scans," Ripley said. "Leila, is your stone acting up at all?"

Leila gripped the deep green stone hanging around her neck. "Nothing."

"Hunze? Any freaky vibes?"

"Also no," she replied.

"Huh. Rika, you and Jo see anything from way up there?"

Rika, circling high, high above, scanned the area with her ship's array of sensors and optical gear. "Nothing, but that doesn't mean they're not here. Remember, they're not only a shimmer-shielded ship, but also the entire crew is wearing them."

"I know, I know," Ripley said. "Eddie's scanning on infra-red to see if anything shows up."

"A shimmer blocks that as well," Rika noted.

"Yeah, but it doesn't block what they're walking on," Eddie interjected. "And if their footwear is anything like Earth shoes, they'll still transfer heat from their feet to the ground."

Rika was impressed. "That's actually a really good idea, Eddie."

"Thanks. And don't sound so surprised. I'm a top-tier AI, after all."

"Ego, much?" Ripley snarked.

"Shut up, you know you adore me."

"Uh, guys? About that scan?" Leila interrupted.

"Right. I'm running scans in all directions, but am concentrating mostly on the area over by the two medium-sized dumb ships over there."

"Dumb ships? Seriously?"

"Rip, you know as well as I do that they don't have an AI installed. So, yes. *Dumb* ships. Anyway, that seems to be the most likely place for them to--hang on a minute."

"What is it?" Ripley said, leaning in close to the readout screen.

"Did you hear the part where I said hang on?" Eddie retorted. "I think I'm getting something. The vibrations are minimal, but if the ship is in a low hover, there wouldn't be the normal impact and vibration associated with the landing gear."

"Craft from my galaxy do not land as yours do," Leila noted. "So if it is here, it is indeed hovering just above the ground."

"And that means... Gotcha!" Eddie exclaimed.

"You see them?" Ripley asked.

"Oh, yes I do," he replied. "Rika, did you copy that? They're here, right where I said they'd land. It looks like they're deploying some ground troops. Twelve of them, judging by the heat signatures of their footprints."

Eddie initiated the rail gun system and diverted the regular sabots from the launch mechanism, fitting it instead with an AI tracker round. It had been decided that he would fire the tracker first, just in case the invaders managed to adjust their shields to stop subsequent rounds.

They would have one shot at this, both literally and figuratively, and he really didn't want to mess it up. And while the craft that had previously invaded the planet had been quite susceptible to his new rail guns, Bawb had expressed his belief that the lead ships of a full invasion fleet would possess far superior shielding.

"Okay, you guys ready for this?" he asked, powering up the system.

"Ready up above," Rika said. "You light up their ship, and I'll target the ground forces."

"You see them?"

"Jo has them on her monitors, plus she's piggybacking your ground scan signal."

"She can do that?"

"She's a cyborg, Eddie. You're not the only brilliant AI brain in this game," Rika said, flashing a grin to her gunner. "You good to go, Jo?"

"You know it. I've got a pretty decent lock on the heat signatures. I might not hit all of them, but the barrage should incapacitate those I don't get directly."

"Good. Maybe we can finally get a little intel while we're at it. Injured have a tendency to talk, when you apply the right pressure," she said with a wicked grin.

"Uh, Rika? You're not regressing on us, are you?" Ripley joked over comms.

The somewhat violent woman circling above laughed in her ear.

It was obvious Rika was free from Malalia Maktan's damaging magical influence, but whether the morbid violence she was anticipating so gleefully was merely her own psyche or a fragment of a holdover from her time as the evil woman's enforcer was anyone's guess.

They were all just glad she was on their side.

"Firing in three. Two. One," Eddie said, then let off the rail gun tracker, quickly cycling to regular ammunition in mere seconds.

The tracking round struck home, blurting out an expletive-laden contact confirmation signal, then settling in to its regular transmission parameters. The invisible ship reacted immediately, blasting out magical defenses in all directions.

From above, Rika rained fire down upon the ground forces before they even had a chance to react, while Eddie did his best to disable the enemy ship before it could make a run for it. The base's auto-cannons also engaged, targeting the impact zone of Rika's rounds.

Eddie had been right. The invaders had adjusted their shields almost immediately. Even the mere seconds it took to switch ammo feeds gave the Tslavars enough time to shift their magic enough to keep the rounds from piercing their hull.

The sheer kinetic impact, however, could only be dampened so much, resulting in the hovering ship being physically pushed back several feet from the force.

Eddie was about to maneuver to get a firing solution that would allow him to pin them down in between two large ships--preventing their escape as Eddie had worried they might do to him--when an enormous burst of magic erupted from the cloaked vessel.

Nearby ships were crushed by the force, while others were sent tumbling.

"Hang on!" Eddie blurted as he hit full throttle, flinging himself skyward with enough force to make his passengers black out from the intense g's so abruptly pulled.

But in his mind, it was far better they pass out than be killed. Fortunately, the violent defensive spell that had been cast by the enemy was only targeting roughly ground-level craft. At altitude, he was safe. Relatively, anyway.

"What the hell was that?" Rika asked. "We just saw some major violence down there."

"Defensive maneuver," Eddie said. "Had to punch it and pull an evasive launch to avoid it. I lost my scanner lock in the process. You guys still see their men?"

"Yeah, several hits judging by the green blood, but no visible bodies. Not yet, anyway," Jo said.

"We'll worry about them later. We have to get that ship before it––"

A blast of force rocked the sky as the Tslavar ship performed a rapid evacuation of the base. They'd come intending to steal some ships and bolster their forces. Instead, they had been compromised and lost several men. And the enemy, it seemed, possessed a shimmer ship of their own. Their plans had just changed, and drastically.

"The tracker shows them heading straight up," Eddie said. "They're making a run to space."

"I'm on it," Rika said, flying skyward, while Jo did her best to lock on to the nascent tracker signal.

"They know we have a shimmer ship now, and they're running rather than engage."

"They don't want a fair fight," Rika replied with contempt. "They just want to camouflage themselves and sneak around like fucking campers. Chicken shits."

A ping rang out from Jo's console.

"I've got a lock on them! They're just exiting the atmosphere, heading into space. The signal's kind of spotty, though. We'll need to––aww, shit."

"Shit, what, Jo?"

"They just warped away. Or jumped. Whatever you call it."

"Can you still track the signal?"

"I don't know."

"Come on, Jo. Follow those breadcrumbs."

The cyborg worked furiously at her instruments, trying to lock in once more on the faint traces of the feeling ship.

"I've got a heading, but it's fading fast. We've gotta go now if we're going to keep up."

"You hear that, Eddie?" Rika asked.

"I did, and I've already synched my warp to follow yours," he replied.

"So you're thinking what I'm thinking?"

"Yeah. Fuck it. Let's do this."

Ripley, Leila, and Hunze were just regaining consciousness after the forces of the hard burn had given them an impromptu nap.

"What's going on?" Ripley asked. "Are we in space?"

"Yep. And we're warping in three. Two. One."

Without even a chance to express her surprise, Ripley and the others vanished in a flash, warping to a distant system in pursuit of the fleeing craft.

"They warped," the AI still active in the base transmitted.

"Yes, I see that," Cal replied. ***"There's nothing we can do about that. I am sending in ground forces to contain the remaining alien combatants. Keep your auto-cannons on containment only, if possible. We hope to take the injured for interrogation."***

"As you wish," the AI replied.

Minutes later, drop ships loaded with armed humans, Chithiid, and cyborgs landed at the facility to see if any of the aliens were still alive.

Far away in the depths of space, a game of cat and mouse had just begun. But who was the predator and who was the prey was still open to interpretation.

CHAPTER TWENTY-SIX

Charlie and his friends had woken to what had seemed like a relaxing morning, and after the exhausting chase they'd been on, it was quite welcome.

With Kip's systems now fully functional, he was ready to fly, his warp equipment all checking out and his newly installed defensive konus functioning well.

Kip wasn't a young AI by any means, but his humble origins as a toaster had actually afforded him a less robust and hardened framework than his major AI brethren. Charlie and Bawb even thought he might be able to cast in some tiny way one day. But for now at least, the konus he bore was simply a silent protection, ready to automatically disperse magical attacks.

He should have been able to get home just fine with that, but for one thing. When Ara notified them all that the Tslavar ship had just jumped away, Kip threw a little monkey wrench in their plans.

"What do you mean you're not going?" Charlie asked. "You still want to come with us? Are you nuts? You've been repaired. You guys should go home."

"No, we should help you. It's the least we can do," the AI ship replied.

"Dukaan, please, talk some sense into him," Charlie pleaded with the ship's pilot.

"I would, Charlie, but Kip is quite difficult like that. Once he fixates on something, it can take quite a lot to sway him."

Bawb and Charlie continued to quickly stow their gear on Ara's harness. *"What do you guys think?"* Charlie asked them silently. *"Do we let him come along?"*

"I do not see how greater numbers can harm our odds," Bawb said. *"And the additional eyes and firepower might prove a valuable asset in this pursuit."*

"I agree with Bawb on this," Ara said. *"We are at a distinct disadvantage, both numerically, as well as in regards to hard intelligence. We could use the assistance."*

That was enough for Charlie. More than because of their bond, he simply trusted the judgment of his friends.

"Okay, Kip," he finally said. "But we're going to be doing something called a jump. It's like a warp, only it uses magic. Now, I've installed a magical device in your ship to help defend you from that sort of attack, but with a little tweak, I should be able to make it sensitive to our magic profile."

"Uh, what does that mean, Charlie? We don't really do the whole 'magic' thing, ya know."

Charlie chuckled. "Sorry. My bad. I've gotten so used to it I sometimes forget. So what'll happen is you'll feel sort of a *tug* in your warp system. It *should* help you follow us as we jump. It's never been done before, so I can't guarantee you'll travel *precisely* with us, but I think it'll work." He turned to Ara. "Actually, could you work on that konus from out here? If it's your magic directly putting the bond in place, it'll be that much stronger."

"I have already done so while you were talking," she replied. "It is an unusual, but interesting, theory. After this first jump, we shall see if it works. But we must go quickly, before the scent fades."

"Right. Everyone mount up!" Charlie said, climbing aboard his friend's back.

They took to the sky, flying in tandem, higher and higher, until Ara notified them she was ready. Kip powered up and waited for her signal, which in this case was a blast of magic that triggered his warp systems simultaneously. A moment later, they were gone.

A small, crackling aura of blue surrounded the pair as they dropped out of warp-jump side by side.

"We came through exactly as we were when we warped!" Kip said excitedly. "And I barely used any power for that."

"Yes, it is most unusual," Ara said, pleasantly surprised. "I too have used far less power than expected. It would appear this form of transit is mutually beneficial for us both. A most fantastic arrangement, indeed."

Charlie did a double-take when he saw the readouts on the scanning display.

"Uh, guys. We have a little problem."

"What is it, Charlie?" Ara asked.

"Kip, you see these scans?"

"Yes, but... Oh."

"Yeah. This is gonna be a bitch," Charlie said. "This system is packed with planets and moons. Dozens of planets and hundreds of moons, to be exact. It could take ages to track them down."

"Well, the sun does have some power emitting from it, so there is that at least," Ara noted. "And that unusual magic I've been smelling is much, much stronger here as well. So, it seems while we may have our work cut out for us tracking that vessel, we may also finally discover the source of this other magical trace."

"Trace? Trace of what?" Dukaan asked. "Is this a form of your magic?"

"Not exactly," the Zomoki replied. "It's actually a little hard to describe. It has the smell and feel of a magical jump, but there's also something odd about it. Almost artificial."

"Could someone be creating a false trail for us to follow?" Bawb asked, his posture straightening with increased vigilance. "Might this be a trap?"

"I do not believe so, Bawb. I sense no additional magic of that origin in the area. No traps that I can discern. And we know there was only one shimmer ship."

The space vampire's posture relaxed slightly.

"Well, there's nothing to be gained from wild speculation," Charlie said. "Let's get to the business of mapping out these worlds and seeing what we can find of these guys. If we don't luck into them on the first few tries, I worry it's gonna be a long process."

"Though they may jump away again, and next time, perhaps to a less crowded system," Bawb noted.

"Time will tell, my friend. At least it's just their one ship against the two of us, so we finally have a bit of an advantage," Charlie said as they began sweeping the planets for signs of the fleeing Tslavars.

"We will start with the planets," Ara said. "We can then circle back and begin surveying the moons should that prove fruitless."

CHAPTER TWENTY-SEVEN

Captain Jimtee was glad to be underway once more. His Drooks had rested and were as close to fully recharged as he could hope for, and, much as he hated to admit it, he had also needed a bit of time outside his ship's walls.

They had been on standby for some time, waiting for the portal that finally brought them to this galaxy to open, and the weeks upon weeks of idleness could have a way of sneaking up on you, sapping your energy.

This new system they had jumped to had something interesting about it. He couldn't quite put his finger on what that might be, not being a natural magic user himself, but the casters on his ship had said there was an unusual magic residue of a type they'd never seen before.

He was wondering what that might entail, when they rounded a small asteroid field. What they saw upon clearing the obstacle was something they had in no way expected, but by all means intended to use to their advantage.

It was a ship. And a good-sized one at that. And armed, from what they could tell.

Captain Jimtee quickly assessed the vessel. It was nothing like any of the craft they had cataloged during their limited time in the system of their adversary. That meant, if he was correct, that this was a new player in the game. Someone who knew nothing of them, or what they had tried to do to that system.

"Drop the shimmer and pull us into visual range," he commanded. "Close enough for a translation spell to function."

"Sir? We do not know if--"

"Just do it," he replied, sharply.

The shimmer spell dissipated just as their craft flew clear of the asteroids. Unless they'd been looking directly at that one spot in space, these new spacefarers would have no idea of the shimmer-cloaking magic the Tslavars possessed.

"Please, help us!" Captain Jimtee said, affecting his best cowardly act. "We are a peaceful trade vessel passing through this system but have come under attack. Can you help us?"

Off-screen, Ulus watched his captain perform a role quite unlike himself, wondering all the while what exactly his plan was. The airwaves remained silent a long time, with nary a crackle or hiss of static.

"Please! We are in a dire situation. Is this transmitting?" he asked, shooting a glance at Ulus.

"Yes, Captain. We are emitting a skree communication signal that should be compatible with any listening device."

Captain Jimtee knew what Ulus was getting at. They had devised a spell that would transmit their magical skree message in such a way that it would be understandable by a wide range of communications devices. It was originally meant for magical tools from their realm, but with the run-in with Earth's strange machines, the men from that distant galaxy had figured out a way to modify it.

But apparently it wasn't working. At least, so it seemed until a gruff voice finally cracked to life over their communication spells, filling the command center's air.

"Alien vessel, power down any weapons systems and prepare to be boarded," the man commanded. "Failure to comply will result in your destruction."

As he completed his sentence, four more ships popped into existence out of the ether. Warp technology, though not of human origin.

Jimtee subtly signaled Ulus to stand down. This new contact could prove most useful if he played his cards right.

"Of course. We are unarmed, as I'm sure you can see. There are no projectile weapons of any sort on our ship. As I have said, we are simple traders, and we welcome you aboard." He then went the extra mile, managing to sound sincere and weak, adding a tremor to his voice. "You're our saviors! We didn't know what to do. Thank you! Thank you for protecting us."

The airwaves remained silent, but the ships that had joined the initial craft had quickly moved into position, surrounding Jimtee's vessel. He signaled Ulus to cut the outgoing transmission.

"So, we are about to be boarded," he said when the outbound spell was silenced.

"Yes, Captain. An interesting strategy."

"I thought so, yes," the Tslavar said with an amused grin. "And given we have no weapons of the sort they will be familiar with, we can play the role of traders just fine. Pass the word to the crew at once. Act meek. No overt signs of military structure. All must act as if we are no more than a motley group of cargo haulers caught out of our depth."

"I'll do so at once, Captain."

"And, Ulus, do make sure the away team is fully geared up and in their shimmers before these aliens board us. We must not let them know our true numbers."

"Or intent," Ulus added.

"Or intent," Jimtee agreed.

His loyal second-in-command hurried off to carry out the

orders, while Jimtee mentally prepared himself for what was sure to be his crowning achievement. If he could pull it off, that is.

CHAPTER TWENTY-EIGHT

"Surprised, scared, and charming. Surprised, scared, and charming," Captain Jimtee quietly repeated to himself over and over, getting into character as he quickly walked to the section of his ship the aliens had been approaching.

Charming would be no problem. Jimtee was known for his silver tongue, as well as his ability to fit in with almost any group. The scared part, however, would take some doing.

His ship rocked slightly as the alien vessel clamped onto its hull. A few moments later, the sound of a retractable inter-ship conduit sealing into place rang out through the ship.

"Open the door," the captain ordered, then stood back to see what fascinating new surprise might be accompanying the sound of boots on the metal deck of the tube linking their ships.

It was a large group of faintly orange creatures with brick-colored hair--all wearing high-collared military-style uniforms--who filed into his ship through the opening.

They entered not on two legs, but moving on all four limbs, much akin to the way apes walk, but somehow doing so with incredible grace. The alien troops fell into line and rose up on two legs, standing at attention. Captain Jimtee took a closer look at his new friends.

Standing erect, he saw they were all fairly tall and lithe, and their sheer, form-fitting uniforms seemed to flow with their bodies in both quadrupedal and bipedal walking styles. They were also carrying strange, curving weapons in their hands. What he assumed were the dangerous ends were all pointing at him.

The Tslavar leader cleared his throat, glad for his translation spell's power.

"I am Captain Jimtee," he said warmly. "Welcome to my ship. I would again like to thank––"

"Save it for the commander," the nearest alien grunted, not lowering his weapon one inch.

Jimtee smiled to himself, feeling the deadly weight of the powerful konus on his wrist, his equally deadly slaap in its pouch on his hip.

"And your commander is?"

"Here," an older man said, striding into the ship.

He had some gray hairs mixed in with the deep brick-colored ones, and judging by the old scar on his forehead, he had seen his share of battle as he moved up in the ranks. Unlike the other troops, he walked upright the entire time, and Jimtee had to wonder if it was a class thing, or perhaps a rank one.

In any case, he had a new guest to charm. Charm, and bring around to his side as an ally.

"Oh, thank you so much for coming to our aid, Commander...?

"Datano."

"Commander Datano. It is an incredible pleasure to have you aboard my humble trading vessel."

"Yes, a trading vessel, eh? I see your men carry knives. Some longer than normal."

"Oh, those are simply tools used to free cargo when it

becomes ensnared in something. The long ones are merely to extend one's reach."

"So you claim."

"Commander, you can see our entire ship is devoid of projectile weaponry of any type. Yours are the only ones aboard."

Datano squinted his eyes, staring at Jimtee with an intense scrutiny that would have made any teenager confess to things they hadn't even been questioned about. But Jimtee was well-trained. By the best, in fact. Many long years had been spent perfecting his skills, and that of diplomacy was one he had found most useful on many occasions.

Despite the setting and unknown species of his counterpart, this situation was in its essence no different.

"Tomak. To me," the alien commander said, summoning what Jimtee assumed was the alien's equivalent of Ulus--the loyal right-hand man always at his side, ready to do his bidding.

"Show me the scans," Datano commanded.

Tomak held up what appeared to be a metal frame of some sort. It was like nothing Jimtee had ever seen. But then, coming from an entirely magical realm, there seemed to be a never-ending stream of novel sights for his eyes in this galaxy.

Lights flashed across the glassy surface within the frame, but as Jimtee looked closer, he realized there was no glass there at all. It was entirely an illusion. An image held within the confines of the metal, floating in the air.

Jimtee glanced at Ulus, who was clearly wondering the same thing.

Ulus flashed a slight uptick of an eyebrow. The meaning was clear despite his lack of words. *"Magic?"*

Jimtee responded with the slightest of shrugs. They had sensed magical potential of an unusual variety, but they'd yet to come across anything tangible. Anything substantial. But these new allies might just be the key to changing all of that.

Once he made them allies, that is.

"Please, Commander, let me show you around my craft. You will be able to see firsthand that we are no threat."

"So you keep saying," Datano replied.

"Surely you saw the damage to our craft when you approached," Jimtee countered. "The burns. The holes rent in our hull. We were simply seeking out new trade when, out of nowhere, we were set upon by a beast most foul."

That captured the alien commander's attention. "Beast, you say? What sort of beast could do that to a ship?"

"Oh, it was terrible. An enormous, red creature with massive teeth, piercing claws, and the fire. Oh, the fire!"

"And you say this beast flew in the void of space?"

"Yes!"

"And it spat fire, even in the vacuum?"

"Yes! Yes!"

Datano turned to Tomak and quietly whispered in his ear. His second-in-command nodded, then hurried off to his own ship. Jimtee couldn't help but wonder what he was up to. But he had a role to play.

"So you see, Commander, we are forever in your debt for this assistance. Without you, we'd have been lost."

"And where's this beast now?"

"Many systems away, I'm afraid. A planet called Earth. Have you heard of it?"

"No."

"It was our destination, a planet intended for peaceful trade. But it has been overrun by hostile beings, this flying beast being one of their deadly force. But perhaps with your obvious might, you could defeat the creature and free the planet for trade once more."

"We'll see about that," Datano said. "For the time being, you will be brought to the Chancellor. Our ships will guide you in."

"In?" Jimtee said, confused. "In where?"

"To the Crux. Our base on a nearby moon," Datano replied. "Follow, and do not deviate from course or disobey directions. If you do, you will be shot from the sky."

Captain Jimtee did his best to appear shaken by the threat, one he had heard countless times in countless engagements over his career.

"Of course, Commander. Whatever you order, we shall obey."

"Good. The Chancellor will wish to speak with you."

"And he is your leader?"

"One of them. You'll be brought to him when we arrive, so I suggest you freshen up. He does not abide uncleanliness."

With that Datano turned and strode through the corridor back to his ship. Moments later his men followed until the area was empty. The seal re-engaged and the connecting tube retracted to the alien ship.

Captain Jimtee looked at Ulus. "How many snuck aboard their ship?"

"Twenty, Captain."

"Excellent," he replied. "This could be a most beneficial engagement after all."

CHAPTER TWENTY-NINE

The ships moved slowly, a deadly flotilla surrounding Jimtee's Zomoki-charred craft. Of course, her flames had not done any serious damage––his casters had deflected them quite efficiently once the initial shock of her attack had worn off.

They had been en route to the mysterious Crux base for only ten minutes when a message came through to them from Commander Datano's second-in-command.

"The Commander wishes your presence on his ship," he informed the Tslavar vessel. "A shuttle will fly to you momentarily. It will seal with your hull at the same point of our last engagement. You will enter the craft and return to our ship. Is this understood?"

"Of course," Jimtee said, a saccharine excitement coloring his voice. "This will be so exciting, seeing your ship. It's such a magnificent craft, I am looking forward to being afforded an opportunity to see the inside as well."

"Whatever," Tomak grumbled, obviously annoyed with what he now took for a spaceship fanboy. "Just be ready."

Five minutes later, Captain Jimtee, the fierce Tslavar warrior and tip of the spear of the entire invading force, was seated docilely in an alien craft, helpless and alone. At least, so he let it appear.

His men had already taken up positions within the alien craft, hidden from sight by their shimmer cloaks. They were to stay put, stay out of sight, and prepare for whatever may come, but Jimtee also knew his men would not allow a hair on his head to be harmed.

If the commander had any thoughts of violence, he and his men would meet a quick end at the hands of Jimtee's men. That is, if the captain didn't simply wield his konus and do it himself.

And that was one of the things of great interest to the man from the magic galaxy. Here he was, armed to the teeth with magical power, and these alien fools had no idea. They simply thought the ornate bands on his wrists were decorative. Little did they know the magic that they contained.

Enough to lay waste to a good number of their forces before they knew what hit them, if needed.

But subtlety and tact were the order of the day. For the time being at least. Jimtee had a plan, and so far, it was going perfectly.

"Commander," he said when he stepped from the shuttle into the vast landing bay of the alien ship. "It is so good to see you again so soon. And to bring me aboard this magnificent ship? I am honored, sir," he said, going so far as to give a little bow.

"Oh, please, don't do that. You are here because the regent wishes to speak with you before we make landfall at the Crux. He wishes to hear your tale firsthand before we bring you to the chancellor."

"I would be glad to speak with the chancellor," Jimtee said. "Please, show me to him."

The crimson-robed regent sat on a low couch in front of a

picture window looking out into space. It was a serene sight, Jimtee had to admit. An old warrior, he had long ago learned to appreciate beauty when it made an appearance, for every such opportunity might be your last.

"Please, sit," the regent said.

"Thank you."

"Tea?" the man offered.

"Why, thank you. Most generous," Jimtee replied, hoping this race's foodstuffs were not toxic to his kind.

He accepted the cup and briefly held his hand over it, as if feeling the warmth. In reality, he was allowing his poison-detecting ring to do its job. At his current position it was not such a concern, but there had been a time that death from within the ranks was a very real possibility. It was long ago, and that uprising had been quashed, but the ring, and the habit, had remained, along with his normal vigilance.

"I am Regent Zinna," the man said. "I am the man on this vessel charged with assessing all who would enter the Crux. Datano has told me your most fantastical story, and I wished to hear it from your mouth, in your words."

"I would be glad to, sir. We are simple traders, you see, and were just arriving at a planet called Earth, many systems from here, when we realized its peaceful residents had been overthrown and the planet was now under the control of machine forces and their deadly henchmen."

"Machines?"

"Yes. Machines and Zomoki."

"What is a Zomoki?"

"It's what my people call the beast that attacked our ship. A giant creature of great power that can rip a ship's armor to shreds without batting an eye."

"In space? But how can it survive the vacuum? And how does it breathe? This is entirely too fantastical."

"But it is true," Jimtee said. "Did you not see the damage done to my ship?"

"That could have been from any firefight, I'm afraid. And if you lie to my commander, and lie to me, why would I ever allow you in the presence of our most honorable chancellor?"

"But I speak the truth," Jimtee said, playing up the desperation in his voice, and even managing to bring a tear to his eye as he wiped his brow, depositing a speck of a carefully placed astringent dried onto his hand for just such an eventuality. The tears came immediately as the chemical burned.

"I think you should go back to your ship and think about whether or not you wish to continue this lie," Regent Zinna said. "I would hate for you and your men to be executed over your falsehoods."

The regent nodded to the guards, who came and grabbed Jimtee under each arm and pulled him to his feet.

"Stand down!" he shouted.

The guards looked at the strange green man with confusion. Was their prisoner actually giving them orders? But no, he was not. In fact, Captain Jimtee was telling his shimmer-cloaked soldiers to refrain from killing everyone in the room. He still had one more trick up his sleeve.

"I can prove it!" he blurted.

The regent, though disbelieving, was nevertheless curious what the man had to offer. "Very well. Bring him here."

Jimtee was walked to a spot right in front of the robed man.

"Well? You said you had proof."

"I do," the Tslavar captain replied, reaching slowly into his pocket.

He removed a small disc of bright metal with intricate etchings covering every inch. It was a very powerful device, and exceedingly rare. A pocket image display device, and one that had been connected to the much larger unit aboard his ship. He had record of the Zomoki's attack, and had key elements embedded in the device for just such an eventuality.

None could ever say Jimtee was not prepared.

He held the device flat on his palm and said, "*Visus.*"

The spell engaged, and the recording of Ara blasting flames as she pursued his ship sprang to life in what, to the aliens, was for all intents and purposes a holographic image. The scene was terrifying. A space monster that could not only fly and breathe in the void, but could produce flame in a vacuum.

The disc sparked and fell to the ground. It was a shame to waste such a valuable device, but Jimtee couldn't risk having these warriors realize he possessed magic. He hoped he would be able to restore the device once safely back aboard his ship.

"Oh, it seems to have overloaded," he said, picking up the smoking unit. "But I hope that satisfied your request."

The regent was a paler shade of orange, his mouth hanging open ever so slightly.

"That, that was incredible," he finally said. "Forgive my doubting you, friend Jimtee. But you may rest comfortably knowing our fleet is more than capable of handling a beast of that nature."

"But I've seen it do harm to many ships at once," Jimtee replied, affecting a worried look.

Regent Zinna chuckled. "Oh, my friend. The ships you have seen are but part of our fleet. Now, come, we will take you to the Crux, where we will offer shelter to you and your crew while you repair your craft in safety. I'm sure the chancellor will want to hear your story."

Jimtee smiled warmly in thanks as he left the chamber, but behind his eyes, the gears were turning.

CHAPTER THIRTY

Ara and Kip had made fairly quick work of the outermost planets, the utterly freezing temperatures of them all, combined with the caustic atmosphere of more than one of them, meant there was almost no chance the Tslavar craft would have taken refuge on them.

Being from their prey's home galaxy, Bawb and Ara knew full well the constraints of their magic and ships, and in this instance, the sheer deadliness of those worlds would have made quick work of them no matter the power of those on board.

The moons orbiting them, however, were not so dangerous. With no atmosphere to speak of on most of them, a flyby survey was relatively easy, and in the absence of life and energy, the traces of Ara's magic stuck to the Tslavar ship would have been easy for her to detect.

"This moon's a wash," Kip said over comms. "It looks like that's it for the ones in the perimeter area."

"Yeah, thank God," Charlie said. "We finally get to start checking the planets in the Goldilocks Zone."

"What is a Goldilocks Zone?" Dukaan asked.

"Yeah, what's that?" Kip chimed in.

"C'mon, Kip. You're from Earth, surely you know the story of Goldilocks. The fairy tale with the three bears?"

"Uh, Charlie, I was a toaster for the early years of my life. They don't really take the time to read us fairy tales. Though I do possess over three hundred settings for proper toasting of bread products and pastry."

"Neat trick, Kip. But yeah, I guess I can see how they might not load you with Earth's classics. I guess you never updated your background files."

"Oh, I've had updates many, many times. But I was first upgraded in a battle situation, so they kinda focused on flight and combat stuff. It was really cool, though. Like, I was flying in there all *Zap!* and *Boom!* And the bad guys were all *aaaaah!* I'll tell you all about it, if you--"

"Kip, you're doing it again," Dukaan said. "No rambling."

"I was just telling a story."

"You said to tell you if you were doing it, so I am telling you."

"You're such a killjoy, Dookie."

The Chithiid ignored his AI companion. They'd had this discussion more than once. "So, Charlie. This Goldilocks Zone you speak of. You were saying?"

"Right. It's basically the part of a solar system where life can take root. Where it's not too cold, and not too hot, but just right. That's where we're heading now. The farthest habitable planets from the sun. Of course, with this many of them in the system, that doesn't mean it'll be any easier to find those bastards. But at least we should hopefully be able to land, pop off our helmets, and stretch our legs a bit."

And after a very long survey of a few small but uninhabited worlds, that was exactly what they did.

"Finally! Fresh air," Charlie said, cracking his back after so many hours riding atop his Zomoki friend.

"And vegetation," Bawb noted. "This world can sustain life."

"I sense a fair amount of it on this planet," Ara said. "But still no sign of the enemy craft." She paused, an odd look on her face as she slowly inhaled the cool breeze.

"What is it, Ara?" Charlie silently asked. *"You okay?"*

"Yes. It is just there is something here. An oddly familiar trace of... I'm not sure."

"Danger?"

"No. Far too faint and old to be of worry. It's just... unusual."

"You want to go check it out?"

"I was thinking the same thing," she said with a little smile.

"Great minds," Charlie replied with a chuckle.

"Wise One, I will accompany you, if you wish."

"Thank you, Bawb, but I will be fine on my own. You should rest and refresh yourself. If I come across game during my flight, I will bring some back for you."

Ara flapped her wings and took to the air, leaving the others behind as they limbered up after their long journey.

"Where is she going?" Dukaan asked.

"Just off to do a little survey," Charlie replied. "She'll be back soon enough."

"Should we accompany her?"

"She'll be fine. She's not about to go engaging any hostiles without us. Just a quick look around to see what she can find, if anything."

Kip powered up his drive systems and quietly lifted into the air.

"Dukaan. You and the guys rest up. I'm gonna go do a survey too."

"But Ara is––"

"She's got her nose, but I've got scanners. Relax, Dookie. I'll be back soon."

Before his Chithiid pilot could say another word, Kip zipped off into the sky, heading the opposite direction that Ara had taken.

"Well, you've got to admit, at least the survey will get done faster this way," Charlie said. "I mean, they're just doing some recon, but knowing Ara, she'll give the whole place a closer read while she's out there."

"And in the meantime, we are afforded the opportunity to rest and refresh ourselves," Bawb said. "I suggest we take full advantage of this time to do just that."

The area they landed in was not only slightly elevated, providing them with a clear view of the lands around them, but they had also performed a basic indigenous life scan when they came in from above.

While small animals roamed the area, nothing large enough to pose a threat appeared to be nearby. Nonetheless, Bawb cast a few protective tripwire spells before lying down in the shade of a small tree. Charlie and Dukaan took his lead and did the same.

"You are going to want to see this," Ara said inside Charlie and Bawb's heads long before they saw her shape approaching from the distance in the sky.

"What did you find, Ara?" Bawb asked.

"Signs of life. A civilization. I will be there shortly and will take you to see for yourselves."

Charlie and Bawb hopped to their feet and gathered the limited gear they had taken with them when Ara deposited them there. Dukaan followed their lead and rose to his feet, scanning the skies.

"What is happening?" the Chithiid asked.

"Ara's coming back. Said she found a civilization," Charlie replied. "Put on your Sunday best, Dukaan. We're going to meet the locals."

"I must inform Kip. He is out there surveying the lands."

"I already pinged him over comms," Charlie said. "Told him to pick up Ara's signal and join us wherever it is she's taking us."

"Wait. He is meeting us there?"

"Yeah, Dukaan," Charlie said with a grin as he watched his winged friend grow close in the sky. "Looks like today you get to ride a dragon."

Ara touched down lightly, lowering herself so the trio could climb aboard her back. She then wasted no time, launching into the air once more, carrying them to the civilization she had told them of. A new world, and new people. Charlie wondered what they'd be like.

"What happened here?" Charlie asked as he surveyed the long-empty structures dotting the landscape.

They had landed in what appeared to be a settlement of some kind. At least, it had been at one time. But now it was no more than a cluster of toppled stones scattered among a few somewhat intact structures. The area may have been overgrown from ages without residents, but only smaller plants had reclaimed a foothold. Whoever had lived there had also done a good job clearing their living area of any intrusive vegetation that might spring back up at a later time.

The long-gone former residents were apparently rather primitive, judging by the lack of tech and living situation of the ruins, but they had also been there in some numbers at one point.

"Do you see that?" Ara asked, nodding toward a blackened stone wall.

"Looks like some kind of dark stone," Charlie replied.

"It is not. It is the same lighter material as the rest of the structures," Ara noted. "But this one was burned."

"But this place looks like it's been abandoned hundreds of years, if not more."

"Precisely. And yet the scorching remains, despite being exposed to the elements," Ara said, again sniffing the air. "There is not much fire that could have such an effect, especially not in this galaxy. Yet something about this is familiar."

"Then that's a good thing, right? I mean, you may understand some of what's going on around here, which is more than any of the rest of us can say," Charlie said.

"Yes, but no. You see, it seems a trace of the power that caused this is embedded in the stone itself. But it just can't be here. It's not possible."

"You're talking to a guy who until a few years ago didn't even believe in dragons, let alone time travel. So *possible* is a matter of opinion these days," Charlie said with a grin.

As if on cue, Kip appeared above, setting down in a clear space beside the ruins.

"Hey, guys. What's with the trashed buildings?"

"It seems the former inhabitants were forced to abandon them," Bawb said. "Though why, we cannot be sure."

Looking around at the traces of destruction, Ara couldn't help but wonder why this place made her so uneasy. "We will perform an assessment of these ruins, then move on. While fascinating in their own right, we have more important problems at the moment."

"Ara's right," Charlie said. "There's still an enemy ship out there somewhere. And there are two of us and one of them. We finally have the advantage. When we find them, they'll never know what hit 'em."

CHAPTER THIRTY-ONE

The moon was one of thirteen orbiting a gas giant situated toward the inner reaches of the system's planets. It wasn't a particularly large moon, nor was it anything special to look at. In fact, aside from having a breathable atmosphere and a surface temperature that was survivable, if not pleasant in its heat, it was totally unremarkable.

Soon, Commander Datano's ship led them across a vast plain, where numerous smaller craft lay parked. There must have been a few dozen of the little ships, but compared to the one they were traveling in at the moment, they seemed of little interest.

Captain Jimtee, however, concealed his blasé reaction to the alien base with a false enthusiasm that even his shimmer-cloaked men almost found convincing.

"This fleet! There are so many of them!" he gushed. "It is magnificent!"

Regent Zinna chuckled at the ignorant trader at his side. "Oh, my dear Jimtee, this is but a small group of the most basic of work ships. No, the full might of our fleet is yet to be seen."

That was music to Jimtee's ears, as he was seriously

beginning to wonder if it was a waste of time conquering these inferior beings rather than continuing their search for a power capable of granting them control of the portal. More than anything, they had to retrieve it from the sun. Only then could their fleet join them in glorious conquest of the new system and the planet Earth within.

The additional ships still surrounded Jimtee's own craft, but were now acting as an escort rather than a guard detail. The technology-based aliens simply did not possess the magic to sense the raw power of the craft they believed inferior to their own. They expected guns to be wielded by their enemies. Magic was simply beyond their realm of experience, or comprehension.

Since showing Regent Zinna the recording of the dragon wreaking destruction upon his simple trading vessel, the Tslavar captain had been taken on a much friendlier tour of the strange new ship. None of the crucial areas, mind you, but enough for him to form an opinion about the resources of this somewhat aggressive race.

He liked what he saw. While it was nowhere near as elegant a vessel as his own magic-driven one, there was nevertheless significant power contained within the craft. Power, and destructive force ready to be unleashed upon their enemies if need be.

Jimtee now only had to further his cause in the most complex, yet simple of ways. He had to sway these people to his side, and as more than just mere hosts.

The ships slowed as they flew toward the end of the plains. A tall mountain range rose before them, its craggy peaks stretching up into the sky. They continued to fly straight without the slightest change of course.

Jimtee was about to ask if it might not be wise to either decelerate or climb high when he saw the juxtaposed outlines of unnatural structures nestled into the multiple alien-built docking bays all along the base of the rocky mass.

Ships. Dozens of ships, and all of them at least as large as the one he was currently aboard, if not bigger. And all were armed. Jimtee was pleased at this development. *Very* pleased, in fact. Here before him was a relatively sizable fleet just waiting to be put to better use.

Like conquering Earth.

The escort ships drew closer to the Crux, fanning out from Jimtee's vessel and docking in available berths on either side. The Tslavar ship, on the other hand, was guided directly ahead, right into a waiting landing bay large enough to accommodate it. Commander Datano's craft headed toward a docking bay just above it to the right.

Now that they were so close to the facility, Jimtee could better assess the alien race's abilities and resources. He wasn't exactly impressed, but what he saw did please him regardless.

It was a vast moon complex, built right into the side of the mountain. Technically, it appeared to be built *upon* the mountain, but Captain Jimtee had little doubt there were certainly parts ensconced within the rocky outcroppings. In any case, it was a substantial facility, and undoubtedly housed hundreds of thousands, if not more, given what he could see from the air.

"It's amazing, Regent Zinna. So many ships. And so powerful!"

The robed man grinned, enjoying his yokel guest's awe at the mighty fleet. "Welcome to the Crux, Jimtee. The pinnacle of Urok power."

"Urok? Is that the name of your leader?"

"No, no. Our race. I thought you knew this already."

"I was unaware."

"Commander Datano really must work on that. We can't have our guests appearing before the chancellor uninformed,"

Zinna replied. "In any case, the Urok inhabit this system, though most of the outer colonies are nothing more than backwater peasants. Ignorant farmers whose lives we protect."

"So your food is grown off-world?"

"Of course. I mean, look at the surface, Jimtee. This is a stark and beautiful landscape, full of raw power and strength. The perfect place for the Urok seat of power. Yet this moon's soil does not lend itself to agriculture. Thus, the lower class are relegated to the outer worlds, where they do their menial work."

"As lesser beings should, Regent."

The regent smiled. "I am glad to see you understand the order of things, Jimtee. It is vital a man know who his betters are."

Commander Datano strode into the observation chamber, where the two men were observing the docking procedure through the large windows.

"Regent Zinna, we will be docked in a moment."

"Yes, Datano, I can see that," he replied, gesturing out the window.

"Of course," the commander replied. "I have received a communication from the Council in response to your message."

"And?"

"They wish to offer our limited hospitality to these trader guests. I also informed them that the Slava crew are unarmed."

"It's *Tslavar*, actually," Jimtee corrected. "But no matter, we are so grateful for your hospitality and protection, you could call us whatever you like," he said with a charming smile.

Regent Zinna laughed, and even Commander Datano cracked a little grin. This was where Jimtee really shined. Yes, he was an accomplished warrior, having led his men through countless conflicts, always emerging victorious. But when it came to the art, the *war* of diplomacy, Jimtee knew few equals.

With merely a well-placed question or an offhand remark, he could subtly steer his quarry's ideals and goals to align with what he wanted of them. He would ask questions, showing great interest in whatever it was that his target was most interested in.

This, of course, created a feeling of familiarity. Comfort. A bonding between them. And once that was achieved, he would dig deeper until they were acting out what the Tslavar wanted of them without even realizing they'd been manipulated.

"Tomak will show you to your ship to see to your men, Jimtee," Datano said.

"Thank you, Commander. We are all thankful for your hospitality."

"You would be wise to have your men dress in their finest attire," the commander added. "One must make a good showing, after all. First impressions are the most important ones."

"You're right, of course, Commander," he said, turning to the regent. "Regent Zinna, it has been a pleasure talking with you. I do hope we may continue our discussions within the Crux."

"I too look forward to that, Jimtee. For a trader, you are a surprisingly good conversationalist."

"I've traveled much, Regent. And I am always eager to learn. And a man as wise as you can surely expand my knowledge greatly."

His ego stoked, Zinna waved his farewell. "Of course, dear Jimtee. I would enjoy that very much. Now, go see to your men. There will be time for us to talk later."

The Tslavar captain was escorted from the chamber and out the airlock onto a ramp leading toward the lower landing bay. The hot air drifting across the moon made for a rather shocking transition from the comfortable interior of Commander Datano's ship.

Tomak noted his charge's subtle shift in posture as they stepped out into the heat.

"The Crux can be a bit hot for many until they get used to it. But do not worry, only the service accessways are exposed as this one is. The rest is enclosed and climate-controlled."

"I was just thinking it might be difficult for my men to dress in their finest attire if they would begin sweating through it within minutes."

Tomak nodded knowingly. "Believe me, Jimtee, we've all been there. But your ship has berthed in the guest landing. The accessway there is entirely enclosed, so that will not be an issue."

"Wonderful news, Tomak. And thank you for your hospitality."

"There is no need to thank me. I am merely doing my duty."

"Yes, but I believe all men, whether they are acting under orders or not, are deserving of appreciation of their efforts. So I say again, thank you."

Tomak blushed ever so slightly, Jimtee noted. His words had the desired effect. Tomak liked him now. Maybe not much, but enough that, come the time for hostilities, he might hesitate a fraction of a second if Jimtee was in his sights. And that would be his end.

They arrived at the landing bay, and Jimtee thanked him again, then took his leave and strode into his ship, sealing the door behind him. Ulus was waiting to greet him.

"Are we alone?"

"We are, Captain."

"Good," Jimtee said, shedding his false smile. "Ready the men. We begin our infiltration shortly."

"An armed incursion?"

"No. The idiots are inviting the entire crew inside their walls for a meal."

"Quite hospitable of them," Ulus said with a wicked grin.

"Indeed. Tell the men to wear their finest clothing. *And* their most powerful konuses. But no magic without my word."

"Yes, Captain."

"And tell them to bring no blades or other weapons these

fools might take note of. We must present as meek and harmless traders, nothing more."

Ulus turned and set to work readying the men, and Captain Jimtee walked to his quarters to prepare. It was getting interesting, now. Soon, if all went according to plan, he would be in command of an entire fleet.

Whether they wanted it or not.

CHAPTER THIRTY-TWO

The great dining hall of the Crux was not terribly impressive by Jimtee's standards. There were ornate columns, vast tables with myriad delicacies--by Urok standards, that is--and music that was not entirely unpleasant to the ear wafting through the air.

But it was not even a shadow of the vast banquets of his home galaxy. Affairs where men and women of great magic would vie for attention, often to the benefit of all gathered in their presence. Grandiose gestures of magical extravagance that pleased not only the senses, but also the pockets of those who knew how to collect traces of the casually wielded power.

Jimtee was one such man, and his private cache of magical devices had grown rather impressive over the years, even for a man of his non-magical status.

The lower-ranking men of the crew were ushered to an outer section of the dining hall, sequestered with other fodder and laborers. They brought the Drooks along as well, affording the ship's power source an opportunity to not only stretch their legs and get fresh air, but also to fill their bellies at someone else's expense.

The Drooks all wore their finest robes, though each and

every one still bore the golden control collar worn by their kind. The devices, however, never had to be used. One painful lesson in their younger years, and all had quickly accepted their fate. Now they simply did their job without complaint.

Of course, Captain Jimtee would have rather kept them safely on the ship, but when the Uroks boarded the vessel, they surveyed all aboard. To leave them behind would be suspicious, and one thing Jimtee did not want was any unnecessary scrutiny. Not at this point in his plan.

"There he is!" Regent Zinna exclaimed warmly as he excused himself from his prior conversation to cross the banquet hall to greet his Tslavar guest. "My dear Captain Jimtee, you certainly cut a dashing figure in that attire. Quite fashionable, for a trader."

The Tslavar was actually wearing his finest for the occasion and was quite sure that he had caught the eye of more than one of the local big-wigs with his unusual, foreign style. But he just smiled as if the regent's offhanded jab meant nothing. And in the grand scheme of things, that was true.

"And now you are held close in the bosom of our mighty civilization," Zinna continued. "It is wonderful to see you here, safe and sound within the heart of the Crux."

"The honor is mine, Regent Zinna. Your people's hospitality knows no bounds, and my men are indeed most grateful for the opportunity to stretch their legs and fill their bellies without fear of attack from the void."

"Ah, yes. The beast. Chancellor Fanti is most intrigued, I must say. He is looking forward to hearing more about this creature from you after the festivities."

"And where is the chancellor? I have not yet learned the caste system of your people."

"He will arrive later, after the banquet. He rarely dines in public, you see."

"Is this customary for your leaders?" Jimtee asked, casually assessing the vulnerability of the influential members of this society.

"Only the chancellor," Zinna replied. "A holdover habit from his ascendancy to power."

"Oh? Was there some turmoil?"

Zinna looked around before speaking in a conspiratorial hush. "I probably should not tell you this, but what harm can come from it? You're just a lower-caste trader, after all. No offense intended."

"And none taken. I know my role in things full well, Regent."

The robed man smiled broadly. "Now that's what I like. A man who knows his place. Very good, Jimtee."

"But you were saying? About the chancellor?"

"Oh, yes. Well, you see, many years ago there was a rival faction set on installing their own party in the Chancellorship. More than one food taster was lost in that unfortunate fiasco," Zinna said, a slight shadow falling across his countenance. "But that's a thing of the past," he said, brightening as quickly as he'd darkened. "Those responsible and their families have all been dealt with."

"Ah, I see. Executed, then?"

"Oh, heavens no. Not when they could provide valuable labor. No, no. They were stripped of rank and assets and shipped off to one of the farming colonies to spend the rest of their days in pathetic squalor with the lowest of classes. A suitable punishment, don't you agree?"

"Indeed," Jimtee said. "Yours are a wise and just people, I can see. We are most fortunate to count you as friends."

A few of Jimtee's men passed by, leading several of the Drooks back to their ship. The robes the slave power users wore were surprisingly fashionable in this setting, almost outshining the closer-fitting attire of the captain and his men. And it caught more than a few people's eyes. As did their unusual accessory.

"You there. Come over here," Zinna commanded.

The poor Drook looked utterly confused. He had been provided a robust translation spell, as had all of the crew--including the dozens of shimmer-cloaked Tslavar warriors now infiltrating the facility--but had no idea how to respond to what was obviously a man of some rank.

Captain Jimtee nodded slightly, giving the petrified man the subtle okay to come closer. "Come. The regent would have words with you," he said, slightly concerned at the unexpected attention directed at his slave.

But his trepidation quickly turned to delight when the regent leaned forward to examine the control collar bound around the Drook's neck.

"This scrollwork is remarkable," he murmured, obviously taken with the shiny object. "And the means in which it clasps with no visible seam. A most beautiful adornment, Jimtee."

The captain smiled to himself. If an opportunity like this was going to present itself, he was damn sure not going to look a gift Zomoki in the mouth.

This was going to be easier than he thought.

"It is a bauble of my people," the Tslavar said, nodding at the Drook and accompanying Tslavars to continue on their way. "I don't normally do this," he said, conspiratorially, "but perhaps I might even be able to procure one for you. A token of our thanks for all you have done for us."

"Why, Jimtee, I don't know what to say."

"Say nothing, then, friend Zinna. It would be my pleasure to offer this to you. I only regret we do not have more for you in way of recompense. You are a great man, and great men deserve great tribute."

The regent smiled broadly, his ego thoroughly stoked.

"Come, Jimtee. Let us join the others. There are many who wish to meet you and hear the tale of your harrowing escape from the horrible creature. You did manage to repair your display device, yes?"

"I believe so, Regent," Jimtee replied. "And I would be happy to show this to all who are interested. It serves both your people and my own well, knowing what hostile creatures wait for us out there in the void, threatening us all."

Perhaps it was laid on a little bit thick, Jimtee thought, but it was of no matter. The regent was wrapped around his finger, and with so little effort. The Tslavar captain allowed himself the smallest of satisfied grins. With a control collar around his neck--willingly, at that--the regent would prove a most useful tool in the next phase of his plan.

But until then, he would eat, he would drink, and he would charm as many of the ruling caste as possible. And then, when the time finally came, he would hammer them all into submission.

CHAPTER THIRTY-THREE

The quantity of planets and their resident moons in this system was making the previously simple task of tracking the scent left behind by the shimmer-cloaked craft exceedingly difficult, Ara found.

Not only was the magical trace hard to track--despite being of her own fiery creation--but she also found many new signatures floating in the void. Unusual traces that mixed with and confused her senses.

Bawb was having a similarly difficult time of it, even with Hunze's powerful gift wrapped around his body. It was going to be a far more labor-intensive task than they had hoped for, but between the magic users and the quirky AI ship flying with them, the odds were still in their favor. It would just take time.

Of course, if the enemy were to jump, that would make things a whole lot easier. The magical signature of that action would provide a blazing road map in the sky compared to what they were currently pursuing. But as of yet, the shimmer ship had remained within the system. Doing what was anyone's guess.

The strange traces of unknown power were stronger among these worlds than in the previous systems they had visited, and Charlie had a hunch the magic-wielding invaders were likely investigating to see if they might make some use of it. At least, he knew that's what *he* would do if he were in their shoes.

The sun was providing a steady stream of power to both Ara and Bawb, so, once again, they had that factor on their side. Both were buzzing with magical potential, and even Charlie felt something of an unusual tingle warming in his bones.

So it was that they flew from world to world, slowly moving farther inward toward the heat of the sun, having left behind the cold reaches of the system for the welcome warmth of the Goldilocks Zone.

For some reason, one blue-green world in particular caught Charlie's attention more than the others. It wasn't anything he could put his finger on, but something about it called out to him.

"Hey, guys," he said over their shared comms. "I don't know what it is, but I'm getting a vibe from that planet up ahead. The one on the left."

"We were going to investigate its twin first," Ara replied. "But given their proximity, I suppose switching the order will make no difference."

With that, she shifted course slightly, heading directly for the world that had caught her human friend's attention. Kip banked and followed, his scanners on high, probing in all directions for traces of the enemy ship—or a potential ambush.

Slowly, the Zomoki and her AI companion vessel entered the atmosphere, taking care to do so in a manner that would not make them stand out like blazing spots in the sky. It was a tricky maneuver, but they made a good showing of it. The odds of any noting their arrival remained slim.

Charlie felt the odd buzz in his head grow a little stronger now that they were within the atmosphere. The scanners showed a breathable atmosphere, so he cracked his helmet once they reached lower altitudes to get a breath of fresh air. What greeted him was a refreshing blast of cool air, carrying with it the smell of a verdant and fertile world.

"Do you see that?" Dukaan asked over the comms. "There appears to be some order to the growth of this vegetation."

Charlie looked closer from their vantage point. He was right. There were lines between certain types of plants, separating them into segregated areas. These were crops. Someone was farming here.

"Guys, this is all current agriculture," he said. "That means there is an advanced civilization around here somewhere. Probably really close. Anyone see anything?"

"I see much, but nothing that impresses me," Bawb replied. "It seems this culture utilizes only the most basic of methods to tend their crops. And I see no trace of any type of craft capable of flight."

The Wampeh was right, Charlie realized as they flew over what appeared to be a moderate-sized farming community. There was a smattering of equipment that seemed advanced enough from what he could tell, but indeed, no flying ships were anywhere to be seen.

"Maybe they just keep them parked somewhere else," Charlie posited. "It's possible this is just a rural area and the more urban ones are where they keep them."

"I'll fly ahead and take a look," Kip said, darting off in a flash before anyone could even reply.

"That ship is not right in the head," Charlie said.

"Perhaps not, but he is one of us," Bawb replied. *"And that gives us the numeric advantage."*

"Yeah, so long as he doesn't keep flying off on a whim."

"Which is warranted in this instance," Bawb noted.

Up ahead, at the base of a series of ragged stone hills, a

larger town was visible in the distance. It was no metropolis, by any means, but at least it was a step up from the rural farming area. Ara flew closer, providing them a better look at the area.

The buildings were all squat and functional, though some appeared to be made from a composite rather than stone and wood as the rustic farmhouses had, for the most part. But the area was still relatively primitive to Charlie's eyes. No real tech to speak of, but signs that there might have been at one time in the distant past.

In fact, the entire area had the look of a colony that had been lost to time. Abandoned and forgotten.

"I think we should go in for a closer look," Charlie said.

"Agreed. It would do us well to discern what information we might glean from the local populace," Bawb said as he watched a small group of lean, light-orange-skinned beings with brick-red hair walk from the buildings, mostly on four limbs, switching to two as they stood tall, staring up at the dragon in the sky. *"And it would appear we have an audience,"* he added.

Ara slowly glided low, then gently touched down in a larger intersection of the roadways, being careful to appear as peaceful and non-intimidating as possible. Being an enormous dragon, that was typically harder than it sounded.

The locals held back, unsure what was going on, but when what appeared to be two men climbed down from atop the beast, their bravery grew, and they came closer, stepping away from the security blanket of the buildings.

Looking around, Charlie thought it really did seem like this was an abandoned outpost or something. There had obviously once been tech here, but it seemed to have all fallen into disuse and disrepair over what must have been decades, if not longer. He just hoped the locals would be friendly enough to provide them with some answers.

Charlie and Bawb removed their helmets, slowly, as Ara had done upon landing. They were the aliens on this world, and sudden movements were a no-no when it came to first contact.

"You casting your protective spells?" Charlie asked.

"You know I am," Bawb replied.

"Good. Then let's do this," Charlie said, walking toward the nearest locals with his hands held up in a non-threatening manner.

"I am Charlie," he said, hoping the translator spell would work with this entirely new species. "And this is Bob. The big one behind me is called Ara. We are visitors from far away, and we mean you no harm."

The orange people were ignoring him for the most part, staring at Ara and muttering among themselves. Finally, one of the braver ones hesitantly stepped forward.

"I am called Boranaz," he said, placing his hand on his chest in way of greeting.

"A pleasure to meet you, Boranaz," Charlie said, placing his hand over his heart in a similar manner. Bawb, likewise, did the same, giving a slight nod as he did. "We have traveled a long distance to reach your world, but we believe there are others not of your system who may have visited as well. Have you seen or heard any signs of such beings?"

"None," Boranaz replied, eyes wide as he stared in awe at Ara.

"Yeah, she's pretty impressive, isn't she?" Charlie said.

"We've never seen an actual *Erenky* before," the orange man said breathlessly, his eyes wide at the sight of Ara's mass.

Ara was shocked. Enough so that she ignored her rule to never speak aloud to any but her closest friends.

"You have seen one of my kind before?" she asked, a great curiosity sparking in her golden eyes.

The crowd erupted into a chattering buzz at her words.

"*Seen* an Erenky?" the man said. "Never."

"But you have a name for those like me."

"Legends. Tales told to all Uroks as children," Boranaz said. "But fierce creatures of great wrath and fire. Not as kind as you appear to be," he said, gathering his courage. "If you come with me, I will show you."

"Show us? Show us what?" Charlie asked.

"The tales of the Erenky."

CHAPTER THIRTY-FOUR

Boranaz was too afraid of the Zomoki to accept a ride atop her back. Charlie couldn't blame the man, though. From what he'd been able to glean from him as they slowly trekked toward the jagged hills outside of town, the *Erenky* were fearsome beasts that killed indiscriminately, burning man, livestock, and anything else in their way without reason.

Sometimes, an Erenky would not even eat what it had slain. Almost like a giant, fire-breathing cat toying with a mouse until it was dead, then leaving it where it fell it once its fun was finished.

A cat the size of Ara was a terrifying image, indeed, and one Charlie had no desire of ever encountering. Fortunately, Boranaz said that these tales were from long, long ago. How long, Charlie couldn't say for sure, as the poor man didn't possess the greatest grasp of history.

But what he did know was what every other Urok citizen knew. From their youth, they'd been brought up on stories of the Erenky, and at one time or another all had taken the trek Charlie and his friends were now embarked on.

They had opted to walk alongside their guide for this

excursion, both to make him more comfortable with the newcomers to his world, as well as to give them the opportunity to gently probe the man for more information.

As they walked deeper and deeper into the craggy hills, Charlie felt that strange tingle in his senses ramping up its intensity. Ara didn't seem bothered by anything, nor did Bawb, and they were both more attuned to this sort of thing than he was. But *something* was up. He just wished he could figure out what exactly that something was.

"Hey, Kip. Just a heads-up, we've made contact with a group of locals. You can track our location from my comms signal."

"Got it," Kip replied. "You need help? I can be there in under three minutes if I burn hard."

"No, nothing like that. But thanks for the concern," Charlie said, though he thought the AI really just wanted an excuse to push his reworked drive system to the max. "So, have you guys found anything? Any signs of major cities, or spaceships?"

"Negative on that, good buddy," Kip said in his overly chipper manner. "Plenty of farming communities of all sizes, but there's nothing we've seen that could get airborne. It's almost like these people are stranded here or something."

Charlie couldn't help but agree with the ship's assessment.

"Okay, you guys keep doing your sweep. We'll let you know what we find here. It seems Ara bears a striking resemblance to some terrible creature from their history. We're being taken to learn more right now."

"There are more dragons on this world? And they are hostile?" Dukaan asked, a note of concern in his voice. "This does not bode well."

"No, they apparently haven't been seen in a really, really long time. But the stories are still strong in everyone's minds, and just one look at Ara kind of set them off, so there may be something to all of this. We just have to go with and find out what. I'll reach out when we know more."

"You guys heard that. Seems like this planet is somehow cut off from the rest of the system."

"Indeed," Bawb said. *"But from what I can tell, this was once a space-going people. Someone reduced them to this."*

"I know," Charlie replied. *"You have to wonder, with all of these crops but so few people, who are they growing all of this for?"*

It was a question that had weighed on all of their minds as they walked the trail leading deeper into the rugged hills outside of town.

"Not much farther now," Boranaz said, hurrying ahead.

"There is something about these people," Ara noted. *"Are you noting anything unusual, Bawb?"*

The Wampeh's brow furrowed ever so slightly as he reached out with his senses. *"Yes, but I can't put my finger on it."*

"I don't know," Charlie interjected. *"It almost feels like there's magic being used here. Like, this is a power-using world."*

Ara looked at him curiously from on high as she circled above.

"This is the place," Boranaz called out a short while later.

The fire-charred rocks on high contrasted greatly with the lighter stone below. Someone, or something, had torched the topmost reaches of the hills with great heat some time ago. It was like the burned wall they had encountered on that other world, and it seemed a similar trace of old magic lingered here as well.

"Down here, under the overhang," their orange-skinned guide called out.

It was easy to miss the hidden cavern unless you approached it from just the right angle. The overhead rocks were large and jagged, and stuck out like the spines on the back of a dangerous beast. That was likely the reason the stone closer to the base of the overhang had never been charred by what Charlie had to assume was an Erenky attack. It was simply too pointy to be worth the trouble.

But time had a way of changing a landscape, and several rockslides later, a clear enough path now existed for Ara to gingerly lower herself to join her friends on the ground far below.

"This is the place of history," Boranaz said. "Where we learn of the Erenky attacks on our people."

Charlie and Bawb strode into the cavern behind their guide, casting an illumination spell as they went. At this point they had already hit the locals with a talking dragon. They really didn't think a minor display of magic would make much of a difference.

What did surprise them was the small device Boranaz held up himself, casting a much fainter glow, but nevertheless emitting light throughout the entire cavern. A device that had no visible power source. A device that smelled an awful lot like magic.

The two looked at one another but decided that was a conversation for *after* they had learned about the Erenky history Boranaz was so excited to show them.

Ara had to crouch low to enter the overhang, but once she had passed the first fifteen feet, the cavern expanded above her, allowing her to rise to her full height. What she saw amazed even her ancient eyes.

CHAPTER THIRTY-FIVE

The cavern's walls were lined with crystals of varying size, all of which had grown there over millions of years, long before the chamber was discovered by the first Urok hunter. From then, it had become a sacred place. A location of safety for a hunted people. And they didn't just have to take their guide's word for it. The story was there for all to see, etched into the rock walls themselves.

"Petroglyphs," Charlie said.

"Petrowhat?" Bawb asked.

"I guess the translation spell doesn't cover that one," he replied with a grin. "Petroglyphs. Ancient carvings in stone that for one reason or another survive thousands of years, if not longer," he said, leaning in closer to examine one of the drawings of what definitely looked a lot like a dragon.

There were more of them all along the wall. A vast tableau of the history of this world's people and their flight from an airborne menace.

"You see this, Ara?" Charlie asked.

The mighty Zomoki bent down, her golden eyes quickly scanning the images before them. "It is, indeed, as he said.

These drawings are ancient, but it truly does appear there was a creature as he described at one time."

Charlie flashed an excited grin. "You know what that means, right? I mean, these Erenky used magic, right? You can feel it in the rocks outside, even after all of these years."

"Oh?" Ara said.

"Yeah, that tingly feeling. So maybe they're some sort of distant cousin of the Zomoki. Or maybe they're even your own ancestors, somehow traveling from galaxy to galaxy. You might not be alone in this galaxy after all."

A curious look settled on Ara's face. *"Perhaps not,"* she mused silently in her friend's head. *"But tell me, Charlie, you have surely noted the device our guide holds in his hands. The one casting light without flame."*

"Yeah, about that—"

"Though these people lack the technology that appears to have once been present on this world, I sense the faintest beginnings of magic use," Ara said.

"You mean these people are casters?"

"Not yet. The device he carries holds a small portion of an indigenous plant imbued with some magical properties. But for these simple farmers to be able to utilize it in this manner... What we are witnessing here is the evolution of a people. The very beginning of a magic-casting society."

The implications were huge. Magic in this galaxy. That meant that maybe humans would one day learn to cast as well. A next, logical step in their history. A step away from tech toward the power flowing all around them.

"Tell me, Charlie," she continued, staring at her bonded friend with her piercing gaze. *"What does the light device smell like to you?"*

"Smell?"

"Humor me."

He walked over to Boranaz and asked to see his light device a moment, then held it in his hands, feeling the power. He didn't even need to inhale for the 'smell' of the magic to reach his senses.

"It's kind of like a woodsy smell, but with a sharp tang to it. Like a battery, but made of a tree or something, if that makes any sense."

Ara looked at Bawb, who returned her very intrigued gaze.

"Now reach out with your senses and see if you can discern where this device's magic source originated."

"What, like see if I can smell more of it?"

"See if you can locate where it is from," she said.

He furrowed his brow, concentrating, when all of a sudden it was there in front of him, clear as day. A faint line, an almost tangible trace leading from the device in his hands to what *felt* like its origin. And somehow, he knew it was an ancient growth in a swampy bog way out on the far side of the township.

"It's from some little plant that managed to survive in a bog on the outskirts of town. At least, I think it is," he said.

Ara and Bawb once more shared that look.

"What?" Charlie said aloud, his voice echoing in the vast chamber.

Ara leaned in close and sniffed the air around him.

"Uh, Ara? That's kinda weird."

"As are you, my friend," she replied. "Can you sense it, Bawb? The change?"

The Wampeh reached out with his senses, his eyes going wide when they touched upon something quite unexpected. "Yes, Wise One, I can. But how is this possible?"

"Uh, guys? I'm standing right here. What's going on?"

"There is something new to your power, Charlie," Ara said, switching to their silent, internal connection. *"Something most unusual."*

"Yeah, you said. But what is it?"

"I smell Ootaki in your magic now."

"You sure it's not just Hunze's hair you're smelling? I mean, Bob's right there."

"No, Charlie. You do not grasp my meaning. Your magic was bound to mine. A blood bond from when we first met. And it has been growing steadily. But now, you also possess Ootaki magic. If I were to guess, I would say that when the three of us shared power so close to the sun's vast energy while fighting the Tslavar invaders in your solar system, somehow, however impossible it should be, you absorbed some of the shared Ootaki hair's magic. Its potential."

Charlie was floored. Suddenly it made sense. Why he could smell magic. Why he could sense things he'd never been able to before.

"But can I absorb power, then? Like you and Hunze?"

"That, my friend, is unknown," Ara replied. *"But Charlie. It seems you are becoming something* more."

CHAPTER THIRTY-SIX

The floating ballet of rock and ice was almost akin to a jagged kaleidoscope, only this wasn't hanging in a child's room, it was suspended in the void of space.

A crackling blue flash interrupted the calm, the pair of warp ships flashing into being with their alarms sounding and warning lights blazing as they both lurched into immediate evasive maneuvers.

"Asteroids!" Jo shouted as Rika pulled hard on the controls to keep them from being smashed to a million bits.

"Gee, ya think?" Rika growled, dodging a floating chunk of ice the size of a large house. "How are the others? I can't take my eyes off of this mess."

Jo quickly spun in her seat, the display in front of her temporarily useless as it attempted to parse the data stream the thousands of space rocks suddenly presented it with.

"Can't see them," Jo said as the ship lurched abruptly to the left. "Going to try to raise them on comms."

"Forget the comms and plot us a way out of here!"

"But the others?"

"There's no time to chat, and Eddie may be a pain in the ass, but he's a skilled AI. Don't distract his flying. Priority one is to find a way out."

"Gotcha," Jo replied, her fingers flying over the scanning units, trying to locate a possible egress from the impromptu slalom course. "Got something, I think," she said a minute later.

"You think or you know?"

"I know. Plotting it into your heads-up navs now."

Seconds later a course through the obstacles stretched out into the distance, suspended invisibly in the empty space above Rika's pilot's console.

"Okay, we're getting the hell out of this mess. Transmit the map to the others. If we're lucky, they're already out, but if not, this may help them."

"On it."

Jo sent the signal as Rika dove and weaved her way out of the heavier debris until, finally, they managed to pull free of the deadly mess.

"Hey, where are you guys?" Ripley called out over comms. "We just barely made it out of that mess. Are you okay?"

"Yeah, Rip," Rika said with a sigh as she loosened her death grip on the controls. "We're clear. Jo sent a map to Eddie. That should help you pinpoint where we—"

Lights flashed on, illuminating the *Fujin*'s cockpit. A moment later, the AI ship's shimmer cloak was dropped so their friends could spot them.

"See ya!" Ripley chirped. "Oh, thank God. I was worried for a minute. Totally wasn't expecting to come out of warp in the middle of a mess like that."

Rika ran her hand through her hair as she tried to force her pulse to slow. "Yeah, what the hell was that?" she asked. "I thought we were supposed to be following a *smart* tracker. Flying us into an asteroid field was anything but smart."

"That's the problem with this sort of AI," Eddie noted. "They're not the most precise of things, you know. And there's really no telling exactly where they might actually emerge from a warp."

"Like an asteroid field, for example?" Leila groused, looking a bit greener than usual.

"Yes, like an asteroid field," the AI ship replied. "But their ship appears to have dropped out of warp outside of the asteroids."

"We call it a jump," Leila corrected. "Magic ships don't use warp."

"Right, I know," Eddie said. "But the thing is, we know it's close. Just not *really* close, if you know what I mean."

"So what do we do now?" Hunze asked. "We can't just warp willy-nilly hoping to find them."

Jo checked her scans again. "We follow the breadcrumbs," she finally said. "The signal trace is working as designed. Now we just have to go after them."

Eddie and Ripley extrapolated the AI tracker's course through the system. They couldn't scan too far ahead due to the power constraints of the little AI tracker, so it looked like they'd be following the slow way. One breadcrumb at a time.

Rika plotted her course and accelerated into the darkness. "Okay, guys, let's get to it."

The soil covering the planet they eventually touched down on was a deep umber, but the vegetation grew in a pale-yellow tone for the most part. The strangeness of a world with breathable air and actual plant life was not lost on the humans in the group.

Though Rika had spent plenty of time off-world in the other galaxy, that had been during her time as a brainwashed slave. But now she was herself again, and this was *her* galaxy. She and Ripley were the first people from Earth to ever set foot on this world, and the rush made her heart flutter just a little.

The Tslavars had been there too, it seemed. Despite their

ship being shimmer cloaked, it wasn't hard to tell, what with all the rudely torn up plant life they found scattered all around the area. Stealth, apparently, was not a priority. But then, they had no idea they were being tracked.

"What were they doing?" Leila asked, shocked at the seemingly random destruction. "Taking out their aggressions on some poor plants?"

"Your guess is as good as mine," Rika said. "But they were here, so that's a start." She walked over to one of the piles of uprooted plants and examined it closely. "Roots were cut off with a blade," she noted. "It looks like they were chopping the hell out of everything within reach."

"Guys, I've got the trail," Jo called out. "It looks like they followed a low flight path that way," she said, pointing into the distance. "It doesn't look like they've warp--I mean, *jumped* again, so let's get moving. Se might catch up with them."

The group dropped the mangled plants where they found them and climbed back aboard their respective craft. The Tslavars were up to something here, but for the life of them they couldn't figure out what. Maybe the next landing spot would provide a bit more illumination.

Unfortunately, all they found were more signs of rough handling of local flora. Besides that, there was nothing of use.

"Shit," Eddie said.

"What?" Ripley asked.

"I picked up another signal from the tracker."

"And?"

"And it came from off-world. They've moved on already."

"Shit."

Rika scrambled for the *Fujin*. "Let's get a move on. Come on!"

Her words jogged everyone to action, and in less than a minute the two ships had leapt into the sky to follow the breadcrumb trail to yet another planet.

CHAPTER THIRTY-SEVEN

"Well, at least they didn't leave the system," Ripley muttered as the pair of ships followed the trace signal left by the Tslavar vessel.

She was right. The shimmer craft had apparently planet-hopped to another of the handful of habitable worlds in the system rather than move on to another system entirely. None of them could figure out what exactly their quarry was doing, however.

As they flew, tracking the signal to a particularly verdant planet, Jo ran a simple analysis of the samples she had taken from the plants the Tslavars had uprooted. There had to be some reason for it, and if she could just figure out what it was, perhaps it would give them a much-needed advantage over their invisible enemy.

Hunze, being a natural power-generating being, had sensed *something* in the system, but was still unable to put her finger on what precisely it was. That was disconcerting for her, but a consolation was that the sun the planets of this system were orbiting was particularly powerful. As a result, her hair was absorbing energy by the minute, even through Eddie's shields and hull.

"That's a pretty big planet," Leila noted as they began their descent into the atmosphere of the green-blue orb. "I hope we are able to locate them."

"With the tracker leaving us that trail, it shouldn't be *too* difficult. If they don't jump away, that is," Ripley replied. "Though that little bastard is acting *really* spotty. What's with that, Eddie?"

"How should I know, Rip?"

"You're the resident AI. And that's an AI tracker. So..."

"Oh, I see. You think because I happen to be an AI that I somehow know the inner thoughts and workings of a freaking barely sentient tracker? One that was shot out of a rail gun, no less––which could damage the psyche of anyone, I'd wager."

"Jeez, okay. Sorry. I didn't mean to offend. Relax, man."

"Sorry," Eddie replied. "It's just a little stressful trying to keep track of everything while we go hopping around the galaxy chasing some invisible ship, ya know?"

"We're invisible now too, Eddie."

"Well, obviously I know that," he grumbled, having partitioned the magic keeping them from detection into a self-regulating sub-routine within his powerful mind.

And the sun of this system had provided them an additional boost of energy as well, supercharging the strand of hair Hunze had gifted him, making it almost effortless to keep the casting going.

"I mean, don't get me wrong," he continued. "I'm enjoying the challenge, but still, it's not exactly easy, ya know?"

Ripley actually felt a little bad for giving her AI buddy grief. It had been good-natured, as usual, but Eddie *was* a really young ship, and she had to remind herself that despite his vast competence, he really was still just a kid, in many ways. And suddenly, he was using magic on top of it all. It had to be a bit of a mindfuck.

But Eddie kept it all under control, reeling himself back in and getting his emotions in check as they dropped into the planet's atmosphere.

Rika kept the *Fujin* on Eddie's tail, but a fair distance back. With the ship casting its shimmer spell, she didn't want to accidentally run into it by following too close.

Aboard the AI ship, a glowing green briefly filled the cabin.

"What was that?" Ripley asked.

Leila looked at the Magus stone around her neck. Apparently, something had triggered it, but only slightly, and just for an instant. Whatever it had been, the green stone was once again silent.

"My Magus stone," she said, tucking it back into the warmth of her shirt. "It must've sensed something. Some sort of danger."

"Do we know what?" Hunze asked.

"I am not able to tap into the stone directly, so I'm afraid I can't give you an answer," Leila replied.

It had been a source of many discussions since she learned the true nature--and true power--of the stone her mother had left her. Apparently, it was a Magus stone of exceptional potency, but as a half-breed, it seemed she was unable to directly utilize the power contained within.

The stone was still bound to her by her bloodline, and it reacted on its own in times of danger, having saved them all from a massive magical attack so very recently. But beyond that, its use was a mystery. One she hoped to someday unravel. But for now, its automatic protective tendencies would more than suffice.

"We've got a lock on the next transmission fix from the tracker," Jo called out over comms. "You see that, Eddie?"

"Yeah," he replied, actually a little impressed the cyborg had picked up the tracker before he did. She was skilled, he had to admit. "Looks like they set down about a thousand miles ahead. We're cloaked, so I'll go in first and see if they're still on the ground. If so, let's hope they drop their shielding when they walk outside the ship, or else we're gonna have a helluva time knocking down their flight systems."

It was something they'd all had on their minds since they had managed to land a tracking sabot on the Tslavar ship. The way they adjusted and adapted their shields so quickly. As powerful as the rail guns were, there was a real possibility their next volley would merely inconvenience the enemy rather than do any significant damage.

But they'd cross that bridge when they reached it. For now, they would adjust their angle of approach and drop down low a few hundred miles away from their destination.

Skimming the ground, Eddie flew up ahead while Rika dropped back even farther, lowering her approach to as close to the surface as was reasonable at those speeds.

"They're around here somewhere," she said to her mechanic-slash-gunner. "We just need to get close enough to finally get a fix on them before they fly off again."

"And if we do?" Jo asked, knowing full well Rika was thinking the same thing.

"Then we do whatever we can to take them down," she replied with grim determination. "They attacked our world. *Twice*. There's no chance in hell I'm playing nice this time around."

They flew in silence for a while, human and cyborg both pondering what might come of this pursuit.

"I've got something weird up here," Eddie called out over comms.

"You found them?" Rika replied.

"Well, not exactly," Eddie said.

"What he means is they were here. Recently. And it looks

like they were tearing stuff up again, like last time," Ripley added.

"So no-go again?" Rika said with a sigh.

"Not exactly. We're dropping the shimmer. Follow our signal and join us here. You'll see what we're talking about."

"Copy that. We're on our way," Rika replied, adjusting her course slightly. "Sounds like something's up," she said to Jo. "You might wanna power up the cannons, just in case."

"Already online and ready to fire," the cyborg replied.

"See? This is why I like having you around," Rika said with a chuckle. "Okay, we're goin' in," she said, then took the ship in to join their friends.

CHAPTER THIRTY-EIGHT

Rika had taken a cautious approach, Jo sitting beside her with her hands on the weapons controls, ready to fire should any hostile actions require it. But all appeared to be calm down below.

What they saw as they circled the area was simply Eddie parked in another clearing. As before, the local vegetation had been uprooted, but there was something else this time. Signs of a fight.

"Keep your eyes peeled," Rika said as she set the ship down and slid her most powerful konus, the one gifted her by Bawb not so long ago, onto her wrist. "Come on."

The pair stepped out of the *Fujin* and joined their friends as they surveyed the area. The atmosphere was quite breathable, and with all of the vegetation of this world, the air was exceptionally refreshing. And there was something *more* to it, it seemed. Something they couldn't quite place.

Hunze, on the other hand, seemed abuzz with excitement as she picked up the remnants of plants left scattered around the landing zone.

"What's she doing?" Rika quietly asked Leila. "She's sniffing them."

"She's an Ootaki," Leila replied. "Her kind not only produce power, but are also sensitive to certain types. And here, on this weird world, she smells magic."

"Magic? I don't feel it?"

"You're human. From this galaxy. Your body's systems are different than ours," the olive-skinned woman replied.

Hunze padded across the upturned ground to her friends. "This is unlike any magic I've ever felt," she said, clearly agitated. "And there's a lot of it in some of these plants. Like, they absorb the power from the sun and convert it to this magical energy."

"Kind of like your hair or Ara's skin," Ripley noted.

"Yes," the golden-haired woman replied. "But this is strong. And dangerous."

"Dangerous? Why do you say that?"

"Something feels wrong about it," Hunze replied.

Jo walked over to a chopped-up shrub and picked up the remains. "Why are they tearing up the plants, then?"

"Because there is power here, don't you see?" Hunze said, on edge. "They appear to be attempting to gather a new source of power. One they can harvest."

"To what end, though?" Jo wondered.

"It is only a guess," Hunze said, "but I think they are trying to gather enough power to retrieve the portal from the sun."

"But you said this magic was dangerous."

"Yes, but maybe they think it's worth it for a one-time spell."

"Uh, guys?" Ripley said, concern in her voice. "You need to see this."

The others quickly made their way to her side. What had caught her attention was a pool of green on the ground.

"Is that Tslavar blood?" Hunze asked.

"From personal experience, I can definitely confirm that,"

Rika replied. She'd slain her fair share of Tslavars in the not-so-distant past. And someone had done the same here. Recently, by the look of it.

"I see signs of a hasty retreat," she noted, scanning the bootprints on the ground.

Rika followed the tracks, pools of drying green blood spattering the ground as the gravely injured aliens fled back to their ship.

"Here. They boarded here," she said, pointing to where all tracks ceased.

The Tslavar ship had been hovering just off the surface, and as a result the ground beneath it was untouched. She bent down and retrieved a shaft of wood from the soil.

"Is that an arrow?" Ripley asked, shocked. "Like, an actual arrow?"

"Yes," she said, noting the blood on the shaft. "But they would have been shimmer cloaked," Rika said, stunned. "I don't understand."

Hunze rushed to her and took the length of wood from her hand, nearly dropping it as she touched the shaft, almost as if it had burned her.

"What is it?" Rika asked.

"That magic again," Hunze replied, pulling her sleeves down over her hands so the wood no longer touched her skin. She brought it up to her nose and sniffed it, recoiling as she did. "There is *strong* magic in this wood," she said. "Magic grown from this system's power. But it feels so *wrong* to me."

"Something in the way the plants absorb it, maybe?" Rika suggested.

"That must be it," the Ootaki woman replied. "This magic, it would have pierced their protective spells. I don't know how they saw through the shimmers, but this weapon could certainly have passed through their defenses."

"Uh, guys?" Ripley said, her voice wavering slightly. "We're not alone."

Some gut instinct told Rika not to spin and open fire. Instead, she slowly turned, making no sudden movements. If these people had taken out a crack Tslavar invasion squad, she had a good inkling she wouldn't stand a chance.

"I guess it's time to meet the locals," she said.

She just hoped she and her friends wouldn't meet the same fate as their green predecessors.

CHAPTER THIRTY-NINE

Rika and the others had given up any thoughts of overpowering their captors when they saw the numbers they faced. A dozen spears and arrows had been pointed at them, ready to fly, so a decision was quickly made.

"We mean no harm," Rika said, hoping her translation spell worked on these natives. "Take me to your leader."

She'd even uttered the line without the slightest hint of a smile, for as instinctive as saying the cliché line was, there was not an ounce of levity in their situation.

Hands held up and open, weapons slung, she and the others stood facing the natives, taking in the details of this new species as they studied them in return.

What they saw was a tribe of tan-skinned humanoids, entirely devoid of hair--something made clear from the sparse clothing they wore--and perhaps six feet tall. They possessed six fingers on each hand, and were well-muscled from what must have been a very physical lifestyle.

And they were tattooed, each with ornate, swirling designs across different parts of their bodies.

Most wore only black ink, while a few others possessed deep

reds, blues, and even a purple pigment in addition to their black lines. A form of ranking, perhaps, Rika thought.

But what really caught Rika's eye in particular were the small swirls at the corners of each of the hunters' eyes.

They could see through the shimmers, she mused, wondering if there might be more to the designs than mere decoration.

"How do you speak our tongue?" the most colorfully inked man said, confirming Rika's theory on tattoos and rank.

"Remind me to thank Bawb for these translation spells," Rika quietly said to Hunze, then turned her attention to the man standing before them. "We are travelers from a distant world. Ours are a people who possess the means to communicate with others from distant lands so we may engage in peaceful discourse with all we meet."

She wondered if that was perhaps laying it on a bit thick, but given the tribal nature of this society, overly formal and respectful seemed the way to go. Better to err on the side of too polite than not, she reasoned.

"A useful skill," the man said, not lowering his spear an inch. "But you come in a flying beast, just as the last invaders did. And we saw you destroying the nagani bush and farzin shrubs. You are defilers. Spoilers of all that is good."

"No, that wasn't us," Rika replied. "Those others, the green men you speak of, they caused this damage. We merely picked up what they had already dug up to understand their motives."

"But you know these others. The ones who attempt to vanish from sight like spirits."

"We do, but not as you think. We are hunting them."

This seemed to catch the man's interest. "Hunting? But they are fierce creatures and harmed several of our farmers before the tribal warriors could come to their aid."

"And you did an admirable job against a difficult foe," Rika said. "You wounded many of them from what we can see."

"You possess the skills to read the signs of battle?" the man said, his guard again on high alert. "A woman?"

"Yes, but I assure you, we do not come here seeking conflict," Rika replied, trying to soothe his agitation.

She looked at the men's wooden weapons. It was hard to believe something as simple as those could disrupt so powerful an enemy. And she could handle the material with no problem, while Hunze acted as if she'd nearly been burned by merely touching the wood. If all beings from that distant galaxy reacted so violently, she could only imagine what being pierced by an arrow crafted from it could do.

"You have very powerful weapons," she said, gesturing to his spear. "What do you enchant them with that gives them such strength?

"Enchant? What do you mean, enchant?" he replied. "These are simply warriors' tools, fashioned from the kakanamaru tree."

"I think this means the native flora absorbs the energy from the sun and converts it to this magic, just as Hunze suggested," Eddie said, his disembodied voice floating out into the clearing.

The natives jumped at the sound, weapons held at the ready.

"Damn it, Eddie," Rika grumbled to herself. "Please, friends, lower your weapons. We mean you no harm."

"This is a spirit voice! One from the beyond come to harvest our bravest!" the leader said.

"No, no. That's just the voice of our flying craft," Rika said, trying to soothe the men. "His name is Eddie. He may not look like the type of creature you are used to seeing, but he is alive."

"That I am," Eddie said. "Sorry if I startled you. Just thought I'd chime in, what with--"

"Enough, Eddie," Ripley hissed at her chatty friend.

"Uh, right. Sorry."

The war party leader cautiously approached the sleek ship. It certainly did not look like any creature he'd ever encountered before, and appeared to be made of some hard material, not flesh like other beasts.

He took his spear and clanged it against Eddie's hull, drawing the point along his side. The ceramisteel didn't even scratch. With the wooden shaft possessing its own magic, the AI ship was just glad the konus he had installed did not react to the action as an attack.

"Like I said, just a being from a different world, far away. He is not what you are used to, I know, but Eddie is our friend, and he means you no harm."

"And the other one?"

"Oh, that's the *Fujin*. My ship. It is not alive. Merely a tool I use to travel great distances."

The man eyed the group distrustfully. But he did not order an attack, so that was something. "You will come with us," he finally decided. "The great ones will decide what is to be your fate. Take their weapons," he ordered his men.

Rika gave a little nod to the others to let them, but, much to their surprise, the natives only took the blades they wore. Their pulse weapons slung on their backs and their konuses were left untouched. Apparently, they'd never seen anything like them before and did not perceive their novel weapons as a threat.

For now, the visitors would play along, peacefully going to meet their leaders, as Rika had asked. The warriors did not trust them, that much was clear, but at least they hadn't attacked them, so that was a good start.

What would come of the meeting back in their village, well, that might be an entirely different matter. Only time would tell.

CHAPTER FORTY

The two humans--three by appearances, if you counted Jo's fleshy cyborg exterior--drew much interest from the villagers as they were paraded into a picketed circle of yurt-like habitations. To see beings of similar coloring, though a lot paler, yet strangely covered with hair was an utter novelty for the relatively primitive people. Rika was a particular favorite among the kids. At least at first.

Then they saw Leila and Hunze.

The greenish hue peeking through Leila's olive-tanned complexion made the survivors of the Tslavar attack wince, afraid she was another of those violent beings. She saw them shrink away and understood their reaction. She knew what had happened to them, and the green half of her family tree was in fact a not so distant cousin of the Tslavars.

But it was Hunze who caused the greatest stir, with children forgetting their fear of the outsiders entirely as they came running up to her to touch her golden locks.

For a race that had no hair whatsoever, seeing a woman with not only bright gold hair, but in such great quantities, was akin to coming across a unicorn. They simply never dreamed such a being could exist.

Hunze smiled warmly at the children, careful to make no gesture or movement that could even remotely be seen as hostile. When it came to kids, she was quite certain this civilization was as protective of theirs as others were, no matter what planet, system, or even galaxy they resided in.

The older tribespeople had more tattoos adorning their bodies than the youth of the village, and, as Rika had assumed, the colorings and density of the adornments appeared to indeed be signifiers of rank and status within their society.

"You will come to meet the elders," their captor/guide informed them. "The great ones."

"Thank you," Hunze said, using her popularity to attempt a bit of diplomacy. "And we still do not know your name, friend. I am Hunze. This is Leila beside me. And those are Jo, Ripley, and Rika, whom you have spoken to at length."

The man looked her up and down a moment, then apparently decided there was no harm in sharing this piece of information. "I am Varahash, leader of the Kalamani warriors," he finally said, puffing his chest with pride.

Hunze flashed her warmest smile. "It is a pleasure, Varahash."

"Yes, thank you for your hospitality," Rika added. "We truly appreciate the honor of meeting your leaders."

Varahash merely grinned curiously, then turned, continuing on toward the largest of the yurts in the center of the village.

"Speak only when spoken to," Varahash said before they stepped inside. Then he drew back the door flap and ushered the alien visitors inside.

It was not nearly as dark as one might have expected within the structure. An ambient light was given off by what appeared to be some sort of glowing moss that had been collected and hung from the rafters, providing a gentle, yellow light.

Seated at the far end were five very old and very inked individuals. The ornate lines covered almost their entire bodies, with great splashes of color woven through the intricate designs.

Three were women. Two were men. All had the bearing of those who have lived through both great and challenging times. The woman at the center leaned forward slightly, as if to better see the people standing right before her.

The tattoos encircling her eyes were far more ornate than those belonging to the hunters, and traces of pale yellow blended with the reds, blacks, and blues on her face. She studied the group a long time, then leaned back in her seat.

"Why have you come here?" she asked in an old woman's rasp.

Rika looked at the others, who gave her a little nod. She was designated speaker, it seemed.

"We are travelers from a distant world, come to your planet in pursuit of a dangerous group of bad men called Tslavars."

"Why pursue them to our world? We have no part in your quarrel," the elder said.

"It was not our intention to come here, but we were tracking them, and this is where they came."

"You can track them through the blackness?" she asked, an ornately inked eyebrow arching slightly in disbelief. "If you possess such power, then why have you not succeeded in your task?"

"Because, as I am sure your hunters will attest, tracking your prey over difficult terrain can be rather problematic. It often takes far longer than you would like."

The woman reached down beside her and picked up a bloody blade. Tslavar, Rika could tell immediately by the design.

"This weapon, made of brightstone, was taken by my warriors when they drove back the first attackers," the woman said. She then reached down on her other side and hefted Leila's long knife. "And this brightstone was taken from you when my warriors captured your war party."

"We're not a war party. We're just—" Ripley blurted.

"Silence!" the woman bellowed in a voice far too loud for her seemingly frail body. "The youth would do well to know her place," she added, throwing a bit of elderly alien stink-eye at the teenager.

"Please, forgive her. She is young and impulsive," Rika covered.

"As the young often are," the elder said, softening her tone only slightly. Nevertheless, she still held two blades in her hands, accompanied by an expression that said more than words.

She didn't trust them, and no matter what Rika said, that was not going to change.

"Many cultures in our world carry knives like these. While they may look similar, ours are not Tslavar."

"So you say. Yet two of our farmers have succumbed to wounds suffered at the hands of the intruders. And my warriors found you uprooting nagani and farzin shrubs, just as the ones you call Tslavars did."

"We were just picking up what they left behind to see if we could understand what they wanted with them, I swear. We did not cut any of the plants ourselves."

The elder was about to make a sharp reply when a murmur spread through the small group assembled in the structure.

A wiry, thin man, far older than the others, slowly strode to the elders. He was an anomaly in this village of tattooed men and women in that, unlike them, he bore no black ink or colors anywhere on his parchment-dry skin.

That's not to say he was unadorned, though, for he was covered in tattoos, the art different than the others. The lines were slender, drawn with an expert hand, yet with none of the ornate, decorative elements so many sported.

And his tattoos were entirely a faint white, the ink seeping into his skin in a way that made them almost invisible from certain angles.

Rika watched him as he stepped closer to the off-world visitors. The fine lines that traced the contours of his body seemed almost alive under his skin, and as he moved, you could nearly feel the power radiating off of him.

He was obviously a shaman or holy man of some sort, and the power he wielded was unlike any the visitors had ever felt. Hunze, being far more sensitive than the others, was almost woozy from the intense buzz of alien magic flowing from the man. The sheer potential he possessed was incredible. Incredible, and dangerous. The magic was unlike any she'd ever experienced before, and she had no idea what it might mean.

The man slowly paced in front of the captives, pausing before each of them, studying them with intense eyes peering out from the fine lines surrounding them. The chamber was silent as he inspected the newcomers. Apparently, his opinion held much weight among the tribe, as even the elders remained respectfully still.

At long last he reached Rika at the end. His head cocked slightly to the side, then he walked away without a word.

"The visitors may stay," the elder said when he had finally passed through the door.

Voices chattered outside the yurt and the former prisoners, now visitors, were ushered out into the fresh air.

"Now what?" Ripley asked.

Varahash turned to the youngster. He still didn't trust the newcomers, but the shaman had spoken. Or *not* spoken, as the case happened to be. In any case, they were to be treated as guests.

"Now we feast," he said. "Come."

CHAPTER FORTY-ONE

The village people of the Kalamani tribe were all hard at work preparing the evening's feast. Fat beasts slain for the occasion were being roasted in a pit fire, while an assortment of plants were being cleaned and placed on long wooden platters.

The seating area was laid out in such a way that an ornately carved piece of timber that served as the village elders' place of honor was at the head, while the other lengths of wood were set up angling away, leaving the look of the rays of a half sun radiating from the elders.

The symbolism was not lost on the visitors. The tribal leaders were what made their entire society function, just as the sun provided light and life for the whole world.

Leila ran her hand across the top of the wood, where they were shown to their seats. It felt strange, as if traces of power ran through it. But different than in other systems. This felt a little off. She wondered how it would have felt if it was fresh wood instead of so greatly aged.

The rough-hewn logs had been transformed into smooth banquet tables, she saw, but not by use of fine tools, but from years upon years of wear, the grain rubbing down to a smooth luster from generations of utility.

"What are they cooking?" Ripley asked. "Smells good."

Varahash looked at her, displeased. "This is not a warrior's task," he replied. "Speak with Darakka," he said, pointing to a large woman with gently curving tattoos running from her chest down to her arms, almost as if the energy from the center of her being was directed to her hands as she prepared the village's meal.

Ripley walked over to where the woman was arranging freshly cooked vegetables on a platter. "Uh, excuse me?" she said.

Darakka turned and fixed her with a curious gaze. "Ah, the invaders," she said. "What do you require?"

"We're not invaders," Ripley replied.

"So you say," she replied, frustrating in her obstinate tranquility.

"Well, anyway, I was just wondering what you were cooking. It smells really good."

A tiny smile teased the corners of the woman's mouth. "You smell the roasted harkaan," she replied, nodding to the animal on the fire.

"Well, it smells amazing, whatever it is. I can't wait to try it."

"It is very good eating, and not too fatty," Darakka said. She looked at the teen a moment, then walked over and carved off a small piece of meat with the stone blade carried at her hip. "Here, you try it," she said, offering the steaming treat to Ripley, who readily accepted.

"Oh my God, this is fantastic," she gushed.

Darakka's little smile blossomed into a full grin. Despite her distrust of the newcomers, the woman's existence revolved around food, and feeding those of her tribe. Making them happy through her efforts brought her great joy, and this strange new visitor was so young she could have been her own daughter's age.

"Now go sit with your friends, Invader. The feast will begin shortly," Darakka said, a bit less standoffish than before.

"Thanks, Darakka," Ripley said, licking her fingers as she walked back to her seat.

A short while later the villagers began filing in for what would be a family-style meal, with massive trays of meats and vegetables spread across the great tables.

"What is this stuff?" Rika asked, picking at an odd, purple vegetable that looked like a cross between a Portobello mushroom and an eggplant.

"Best not to ask," Jo replied, her cybernetic eyes taking in all aspects of the gathering as quickly as she could. "Scans showed nothing toxic in the area when we landed, so I say just smile and eat."

Rika cautiously took a small bite, the plant snapping under her teeth, its purple juice running down her chin.

"Crap," she managed through her full mouth. "Hey, this is actually pretty good."

"And the roast harkaan is freakin' delicious," Rip added, tearing off a giant piece and eating like a hungry savage.

Hunze and Leila, however, were not so enthused by the meal. In fact, aside from a light-yellow porridge from some sort of ground grain, neither touched the impressive spread.

"What's the matter, you guys aren't hungry?" Ripley asked.

"No, it's not that," Hunze replied. "It's just these vegetables are very rich in the strange magic of this world. It is uncomfortable to touch, so, as you can imagine, ingesting it would likely cause great distress."

"You too, Leila?" Rika asked.

"Yeah, but not as much as Hunze. She's a lot more sensitive to this than I am. But I can definitely feel the power in the plants." She took a sip of her porridge, judging it before finally swallowing. "At least this stuff is only barely touched by it."

"Well, this won't do," Rika said. "I'll tell them we need to return to our craft after dinner. Eddie said he'd trace the Tslavars solo and let us know over comms if they left the planet. So far there's been no word, so it looks like the tracker is still pinging on the planet."

"That would be ideal," Leila said. "Hunze and I have a supply of food we can eat on the ship. I just don't think we can chance it with this stuff."

The visitors sat and ate, or didn't eat, as the case may be, observing the social structure of the Kalamani people as they interacted and dined together. It was a crash course in primitive culture sociology, but by the end of their meal, it seemed they had a decent feel for the flow of tribal life.

The children were afforded a leniency of sorts until they reached a more mature age. They guessed that to be roughly ten years old, at least by Earth standards. The younger children were pampered to an extent, allowed to play and chatter, while the older kids helped with chores.

Several had taken quite a liking to Rika for some reason, bringing her fruit and flowers then running away, giggling. It was a bit odd for the woman who never really liked kids, but she found herself rather taken with them.

"I trust you have dined well?" Varahash said, checking in on the newcomers as the feast wound down.

"Yes, it was excellent," Rika said. "Thank you for your hospitality."

"The Haka says you are to be treated as guests. So you are treated as guests."

"The Haka? Is that the shaman fellow we met earlier?"

Varahash nodded.

"I'm glad he decided to trust us. We're not like the Tslavars, you know."

"Trust is earned, not given," the war party leader said. "But hospitality may be offered, even to an enemy."

"But we are not your enemy. Please believe me when I say we do not wish you or your people any harm."

"We have taken your weapons. You could not do harm even if you wanted."

"We could. But we choose not to," she replied, managing to make it sound like a statement rather than a threat.

Varahash simply laughed. "You would find we are most formidable when pressed," he replied. "Do not test our hospitality, Invader."

Rika didn't much like the sound of that, but decided to let it go for the moment. They had other issues to deal with, so no use muddying that water.

"Listen, Varahash," she said, changing subjects. "Leila and Hunze need to visit our craft for a bit. There are things that should be attended to sooner than later."

"You are to remain here for the time being. It is the elders' wish."

"But the rest of us will stay here," she countered. "Please, they need to check our craft and will be back shortly."

Varahash thought on it a moment. The elders wanted security, but if three of them were to remain under his watchful eye, that would satisfy their wishes.

"Very well. But they return shortly."

"We will," Leila said, getting to her feet. "Come on, Hunze, let's get moving."

The two quickly left the village, heading back toward the empty field, where they'd been captured. Of course, shimmer-cloaked Eddie would just drop down nearby once they were clear of the village, but the warrior didn't need to know that. So long as none of his ilk were present, the others would not be able to see the invisible ship when he touched down.

"Come!" a small child said, pulling Rika by the hand, oblivious to the tension in the air between her and Varahash.

The warrior looked at the youth, then at Rika. His eyes softened slightly, and he gave a subtle nod, which Rika returned, then followed the child, pulled by her tiny hand.

The elders and shaman shared an uneasy look as they watched the proceedings from their seats of honor. Whatever was afoot, the newcomers would need to be closely watched.

CHAPTER FORTY-TWO

Standing at one of the many observation windows afforded the upper class of the Crux, Captain Jimtee looked calm and relaxed as he stared out at the expansive fleet of powerful vessels.

He was anything but.

His request to see inside some of the larger ships had been posed at the most opportune moment, right after an engaging discussion with the upper crust of Urok society, Jimtee dazzling them with stories of the surprising adventures of a simple space trader. All were wondrous lies, and he was a hit, and as Regent Zinna was the one who had brought him to the Crux, the diplomat had found his social worth increased for it.

So it was that after a particularly pleasant evening of wine and talk, Jimtee finally broached the subject of the Urok protection being provided to him and his men as he and the regent walked the spacious halls afforded the wealthy.

Commander Datano followed the men, at Jimtee's request, though he had carefully made it seem as if the idea had been Regent Zinna's.

To seize power, he would need to understand their military as well as their political structure, and his fortunes were looking good as these two men were his first contact with this new race, and they had benefited socially from their association.

"We are glad to be your friends and protectors," Commander Datano said, "but rules still apply. You would be wise to remember that and watch your step, as well as your tongue, alien."

"I'm sorry, I meant no offense," the Tslavar captain replied, acting meek and apologetic. "I merely wished to better marvel at the incredible power your people possess."

Regent Zinna rested a hand on his shoulder. "My dear Jimtee, we understand how it must be for a relatively primitive race such as yours to suddenly find themselves surrounded by all of this," he said, gesturing at the technological wonders around them. "But Commander Datano is correct, if a little harsh. We simply cannot take outsiders--especially lower-class ones--aboard our military vessels for a look around. It simply would not fly with the captains, and is thus entirely out of the question."

"Again, I meant no offense by it," Jimtee said, his eyes fixing on a seemingly empty space a ways to his left. "Walking the mighty decks of those craft is something I am sure any of my men would very much like to do. After all, understanding the workings of so marvelous a fleet would only bolster their confidence in your might and ability to protect us from the horrible flying beast."

Commander Datano turned a curious glance to the space Jimtee had been looking, but nothing was there. For just a moment he could have sworn he felt the slightest of breezes, as if something had moved past him, though his eyes told him nothing had.

"Gentlemen," Jimtee continued, "it seems I have unintentionally crossed a line of decorum, for which I am truly apologetic. But I hope you can forgive me and understand how a simple people such as the Tslavars would have a natural curiosity and desire to learn more about the Uroks. You are such a powerful race, and will be a mighty ally to my people."

"I don't know if we can call ourselves allies," Zinna said, ever the diplomat. "Rather, we are more akin to your protectors. The Tslavars are obviously a sophisticated enough people. You possess the means for space travel, after all, though your lack of weaponry and defense is quite disappointing."

"We are simple, peaceful traders, so the need for such things has never arisen," Jimtee managed with a straight face.

"Even so, to go out into the wild naked, essentially. It is foolishness," Datano interjected. "To do so is to court subjugation at the hands of a greater power."

"Or to find protection from one," the Tslavar replied.

"Yes, protection," Regent Zinna said, reflecting momentarily on Commander Datano's words.

Perhaps the Tslavars would eventually bend the knee and become another subservient faction within the Urok empire. If so, his role in securing this new resource for his people would go far in increasing his standing and rank. But Regent Zinna merely smiled pleasantly at his simple guest. What he didn't know wouldn't hurt him. Not yet, anyway.

Jimtee, for his part, likewise assessed the potential of this new race. They were cocky and self-assured, but he had to admit their ships and weapons appeared to be rather formidable, if limited in numbers.

Once they recovered the enormous portal trapped within Earth's sun and his full fleet passed through, then they would see who would be subjugating whom.

Ulus joined his captain in the corridors later that evening as he walked the Crux, slowly making his way back to their ship. It was amazing watching his normally strict and demanding captain acting like a weak-willed dandy, but Ulus had to admit, the man excelled at both diplomacy and deception.

He mingled and charmed the high-ranking inhabitants of this section of the Crux as they casually walked, a green-skinned novelty of the moment for them to amuse themselves with. Finally, he and Ulus reached a quiet stretch of hallway as they passed between sections of the facility.

Jimtee quickly and quietly cast an obfuscation spell, blurring their speech to others, while leaving their own translation spells active so they could fully understand those around them if need be.

"How did it go, Captain?" Ulus asked.

"Not as well as I would have liked. They refuse to grant access to their warships, even for Jimtee, the friendly trader."

Ulus chuckled.

"Something funny, Ulus?"

"Oh, no, sir," he said with an amused grin. "I merely cannot wait to see their faces when they realize whom they've been underestimating all this time."

Jimtee smiled. Yes, he too would take great pleasure in bringing this entire culture to its knees.

"So, shall I begin collaring them by force?"

"No, Ulus. Not yet. There is still much to learn, and we must be very strategic with our control collars. We simply do not possess enough to effectively dominate all who would be of use to us. But never fear. Plans are already in motion in that regard."

Jimtee saw another throng of chattering diplomats and elite walking their way and reversed his obfuscation spell. Duty, it seemed, called yet again. But he would grin and bear it, knowing full well that all throughout the Crux, and now even aboard some of the Urok ships, his shimmer-cloaked men were scouring every accessible area, gathering all the intel they could.

"Fetch the others," he said, then turned up the exhausting smile he'd had plastered to his face ever since they'd arrived and readied himself for another tedious engagement with the vapid Urok elite.

Soon, it would be time to put his next phase into play. Then they could get on with the real task. That of retrieving his fleet and bringing Earth to its knees.

CHAPTER FORTY-THREE

To allow any but the most senior of the crew into his personal quarters would have been an idea met with ridicule and scorn just a short time ago, but Captain Jimtee found his chambers crammed with invisible Tslavars when he finally returned to his ship.

"Uncloak, we are secure in here," he said.

The two dozen men dropped their shimmers immediately, standing at attention before their captain.

Jimtee looked at the sheer number of men crowded into the room and felt his irritation flare. Not at his men, though. At the ridiculous Uroks who had forced him to take such drastic measures.

There was an element of trust from their hosts, but one intermingled with an abundance of caution. As such, regular patrols walked not only the landing bay in which the Tslavar craft rested, but also the corridors and rooms of the ship itself.

Given the constant supervision of their hosts both within the Crux as well as the ship, only the captain's personal space was left unobserved. Of course, the invisible, shimmer-cloaked men had to maneuver around the periodic foot patrols to get there, but all had years of experience and viewed it as more of an interesting challenge than a dangerous obstacle.

Jimtee looked over his men. The majority were either still out in the dining hall or in other public places. His crack shimmer team, however, were making rapid strides in gaining intel on their hosts. A good half of their number, he noted, were not with them this evening. That meant they were still gathering information somewhere on the base.

"Tell me what you've learned," he said.

The ranking Tslavar stepped forward to give the situation report for the team members present, as well as what he knew from those still out in the field.

"The powers that drive their systems are incredibly inelegant and unnecessarily complex," he began. "They call this '*technology,*' which seems to equate to a form of magic they use to operate devices and vessels."

"Yes, I've seen much of this technology within this facility. But what of their ships? What have you learned about their fleet?"

"Many of our men are still aboard those craft. Due to the nature of their doorways, we found ourselves unable to merely negate the force spell sealing a door to pass through. Rather, we had to wait for a doorway to be opened to pass to the next chamber. It slowed our progress greatly and made staying unnoted extremely difficult. Especially in double-door protected areas."

"Why double doors? That seems excessive, even for these creatures."

"It would seem to be a safeguard against loss of pressure within the vessel should there be a breach."

Jimtee shook his head in disbelief.

"It would be so much simpler to just have a force spell to protect against such matters. For all their seemingly advanced ways, these are nevertheless a primitive people."

"I would agree, but only to a point," Ulus interjected.

"You have something to add?"

"Yes, Captain. I have discussed the general mechanisms behind the Urok craft, and from what I have been able to glean from their crews--thanks to many drinks from their grateful and generous guest--is that despite the crude manner in which they operate, these are nevertheless craft of great power."

"But I sense no magic."

"Not that sort of power, sir. They rely on an entirely novel form of energy. It propels their craft without Drooks, even allowing them to perform a maneuver they call a 'warp,' which is similar to a jump. And it does all of this as well as charging many of their larger weapons."

"Hmm, interesting," Jimtee replied. "And what of these weapons? If they can maintain a system capable of jumps, I wonder just how much destructive force they can muster."

Ulus shifted on his feet uneasily. No one ever wanted to be the bearer of bad news, especially not to Captain Jimtee, but intel was intel, and it must be shared.

"It is my assessment, sir, that this strange, yet powerful means of operating their systems and weapons could give our own craft a run for their money in smaller engagements. Perhaps even defeat them."

"These buckets could hold their own against our mighty fleet? I find that hard to believe."

"Not the entire fleet, no. But do not underestimate the destructive force contained in these craft. Their weaponry is quite sophisticated in its own way."

Jimtee's mind churned with the possibilities. They were outnumbered should they attempt to retrieve the portal from its resting place within the Earth's sun. Even a short foray into that system had shown those adversaries to be--while not magical--quite formidable opponents.

A fleet of these *technology* ships, however, could turn the tables.

"Can we commandeer them?" Jimtee asked. "Steal them and repurpose them for our own use?"

Ulus turned to one of the men standing silently by. "Tell him what you discovered."

The man was a bit older than the others. More experienced, with a longer history of service under Captain Jimtee. As such, he was somewhat comfortable when discussing the realities of the situation.

"I'm sorry, Captain, but I do not believe we can steal these vessels. I have been aboard several of the smaller ones under protection of my shimmer cloak, and what I have seen on each of them reinforces that belief."

"But surely we could take the command centers without much difficulty."

"Oh, yes. That would be relatively straightforward," the man agreed. "However, the craft are guided by a very complex means of control. Buttons and levers, and strange types of display that both hang in the air, almost like a spell, but are also projected onto flat surfaces. It is not that we could not eventually learn to understand these things, but I fear it would take an unreasonably long time to gain enough expertise in this incredibly crude control system to put the ships to any constructive use."

Jimtee thought on it quietly a moment. "So we're locked out."

"Quite."

"Very well, then," he said after a long pause. "We will use the collars."

The following afternoon, the chime to Regent Zinna's offices softly rang just past lunchtime, announcing the arrival of his Tslavar guest.

"Yes? What is it?" he asked as he opened the door. "Oh, Jimtee. I did not expect to see you this afternoon. I am rather busy today, is there something you need?"

"Need? Oh, no, Regent. I merely wished to make good on my offer of the other day," Jimtee said with his best disarming smile.

"Offer? I don't recall an offer," Zinna replied.

Jimtee made sure no one was near, and once he was assured they were alone, reached inside his jacket and removed a gleaming, golden collar, complete with finely etched and rather ornate rune markings.

"I was able to procure this for you. A gift, as I had mentioned." Jimtee looked around conspiratorially. "But don't tell the others. This is something special, just for you."

He handed the golden collar to the regent, the gleam in the light bouncing off the man's eyes. The little spell Jimtee had cast to enhance its shine also didn't hurt.

"Oh, it is beautiful, Jimtee," he said. "Such intricate scrollwork, as if it were a living part of the metal itself." He held it up close to his eye and studied the design. "But, Jimtee, I see an open end, but no hasp or hinge. How does the clasp mechanism work?

Jimtee smiled his warmest grin. "Here, let us step into the privacy of your offices a moment and I will show you."

CHAPTER FORTY-FOUR

"You see anything?" Charlie asked over their comms.

"Nada," Kip replied. "All me and Dookie see is a whole lot of nothing."

Dukaan sighed, but let it go.

"All right. You guys stick to the far side and keep your scanners open wide. We're gonna be sniffing them out from the other hemisphere. If they're anywhere near this planet, Ara will find them."

"And then we kick their asses."

"Yes, Kip. Then we kick their asses. We've still got not only the element of surprise, but numbers too. So stay sharp, and be ready to hop in and help if we engage. Obviously, we'll do the same for you."

"Got it," Kip said, then banked off for another run of the area.

They'd been slowly narrowing down the planets on which the traces of magic could be coming from, but the interference from the system itself was still messing with Ara's senses. Back home they'd have already pinpointed the ship and taken action, but here, in this insanely dense system, it was like searching for a penny in a murky wishing fountain.

Charlie wasn't stressed, though. He knew Ara's skills, and he was fully confident she would pull out a win soon enough. On top of that, his own odd, new, tingling sense seemed to be buzzing sharper now. Getting stronger, and quickly. It was all new to him, but he was pretty sure it meant they were getting closer.

Ara glided through space above the small planet, the ambient power a little thinner around this world.

"I think I sense something," she said, flaring her nostrils at the passing whiff of power.

"I feel something too," Charlie said. *"Just past the little moon, I think."*

"Prepare yourselves. We may have found them," Ara said, changing course.

"Guys, keep your ears on. We think we may have something."

"You found them?" Dukaan asked.

"Not sure. But we'll know in just a--"

Ara abruptly pulled up short. Then she turned and flew away as fast as she could. The massive starship firing beam weapons at her followed close on her tail.

"Contact! Contact! We're under attack! Get your asses over here!"

"On our way. Is their shimmer on?"

"It's not the Tslavars," Charlie said, hanging on tight as Ara somehow avoided the barrage of beam weapon blasts flashing through space around her.

Kip punched it, arriving on the scene in just a few seconds. "What the hell is that?" he blurted. "I've never seen a ship like that."

"I don't care. I can't raise them on our comms. Hit them on all frequencies and tell them to stop firing. We're peaceful!"

"I've got a signal, but I don't recognize the language," Kip replied.

"But don't you guys have files for all the known races?"

"Yes, but this one is new."

Charlie realized what was happening with a sinking feeling in his gut. This was first contact with a new alien species, and it started with a shooting war and no way to call it off.

"Bawb, can you use the translation spell?"

"They are too far from us to accurately apply."

"And if they're any closer, they'll be able to hit us."

"Precisely."

Charlie kept trying to hail them over their comms array, but it was to no avail.

"Why the hell are these guys so pissed at us? They don't even know us!" Charlie yelled in frustration as a beam blast came incredibly close to scoring a hit.

None of them knew if their magical defenses would adequately repel this novel type of weapon. If it was related to a laser or pulse weapon, then the answer was yes. But if it was something else, their odds of success were entirely unknown.

Meanwhile, the captain of the alien vessel shouted commands to his gunners and comms crew as they pursued the red space beast.

"Inform the Crux we have found and are actively engaged with the hostile space beast. Forward our location and request immediate assistance."

"Immediately, Captain Hoovar," his comms officer replied.

The message reached the Crux within seconds, and a half dozen ships immediately began launch procedures to come to the aid of their comrades. Not more than a moment later, the shimmer-cloaked Tslavar troops quietly relayed the information to their captain.

Flight teams rushed to their craft, the commanders and key crew members taking their places on their command bridges. They moved with urgency, yet if one were to pause to really watch, it would become apparent that *something* was a little off about them.

Jimtee could have told you, as could any of the Tslavars who had helped him apply the control collars around the necks of the key members of the Urok command chain. It was Regent Zinna, the first to wear a collar, who had eased the transition of power.

His first attempt at defiance resulted in such a life-altering pain through his entire body that he had become a willing accomplice so long as the Tslavars would not inflict the torturous agony upon him again.

"Yes, Commander Ripsal, right this way," the regent said, luring another flag officer into the trap. "I just need to go over a few particulars of the mission brief before you and your ship depart."

The commander followed him into the regent's offices, where five shimmer-cloaked Tslavar commandos immediately seized him, quickly affixing a control collar around his neck.

And so it went. Once they had the key piece in the regent, the rest quickly fell in place, as planned.

"We mean you no harm, Zinna," Jimtee had said. "Just summon a few of your top aides to come teach us your obviously superior ways and we will leave, taking this knowledge back to our leaders. I regret resorting to such methods, but there is no way we could possibly replicate what you have here. We can, however, learn. And if you help us, there will be no more pain."

The regent most certainly didn't want any more of that. "Well, if you only want to learn, I suppose it can't hurt," he said, convincing himself that was all the Tslavars wanted as he recovered his senses following the collar shock.

By the time he realized, or accepted, what was really happening to his people, it was too late. Zinna knew his career--perhaps even his life--was over if his role was discovered. So he did what so many do when faced with such a decision.

He doubled down.

And that was how the mighty Urok fleet fell under the control of a Tslavar captain without a single shot fired.

Not terribly far from their location at the Crux, Ara and Kip were dodging and weaving as best they could, avoiding the continuous barrage from their silent attackers. Charlie kept trying to hail them, while Bawb cast his translation spell over and over. Even with the boost from his Ootaki hair, it didn't seem to be working.

"This makes no sense," he said. "They should be close enough. We can understand them now, so they should understand us too!"

"But they're not responding," Charlie grumbled as he cycled through another frequency, wondering if their attackers perhaps used some odd sort of communication system they simply weren't able to reach, for whatever reason, though he and his friends could hear their chatter just fine.

Bawb turned to Charlie. "You know, we have the magic to easily stop this ship. To blast it from the sky."

"We can't, Bob. I mean, this is first contact here. And what if it's just a communications mistake? No, we've got to avoid fighting them."

"They didn't seem to get that memo," Kip chimed in. "You know, in case you hadn't noticed."

"Shut it, Toaster," Charlie shot back. "Okay, we have to get out of here and buy ourselves some time to think. To plan, while not under attack, ideally. Ara, can you jump us a few planets away? Just far enough to be out of their reach but close enough to make contact when we're ready?"

"I can do this easily," she replied. "Kip, are you ready?"

"You bet I am," he said.

"Then we jump in three. Two. One."

The giant red monster flashed from sight, leaving the Urok attackers wondering where it went. Little did they know, they'd soon have far more to worry about than a lone Zomoki.

CHAPTER FORTY-FIVE

It took only minutes for multiple Urok craft to flash into being where there had previously been nothing, occupying the space near the lone ship that had been pursuing the red space beast.

"We are here, Captain Hoovar," Captain Sarak's familiar voice greeted the ship's commanding officer. "Where is this evil creature? I see nothing on our scans."

"Gone," Hoovar replied. "It seems to have warped away."

"Warp? How can an animal warp?"

"Your guess is as good as mine, Sarak. It was here one moment, then gone the next."

"Did you observe it emitting flame in space as the newcomers claimed?"

"No, I did not. In fact, it did not seem to be capable of much more than running away."

Sarak chuckled. "You are flying one of the finest ships in our fleet, so that should not be terribly surprising."

"I suppose," Hoovar replied. "But I expected more from it. And there was something else. Something unexpected."

"Oh?"

"Yes. It was accompanied by a small craft. It avoided my cannons as well, and warped away before we could disable it."

"Most unusual," Sarak mused. "Good fortune you happened to be patrolling the area, though. Otherwise it might have gone unnoticed until it was upon the Crux itself."

"The thought had crossed my mind. Though, with the knowledge the animal can warp, I fear we will need to adjust our strategy to address this disturbing new facet."

"Yes, I think that will be a revelation to the higher-ups," Sarak said. "Did it attempt to make contact? The ship flying with the beast, I mean."

Captain Hoovar turned to his comms operator, a young woman in a role of considerable importance for one her age.

"No, Captain. There was no contact from the vessel or creature," she said, absentmindedly feeling the slender, golden collar inside her uniform with her fingertips. "I will inform you the moment there's a change."

"Well, there we have it, then," Hoovar grumbled. "Take your ships and fan out. We will survey the nearest moons first. Though I'm amazed it even possesses the ability, I doubt a beast could warp far, even with that skill. If anyone makes contact, we all converge and end the threat before it has the opportunity to warp away again. Agreed?"

"A good plan, Captain," Sarak replied. "I'll have my people get right on it."

The comms line went dead, and he set to work dispatching the smaller ships under his command to begin their reconnaissance. With any luck they would make quick work of the creature and its mechanical sidekick.

Captain Hoovar certainly hoped so. He had been summoned by the regent himself, but was already underway when the message arrived. He couldn't help but wonder what so powerful a man could want with him. A promotion, perhaps? It seemed unlikely, but the whims of the ruling class were difficult to understand on the best of days.

Meanwhile, back in the Crux, Jimtee and his men were making quick work of collaring key military personnel before they shipped out to join the search. There were simply not enough collars to go around, but if they were frugal with their placement, Jimtee and Ulus thought it quite possible to control nearly half of the command level vessels via their leadership.

But Jimtee was not concerned. He'd seen this before and knew it well. Control the leaders and the minions will follow.

Some of the newly collared officers tried to fight the magical binding. At first, anyway. A few sessions of excruciating pain, courtesy of the control collar now fastened around their necks, quickly put a stop to any such thoughts of rebellion. And now that the first wave of ships had flown, Jimtee allowed himself a moment to enjoy the fruits of his labors. It seemed his plan was going to be a success.

Meanwhile, on a small, hot planet at the very innermost edge of the Goldilocks Zone, Ara and Kip sat parked beside a pool of hot water bubbling up from the depths of the planet's rocky crust.

"Play it again, Kip," Bawb said, scrutinizing the image on their AI ship companion's display.

"There. You see it?" Charlie asked, pointing to a section of the image captured at the instant they had jumped away.

"Yes, I do," Bawb replied. "Another ship, apparently of similar origin as the first."

"Kip, can you run a spectral analysis of the energy pattern around that ship when it first arrived? It looked a hell of a lot like it warped in."

"Already did that," the AI said. "And yeah, it's definitely a warp of some sort. Different than mine, but hey, different tech, different warp styles, am I right?"

"It would make sense," Charlie admitted. "But why would they attack us like that? I mean, there was no warning shot, no hailing, no nothing. Just wham-bam attack you, ma'am."

"I am quite perplexed as well," Ara said, sipping the hot water bubbling up from below. "They are not who we are after, nor did we display any overt hostility toward them."

"They could just be a warlike race," Dukaan noted. "Believe me, my people know more than they ever wanted to about creatures like that. Those who prefer conquest and destruction of all who are unlike them over peaceful coexistence."

"Unfortunately, without them responding in any way, the only thing we know about them is they're a force to be reckoned with," Charlie said. "Whatever those weapons were, they had some serious oomph to them."

"Yes, I sensed the energy signature quite acutely when my wing was nearly singed by one such burst," Ara noted. "Fortunately, it was only a tiny jump to get clear of their line of fire, and my senses tell me the Tslavar ship does not appear to have jumped yet."

"I know," Charlie said. "The trace is still here in this system."

"You can sense this now?" Ara asked, sharing a curious look with Bawb.

"Most interesting, Charlie. Are your powers becoming attuned with this?" the Wampeh added.

"I guess so. I can't really say, guys. It's just, it kinda feels like it's here, is all," Charlie said.

Dukaan began pacing, nervous about their next moves. He preferred an ordered life, and this was anything but. This was chaotic, and it was chaos that shot back.

"Do we keep pursuing them?" he finally asked. "What I mean is, do we pursue them in this system, knowing there is a hostile force waiting to attack us if we encounter them again? Or do we wait for them to jump and just follow the trail?"

"I don't know," Charlie said. "The Tslavars are still here, so until they jump, we stay put. But if we're lucky, they'll have an even worse greeting than we did from whoever the hell those guys were. For all we know, this new race we stumbled upon might do our job for us."

CHAPTER FORTY-SIX

The Kalamani elders listened to Rika explain again how the men they were chasing were bad, while she and her friends were good. She was not convincing them.

"Why should the Kalamani take your word for this?" the heavily tattooed man seated at the end of the five leaders asked. "You have been shown hospitality in our village, and eaten food with our people, but only because you are defenseless and weak. If our warriors had allowed you to retain your brightstone weapons, how do we know you would not have attempted to harm our people, as these invaders you call Tslavars did?"

As designated point person, it once again fell to Rika to clarify the situation.

"As I've said, revered elder, these men have attacked our world not once but twice. We have chased them for many stars distance to end their threat once and for all."

"Many stars, she says. No one has such power," the eldest grumbled.

"But it is true. You have seen our vessels and know they are capable of flight. This is just an extension of that ability."

Varahash was watching the exchange with great interest.

That the elders even granted an audience to the invaders was highly unusual. And now they were talking back to the most revered? Unheard of.

"And what of this trickery these Tslavars use?" Varahash asked, his rank granting him the right to speak openly in front of the elders.

"What do you mean?" Rika asked.

"They attempt to hide themselves from us. Attacking our farmers and those not possessing the sight," he said, tapping the tattoo around one eye with his finger.

"Oh, that. It's called a shimmer spell, and it is very powerful magic," Rika explained. "And your warriors got lucky last time. Now that they are aware some of you can see through their camouflage, I guarantee they'll change their tactics. Tslavar mercenaries are deadly, so if any of your people sees them, they have to run."

"Run? A warrior does not run from battle."

"Then many warriors may pay the price of foolish pride," Rika replied.

Varahash puffed his chest, offended by her words.

"Look, I don't mean to be rude here, but someone has to speak the plain truth to you, for the sake of all of your people. If they return and you face them head-on, it'll be a bloodbath," Rika said. "But we can be of help."

"Help? How?"

"Allow us to look around. To see if we can find them using our ship's tracking systems."

"Tracking?"

"It's like following an animal's trail, only this is one you cannot see. But our vessels have the means to see what we cannot. Please, allow us to do this thing. It will help both of our people, and may be crucial in keeping yours safe."

Rika stood silent for what seemed like minutes as the elders whispered amongst themselves, casting distrustful glances at the newcomers. Finally, the eldest spoke.

"Very well. You may go and look for your Tslavars. But we are keeping your weapons for now."

"But we've got--" Ripley started to say.

"Thank you, Ripley, you're right. We've got a lot to do," Rika said, flashing a look at the teen. "A most reasonable decision, which we thank you for," Rika said. "We will return by evening time."

With that, she and the others rose and walked from the village, accompanied by a small group of warriors, who, while armed, were at least not pointing the sharp ends of anything at them this time.

The pair of ships decided to stay together for the initial survey run. The Tslavars were crafty bastards, and even though Eddie's shimmer spell was working perfectly, having the firepower of two ships instead of one would make any engagement that much more lopsided in favor of the Earth vessels.

"Keep an eye out for any anomalies," Rika said over comms as she took the *Fujin* into a gentle banking turn over what seemed to be a good landing spot, with what appeared to be more uprooted plants. But the Tslavars weren't there. The remains of their pillage, however, was.

"I can't get a fix on them closer than a hundred miles," Eddie griped. "There's some really strange interference going on around this planet, that's for sure."

"What do you mean?" Ripley asked her AI friend.

"I mean, I can see the tracker is functioning fine, but its trail is jumbled up with this outside energy. I don't know why it's doing that, but it's making it really hard to track."

"Can you follow them if they jump?" Ripley asked.

"Oh, yeah. Once they're out of the atmosphere it should be

relatively easy to pick up their normal trail. But down here? Not so much."

"Well, shit," Rika griped. "I guess we just keep doing what we've been doing, then. Let's get down there and see what they left this time."

It was the third torn-up landing site in as many hours, but these plants were different from the others, and Hunze had a far more visceral reaction to them.

"The power. It's so strong," she said, not even touching the sap-leaking branch of a small tree.

"Right. The native flora absorbs the sun's energy, kind of how you and Ara do on Earth. But what were the Tslavars doing?" Leila asked.

She moved closer to the sappy branch, and her Magus stone began to glow a deep, foreboding green.

"Uh, Leila? I don't think it wants you to do that," Ripley said.

The olive-skinned woman quickly backed away, the glow in her protective pendant fading as she did.

"Huh," Rika said, picking up the branch. "That much power in one little branch? We really should get samples of all this stuff back to Cal. The labs on Earth will have a field day seeing what they can make of this stuff."

"We should stay," Jo said. "It should be Eddie who flies back. For one, he has greater storage capabilities than we do. Second, you are the one person the Kalamani seem to respect. At least somewhat. We should stay with them and track the Tslavars as best we can until the others get back."

"We don't all have to go," Leila said.

"You two need real food. More than just a few days' worth. And protective gear, too, if you're going to be in contact with this plant life. It shouldn't take you much time at all to gather some things that'll keep you safe from accidental contact with it."

"She does have a point," Hunze noted.

"I know she does. But it doesn't feel right leaving her here all alone," Leila said.

"*Ahem*?" the cyborg at her side said.

"You know what I mean, Jo."

Rika pondered the situation a moment. "No, Jo's right. This is first contact with an entirely new race. One that uses primitive weapons but that can somehow overcome some of the most powerful Tslavar magic. They may not be an advanced culture, but Earth needs to represent. And we need to do it right. You guys take the samples and do a quick warp back to Earth. It shouldn't take you too long to backtrack. Once you're there, Cal will have not only the raw materials to study, but also the star map to this system. From there, humanity will have a new species to build an alliance with, hopefully."

"But you'll be undermanned," Ripley noted.

"Don't worry about us. Even if we find them, we've got no intention of engaging the Tslavars until you get back."

"Promise?"

"Promise."

Ripley mulled it over a moment longer. "Well, all right, then. Help me stow all of this stuff in one of the cargo holds and we'll get going."

The humans and cyborg made quick work loading the magically potent plant matter into the ship, while Leila and Hunze stood clear. They felt strange just watching their friends labor, but given each of their reactions to the material, it was far better than the alternative.

Soon, the ship was packed up and ready to depart. Ripley gave Rika and Jo each a giant hug.

"Don't you guys do anything until we get back, okay?"

"Promise," Rika said with a little laugh. "And hey, by the time you're back, maybe we'll even have found them."

A minute later, Eddie took to the sky and left atmosphere. Backtracking their route should be relatively simple, and from there, star charts would help them plot a much more direct route back.

"Okay, Jo, it's getting kinda late. Let's get back to the village."

With that, the human and cyborg lifted off in their technological wonder, heading back to as primitive a culture as they'd ever seen.

CHAPTER FORTY-SEVEN

It only took a couple of warps for Eddie to map out a faster route back to Earth, his powerful AI processor calculating the enormous equations required for such a lengthy warp in mere minutes. Given the distance spanned multiple solar systems and millions of light years, it was remarkably fast.

But then again, being one of the newest generation of AI ships to be born on Earth, it was to be expected.

"Uncle Cal, we're coming in hot!" Ripley called over their comms.

"Ripley, you do not appear to be entering the atmosphere any faster than normal," Cal replied.

"Figure of speech, Uncle Cal. What I mean is we've got important stuff for you and your buddies to analyze."

"Aah, so it was a productive pursuit, then. Very good to hear. We analyzed the blood at the facility in Sicily after your hasty pursuit. It was Tslavar, as I assume you likely realized by now."

"Yeah, we know. Believe me, we know."

"So, were you successful in eliminating the threat?"

"Uh, not exactly."

"I see. But tell me, where are Rika and Jo? Sid tells me he has not

picked them up on any of his scans, and surveillance relay satellites are likewise showing nothing."

"They're fine," Ripley said. "But that's where it all gets a little bit more complicated. I'll need you to have a few people standing by when we touch down to carry stuff inside. Leila and Hunze have a really strong reaction to it."

"Oh? Only the people from the other galaxy are affected?" the mighty AI mused, the gears of his great intellect already turning. ***"Now that is rather interesting. I'll have a team standing by momentarily. Eddie, you know where to go, yes?"***

"Yeah. The new spot you were spooling up the other week, right?"

"Correct."

Eddie swooped down through the clouds on a rapid descent direct toward Los Angeles, right to Cal's new research facility. His prior command hub would take some time to rebuild after the last Tslavar attack had essentially leveled the facility, along with the equipment and people within.

Fortunately, the massively powerful AI's actual mind was housed in reinforced processing center far from that location. A fact the invaders, with their ignorance of the functioning of AI technology, had failed to realize.

They could destroy facility after facility, but Cal would remain unscathed. He had managed to avoid the AI virus that had eliminated so many of his brethren during the Great War, and since then, a great many new precautions had been installed to buttress his already-robust safeguards.

Eddie touched down outside the new research location just west of Downtown.

"Door-to-door service," he said, popping the airlock open.

Ripley hopped out, breathing deep the fresh air of Los Angeles, the slight salty tang from the Pacific wafting in on the breeze from the coastline.

"Home sweet home!" she said with a broad grin.

She knew from history lessons that the Los Angeles basin had once possessed some of the worst air conditions in that part of the continent. But with the eradication of almost the entirety of the human race during the Great War, the planet had long since reclaimed the environment for itself.

Pollution had been absorbed, broken down, and replaced with fresh air and water, over time. And with such a small global population now, it would take centuries of actively trying to damage the planet to return to anywhere near those levels of pollution.

Of course, technology also rendered the combustion engines and other particulate and smoke-producing means of power generation obsolete, so it really wasn't even a concern.

Leila and Hunze had adapted to California coastal life when they'd arrived in their new home, and the familiar warm, fresh breeze was invigorating to them as well. More so for Hunze, as she was so attuned to the Earth's sun's powerful energy.

"That feels wonderful," she said, stretching luxuriously like a cat in a patch of sunlight as the magical rays absorbed into her golden hair, bolstering its power.

Four men––cyborgs by the look of their gait, though with most it was almost impossible to tell––jogged up to the ship in perfect unison.

"Cal told us you required assistance with some cargo. What can we be of assistance with?"

Eddie popped open his aft cargo hold. "In here, fellas," he said. "A bunch of botanical stuff. It's mostly in containers now, but a few of the odd-shaped pieces are wrapped up in a kind of makeshift containment bundle. They're not that heavy, just a bit awkward to carry."

The cyborgs' leader chuckled. "I think we'll be fine with the weight," the mechanical man replied. "Okay, you guys, let's get this stuff inside. Cal wants it in labs two and three."

"What is it, anyway?" one of his men asked.

"Don't know. Don't care. Just get it inside and let the big brains do their thing."

"On it."

The four-man team moved quickly, each carrying individually what had taken several trips for the humans when they loaded the ship. In mere minutes the cargo hold was emptied of its alien prize.

The cargo hold sealed shut as soon as the last man exited.

"I'm gonna run a decontamination protocol in there," Eddie informed them. "Should only take about twenty minutes. I just want to be sure there's no trace of anything Leila or Hunze might have a bad reaction to."

"Good idea, Eddie. Thank you," Hunze said. "Your consideration is much appreciated."

"Yeah, thanks for looking out for us," Leila added.

"It's my pleasure."

Ripley turned to follow the cyborgs into the facility, then paused. "Hey, why don't you guys go and stock up on food you can actually eat while we're here? Eddie's got plenty of cold storage for fresh stuff, plus we can maybe refit his food fabricator to handle a wider range before we ship out again."

The two alien women nodded in agreement.

"Not being poisoned by our meals *would* be a nice option," Leila joked. "And while we're at it, I'm going to see if that odd AI with the fascination for clothing might fabricate us something lightweight that could still protect us from the magical vegetation back there. From what Cal said, he may be a bit strange, but there's no better tailor on Earth."

"That would be ideal," Hunze said. "And ask for gloves. I nearly burned my hand with sap from that one plant." A strange look flashed across her face at the memory. "It still amazes me."

"What does?"

"This magical power present in this galaxy. It has such potential, but it seems none have harnessed it."

"Case in point, people hunting with bows and arrows."

"Yes. And for whatever reason, *that* magic seems to clash with my own."

"And mine, even though I've only got a drop of natural power. But I presume it's just like an allergic reaction to it from people from our galaxy. It's the only explanation I can think of."

"Perhaps," Hunze replied. "I will be most interested to see what Cal uncovers."

CHAPTER FORTY-EIGHT

Ripley quickly strode through the halls of the new research facility, hot on the heels of the cyborgs carrying the armloads of samples from the distant alien world.

"Uncle Cal?"

"Yes, Ripley?" his voice rang out in the corridor's air.

"I was wondering, have we heard from Aunt Daisy? I know she's been out on a big survey mission, but this sort of thing really seems to be kinda up her alley."

It was true, Ripley's notorious aunt was indeed something of a legend when it came to dealing with insurmountable odds and utterly unexpected situations. Even more than her own parents, the teen idolized the multi-faceted woman whose efforts helped eventually end the Great War.

Growing up with the stories straight from her aunt's mouth was different than what they taught in class. Even her uncle Cal, for all the amazing things he had done during the war, couldn't hold a candle to the sword-wielding badass woman in whose presence she'd been raised.

"Daisy's mission is a bit overdue," Cal replied. ***"But we know***

how she can be. She has a nose for trouble, but of all our varied teams out there, it is hers I am least worried about."

"Well, yeah," Ripley agreed. "I was just hoping she was back is all. We're getting into some really crazy stuff out there."

"Apparently. Now, while my research assistants prepare the samples, tell me, what exactly did you find?"

"We went really far, Uncle Cal. Like warp after warp. But the tracker worked pretty well, and eventually we found the planet the Tslavars had landed on."

"Eddie already shared the coordinates. You were many solar systems away. Quite a distance, really. Their magical jump power must be rather robust to have accomplished that in such a short time."

"Yeah, it was way out there. But that's where it gets kind of strange."

"You mean the interference with your tracking?"

"Yeah. When we got there, something else was going on. Something that was messing with Hunze's magic pretty big time. And even Leila's Magus stone reacted."

This got Cal's attention. He knew by now the power contained in the deep green pendant she wore. He also knew that it protected her with a ferocity that could only be explained by its deep magical bond to her and her alone.

"So there is a magical threat beyond the Tslavars? Is that what you're saying?"

"Yeah, exactly. The sun in the system we finally tracked them down in is really strong. Not like ours, exactly, but Hunze could feel it."

"She is a magical being of unique sensitivity."

"Totally. But in this one, it seemed the energy was being absorbed into the plants and animals directly."

The cyborg team split the cargo between them and hurried into two lab facilities, arranging the materials as instructed while Ripley waited outside. Cal, of course, was everywhere, both monitoring within the labs as well as talking to his young friend.

"So the local flora and fauna acts as a sort of magic sink of sorts, storing up power in the manner Hunze's hair does," Cal realized. ***"Though I suppose the animals could also absorb the power through ingestion of the plant matter."***

"Right. And the Tslavars were apparently taking samples of all sorts of plants. We found their landing zones and took samples of the stuff they had been collecting. One of them was so strong it nearly knocked Hunze down when she touched it."

"That is powerful, indeed."

"I know, right?"

"But if the magic is harmful to those of their galaxy, what could the Tslavars possibly hope to accomplish with it? Wielding it—even if they could find a way—would be incredibly dangerous, if not outright fatal, I would think."

"We had a theory about that," Ripley replied. "Rika thinks they're collecting it to build something with enough magic to pull the portal back out of the sun."

Cal was silent a moment as he ran a few million calculations.

"If they cast a self-perpetuating spell, from what Bawb and Ara have informed me in prior discussions, it might be possible to use such an energy source to gradually retrieve the portal from the sun, as it was placed there using magic bolstered by this system's sun's energy. If it is not entirely extra-galactic in nature, perhaps this new energy source could achieve their goal."

"Which would be bad."

"Very," Cal replied. ***"But tell me, Eddie also mentioned you made first contact with a new species."***

"The Kalamani. Yeah, they're a totally primitive tribe. No electricity, no metals. Hell, they hardly even wear any clothing."

"Yet they repelled a Tslavar mercenary team. One with shimmer magic, as well. Quite impressive for primitives, wouldn't you agree?"

"Oh, totally. That's the thing, though. They have these weird tattoos around their eyes. Well, the hunter-warrior guys do, anyway. While we were flying back, I was thinking about that. I don't know, but, maybe, that's what let them see through the shimmer."

"If the pigments were made from the magic-powered vegetation, then perhaps it enhances their vision in some way. It would seem logical, as you describe its used only for hunters and warriors, whose positions require sharp eyesight."

"But they have no guns, or even normal knives. Theirs are made of sharpened stone. And they pretty much only use bows and arrows, ya know? Spears and that kind of thing."

"Ah, let me guess. Made of this magically imbued wood, correct?"

"Yeah."

"Which reacted with the Tslavar magic in an unexpected manner, I assume."

"Went through it like it wasn't there."

"Hmm. You did well bringing these samples back, Ripley. I do not wish to overstate this, but I believe you may have stumbled upon a tool that could give us the upper hand in combating this enemy."

Ripley felt a little glimmer of relief well up in her chest. She'd seen and done a hell of a lot in recent weeks, but she was still just a teenager, and it was all more than a little overwhelming when she let herself stop and really think about the enormity of all she'd been dealing with.

"Any word from Charlie and Ara?" she asked. "And Bawb? I know Hunze is worried about him."

"None yet," Cal said. ***"But they are more than capable of handling themselves, as you know."***

"Yeah. But if they're not back yet, we only have our regular weaponry to fight with. Rika's waiting for us back with the Kalamani, and it seems pretty likely we're gonna eventually have to confront the Tslavars on our own. If the big-gun magic users aren't with us, it's gonna be tough."

"Might I make a suggestion?" Cal asked.

"Of course. What were you thinking, Uncle Cal?"

"You and Rika have been trained in the use of magic. She more than you, obviously, but nevertheless, you possess some skills now. And she can help you acquire more."

"Don't forget Hunze. Bawb's been dumping all sorts of stuff into her head," Ripley said.

"How do you know about that? He requested secrecy when I helped configure his neuro-stim unit."

"Yeah, I know. Don't tell him I know about it, but Hunze mentioned what he was doing for her when we ran into the Kalamani. But she still can't seem to make any of it work."

"It's her nature as an Ootaki. Destined to possess and create incredible power, but never wield it herself."

"That sucks."

"Yes, Ripley. It does. But back to the matter at hand. I think in this circumstance, you and your team should gather all of the magical weaponry you can prior to your return to that world. There's no telling what you may face, and I want you as protected as you can be."

"But they can block our attacks. You've seen it."

"And they will not be expecting you to switch to magical ones. Utilize that surprise to your benefit. We will also arrange for additional ships to come with you this time, but our conventional weapons may not be the most effective against them. Nevertheless, numbers do count for something in a situation like this, and if you can disable their shimmer-cloaking spell, the task of tracking and pursuing them will be much easier with the additional resources."

"How long, Uncle Cal?"

"Ships are just trickling in from their long-range surveys, but I think within a day or two we should be able to retrofit them adequately for our needs. I suggest you take that time to go home, rest, and prepare yourself. I'll let you know as soon as I've made any progress on these samples."

Ripley didn't know what else to do. It was a waiting period, and there was no way around it. As much as she wanted to hurry back to help her friend, she knew Rika and was confident in her ability to take care of herself for just one more day.

"All right," she said. "But we should go as soon as possible."

"Of course," Cal replied. ***"Now, go home. And please, send my greetings to your parents."***

Ripley was awash in emotions as she walked back out to her waiting ship. It was going to be a difficult wait, but there was little else she could do.

CHAPTER FORTY-NINE

The flash of blue was relatively small, given the extremely short warp Kip had just performed. Only a minimal amount of warp power had been required, and the resulting crackling trace of his arrival was dispersed in under a second.

"Everything off?" Dukaan asked from the cozy confines of his four-armed space suit as Kip performed a rapid shutdown sequence for all but the most essential, core systems. Everything else went dark, including life support.

"That's all of it," Kip replied over the short-range helmet comms. Even his internal speakers had powered off.

And for good reason.

The AI craft had warped from their hiding place several worlds away, leaving Ara and the others safely concealed while he and Dukaan gathered data. Ara was fully capable of flying out as well, but the recording and surveillance array Kip sported was far superior to the tiny makeshift tech hastily wired to Ara's harness.

His task was simple. Or, as simple as flying smack in the middle of what was likely hostile enemy territory could be. Kip would arrive and go dark, hopefully blending in with whatever other floating debris was in the area. Then he would spy.

"We need intel on these aliens," Charlie had said. "We were so busy running for our lives, we didn't really get a chance to properly size them up."

"And that's where you come in," Bawb said to the AI ship. "If you're up for it, of course."

"Me? I'm up for anything!" Kip had replied, perhaps a bit too enthusiastically for his partner's taste.

"What Kip means is we are prepared to undertake this mission to the best of our abilities," Dukaan said. "And, should we go unnoticed, we will bring back whatever intelligence we can about this unexpected foe."

And that was exactly what they did, warping to as close to the area of the previous attack as they deemed safe. From there, Kip would drift and scan until he made contact with the ship that engaged them.

"Do you see anything?" Dukaan asked once they'd arrived at their destination. "The short-range scan still online is experiencing some disruption."

"Yeah, there's trace of a drive system's output showing on one of my readouts. I've tapped the power just slightly to give us a nudge in that direction. I'll use the air thrusters to slow us down if we find them."

"A wise decision. They'll likely not detect a mere air thrust, whereas any energy signature would likely read on their systems if their technology is anywhere near as advanced as ours."

"And given what we've seen so far, yeah, that's probably a pretty good bet," Kip said.

It was a few hours before the little ship's high-speed drifting finally resulted in contact. And when it did, Kip and Dukaan were very glad they'd flown in with systems dark.

"Scans just flashed over us," Kip said over the suit comms.

"They must be fairly close by and looking for us, but we can't see them yet."

"That means they possess formidable scanning technology. Are we safe?" Dukaan asked, shifting uncomfortably in his seat.

"As safe as we can be, I guess. If anything gets shot our way, I can power up drive systems in two seconds and achieve full power in four."

"That's a long time with beam weapons shooting at you," Dukaan noted.

"Yeah, but I can also use the air thrusters to maneuver out of line of any if they're a ways out. From far away it doesn't take a lot to throw off a shot's accuracy, after all. Hell, I learned that up on the moon when Sid and the gang first had me running combat simulations. Man, that was something else. I mean, can you imagine? Being thrust from a minimal AI existence into a ship with guns? It was sooo cool. Remind me to tell you about it later."

"If we survive this, I will listen to the tale," Dukaan replied somberly. "Again."

"Well, duh. But we'll survive, Dookie. I give you my word."

"If only the fates bowed down to your will," the Chithiid replied with a resigned sigh.

In a relatively short time, two blips showed up on the AI ship's readouts.

"Contact," Kip said. "And yeah, two of them. That second ship definitely arrived just as we warped."

"Might there be more?"

"Safe to assume there could be. But that's not our concern right now so much as just getting close and gathering intel on what the hell we're dealing with," Kip said. "All right, take a deep breath, 'cause I'm taking us closer."

With that the little ship tapped his thruster nozzles and directed their floating form closer to the pings that now read steady on his display. He had to do so slowly, though. Any fast movement would undoubtedly raise an alarm, and once they got in close that would be a bad thing.

Very bad.

No matter how fast you can power up, it won't do any good if the people shooting are right on top of you.

Fortunately, the Urok ships took no notice of the cold debris around them, and thus Kip's powered-down shape went unnoticed. He and Dukaan gathered as much information as they could, from power signature readings, to comms chatter between the ships, to as many images from as many angles as they could safely get.

They then nudged their course away from the two ships and drifted behind a small asteroid cluster not terribly far away. Once safely blocked by the floating rocks' mass, they executed a rapid power-up and warp, not giving the aliens enough time to read, track, or follow them.

"What the hell is that thing?" Charlie wondered as they assessed the images and data Kip had brought back. "Bob, you ever see anything like this?"

"Of course not, Charlie. You know my galaxy does not utilize this type of machinery."

"Right. Sorry. Brain fart," he replied. "Kip? Dukaan? Either of you ever see anything remotely like this?"

Unfortunately, neither of them had the foggiest idea what they were looking at. Obviously, it was a pair of fairly large ships, and by the design, they were a rather technologically advanced race. Beyond that, however, they were at a loss.

The energy signatures suggested a warp system somewhat akin to those used by Earth forces, but this one was quite foreign in its power source.

"That is what I was sensing," Ara noted. "The unusual

energy for a few systems, now. It was residual traces of their warp power."

"So, they're *very* advanced if they have warp tech," Charlie stated. "We don't know who they are. We don't know what they want. We don't know anything, really, other than we've just made first contact with a whole new species and immediately got off on the wrong foot."

"Technically, *they* got off on the wrong foot," Kip noted. "I mean, they started shooting first."

They all agreed, the AI had a good point.

"What are the odds the Tslavars were already destroyed or taken prisoner by them?" Dukaan asked.

"If they were a normal craft, I would give fairly good odds on that," Bawb said. "However, since the Tslavars fly a shimmer-cloaked ship, I would have to say odds are slim."

"Damn," Kip griped.

"Indeed," Bawb agreed. "But given what we've seen, I will say one thing. Heavens help them if they uncloak anywhere near these craft."

Charlie nodded in agreement as he flipped through readout screens from the scanning run. "Hey, Kip. What's this here? It looks like a trail of some sort."

"That's the residual energy from their warp system. It's strong, but kind of leaky. Probably why Ara could smell it so easily."

An idea was forming in Charlie's mind.

"I know that look," Bawb said. "What are you thinking?"

Charlie grinned. "Just that what if we use these scans and backtrack the energy directionally? If we do that, maybe we can get a rough idea where the ships actually came from. If Ara smelled it that much stronger in this system, my best guess is they're likely based out of here. That, or they at least have some sort of shipyard facilities in the area."

"Well, that's all fine and dandy," Kip said. "But they're bigger than we are. How do we fight them?"

"We don't."

"I'm sorry, it sounded like you said we don't."

"Yep," Charlie reiterated. "We're here to make peaceful contact, not start an inter-system war."

"And what if they don't care about your peaceful intentions?" Kip asked.

A slightly grim look flashed across Charlie's face. "If it comes to that, we have a *lot* of magic on our side. But let's hope for the best. Just rest easy that if it does come to fighting, we're more than capable of holding our own."

CHAPTER FIFTY

The golden collars worn by a great many of the leaders and key crew on several of the Urok fleet's flag ships remained mostly hidden by the cut of their uniforms' moderately high collars.

While this kept them from overt sight, crew members nevertheless noticed the unusual adornment so abruptly worn by some of their superiors. But as the lower ranks so often do, they said nothing. Whatever was going on, it was far, far above their pay grade.

Regent Zinna, collared and wearing the gleaming band overtly, chose to present it as a conscious fashion decision rather than a clear sign of his new, reduced status as a slave doing the bidding of the Tslavar "trader" he had so greatly underestimated.

It was a bit of an eye-opening experience for the man so accustomed to being the one pulling the strings of power and guiding the machinations of government both in front of as well as behind the scenes. And now here he was, another's marionette, all the result of his endeavoring to pull just a few more strings to elevate his standing.

The irony was not lost on him.

"Zinna, I wish to have a private meeting with the chancellor," Jimtee informed his slave.

"Ah, yes," Regent Zinna stammered. "The others were a bit easier. Military are always looking to advance their rank, after all, so they were more open to an unusual meeting. The chancellor is, however, somewhat more difficult."

The look of irritation on Captain Jimtee's face made Zinna wince, subconsciously touching the control collar around his neck. He had felt the power of the device once already, and that low-powered shock had been more than enough to make him fall quickly in line with his new leader's wishes.

But this? This was a bit more difficult. He just hoped Jimtee would be amenable to what he had managed to arrange.

"Sir, what I mean is, the chancellor is a very busy man, and as he is already in a position of such considerable power, maneuvering him toward any wishes other than his own requires a bit more finesse than the others."

"What are you saying, Zinna?" Jimtee asked, leveling a cool gaze at the man as he sipped a steaming cup of a local beverage somewhat akin to Azarus tea from his own world.

"What I am saying is he will have an audience with you."

"Excellent."

"*But,* it will not be until this evening, I'm afraid."

Jimtee had actually not expected the man to be able to arrange a private meeting so quickly. This was a pleasing turn of events, though he would not tell Zinna that, of course. Keeping the man on his heels, wondering and worrying about his performance was a surefire way to make him over-perform.

"Very well, Zinna," the Tslavar said with an exaggerated sigh. "I suppose that will be acceptable. And what of the remaining captains and commanders?"

"As you requested, I have drafted a list of leadership caste, broken down not only by rank, but also by contacts, both within government as well as military. Some who appear strong are actually quite weak, you see, while others play their roles quietly but have amassed quite substantial power and influence in the process."

"All while appearing to be less than they are," Jimtee added with an amused grin. "Sound familiar, Zinna?"

His words stung, but not nearly as much as the collar around his neck would if he spoke his true thoughts on the situation.

"Yes, sir. Very clever of them, as it was of you. I have learned much in the ways of deception from your play. It was masterfully executed, I must admit."

He knew he was kissing ass, as did Jimtee, but sometimes both parties in a situation such as theirs needed to play those parts overtly, even if the dynamic was already well established.

"Well said, Zinna," the Tslavar captain said. "Now, I have heard word the Zomoki has been sighted again?"

This surprised the regent. How the Tslavar had managed to acquire intelligence so quickly from ships he was not in direct contact with was beyond him. It was uncanny how the man who had only just begun seizing control of the Urok forces nevertheless seemed to already have eyes everywhere, yet nowhere at all.

It was something that also negated any thoughts of deception he might have immediately for fear of being caught. He had a good idea what that would result in, and it would not be pleasant.

"Yes. At least, we believe so. One of our smaller scouting satellites captured a blurry image, but it appears the red beast was briefly in the area around one of the smaller moons orbiting an inner-ring planet."

"Habitable?"

"Yes, but far too hot to be useful for any length of time."

"But they are using it as refuge. And for that, they will not require a lengthy stay."

"Well, I thought––"

"You are not to think, Zinna, you are to report and do my bidding."

"Yes, of course, sir."

Jimtee enjoyed making the pompous man squirm. He'd never liked the aloof power players he was so often required to mingle with––typically while maneuvering them subtly to do his leaders' bidding, while believing it was their own idea. But perhaps he was exerting a bit more force than was really necessary with this one. Still, it was the simple pleasures that made his work rewarding.

In any case, Jimtee's plan was coming together, and far better than he had dared hope when he had first stumbled upon the Uroks and their potent fighting ships. It was an opportunity he had not anticipated, but one he was glad to seize with both hands. Improvisation, the old soldier knew full well, was often the difference between success and failure.

"Have the entire fleet prepared to launch as soon as I've had my 'meeting' with the chancellor. Once that has been accomplished, there will be no pushback from on high."

"The *entire* fleet?"

"You heard what I said, Zinna. The entire fleet. The beast is dangerous, and its very survival could pose a great threat to my ultimate goal."

"And what exactly is that, Sir?"

Jimtee uttered a word quietly. Far too quietly, it seemed, to cause the searing pain that shot through Zinna's body, dropping him to the ground in a twitching heap. The Tslavar canceled the spell and smiled. Yes, his magic still functioned just fine in this realm, and for all their technological prowess, these cock-sure Uroks had no defense against it.

"You would do well to remember your place, Zinna," he said to the man at his feet. "Now, go clean yourself up. You've made a bit of a mess."

The regent scrambled to his feet, bundled his robes, and

hurried from the chamber as fast as he could, lest he face further ire from the man pulling his strings.

"Well, that was interesting," Ulus said, uncloaking from his shimmer when the men were alone.

"Indeed. It seems we are making far better progress than anticipated," Jimtee said.

"The regent is a particularly weak man," Ulus noted. "Weak, yet very, very well connected."

"Which plays into our new plans perfectly," his captain replied. "We will hunt the Zomoki and destroy it with the full force of the Urok fleet. It is inelegant, and excessive, I know, but if we hope to subjugate that troublesome planet and retrieve the portal from their sun, we cannot afford to have a magic-wielding foe as powerful as that. We've felt the beast's magic, and it seems it possesses enough power to actually damage our ship, despite our defenses."

"Meaning it must be a very old Zomoki, indeed."

"Yes. Old and unusually strong. And you know what that means."

"We go on a hunt," Ulus said with a grin. "Good. I could do with some violence of the overt variety for a change."

"And that you shall have."

CHAPTER FIFTY-ONE

The meeting with the chancellor had finally taken place, although far later into the night than Jimtee would have preferred. Nevertheless, despite the inconvenience, the Tslavar captain had left the encounter with precisely what he needed, and the chancellor with a startling realization just how vulnerable he actually was.

Excruciating pain had a way of cutting through the pompous bullshit he had been so accustomed to spewing. A few minutes of agony, and the chancellor was more than willing to do whatever it was the green-skinned man wanted, so long as he just made the pain stop.

Ulus had watched the entire exchange from behind his shimmer cloak, and the man's reaction to what for most was only a moderate amount of torture was a topic of some amusement when Jimtee returned to his quarters.

"Show yourself, Ulus," he commanded.

His number one shed his shimmer. "Well, that was enlightening," Ulus said with an amused grin. "It seems that for all their bluster, once you get past their weaponry, these Uroks are quite a soft people. Disappointing, really."

The captain would agree, but only to a point. It was true, the elites and politicians were weak and easily swayed. But several of the fleet's captains and commanders had shown admirable resilience.

Commander Datano had been a particularly stubborn one, in fact, and had for a short time made Jimtee wonder if he wouldn't have to kill the man to make a point to the others.

But he, too, had eventually broken. A good thing too. Explaining the sudden disappearance of a high-ranking flag officer would be difficult, even with dozens of control-collared Uroks doing their bidding.

"It seems we are prepared," Jimtee said, allowing himself a momentary sigh of satisfaction. "Though I had hoped to begin this evening, tomorrow morning will suffice. At daybreak, the Urok fleet shall launch, under *my* command. The entirety of these forces will hunt the Zomoki down and destroy it, clearing our way to complete our new mission and backtrack to that cursed blue planet."

"Might we possibly send a portion of the Urok fleet ahead, to soften up the Earth defenses in advance of our arrival?" Ulus asked.

"Would that we could, Ulus, but I fear we may need every last one of them if this Zomoki is as wily a creature as I am coming to believe it to be. And it appears to have some sort of small craft accompanying it, I now hear. Strange things are afoot, and we will be far better served coming at them with overwhelming force. If not, there is no telling where or when the Zomoki might pop up and cause actual damage to our vessel."

"It is a strong one, that is for certain," Ulus agreed.

"Yes, and one with that much magic potential must not be taken lightly. But now we shall rest and gather our energy. Come morning, the hunt is on."

. . .

As the sun crested, washing the harsh landscape surrounding the Crux with its orange glow, the men and women of the Urok fleet were already fast at work readying their ships for launch. In the span of less than a half hour, every last one of them had taken to the skies.

"Quite a sight, the full might of the Urok fleet," Regent Zinna said, standing beside Captain Jimtee on the bridge of the Tslavar ship.

The captain had thought it best to keep him close, despite the extended range of the control collar the man wore. It was easy enough for him to make excuses to the other captains, saying simply that he wished to experience firsthand the novel practices of the Tslavar trading ship. They were new allies to the Uroks, after all, and it would do them all well to understand their ways.

If only the real reason were known, the other captains would have turned their guns on the lone craft and rent it from the sky. That is, if they, too, weren't securely under the thumb of Captain Jimtee's control collars.

Not all of them, of course. But enough of the key players to lead the rest of the fleet, who would follow their lead blindly.

"My dear Zinna, would you please ask Commander Datano to have the fleet fan out across the system in the quadrant the beast was last sighted?" Jimtee asked.

It was not a question.

"Of course, sir," the regent said with a little bow.

The man had taken to his subservient role quite well, it seemed, as men of power often did when the burden of decision-making was suddenly removed from their shoulders. It was freeing in a way, not having to think, only to act. But his acts would send his very people on a collision course with a foe far greater than they realized.

"There has been contact reported!" a voice blurted over the open comms channel a short while later. "A stationary asteroid-mounted survey unit noted unnatural movement, and our techs initiated a manual redirect of its cameras and scanners. It's a big, red creature, all right," the lowly comms operator said, excited to relay news of some significant importance.

"Pinpoint its location and transmit coordinates to the nearest ships with clear warp paths," Commander Datano's voice crackled over the channel.

"Done, sir."

"How many ships?" Datano asked.

"Fourteen have a clear path."

"That's not enough," the commander growled.

"I'm sorry, sir, but the location of the creature is in the direct path of several of the smaller asteroid fields, as well as a series of small moons. Warping ships through that would be potentially disastrous."

The commander knew he was right, but the plan was an overwhelming assault. Enough to eliminate the threat before it had even realized it was under attack.

"Private line," he barked to the control-collared comms operator. "To the regent."

"Open, sir."

Datano turned from the others, speaking quietly into his comms. "Regent Zinna, you heard the situation. What does our friend wish to do? We only have fourteen ships at our disposal, and I know this is far less than he wished for."

Jimtee was listening, of course, but remained silent, opting to let Zinna reply for him. He gave the man a nod to go ahead anyway.

"He wishes us to proceed regardless," Zinna said. "Begin the attack at once."

Ara and her passengers, meanwhile, were taking a cautious flight to survey nearby moons for resources that might be of use to them, while Kip stayed a decent distance away, scanning for possible hostiles.

"I don't see anything," the AI ship said. "I think it's all clear in this sector. But if we start a backtrack following the traces of their warp signatures, I think we may be able to––"

A half dozen flashes lit up the darkness around Ara. Moments later, eight more joined them.

"Ara! Get us out of here!" Charlie yelled in alarm.

Dozens of beam weapons were already spooled up and firing on them, all of their destructive force pinpointing on the lone Zomoki and her friends.

"We've got them trapped!" Commander Datano exclaimed as the beams flew true. "In mere seconds, the beast will be no more."

And he was right. At least, about part of that thought.

The massive convergence of energy beams struck one another, triggering a cascading wave of detonating power. When the blinding light faded, there was no sign of the red-scaled beast.

The Uroks celebrated aboard their ships, cheering the successful annihilation of their target. But aboard the Tslavar craft, Captain Jimtee was decidedly *not* amused.

"You saw it, did you not?" he asked Ulus.

"Yes, I did," he replied.

"I saw it too!" Regent Zinna exclaimed enthusiastically. "The beast has been destroyed!"

"No, Zinna, it has not," Jimtee said with an annoyed sigh. "It jumped away."

CHAPTER FIFTY-TWO

"Okay, so they're *definitely* hostile," Charlie said once his heart rate had dropped down from its adrenaline-fueled jackrabbit staccato. "Holy shit, did you see that? I mean, one ship, it can be chalked up to a misunderstanding. But how many was that? A dozen?"

"Fourteen," Bawb replied.

"Right. Fourteen. That's a lot of fucking ships!" Charlie exclaimed. "And how the hell did you count them in the heat of combat so quickly, anyway, Bob?"

"Force of habit," the assassin replied calmly.

"Yeah, yeah. Deadliest assassin in thirty systems. I know, I know."

"More than that, which you know as well," the Wampeh said with a wry grin. "But the actions of this strange force make no sense. Even for a hostile race, some form of contact is almost always attempted. Only the most primitive cultures attack on sight, and even then, it is typically because one has accidentally crossed a cultural line and given some sort of offense. But this? This is anomalous."

"You can say that again. Ara, what do you think?"

"I agree with Bawb. And even if this were a primitive culture, which it is clearly not, this hostility is exceptional in all regards," the dragon said, having taken up a hiding place under a rocky overhang on a small moon.

Charlie was at a loss. He had thought they might find some way to open channels of communication with the hostile beings. A first dialogue to set things on the right foot. But that simply did not seem to be in the cards.

"Where's Kip?" Charlie asked. "Was he caught up in the crossfire? I think he should have been clear, but in all the craziness, I just couldn't track him with all that was going on."

"Well, I would advise against any longer-range comms at this time," Bawb said. "The odds of our signal catching the attention of the aggressors is far greater than before."

"Yeah, I know. I just hope he was able to link to our signal when we jumped. Otherwise it's going to be a real chore tracking them down while avoiding those ships."

"Hey, guys!" Kip said. "Holy crap, did you see all of those ships?"

The AI pulled a tight turn and settled down beside the hidden Zomoki.

"Okay, that answers that question," Charlie said with palpable relief.

"Boy, I'm glad I was able to lock your signal before you jumped. It would have sucked being stuck out there with all of those bad guys. There have to be over thirty of them!"

"Bob says he only counted fourteen," Charlie said.

"Oh, yeah. At first there were fourteen, but after you jumped, a bunch more started showing up just a few minutes later. And some of them were *big*!"

"This is *so* not good," Charlie groaned.

"No. Not good at all," Bawb agreed. "Dukaan, were you able to capture images of the vessels?"

"Of course," the Chithiid pilot replied. "But I must say, at this point, it would seem we are facing a far larger, and far more dangerous foe than merely the Tslavar craft."

"And they won't talk to us," Charlie lamented. "I still can't help but wonder what kind of misunderstanding would cause this sort of thing to happen."

A curious look spread across Bawb's face.

"What is it, man? You look like you're plotting something."

"Perhaps," the Wampeh replied.

"People tend to die when you plot things, Bob."

"Often, yes. But perhaps that eventuality might be avoided, with your expertise in this particular matter."

"*My* expertise? Uh, what've you got up your sleeve?"

"A proposal. A rather unusual one at that." He turned to Kip and Dukaan. "Tell me, before you warped to join us at this location, did you observe any other craft in the system? Perhaps spread out and searching for us?"

"In fact, yeah," Kip said. "It did look like a bunch of their smaller ships were heading in all directions after you jumped. My guess is they're running a search pattern, ya know? Casting a wide net."

"Hmm," the Wampeh murmured. "Then perhaps it is possible."

"*What's* possible, Bob? You're killing me here."

The assassin smiled a pointy-toothed grin. "For you to return to your roots, my friend."

"You need an engineer?"

"No, not that. I need a space pirate."

Charlie did not like the sound of that one bit. "That was a long time ago, Bob. And what exactly did you have in mind?"

"We capture one of their ships, of course," he replied.

Dukaan was more than a little shocked at the suggestion. "You propose attacking *them*? That is madness."

"Perhaps, but that seems to be the only way we are going to be able to have a conversation with our pursuers. And I, for one, wish to understand why, exactly, they are so determined to destroy us when we've only just met."

Charlie was not liking the sound of that one bit, but he had to admit, the Wampeh had a point. And with his specialized skills learned during his short stint as a pirate, along with Bawb's formidable fighting skills, and all of their combined magic, they just might be able to pull it off against one of the smaller ships.

"So, we ambush them," Charlie said, the pirate gears in his mind already turning. "Wait for one to pass behind a moon or asteroid belt so they're off visual of the other ships. Then take them down fast and hard."

"But they obviously have comms between their craft," Dukaan pointed out.

"I've got readings of them, Dookie. Their tech is alien, obviously, but their comms transmission systems are pretty similar to ours in some ways. I can leverage a few exploits I noticed and scramble them for a brief while," the AI ship said confidently.

"Really?" Charlie said. "You've already figured out a totally alien tech in this short a time frame?"

"Well, from what I've seen, they're flying their ships manually. If there's no AI involved, then there's simply no way they can keep up with me when it comes to coding. No meat brain can."

Charlie looked at his friends, each and every one of them ready to dive in headfirst and follow him on this insane undertaking. And it warmed his heart.

"Okay, then," he said. "Let's go bag us a ship."

CHAPTER FIFTY-THREE

The Urok ship circling the small moon was a fairly well-armed vessel. Its exterior was not bristling with weaponry and defensive arrays as some of the larger warships in the fleet, but it nevertheless packed a sizable wallop for a craft of its size.

As such, its captain flew with the confidence of a predator, sure in her knowledge that they could easily handle themselves against nearly any foe.

They had just passed into the shadow of the moon, blocking them from visual contact with the rest of the fleet for a short while, when their communications systems suddenly went from continual chatter to eerie, static-filled silence.

"Basha, what the hell is going on with my communications?" Captain Pril demanded.

"I don't know, Captain," her confused comms operator replied. "Everything was working just fine a second ago."

"Well, fix it. We don't want to miss out on the fun when the target is finally located."

She had just barely uttered those words when the ship was rocked by a massive blast of magical fire, its shields crumbling under the sheer force of the onslaught.

"Weapons! What hit us? Do you have a firing solution?" Pril bellowed.

"All systems are operational, Captain. But we don't seem to have anything to lock onto. There was a blip, but just for a few seconds, then the screen went blank again."

Captain Pril was livid. Somehow her crew had slacked off, and now their ship's shielding was damaged. If she didn't rectify the issue, and soon, the promotion she'd been pushing for would all but evaporate before her eyes. Worse, the alien in their midst would be *very* upset, she thought as she touched the golden collar hidden beneath her uniform.

"Comms, call reinforcements. Tell them we had contact with the beast."

"But it hasn't been confirmed, Captain," the comms operator replied.

An icy glare froze her in her seat.

"Are you refusing an order?" Pril growled.

"No, of course not, Captain. I'll transmit immediately," Basha quickly replied. "But with the glitching in our system, I can't guarantee the message will go through."

Pril's sixth sense was tingling on high alert. Something was up, and there was danger, she just knew it. Somewhere out there, somewhere close, was her enemy. And she'd be damned if it would slip away from her grasp.

"All scans to maximum, weapons charged and primed," she commanded. "I want all eyes on the skies. The second we have so much as a pingback, target and fire."

"But shouldn't we confirm--" the weapons chief said.

"We know our own ships, and anything else out here that's not transmitting a Urok ident code is fair game."

"Yes, Captain," the chief replied, then quickly set to work assuring his teams were ready for a fight.

All the myriad scanning tech was pointed out into the inky

black, searching for any trace of the beast. If it came back, they'd be ready. It wouldn't stand a chance.

Meanwhile, the two space-suited figures stealthily deposited on the ship's hull in the confusion immediately following the blast were making their way quickly toward the designated breaching point.

Kip had determined what appeared to be the most likely command center location on the vessel, and, as luck would have it, there happened to be a perfect section of hull very close by that was devoid of external defenses and surveying apparatus. Ideal for what Charlie had in mind.

He and Bawb hustled to the breach point and secured themselves to the hull with clips and straps. There shouldn't be any violent atmospheric change if Charlie cast the spell right, but it had been years since his pirating days, so they both figured it was far better to be safe than sorry. Sorry and drifting off into the depths of space if a blast should knock them from the hull.

"Okay, you ready?" Charlie asked.

"Oh, indeed," Bawb replied, looking forward to the action.

"All right. I'll cast in three, so be ready."

"I've *been* ready, Charlie. Just do it already."

Charlie could almost hear the grin in his friend's words. Bawb, for all the calming effect Hunze had had on him, was still an assassin, and no domestic bliss could take the training and thrill of action entirely from his system.

The spell was a simple one. A pair of them, actually, to be specific. One to create a force bubble around the two men and that small section of hull, and a second to tear free a clean hole in the ship's skin. If it worked according to plan, only a tiny puff of air would escape, filling the small force pocket but not venting into space.

If Charlie did it right.

Fortunately, his memory was true, and the results were near

perfect. He cast the spells simultaneously, the magical seal locking in place just as the metal gave way.

"Go!" he shouted over comms, but Bawb, naturally, had lunged inside the instant the piece of hull was clear, a full second before Charlie could even open his mouth. Say what you might, but there was no doubt as to the Wampeh's reflexes and skill set.

Charlie's boots slapped the deck as the artificial gravity took hold once he'd passed inside the ship. Bawb was up ahead, already moving quickly toward the command center. Two lean, orange-skinned aliens were down on the ground, though it seemed Bawb had refrained from landing any killing blows on their prey.

And that's what Charlie thought of them as now. Prey. Not opponents, but victims. For with his and Bawb's skills in play, there was little hope for the crew of the small ship, even if they did manage to raise an alarm.

They did, in fact, sound an alarm just as Charlie and Bawb reached what seemed to be the command center doors, a heavy-duty set of sliding panels that stood before them. The goal was at hand, but it would have to wait a moment longer.

From down the corridor the sound of boots racing toward them rang out in the otherwise silent ship.

"Shit. Sounds like we've got company, Bob," Charlie said, dropping to one knee to provide a smaller target for their enemy as he prepared to cast stun spells.

A hand rested on his shoulder.

"Allow me," Bawb said, closing his eyes and extending his arms as he chanted a quiet incantation just as a large group of alien crew rounded the corner, speeding toward them as they raised their weapons.

The Ootaki hair within his armored vest began to glow brightly, the light seeping out through the gaps for an instant before a massive stun blast released from Bawb's arms--a precisely focused blast set free just above Charlie's head.

The spell passed through walls with ease, the stun magic knocking every single person on that level to the ground. The troops who had been charging at them all unceremoniously dropped to the deck in an unconscious pile.

"Holy shit, dude," Charlie marveled.

Bawb merely smiled. Perhaps it was a wee bit excessive, but damn, it felt good. "Worth the expenditure of power," he said, satisfied. "Now, shall we?" he asked as he forced the command center doors open.

"After you, then," Charlie replied.

The duo quickly sealed the bridge behind them, just in case attackers from a distant part of the ship happened to come see what was going on and why their buddies weren't replying. Never leave an enemy at your back, Ser Baruud had taught Charlie. He had no intention of dishonoring his teacher by forgetting that lesson now.

"Bind their hands and disarm them of any weapons," Bawb said as he quickly tied the wrists of everyone he came to, while removing their sidearms and stowing them in a bag brought for just such a purpose.

Once back with the others, they could examine and reverse engineer the technology at their leisure. But for the moment, speed was of the essence.

Charlie moved one of what appeared to be the command officers to a position to better tie her limbs when her uniform shifted. What he saw horrified him.

"Oh, shit," he gasped. "Fuck. Bob, come look at this."

Hearing the tone in his friend's voice, the Wampeh rushed to his side. "What is it, Charlie? You sound alar--"

Then he saw what had so shocked his friend. The device resting against the unconscious alien's orange skin.

"That is a control collar," he said flatly. "A Tslavar one, from what I can see."

"Yup," Charlie said, sinking into an empty seat. "You realize what this means, don't you?"

"Yes. If the Tslavars brought control collars with them and have enough to have seized control of this ship, then they have already made contact with these aliens and taken the reins of their vessels."

"And not just that," Charlie said. "To have been already carrying that many collars means they were planning on using them long before our little pursuit took place."

Bawb scowled at the thought. "They meant to subjugate Earth's population," he spat.

"Yeah. Or at least the key individuals," Charlie added. "We are so fucked."

The vein in Bawb's temple that only throbbed visibly when he was truly angry was beginning its little *thump, thump* dance as he clenched his jaw. "I will not allow Hunze to wear a collar ever again," he said in a low growl. "I will die before that happens."

"We've got to do something, Bob. This changes everything. These aren't enemies, they're innocents being used against us."

"Ara," Charlie called out with the silent link shared between them.

"Have you succeeded, Charlie?" she replied, from some distance, it seemed, given the faintness of the reply.

"Big change of plans," he said. *"The crew, the officers, at least, are all wearing Tslavar control collars."*

"You are certain?"

"Yes. And Bob confirms it."

"Well, then. This changes our tactics rather drastically, don't you think? We must try not to harm these innocents, if possible," Ara said.

"I know. But they're under Tslavar control, and I don't know if we

can effectively disrupt enough of these collars to free them from their effects."

"Do what you can, Charlie. I have the utmost confidence in you, and I know you will do all you can to not harm them, if you are able."

"And if that's not possible?"

Ara paused a moment.

"Then kill them as quickly and humanely as you can," she finally said, and even Bawb, the seasoned assassin, was shocked by her words.

CHAPTER FIFTY-FOUR

"We can't just kill them, Bob," Charlie said as he paced the command center. "She was kidding, right? She had to be kidding."

Bawb watched his friend with both concern and a bit of amusement. "I am quite certain she was deadly serious," he replied. "But I am also sure that she would only recommend that action as a last resort. And we have other options at our disposal."

"So you're against the idea too?"

"Just because I am an assassin does not make me wish to be party to the mass murder of a few hundred beings, most of whom are unconscious, I might add."

It was true, the spell had done far more than Bawb had originally anticipated. It was a stun spell, and a very powerful one at that, but the Ootaki hair he wore had supercharged its potency far beyond anything he'd expected.

The resulting blast of magic had apparently spread beyond the deck they were on, knocking out crew on several other levels of the craft as well. Only those stationed at the farthest reaches had escaped untouched.

"It may have come out a little more powerful than I anticipated," Bawb said.

"A *little*?" Charlie shot back sarcastically.

"Okay. Maybe a lot," the Wampeh replied sheepishly.

Bawb had channeled too much power to the spell, and there was nothing to be done for it. They'd just have to improvise.

Charlie paused in his pacing, a light bulb idea flashing in the churning processor of his mind. "What if we join our power and remove the collars?" he suggested. "We don't have a plasma cutter, but we do have some pretty potent magic."

Bawb bent down and studied the collar on the sleeping comms operator's neck. "I'm afraid these are particularly robust, Charlie. The removal with magic alone would require a great deal of power."

"Which we have."

"Yes, but which we would be fools to expend on something so uncertain as this when we may very well need that power to save our very lives should the fleet locate us."

Charlie knew he was right before he'd even finished his sentence. It didn't make the reality of the situation suck any less, though.

"So what can we do here? I mean, it's not like we can take their ship. Neither of us knows how to fly it anyway, and I'm sure they've got the means to track their own craft. Like an ident beacon or something."

"Most likely, yes," Bawb agreed.

"Right. So taking the whole ship to pick apart at our leisure is out of the question, and we can't remove the collars, but we need intel. We just don't have the time to properly gather any, it seems. From what Kip said as we came in, the other ships in the fleet will be in visual and scanning range soon. And when that happens, when this ship fails to respond to hails, the game will be up."

"Yes. And, unfortunately, my stun spell seems to have

actually been a *lot* more overpowered than I had originally thought."

"But they'll wake up, right? You didn't fry them or anything?"

"They will all recover, in time," Bawb replied. "However, the spell I used to subdue the crew in the immediate vicinity as we stormed the command center was a particularly powerful one."

"Nothing wrong with that. Better we knock them out than kill them, right?"

"Well, yes and no," Bawb said. "The problem is the Ootaki hair Hunze gifted to me is occasionally surprising in its strength. Yes, I am learning its capabilities, but a lot is still trial and error. In this case, the error being a far more potent spell than anticipated."

"How much more?" Charlie asked, uneasily.

"I can't say for certain," Bawb replied, "but I would guess ninety percent of the crew were affected by it."

Charlie's eyes widened at the number. "You knocked out almost the entire crew with that thing?"

"Well, yes. But it is not ordinarily possible. Only the confined nature of the ship, along with our proximity to the targets allowed this to happen. In the wild it would be a far less potent casting."

"So lemme get this straight. You not only knocked out pretty much the entire crew with that thing, but now it looks like we have no idea when they'll even wake up so we can ask them some questions?"

"More or less," the Wampeh said, apologetically.

"Jesus, Bob. The plan was to gather intelligence, ya know? Grill one of the officers and get some answers."

"Though we do now know they are under Tslavar control, so the question of our being attacked has been answered."

"Yeah, but there's so much more we need to know. Like how many of these guys are out there? And what kind of firepower are they packing?" Charlie began pacing again. "Shit, shit, shit. We are so screwed."

Bawb cocked his head to the side ever so slightly, then unfastened a tiny pocket on his weapons belt and drew out a single strand of Hunze's golden hair.

"What are you going to do with that?" Charlie asked. "And why do you have one hair in your pocket when you're wearing a massive braid of the stuff?"

Bawb smiled a toothy grin. "I keep this handy for just this sort of occasion," he replied. "It is too time-consuming to unbraid the mass of hair I possess to retrieve just one strand. But keeping this one ready for use, safe in its own hidden pocket? Why, that's not difficult at all. And it seems to have come in quite handy today," he added, bending down and wrapping the hair around the collar of what appeared to be one of the ship's officers.

"Of course," Charlie said, flashing back to his own captivity when the space pirates who had snatched him from the street had wrapped a small cloth of woven Ootaki hair around his collar. That act had effectively muted it from tracking, while also negating its owner's ability to harm or kill the wearer.

The hairs that cloth had been made of were far greater in number, allowing for an actual fabric to be woven. Hunze's hair, however, was magnitudes more powerful, and just a single strand could easily accomplish what the pirates' cloth had managed.

"Kip, we're going to need you to come to the downed ship ASAP," Charlie called out over comms. It was decision time, and with the use of that piece of Ootaki hair, Bawb had just made it for them.

"Wait, but I'm holding position for surveillance of the fleet. This isn't the plan," Kip replied, a bit concerned.

"No, but plans change, so get your ass over here."

He was not thrilled with the unexpected change, but,

reluctantly, Kip pulled away from his hiding spot and maneuvered toward his friends, being as careful as he could not to draw the attention of the several ships nearby.

"If they see me, we're going to have to boogie out of there, and fast!" Kip said as he raced toward the Urok ship.

"Yeah, we know," Charlie replied, hoisting the unconscious female over his shoulder.

She was the captain, he believed. That is, unless he totally misread the symbols on the crew's uniforms and had accidentally taken the lowest ranking person rather than the highest. Time would tell, but for now, the first step was getting clear of the disabled ship in one piece.

The human and his Wampeh friend raced the corridor toward their breaching point, hopping over the unconscious bodies of the crew as they ran. Bawb was right, his spell was a lot more powerful than either had imagined.

Sure, it made escape easier, what with everyone passed out on the ground. But Charlie couldn't help but worry that their captive might only wake once all the action had already passed, and that would not be helpful at all.

The breach was just as they'd left it, the vacuum of space held at bay by the powerful magic sealing the hole with a tiny bubble stuck to the outside of the ship, like carbonation to the side of a champagne flute.

Kip was already approaching, his soft-seal docking mechanism deployed to create a safe path for them to transfer their prisoner. The AI ship stuck the connection expertly, and within seconds, a secure path with breathable atmosphere was in place.

"You guys had better hurry!" Kip called over his speakers. "We don't have long."

Charlie handed his unconscious burden to Bawb as they stepped out into the zero-g of the umbilical. "Get her inside. I've got to seal this before we go."

Bawb didn't hesitate, taking the woman's unconscious shape from his friend and hurrying into Kip's waiting hull.

"Who is this?" Dukaan asked, helping Bawb strap the unconscious form into an empty seat.

"A captive," he replied. "Hopefully one who can shed more light on the situation when she awakes."

Charlie, still in the umbilical, quickly lifted the breached metal piece where it sat floating, right where he'd left it. In just seconds, he was slapping it back into place, then applied a hasty welding spell, drawing the edges of the ship and the fragment together, creating a solid hull once more.

It wasn't his best work by any stretch, but it would keep the sleeping aliens from venting into space when the spell holding the air inside was removed.

"Come on, Charlie! We've gotta go!" Kip blared out over both speakers and comms.

"Okay, okay," he replied, scrambling aboard the ship. "I'm in. Punch it."

Kip didn't need to be told twice, and in a flash, he engaged his warp core. And none too soon, for moments later the Urok ships moved to within visual and scanning range. But the little AI ship was already gone, and the crackling blue remnants of his warp had already dissipated.

CHAPTER FIFTY-FIVE

Rika had been explaining the magic wielded by the Tslavars to the Kalamani elders for the umpteenth time when Varahash interjected yet again.

"But the higher you go, the harder it is to breathe," the warrior leader said. "When our young endure the trials of passage to enter the warrior band, they must climb to the peak of the mountain you see in the distance. It is a difficult journey, and the climb is treacherous."

"I can imagine," Rika said.

"At the summit, it is so hard to breathe that many, even the strongest, have lost consciousness for a time."

"Also to be expected," she replied.

A curious expression formed on Jo's face. "But isn't it wasteful, losing the lives of young men for what is essentially a test of one's courage? I can't imagine it would be of benefit to thin your ranks of the young and sturdy over something so avoidable."

Varahash snorted with amusement. "We do not kill our young in this test. We have older warriors, those who are better suited to those heights, watching the attempts. Only very rarely does a young aspirant pay the highest price."

"Well, that's good to hear," Rika said. "But back to travel by spaceship. They fly high, yes, and even travel out of the planet's atmosphere into space. But the inside of the craft is sealed and pressurized."

"What does that even mean?" the warrior asked.

Rika sighed. It was getting exhausting trying to explain technology that simply didn't exist on this planet in any shape or form.

"It means we can go places your people cannot. And the Tslavars who attacked your farmers have a very powerful craft, it seems."

"Ah, yes. The thing that attempts to hide from the eyes of the Kalamani warriors, just as the invaders tried to trick our senses. But we pierced their deception," he said proudly.

"Yeah, and a few of their bodies as well, thanks to those arrows and spears you crafted. They seem to disrupt their defenses, which I can assure you was a very big surprise to them. They're used to being able to sneak around and do as they want. For a less technologically advanced people to disrupt their shimmers so easily, it must have been quite a shock."

Varahash smiled with pride. Of course his warriors had defeated the invaders. They were the strongest of the tribes in the region and had long been known for their skill and prowess. And with their shaman's arcane skill in applying the sacred lines to their bodies, the Kalamani warriors would never know defeat.

Or so he thought, right up until the screaming started at the outskirts of the village.

A young woman rushed into the elders' yurt, a splash of green blood on her skin that certainly did not appear to be her own.

"Tslavars!" Rika realized. "Jo, we're under attack. See if we've got a path to the *Fujin*, then help the Kalamani civilians get clear."

The cyborg jumped to her feet, smoothly swinging the pulse rifle from its sling. "On it," she said, rushing outside toward the sound of fighting.

Judging by the cries filling the air, the Tslavars were doing far more than just probing the natives' defenses.

"Keep the elders safe," Rika said as she raced to join the fight, her pulse rifle ready and her magical weapons fully charged.

"You do not even possess weapons," Varahash replied. "Your brightstone blades are still safely in my possession," he said with an overconfident snort. "And you do not tell the leader of the Kalamani forces what to do. The elders are safe. My warriors will make quick work of these Tslavars you seem so concerned about."

"You don't understand. This isn't a small group being taken off guard. They *know* your people can see them, and they'll have adapted and adjusted their tactics accordingly."

At that moment, Jo's voice crackled over Rika's comms. The unit was set to open broadcast, not in-ear only. The voice in the air startled the Kalamani.

"Rika, it's a mess out here. It's an all-out assault, and they've surrounded the village," Jo informed her. "They're all shimmered, and since it's only the warrior members of the tribe who have the means to see them, everyone else is running around blind. They're picking off the civilians as they push in closer."

"Shit. Is there any chance of getting to the *Fujin*? With its firepower, we might stand a chance at pushing them back."

"Negative. There's no way we can get through all of those shimmered bastards to get to the ship. It's too far away, and we'd be picked off."

"So the ship's safe, you think?"

"We left it a ways away, and its auto defenses are still registering no contact so far as I can see, so I think they've either missed it or are ignoring it, opting instead to strike the village with everything they've got. The locals are making a good showing, though. Varahash's warriors, I mean. But if they get past them, we're going to be overrun."

Rika quickly ran through their limited options. None were good.

"We could run the remote startup protocol. Recall the ship and have it auto-land at my location."

"But it's not configured for a rapid combat auto-flight. It'd be a sitting duck as it came in."

"Shit, you're right," Rika grumbled. "Just leave it, then. We can't risk losing it to a lucky shot, or worse, having the Tslavars take it."

The sound of pulse rifle fire rang out over the comms.

"What are you shooting at?"

"Just popping off shots where the warriors are attacking. They can see them, so I'm using them as a sort of targeting mechanism."

"Clever," Rika said. "I'll be right there, hang tight." She turned to Varahash once more. "Keep them safe," she said, then raced from the tent to join the fray.

CHAPTER FIFTY-SIX

Bodies lay in the dirt, broken and bent where they had fallen, victims of the Tslavar spells. The killing had been indiscriminate. Women and children were fair game, it seemed. The invaders were not interested in capture. They had come to wipe them out.

The warriors were putting on a good show, Rika had to admit. It seemed their arrows and spears flew true more often than not, and the Tslavar defenses were simply not designed to handle the unusual magic contained in the primitive weaponry.

Also of note was the way the tattoos around their eyes seemed to faintly pulse with a self-contained light, despite the ink's black color. And the designs on their arms acted in a similar manner as they launched their weapons.

For all Rika could tell, they were drawing from the magically charged pigment of their designs, using the power to help drive their attacks home. It was fascinating, and certainly worthy of study, but the heat of battle was definitely not the right time.

Varahash was following fast in her footsteps, an arrow already nocked on his bowstring and ready to let fly.

"I said protect the elders!"

"You do not dictate my actions, Invader," he replied, letting the arrow loose.

A shriek and spray of green blood where there appeared to be no one was evidence the shaft had flown true.

"Thanks for lighting him up for me," Rika said, unslinging her pulse rifle and letting off a pair of blasts.

The injury had apparently distracted the Tslavar mercenary from his defensive spells, and that was enough for her shots to land. The man didn't even have a chance to scream as his torso blew apart, the shimmer spell fading with his life force.

Varahash looked at Rika with an expression of true shock. Here he had thought he had disarmed them of their weaponry. The brightstone blades were fine and deadly, and all they possessed were the clunky things on straps they carried. Clunky things that apparently contained great power.

The appearance of pulse weaponry in the mix caused the Tslavar troops to shift their tactics, targeting the area the novel power was originating from.

"They're coming in heavy," Jo called out as Rika and Varahash joined her at the front lines. "But the locals seem to be holding them back for the most part."

As if to disprove her point, several of the innocent villagers cowering behind what limited cover they had were struck down by a flurry of Tslavar spells. It was brutal, and even the seasoned eyes of Varahash were shocked by the horrors inflicted upon his people.

"Fuck you!" Rika bellowed, unloading her pulse rifle in a spray of fire, laying waste to a swath of ground, taking a few Tslavars out in the process and damaging the shimmers of others by sheer luck.

A mercenary with a damaged shimmer spell rushed forward, mostly visible now, charging toward them. She targeted him and pulled the trigger.

Click.

"Shit. I'm out!" she called to Jo.

"I'm on my last reload!" the cyborg called back, now holding a spear taken from a fallen warrior.

Rika threw her rifle aside and prepared herself, drawing upon the magical combat knowledge still locked in her brain. She chided herself for relying on the pulse weapon in the first place, but sometimes old Earth habits died hard.

The Tslavars would now die harder.

Varahash watched in awe as the woman he had considered a disarmed invader drew upon some secret store of power, unleashing devastating magic upon their attackers.

This was a type of attack the Tslavars were used to facing, but they had adjusted their defenses for the pulse weapon threat at hand, and as such, their usual magical shielding was not ready for the sheer power of the attacks Rika launched at them.

A dozen men fell to the first series of spells, while another handful were seriously injured, their bodies flying through the air as the invisible attack grabbed a hold of them, hurling them with brutal force.

Rika was putting on quite a show, and the Kalamani could not help but take note of the ferocity with which this strange woman was defending their village. The elders had emerged from their yurt, watching with interested gazes that were just as awe-filled as Varahash's.

Another set of eyes was watching with great interest as well, the white-inked shaman assessing this strange woman with growing interest.

Varahash, for his part, was simply stunned. This seemingly harmless woman could have killed them all with a wave of her hand at any time, yet she had chosen not to, opting to submit to their will. He had, it seemed, greatly underestimated her.

"Rika, on your nine!" Jo called out.

Without hesitation, Rika spun and loosed a crippling spell, the mostly shimmer-cloaked Tslavar falling to the dirt in a partially camouflaged heap. The resulting retaliatory strikes shook the ground, nearly knocking her from her feet. Her defensive spells held, for the most part, though a few small cuts blossomed on her body.

But Rika ignored them, shrugging them off in the heat of battle.

Screams of fear caught her attention. Deep within the enemy-occupied area of the village, a young girl crouched beside her parents, shaking them in desperation. But to any observing, it was clear they would never hold their daughter again.

Rika locked eyes with Varahash, then Jo. Then she turned and ran headlong for the child. "Cover me, Jo!"

"Rika, no! You'll be killed!" the cyborg shouted after her. "Quickly, cover her!" she yelled as she spun to face the Kalamani warriors.

The men loosed a volley of arrows in an attempt to clear a path for her. They were only partially successful.

Unable to see most of the Tslavar fighters in her path, Rika fired off spells blindly, some landing, but many not. As she passed the invisible men, her magical defenses stopped their spells from landing, but were not able to prevent their blades from driving home.

Myriad wounds opened on her body, blossoms of crimson spreading on her clothes as they absorbed the flowing blood. But Rika was locked on her goal, ignoring the damage being done as she ran for the girl.

The elders watched in amazement at the efforts of this stranger, her willingness to die if need be to save the life of this child. She arrived at the girl's side, and without hesitation snatched her up under her arm, turning and running at top speed from the battleground.

Magical blasts shook her as she ran, but she somehow kept to her feet. The Kalamani warriors with their enhanced vision unleashed a flurry of arrows, granting her a temporary respite from the barrage.

It was enough, but only just.

Rika darted behind cover, then raced to the nearest group of Kalamani, handing the terrified girl off into their waiting arms. Finally in the safe embrace of her people, the child looked up at her bloody savior, her tear-filled eyes brimming with confusion and fear, but also gratitude. And at that moment, as the adrenaline began to fade and the severity of her injuries became apparent, that look was nevertheless enough for Rika.

The ground shook violently. Far more violently than before.

"Their ship," Jo called out. "They're moving for an aerial attack!"

Rika summoned what energy she still had, her clothing slick with sticky red, and turned to the source of the magical barrage. They had casters aboard that ship, but in using them, they'd given away their position, at least momentarily.

Relying purely on instinct, she focused the power of all of her magical devices into one massive spell, casting with the intent to do great damage to the invisible craft above. The konus Bawb had given her flared to life, the incredible magic contained within drawing from all the other devices on her body, even those she was not actively wielding, focusing them like a rifle shot of deadly magic.

The spell flew true, and the lone woman standing on the ground beneath them actually shook the massive craft in the sky above her.

The shimmer cloak fell, and bits of the ship cracked and fell away as the pure intensity of Rika's spell battered it like no spell it had ever experienced. It was an arcane spell. A secret, last-resort weapon that Malalia Maktan had implanted in her mind when she was a brainwashed mercenary doing her bidding. A fail-safe, of sorts. Only now, she was a free woman, and though it might just kill her, she called upon that powerful magic willingly.

The Tslavar captain was shocked at the damage inflicted. There was a true power user among the natives, it seemed, and a strong one at that. One that, from what it appeared, possessed the power to knock them from the sky, given the chance.

A very hasty retreat was ordered, the ground forces scattering to the wind in an instant, racing from the village to be collected a safe distance away, many taking magic-laced arrows in the back as they ran.

The Tslavar ship fled as well, letting loose a barrage of deadly spells, all aimed at the magic user in hopes of distracting them long enough to allow for an escape.

Little did they know, the poor woman was all but tapped out.

She did all she could to defend against the onslaught, draining the very last of her power in the process. Somehow, she managed to deflect the deadliest of the spells, but enough of the attack made it through to drive her to the ground.

She had not only saved a child, but the whole village it seemed, but floating in the inky black of unconsciousness, she was entirely unaware.

Varahash picked up her blood-soaked body with reverence, carrying her toward the village elders when the shaman stepped in front of him. The holy man did not say a word, but merely gave the warrior a look, then turned for his tent. Varahash glanced at the elders once, each giving him a slight nod, then turned and followed.

CHAPTER FIFTY-SEVEN

The villagers emerged from shelter and began the arduous task of clearing the dead from the ground, both the invaders, as well as their own.

Streaks of green blood trailed off into the brush at the outskirts of town, a grim reminder of the Tslavars who, despite the Kalamani's best efforts, nevertheless lived to fight another day, though likely not for some time, depending on their injuries.

And judging by the hasty retreat of the green-skinned aliens, it did not seem as though they would be coming back anytime soon, if at all.

The Kalamani were efficient in their grim work, quickly restoring their village to a less grisly state. But while all of that was taking place, others were working intently, the outside world tuned out entirely.

Varahash had laid Rika's body on a thin mat rolled out on the shaman's floor, then stepped back, ready to serve the holy man however needed. He was covered in the woman's blood, but barely seemed to notice.

Jo, on the other hand, was acutely aware of everything in the chamber, from the candles to the smoldering incense, to the odd implements the shaman was slowly and precisely laying out beside the critically wounded woman.

The cyborg was beside herself with grief--one of the drawbacks of an AI possessing emotions as a true intelligence and not a mere imitation of one. Jo was suffering because of what had happened to her friend. Rika was hurt, and no matter what anyone might say, she felt it was her fault.

Rika had wanted to leave. To go back to Earth with the others to analyze the samples they had collected. But it was Jo who convinced her to stay behind. To remain with the Kalamani and track the Tslavars until the others could return with reinforcements. And now she was near death because of it.

It wasn't the first time Jo had experienced the sensation of guilt, but the overwhelming nature of this experience had shocked her with its intensity.

And so it was that she came to stand above her friend, keeping watch over her as only a cyborg could. Not moving. Not tiring. Not leaving her side. She would remain with Rika and not budge an inch until her friend either pulled through, or needed her to carry her remains back home to Earth. Either way, she was going nowhere.

Varahash was somewhat unsettled by the lack of life the woman looming over her friend showed. It wasn't natural. Jo, of course, could have explained her true nature to him, but that would only complicate things. That, and she had no interest in anything but Rika at the moment.

The shaman, however, was not interested in the stock-still woman in the least as he set about his work. He had already lit the special incense taken from a small recess in a piece of knotted wood acting as a shelving unit standing against the far wall of his tent. The sappy resin ignited with a bright spark, emitting a most unusual smoke that seemed to almost illuminate the air rather than muddy it.

He then arranged a collection of fine bone needles, mounted in ornately carved wooden handles. A small mallet lay next to them. There had been a number of such implements to choose from within his collection, but these seemed almost untouched, as if reserved for only the most sacred of occasions.

The shaman crossed the tent again, carefully pressing a series of knots on the shelves. With the slightest of clicks, a seam appeared where none had previously been, and a small drawer slid open.

From this, he withdrew a sealed bowl of what appeared to be sap or pigment from some sort of plant, but one the visitors had not come across in their survey. The pure white substance was faintly glowing of its own accord, as if a living pool of energy resided in the container.

Without a word, he sealed the drawer again and sat down next to Rika, then began stripping her of her clothing.

"What are you doing?" Jo asked, her defensive instinct flaring.

The shaman ignored her entirely, continuing his work without pause.

"He is preparing her," Varahash said.

"Preparing her for what?"

"To be healed," the warrior replied in a quiet voice. "It is a great honor to receive this gift."

Within minutes, Rika lay completely nude, the dozens of wounds inflicted in the course of battle showing their gaping puckering of flesh plainly in the torchlight. The shaman had startlingly steady hands, despite his apparent age, and had her body cleaned of all blood in no time.

The wounds themselves he dressed with clean cloth, but she had lost so much blood, there was little danger of them being soaked through. One by one, he placed a dollop of the white substance within the rent flesh, then began stitching the flaps of skin shut, sealing it inside.

It took nearly an hour to complete the task, but when he had finished, you could barely notice the severity of the injuries, so skilled was his needlework. That, and the white substance had apparently already begun its healing process.

If the act had been performed on a being from the other galaxy, it would have undoubtedly been instantly fatal, as they'd seen the severity of the reaction they had to this system's magic. But for this woman, born on Earth but molded into what she was in the other, the best of both worlds flowed in her veins. The strength to survive the infusion, as well as the magical skills to bind and use it.

"So now we wait," Jo stated, still having not budged an inch.

"No," the shaman said, speaking for the first time she'd heard, the strength in his quiet voice shocking the cyborg. "Now we begin the real work."

He then picked up a multiple-needle implement and dipped the points into the pigment, then crouched over Rika again, pressing the needles into the flesh above her heart.

"What are you doing?" Jo asked.

"Placing the Wellspring," he replied, tapping the handle of the needle rod with his mallet, beginning to lay down the first lines of a dense, intricate design inked into her skin with the almost translucent white pigment.

"The what?"

"The prime," the old man replied, not pausing in his work. "That from which all power flows. That which connects and binds."

"I don't understand," the cyborg said.

"He is healing her," Varahash said. "Making her strong. This is an honor never bestowed, not even upon our own people." The look of sheer reverence on his face as he watched the man work spoke louder than his words to the importance of what was happening in that tent.

"But the ink. It glows."

"Yes," the shaman replied with a knowing look. "The rarest of the rare. Known only to the chosen few."

Rika's body trembled slightly as he connected the first of the lines together with a series of precise taps of the mallet, his steady hands inking her with even more precision than an AI-guided tattoo unit.

A flash of light blossomed from the ink in her skin, which then faded to a barely visible white hiding within her flesh. The trembling stopped, her body once more going limp.

"Is she going to be okay?" Jo asked, still uncertain what exactly was happening, but watching with great interest.

For the first time, the shaman paused and looked up at the woman, the glow in his eyes and tattoos almost disconcerting, were it not for the other things already seen this day.

"It will save her," he replied. "Or kill her. One way or another, she will move on to her next form."

CHAPTER FIFTY-EIGHT

Some in the Urok fleet might have thought it odd that the smaller alien craft would be flying beside their mighty flagship as the fleet swarmed the solar system in search of the rogue Zomoki.

But that sort of thought was way above their pay grade, and whoever had approved the unusual flight configuration was obviously very, very high up the food chain. So the great many ships comprising the Urok fleet quietly accepted the anomaly and flew forth, carrying out their objective without a further doubt.

As for Jimtee, flying his ship entirely uncloaked was a rather novel experience. He'd become so accustomed to the silent-running stealth procedures adopted over the years he had commanded his vessel that to be among so many great alien craft, visible no less, was a disconcerting experience, despite the iron grip he held on their commanders.

"Ulus, have you confirmed the positioning of the ships we control?" Captain Jimtee asked.

"Yes, Captain," his number one replied with a satisfied smile. "More than half of the larger ships are now commanded by captains under our control, as planned. Additionally, a full quarter of the smaller ships following in their wake are as well."

"Good," Jimtee murmured. "The rest, as anticipated, will follow the others blindly. Such a simple yet significant flaw in the command and control structure of so many military forces, wouldn't you agree?"

"I would, Captain."

"Just a small amount of independent thought, and any single one of their ships not under our control could throw the whole plan into disarray. Yet they are regimented. Military. Loathe to break ranks."

"And that is their downfall," Ulus said, finishing the thought.

"Indeed," Jimtee agreed as he scanned the vastness of space around them for any sign of the troublesome Zomoki.

He'd received word that one of their ships may have had a run-in with the beast. However, nearly the entire crew, but for those in the deepest depths of engineering at the far end of the ship, seemed to be unconscious, though there was no apparent physical reason why.

Jimtee and Ulus shared a knowing look at the news. Only one sort of thing could cause that type of effect. A stun spell, and from what it sounded like, a ferociously powerful one at that. The Zomoki was far more clever than they'd anticipated. Clever, and strong.

Of course, they couldn't admit as much to the Urok fleet. To do so would court panic among the crews if they learned the creature could render them unconscious from a distance without ever needing to fire a conventional weapon at them.

No, it was best to keep this bit of information secret as they paired up and ran a new search pattern. No ship was to fly alone, so groups of two or three headed off to scan the system for their prey, each one covering the other's back as they moved.

. . .

Nearly the entire day had passed when the ships yet again reported no sign of the creature, despite searching pretty much every rock, moon, and planet in the system. The thing was, even with the full might of the fleet and all of its numbers on their side, it was simply too easy for a lone target to avoid them if they were at all alert.

And the Zomoki was most certainly alert.

Finally, Captain Jimtee found himself forced to make a tough decision. One he was not at all happy about, but which circumstance had finally dictated.

"Ulus," he said to his right-hand man. "Bring me the regent. It is time we moved on to the next phase of our little endeavor."

"At once, sir," he replied, hurrying off to fetch the robed politician.

A few minutes later, the weary man was ushered into the command chamber of the Tslavar vessel. From the look of him, he had been napping, though somewhat fitfully judging by the red rimming his eyes.

"You called for me?" he asked, stifling a yawn to the best of his ability.

"Yes, Zinna. I need you to prepare the fleet to jum--I mean, *warp* to our ultimate destination."

"Ultimate destination?" the man echoed, confused. "But what do you mean, Jimtee? I thought we were hunting down this space creature for you."

"And that you are. But that is merely a beginning step in the plan. Now we are going to wield the might and glory of the Urok fleet in its full force. We will take these ships and recover the portal leading to my people from the sun of the enemy's system. Then we will show them the true glory of my fleet and will annihilate the defenses of Earth and its pathetic moon base."

The regent went paler than he already was. "Did you say you wish to invade a *planet*?"

"That I did. Once we recover the device which is the key to

joining forces with *my* fleet, then we shall show them what *true* power looks like," Jimtee replied with a wicked smile. "Not that your ships aren't impressive, Zinna. But compared to the might of our own, your vessels seem but mere toys."

The regent wisely kept his mouth shut, though the sheer confidence of the Tslavar captain certainly left him feeling ill at ease. The Urok fleet was a force to be reckoned with, and for this man to dismiss it so offhandedly made him wonder just what sort of leaders he truly served under.

Jimtee was buzzing with energy now that the decision to move ahead had finally been made. "Ulus has prepared the star map coordinates and had them distributed among the fleet. It will require a few warps this first time, but once the path is finally dialed in, we should be able to cover it in a single jump as needed in the future."

"But what are we to do once we arrive? And where are we going, for that matter?" Zinna asked.

"We are jumping--or as the Uroks say, 'warping'-- to the Earth's sun," Jimtee replied calmly.

"A sun?"

"Yes. And with your help, we shall retrieve what was lost."

Zinna didn't know exactly what he meant to do. It was all still confusing to him, this talk of portals and fleets coming from the sun. But with the collar around his neck, he knew better than to question the green man.

"Of course, Captain. I will inform the commanders of the fleet and have them prepare," Zinna said.

And less than an hour later, the entire Urok fleet warped away in unison, leaving the system silent in their absence.

"What the hell is that racket?" Donovan asked as he walked through Dark Side moon base's Hangar Three.

Alarms were blaring a cacophonous medley of sirens and klaxons, which echoed throughout the base.

"A massive fleet of unidentified craft has just exited warp near the sun," Sid informed him over comms. "I have already alerted Cal and the AI network," he added.

"Oh, shit! Are we under attack?" the pilot asked.

"It does not appear that way. At least, not yet. But they are definitely doing *something* near the sun, it would seem."

Given what had just recently happened with the motley band of magic-powered aliens fighting to save the Earth, they all had a pretty good idea what any hostile force would be doing so close to the resting place of the portal to another galaxy.

"Are they trying to retrieve it?"

"I am reading some very strange energy emissions from the area," Sid replied. "Yes, I believe that is what they are attempting to do, though I do not know how."

He was correct in that assessment. Jimtee had focused all of the considerable magic of his casters at the portal, trying to pull it free while the Urok ships used their beam weaponry to create small detonations within the molten plasma beneath it in an attempt to nudge the magical device out of its blazing home. So far, however, they had not been successful.

"How many are there?" Donovan asked as he raced for his AI ship.

"It is difficult to tell with all the interference so close to the sun," Sid replied. "But if I were to hazard a guess, I would estimate just shy of one hundred ships of varying sizes."

"That many?" the pilot gasped. "Okay, we need to get everyone in the air, pronto. Tell Cal to scramble whatever he's got and get them en route immediately. We'll join up with them on the way."

Meanwhile, Captain Jimtee observed the progress, or lack thereof, from his command chamber. The portal was simply too embedded to move, and while the beam weapons were exerting small force upon it, the amount would clearly be far too little to push it from the sun's grasp.

"Have them cease fire," the Tslavar leader said with a resigned sigh.

Regent Zinna relayed the command, which was then passed down the line until all firing had ceased.

"Captain Jimtee, it would seem this tactic requires a good deal more power than we have at our disposal."

"Yes, Ulus, I am aware," he grumbled.

Ulus paused, watching the gears turn in his captain's mind.

"What would you have us do, sir?" he finally asked.

Jimtee thought a long moment, then stood tall, cracking his neck as he readied for the next phase of his task. The backup plan.

"So be it," he sighed. "Prepare the fleet for an all-ship assault."

"Sir?"

He turned to his number one. "Now, my dear Ulus, we redirect our efforts. If we cannot retrieve the portal, and thus our fleet, then we shall conquer this world on our own with what we have at hand."

CHAPTER FIFTY-NINE

The sudden departure of not one but all of the Urok ships from the system had surprised Charlie and his friends. It also posed an interesting dilemma.

"Do we still backtrack to their launch point?" Dukaan asked. "Kip and I have narrowed it down to just a few options once the fleet launched. With that many signatures trailing back to the same sector at once, it only leaves a few options."

Charlie and Bawb shared a look as they picked up their helmets and prepared to depart. The brief respite on the habitable world was much needed and had given them an opportunity to question their captive. That is, it would have, if she had actually woken from the stun spell she'd been hit with. But now, with or without the information contained in her head, they both knew full well what had to be done.

"No, Dukaan, we don't follow the trail to their base, or planet, or wherever they launched from," Charlie said.

"Indeed," Bawb agreed. "Now that we know for certain this fleet is under Tslavar control, we must assume they are acting as an extension of the ship we are following."

Ara spread her wings as she prepared for what would be a

very long jump. "I have their scent quite clearly, as well as the energy traces of the other craft," she added. "It seems the entire fleet has departed with the shimmer ship as a single unit. And all to the same destination. Following them with this road map will be quite simple."

Charlie could sense it as well. Whatever had been growing inside him had only strengthened in the light of the system's sun. Part Zomoki power, part Ootaki, yet all human, he was something that had never before been seen in either galaxy.

"I smell it too," he said, searching for the right words to describe the sensation. "Like a bunch of similar aromas mingling together, but still distinct in their own way."

Ara looked at him and smiled. "Yes, that is rather similar to how I experience it as well. Very interesting, Charlie. You are growing much stronger, it seems."

"Yeah. Whatever that means. But listen, we need to pack up and get a move on. No telling where the hell those bastards are heading off to, but it can't be good."

"No, it cannot," the Zomoki agreed. "And it appears they have retraced their steps with this first jump," she added.

Charlie wasn't adept at determining celestial direction yet, the nascent ability only just making itself known to him. But if they were heading back the way they came, then there was one possibility that was very disconcerting.

"You don't think they're heading back to Earth, do you?" he asked.

"With a fleet of this size, it is entirely possible," Bawb said. "We've already seen the confusion they have attempted to sow with just their one shimmer ship. Possessing control of an entire fleet? I would be concerned, at the very least."

"Shit, we've gotta go," Charlie said, urgency in his movements as he readied for departure. "Dukaan, is our guest still securely bound in her seat?"

"Yes. And Kip and I are keeping close tabs on her."

"Okay, good. Then that's it. We follow them and see what we find. Be ready for an emergency warp just in case we arrive on top of them. But let's hope that's not needed."

With a fire lit, driving them to action, the team prepped and launched in just minutes, heading off on a chase that they feared might take them exactly where they wanted to be.

Back home.

Several jumps ahead of the pursuing Zomoki and her tagalong AI companion, the Urok fleet had already been broken up into multiple groups, each led by control-collared captains doing the bidding of their Tslavar master.

They didn't know it, but under most circumstances the collars would not function at distances greater than a very long line of sight. These collars, however, had been robustly bolstered with additional power as the Tslavar captain's plan took shape.

It had been a huge use of their main caster's magical reserves to do so, and had taken him days to recover his energy, but the result was worth the expenditure in Jimtee's eyes. The collars now had a far greater range. One that might not allow him to kill disobedient wearers outright if they were, say, on the opposite side of a planet. But enough to allow him to rule with a strong hand.

"Attack wings are prepared and weapons charged," Ulus informed his captain.

"Excellent. Have them spread into their respective assault formations and begin the attack," Jimtee said, watching the ships organize and arrange themselves into deadly clumps of large and small craft.

They were making a rapid approach, moving on quickly from their failed attempts at the sun's edge. They knew their presence had surely been noted––there was no way a fleet that size wouldn't be––so there was no use in attempting stealth.

Instead, they simply prepared to hammer the planet and its moon base with unrelenting force, subtlety be damned.

"We are growing near," Ulus reported. "The smaller wing is aligned for a direct assault on the moon facility, while the remaining vessels are prepared to strike with all of their might at all major cities and vessel landing facilities on all continents."

Jimtee couldn't help but smile. The destruction would be of a grand scale, and there was nothing the paltry terrestrial forces could do to stop them.

"Begin the assault," Jimtee said. "And instruct Commander Datano that--"

A massive blast rocked their ship, the magical shielding they had just ramped up in preparation of the hostilities the only thing keeping the shimmer craft from being severely damaged by the impact.

The Urok ships around them did not fare so well, and several of the smaller ones were destroyed outright in the fusillade, a few even crushed as the larger ones veered into them as they spun away in a panicked defensive maneuver.

"We are under attack!" Regent Zinna cried out in shock. "Who would dare attack the Urok fleet?"

His question went unanswered as another volley of pulse blasts and plasma bursts scattered the carefully positioned ships.

Closing in fast, Captain Harkaway watched the carnage from the bridge of the *Váli*, his massively retrofitted ship, as it continued blasting away with its new cannon array. The rest of the combined human and Chithiid fleet were zeroing in on the enemy right along with him, tearing into the invaders without mercy.

"Blow those fuckers to pieces, Reggie!"

"On it, Captain!" his pilot said, loosing another round on the enemy.

Aboard the Tslavar ship, the confusion was thick. "There

were no such forces at this planet!" Ulus blurted. "Where did all of these craft come from?"

Jimtee watched the unfolding scene with dispassionate eyes, quickly assessing his new options as the large--and deadly--conglomerate of ships ripped into his fleet, disrupting his carefully laid plans.

Comms chatter was thick, the confusion of battle hanging in the air, or lack thereof, as the battle raged on. Sid, being the closest of the massive AIs, directed much of the assault, using his satellite arrays as well as the spotter ships he'd deployed the moment the enemy craft had arrived at the sun to direct their forces.

Zed, the main AI command ship of the joined Earth forces, was likewise steering the craft under his command, his mighty processors seeing gaps in the enemy's formations at the speed only a supercomputer could.

In tandem, the two AIs were picking apart the invaders, keeping them from regrouping for a secondary attempt.

Captain Jimtee could read the writing on the wall. The tide had turned, and he was on his heels. Only the stubborn pride of the Urok captains kept them from turning tail and fleeing. The one benefit of their egos running the show.

"Use magic," Jimtee said to Ulus.

His number one glanced at the regent, then back at the captain, an eyebrow raised in query.

"Yes, I know he's here, but that no longer matters. All casters, engage now."

Ulus didn't hesitate any further, passing the command to the magic users immediately.

"Did you say magic?" the confused regent asked.

"Be silent and observe the true power of your new rulers," Jimtee replied.

The bravado with which he spoke was false bluster, however. A display put on for the benefit of the Urok should they make it out of this alive. Something he suddenly had the beginnings of a reason to doubt.

The Tslavar ship began hurling magical attacks into the oncoming Earth ships, the invisible barrage passing through many of their shields, sending the craft tumbling. Apparently, not all of them were properly prepared for this battle, Jimtee realized. And that meant, perhaps, he might still have a chance at victory.

And he was right about that one aspect of the engagement. The recently returned fleet had been hastily pulled from their survey missions when every available warp ship had been sent out to find and recall whoever they could as soon as the aliens attacked the planet.

Most had been relatively close to their original destination systems, and thus able to be tracked down, though quite a few of their vessels had moved on, surveying farther away, totally unable to be reached. Regardless, enough had come home to put up a significant defense of their planet.

They'd been invaded and nearly wiped out once before, and they were sure as hell not going to let that happen again. If it came down to it, they'd go down fighting.

CHAPTER SIXTY

Ara and Kip flashed out of their shared 'jump-warp' to find themselves in close proximity to the sun. Bawb and Charlie immediately cast shielding spells, while Kip ramped up his shields and pulled away to a safe distance.

Ara, on the other hand, reveled in the sun's rays, the energy rejuvenating her with its power. The Ootaki hair within Bawb's armored vest was likewise growing stronger by the minute, absorbing the magic flowing from the glowing orb.

Even Charlie felt the effects now, the combined magic within him somehow seizing upon the energy source and strengthening its hold on him, merging into every cell in his body.

"I can smell them clearly," he silently exclaimed as the distinct signature of the Tslavar ship coated with Ara's magic suddenly stood out like a glowing light in the dark. *"I can feel them. And the energy, it's all around us, ramping up, growing in intensity,"* he said, reveling in the sensation. *"The sun, it's making this power in me build, whatever it is."*

"I had wondered if it would do as much once we returned to this system," Ara replied. *"We already know how Hunze and I react to*

the power of your world's sun. And now it appears you are a part of that chain."

Charlie couldn't help but wonder what that would mean going forward. Would his abilities grow the longer he was within reach of the sun's rays? Earth was his home, so if that was the case, there was no telling how much power he might gain over time as he passed every day in its warming glow.

"I am glad you are strengthening, Charlie," Bawb said. *"For we are now called upon to protect our own. When we left, they were dealing with a single vessel on the surface, but now we know the enemy's true plans. They mean to subjugate those we care for. I will not allow that to happen."*

"Right there with ya Bob," Charlie replied. "Okay, guys," he said over comms. "You ready for this, Kip?"

"Yes indeedy," the quirky ship replied. "About time we get to have a little fun on our own terms."

"You do realize we're facing an entire enemy fleet, *plus* a shimmer-cloaked alien ship wielding magic, right?"

"Well, yeah," the AI replied. "But we're home. And our buddies are back," he said with a chipper tone to his voice. "This is home field advantage, right?"

"I suppose you're right," Charlie replied. He couldn't help but respect the quirky ship's enthusiasm and confidence. "So let's join up with the others. Fly in wide and stay out of sight as long as possible. They all seem pretty preoccupied with the madness going on down closer to Earth. If we can pull in from their blind side, maybe we can get lucky and land a shot on the Tslavar ship."

"But it will be cloaked," Dukaan noted.

"Maybe, but if I can smell the traces of Ara's magic still lingering on it, I know she can. Even invisible, we can target it. And when we do, you fire at the same location. Combined, we may be able to damage it enough to render it somewhat visible."

"And if that happens, the rest of the fleet can lock on as well," Kip stated.

"Exactly. Transmit the plan to the others. And let them know the enemy ships are under Tslavar control, but we don't know if any of them are actually fighting our forces willingly. For all we know, this may be a puppet fleet forced to do the Tslavars' bidding."

"Even so, they are just as deadly," Bawb noted.

"Yes, but if we can disable without destroying, then we should make an effort to do so."

"That would be appreciated," a groggy woman's voice said quietly.

Dukaan spun in his seat, fixing his gaze on their captive. Captain Pril, for her part, handled the sight of a four-armed, four-eyed, seven-foot-tall alien with surprising calm.

"You have awakened," the Chithiid said, the comms line still open.

"Yes, obviously," she replied. Her bound hands went to the collar around her neck.

"Do not fear, we have disabled the collar's abilities," Dukaan informed her.

The tension in Captain Pril's shoulders visibly released. "So, you possess the technology to counteract those green-skinned bastards' control devices?"

"It is magic, actually," Bawb said over comms.

The captain didn't seem surprised at the sudden appearance of the voice that had been listening in.

"Magic?" she said incredulously. "You expect me, a captain of the Urok fleet, to accept this was *magic*?"

"Trust me," Charlie interjected over the comms, "I had the same reaction at first, and you'll save yourself a lot of headache if you just accept it for what it is. Magic, power you can't understand from a distant galaxy, whatever it is. It's not tech, that's for sure. At least not like we're used to, so just call it magic, and save yourself a headache."

She considered his words a moment, then nodded slightly as she surveyed the interior of the ship in which she was confined. *It* was most definitely technology, though different than that of the Urok people. But advanced, clearly.

"So, you are familiar with this Captain Jimtee, I take it?" she asked.

"Oh, is that who's running the Tslavar ship?" Kip chimed in.

"Another voice," Pril replied. "How many are you out there?"

"Oh, I'm not out there. I'm Kip. You're on board my ship right now."

"Ah, the captain."

"No, the AI. I *am* the ship," he clarified. "Though I noted your culture doesn't seem to have artificial intelligence yet, so I guess that's gotta be kind of a head trip for you."

"You are the ship? You mean this craft has a consciousness?"

"Yep, that pretty much sums it up," Kip replied. "Anyway, nice to meet you, now that you're awake. We were all hoping you wouldn't be some warmongering asshole."

"Pardon our friend," Charlie said. "It's just that we've been attacked relentlessly since we stumbled upon your people, but once we discovered the control collars, we realized you were being used."

"But that does not necessarily preclude a hostile intent," Bawb added. "We are pleased with your demeanor. I am Bawb, by the way. With me are Charlie and Ara."

"And I am Dukaan," the Chithiid added. "You've already met Kip."

The captain sat up taller in her seat, bound as she was. "I am Captain Pril of the Urok armada."

"Welcome to the good guys, Captain," Charlie said. "Now, if you'd be so kind as to help us figure out how to stop all this fighting, we'd be ever so grateful."

CHAPTER SIXTY-ONE

Freed from her restraints, Captain Pril slid into the co-pilot's seat at Kip's command and control center. It was still rather disconcerting, having the ship itself chattering at her as it flew them toward her fleet and its control-collared friends and colleagues, but she was gradually getting used to the idea.

The idea was to get on the comms band she had specified so she could warn the others that many of their leaders had been compromised. It went against every fiber in her being to essentially call for mutiny, but given what had befallen her fellow captains, Pril believed it to be the only honorable course of action.

Unfortunately, she quickly learned that, despite her best efforts, the message simply would not go through.

"It's transmitting," Kip said, confused. "And I can see the signal has reached the fleet. So why aren't they responding?"

"I'm afraid I know why," Captain Pril replied. "I was worried this might happen. The invaders have taken control of the communications centers of the flagships to the fleet. It is through those hubs that all subsequent communications are filtered out to the rest of the ships."

"But if they've been compromised––" Charlie said.

"Then the message would never be allowed to circulate. My warning to my comrades will never make it past that firewall. Even with my verification and personal ident code, it seems these Tslavars have cut off our one means of warning the others."

Charlie thought on it a moment. "Hey, Kip? Do you think you could rig a burst transmission that could override the flagships if we moved in close enough?"

"I suppose so," he replied. "But we'd have to be pretty close. And it would only get through for an instant."

"An instant is all we'd need, if I'm not mistaken. Your ships all automatically record any transmissions, is that correct?" he asked Pril.

"Yes. That is standard operating procedure."

"So even a short message would be archived. Archived and ready for replay and subsequent transmission among the ships of the fleet, yes?"

She saw what he was getting at and had to admire the unusual tactic. "I think it might work," Pril replied. "But we will have to be much, much closer to achieve a powerful enough transmission to override the main feed."

"Leave that to me," Kip said, excited for the opportunity to do something interesting and more than a little daring.

Ara and Kip split up, the dragon taking point, the small ship following behind while she cleared a path for him to try to send the pirate signal to the Urok fleet. If they could just break through somehow, there was an actual chance the fighting might be stopped.

In the meantime, however, it was a space battle in full force, with pulse and beam weapons firing in all directions. The carnage was spectacular, but not nearly as much as it would have been if both sides' shielding systems hadn't been able to adjust to handle the opposing force's unusual weapons systems.

They were in the no man's land between the Earth and the moon, pushing closer toward the Urok ships as the fighting intensified all around them.

"Almost there," Kip informed them over comms. "Pril thinks we should be able to attempt the transmission in about--"

His words were cut off as a blast rocked him off course.

"Kip, are you okay?" Charlie called out.

"We are experiencing some technical issues from the impact," Dukaan replied with strain in his voice.

"Fly clear. We can regroup and try this again later. Protect yours--"

A new blast came through from one of the Urok ships, this time targeting Ara herself. And despite the magical shielding being cast by all three of them, Ara suffered a substantial blow.

Charlie and Bawb, connected to her by their shared bond as they were, both felt the impact shake their friend, injuring her. This wasn't just a little knock, she was actually hurt.

Without thought, and acting on pure instinct, Charlie felt the new energy within him rapidly swirl and increase in potency as his gut-level anger flared. He was carrying significant power within him when he merely shared the Zomoki's magic, but now, with the Ootaki power as well as the boost from their flight to the sun, he was supercharged with potential.

Not even forming a specific spell, Charlie lashed out on a primal level with his magic, emptying his reserves in one massive outpouring of energy, targeting the general direction of the ship that had hurt his friend.

The magic ripped through the vacuum, the Urok ship in its path catching the full force of it, tearing to shreds and bursting apart from the sheer magnitude and ferocity of the casting. The ships that had been in a loose formation with the craft quickly scattered, unsure what had just happened, but wanting no part in that particular fight.

The surge of power finally reduced to a trickle, and Charlie felt his head go light as he slumped over, exhausted.

"Get us out of here, Ara," Bawb urged his friend.

The Zomoki did not need to be told twice, and, thanks to the clear space created by Charlie's display, she managed to circumvent any further contact with the enemy as she raced painfully for Earth's welcoming surface.

Kip headed straight for Cal's new research facilities, guided in by the brilliant AI as soon as the duo broke atmosphere. Ara, however, had a different destination.

"Get me home, Ara," Bawb had said, the urgency clear in his tone. *"Get me to Hunze."*

He had very nearly lost her once before, his love having been frozen by a massive stasis spell. He was not going to allow such a thing to happen to her again, and there was simply no way another collar would be placed around her neck while he still drew breath.

Ara touched down roughly just outside of Bawb and Hunze's home, the Wampeh leaping to the ground and racing inside.

"He'll be fine," Charlie said as he slowly recovered his wits and energy under the Earth's golden sun. *"She's home. And she's fine."*

Ara raised a scaly eyebrow. *"You can sense this?"* she asked.

"Can't you?"

"Of course. But for you? This is something new. And so shortly after such a draining display of power, no less."

Charlie realized she was right. He'd been taking the new gift for granted. Something that was just a normal part of him.

"I hadn't even thought about it," he replied.

"No, obviously. But, Charlie, the power growing in you has taken on a new potency. One far greater than before."

"Yeah, tell me about it," he sighed, recalling his magical rage casting so recently.

"You need to build up to that sort of thing, Charlie. You could have hurt yourself drawing down your magic so fully and so quickly."

Charlie surveyed his own powers, trickling through his body, and realized she was right. He had tapped himself out, far beyond the levels of safe casting. It was only neophyte's luck and his link with Ara that had kept him from severely crippling himself.

He'd take it slower from now on.

Then he sensed something else. His bond with the Zomoki told him something else.

"You're hurt."

"I will be fine, Charlie," she said. *"I just need a little rest."*

Charlie thought it might be a little more than that. *"Get me home, Ara. I've got something for you."*

CHAPTER SIXTY-TWO

Leila was already waiting outside their home when Ara touched down. Her heart surged with heat and relief when she saw Charlie climb down from their friend's back. He was hurt, but he was alive.

"Let me help you," she said, rushing to his side as he stepped free.

The banged-up man was not about to decline the assistance, but first there was something he needed to do. He pulled Leila in close, hugging her with a ferocity of emotion repaid in kind by his olive-skinned queen.

"Missed you, babe," he muttered into her hair, his face buried in her scent.

"Missed you too," she replied, her stress melting in the warmth of his arms.

Charlie felt a twinge at the edges of his power, the sensation reminding him of his other task. "Give me a hand, will ya? I need to get something out of the vault." He turned to his Zomoki friend. "Wait here a minute, I'll be right back."

Ara was glad to comply, lying down and spreading her wings

wide, absorbing as much of the sun's energy as she could on the cloudless day.

"What the hell's going on up there?" Leila asked as she helped Charlie rush through their home to the rocks and boulders of their little Zen garden out back.

It was the one touch Charlie had added to the estate when they'd settled in, a little homage and remembrance of Ser Baruud and his teachings.

"Tslavars," he replied. "The invaders are Tslavars."

"Yeah, we know."

This got his attention. "Is everyone okay?"

"Yeah. We had to leave Rika behind while we brought samples of the magic-harnessing plants we found, but she was okay when we left her with the Kalamani."

"The what, now?"

Leila allowed herself a little smile. For once, she was the one with the surprise. "First contact, Charlie. We chased the Tslavars when they jumped away and found a new species out there. Primitive, but the sun in their system is powerful, and the plant life absorbs the energy. Their spears and arrows actually pierced the Tslavars' defenses."

"Holy shit," he said with a little smile. "Taken down a notch with sticks and stones? That must've messed with their heads."

"I'm sure it did. But what about you? There's something huge going on up there. Cal said there was a full-on battle taking place, and against an advanced fleet. Tech users, not magic," she added.

"Yeah, about that," Charlie said. "You're not the only ones to make first contact."

"You're kidding."

"Wish I was. But the Tslavars found them first."

"So they're allied with them now?"

"No, it's far more complicated than that," he replied. "If they'd just joined forces, we could blast them indiscriminately.

But we captured one of their ships, and you'll never guess what we found."

"Control collars," Leila said. "They're using control collars."

"Well, shit. I guess you *will* guess," he said.

"It seemed obvious from what you'd said," she replied. "You made it sound like they were unwilling allies. That could only mean one thing."

"Yeah. We tried to contact the members of their fleet who aren't under Tslavar control, but they managed to block all comms, and damn near took out Ara in the process," Charlie said. "Which brings us to this," he added, turning his attention back to his rock garden.

Charlie reached for his magic, the power deep within him slowly flowing back through his body as the movement spell took hold of the largest boulder and began shifting it. The mass flopped back to the ground after lifting only a few inches.

"Shit. I'm still drained, babe."

Leila was shocked seeing him so weak. Whatever they'd gotten themselves into up above, it must have been something far more substantial than she'd originally guessed. She slipped the konus from her wrist and handed it to him.

"Here. You're better with it than I am."

He accepted the loan, sliding the band onto his wrist and drawing on its stored power, quickly casting his spell. The several-ton rock lifted and moved, revealing a solid ceramisteel door, warded with a dozen trap spells to prevent nosy visitors from accessing the trove within.

Charlie took off the konus and handed it back to his queen. "Thanks," he said. "I can disarm the rest without it."

He did so, quickly climbing down into the small panic room-sized chamber to retrieve not only a few choice weapons to bolster his diminished magic, but also the last bottle of his most precious possession.

"The Balamar waters?" Leila asked as he climbed to the surface, the thick container in hand.

"Ara's hurt," he said. "And we simply can't afford to wait for her to heal up normally. Even with the sun's help, it'll take too long, and we need her at full strength."

Leila took his arm and fixed her gaze on him, concern etched on her face. "Then you take some too," she said.

It was not a suggestion.

Charlie knew better than to argue by now, merely nodding and opening the bottle, taking his first sip of the magical healing water in a long, long time.

The rush of energy felt like quicksilver flowing through his veins, his magic bolstering and starting to roar back to life with a visceral jolt. To have such a reaction to the waters, now that he had the additional magic within him, was a bit shocking. But, then, he was the first human-Zomoki-Ootaki-powered hybrid ever, so anything was possible, he guessed. He still wasn't anywhere near back to one hundred percent yet, but he was improving rapidly.

"Ara, I have something for you," he said as he and Leila emerged from their home.

His enormous friend fixed one of her golden eyes upon them, but didn't get up.

"What have you brought, Charlie?"

"Say 'aaaah,'" he replied.

She saw what he was carrying, the scent of the water crisp in her senses as soon as he opened the container.

"But this is the last of it," she said.

"It is," Leila agreed, "but you need it, and what's the good in having an emergency stash if you don't use it in an actual emergency?"

Leila was right, and Ara knew she was going to be double-teamed by the stubborn couple. There was no way she'd convince her friends to change their minds, so Ara simply nodded and opened her mouth, allowing Charlie to lean inside and pour out the last of the jug onto her tongue.

It was by no means a massive, life-altering amount like she'd ingested so many years ago on the Balamar Wastelands, but even this relatively small drink of the waters immediately set her body healing, her powers spiking along with her flesh as both were bolstered by the magical fluid.

The waters did their work, and fast, and Ara's scales had already taken on a greater luster just moments later as she rose to her feet, ready for battle.

"Lookin' good, Ara," Charlie said appreciatively.

"Feeling good, Charlie," she replied with a smile. "Now, we should join up with Kip and Dukaan and go over what insights our new Urok ally has been providing them in our absence."

"And Bawb?" Leila asked.

"Let them have a moment's respite," Charlie said. "He was really worried about her."

"After what happened last time, it's understandable," she replied.

"Exactly. We'll take care of this with Cal and just have Ripley give them a lift to join us when they're ready. Sound good?"

Leila nodded her agreement, as did Ara.

"Okay, then. Let's see what intel our Urok friend has for us."

CHAPTER SIXTY-THREE

The deadliest assassin in more than thirty systems sat quietly with Hunze on the grass overlooking the Pacific Ocean. They stared at the beauty of the coast's unique brand of nature tranquilly, his arms wrapped around his golden-haired love, holding her close as they reveled in each other's presence, comforted in the simple act of doing nothing but being.

Bawb had been incredibly concerned for her well-being the entirety of their time away, though he hid it well. But now, knowing she was safe and under his protection, he felt the little knot of worry he'd been carrying since their separation dissolve.

But he knew it would return when he left her alone again. And there was no doubt in his mind he would have to do just that when they went into battle once more. He would not be able to be present to protect her, and that was simply not acceptable to him. Not this time.

Bawb loosed his arms and gently took Hunze's face in his hands, looking deep into her eyes. He had a plan. A crazy, mad, but inspired plan. One that he didn't even know would work, but he had to at least try.

"You know what we are facing," he said, his concern palpable in his voice.

"Tslavars," she replied. "Yes, I know, love."

"I will not allow them to harm you, Hunze," he said, emotion burning in his eyes. "I will not allow you to be a slave again."

"I know you will do all you can, Bawb," she replied, softly caressing his cheek.

He shivered at her touch, emotions welling up. With that, any doubts melted away.

"Do you trust me?" he asked, taking her hands in his.

"With all that I am," she replied. "But what is troubling you? You're trembling."

The deadly assassin quickly regained control of his emotions, focusing hard as he knew he must. This was not going to be easy by any means, and he would be stretching his knowledge and abilities to the very limits and still might fail in his attempt.

"I've been thinking long and hard," he finally said, putting thoughts into words. "I want for you to do something for me, Hunze," he said, pulling out a small, wicked-sharp blade from its hidden sheath.

"Anything," she replied without hesitation. She felt no fear. Bawb would not hurt her. Not now. Not ever.

He looked at her long and hard, taking in her fine features, the lines of her cheekbones and eyebrows, the way they framed her expressive eyes. And her hair. The massive length of golden, magically charged hair.

He took a breath. This was it. What he had been preparing for.

"Hunze, I want you to give me all of your hair," he said.

Hunze, so long used as a mere magic-storing vessel, did not flinch, nor did she show any sign of doubt.

"It is yours, my love. All of it. Freely given to you and you alone, and out of love," she said, the act and intent behind it rendering her locks forever bound to Bawb, their magic supercharged by her selfless act of giving.

She felt a little weak for a moment as the link was made and the control of all of that hair atop her head transferred. There was just one thing left to do now, and she willingly leaned in close, ready for him to do the deed.

Bawb raised the knife, the sun glinting off of the razor-sharp blade. But rather than reaching out and shearing the locks from her head, he instead pressed the blade to his palm, the knife's edge so sharp he barely felt it separate his flesh.

Blood flowed, but he ignored that, taking Hunze's hand in his and repeating the act, cutting her palm as he had his own, swearing to himself that it would be the only act of harm he would ever inflict upon her.

Through it all, Hunze did not hesitate, trusting him completely as he pressed his palm to hers, wrapping their hands with the end of the length of magical hair growing from atop her head.

With all of his might, he focused, channeling the incredible amount of power now in his possession, using it to bolster the ancient, arcane spell he had never thought he would ever use.

It was old. Powerful. Something stumbled upon in the dustiest of spell books within the archives of the Wampeh Ghalian in his early days of training. Memorized more out of novelty than any thought of actually attempting the deadly spell, for just one misstep could prove fatal for both parties involved.

But today would not be the day that happened. He had prepared as thoroughly as any from either galaxy could, even using the neuro-stim--with Cal's assistance--to ensure his recall of the spell was perfect.

Beads of sweat formed on his brow as he leaned forward, pressing his forehead against Hunze's, his hand squeezing hers tightly as their blood mingled, and with it, the spell that was worming its way into both of their cores, doing the bidding of the Wampeh, superpowered by the Ootaki hair.

There was no guarantee it would work, but with Hunze's locks bolstering the spell to unheard-of levels, this was as good a chance as any ever had or would have of success. Certainly more than those few who had attempted the feat in the thousands of years since the spell was first committed to the dry parchment of the ancient assassin order's records.

A surge of magic swirled around the pair, a burning heat flaming within their tightly clasped hands. Then, with a flash of golden power, they separated, both falling to the ground, unconscious.

How long they would stay that way was anyone's guess, but both still lived, and as they lay there, the bleeding wounds on their hands slowly staunched their flow. All that remained now was time and waiting.

But how long that might be no one had known for thousands of years.

CHAPTER SIXTY-FOUR

Captain Jimtee was changing his attack plans on the fly, his orders no longer relayed through Regent Zinna but barked by the Tslavar captain himself. Whomever among the Urok fleet questioned this strange voice issuing commands said nothing. Their superiors were following them as though they were spoken from the chancellor himself, so who were they to ask why?

"Ulus, the Zomoki. Did you see where it went?" Captain Jimtee asked of his right hand.

"Not exactly, Captain, but one of the Urok ships did manage to land a blow to it. The Urok ship, however, was utterly destroyed by a very powerful spell unlike any I've ever encountered."

"Yes, the violence of the magic was exceptional," Jimtee agreed.

"Likely cast in panic by the beast, as I believe it was injured in the exchange."

"A Zomoki carelessly expending its magic? This may be our opportunity, Ulus."

"I agree, Captain. We tracked its path to the surface, and if we pursue it immediately, we may still take it while it is recovering from the event."

Jimtee thought on it a moment. The battle was here, in space, but Ulus had a very sound point. This might be the best chance they'd ever have to catch the beast while it was vulnerable. Opportunity favored those who grasped it, and Jimtee was not about to let this slip through his fingers.

"Plot the course," he said. "We take the Zomoki."

The Tslavar ship, visible to the Urok fleet all this time, engaged their shimmer cloak, suddenly disappearing in front of the flagships they controlled. That simple display of power served twofold. One, it allowed them to begin their pursuit in earnest. Two, it revealed to the commanders of the fleet under their control just how powerful their new masters truly were. Obedience was all but assured at that point.

The invisible craft evaded a cluster of Earth's defensive ships, then dove through the atmosphere, making a straight shot for the coast of Malibu, where the Zomoki had been headed.

Ara had already departed the sleepy beach community, ferrying her friends downtown to meet with Cal and their new Urok ally, now that her control collar had been effectively muted. But Captain Jimtee and his crew were unaware of that, and thus headed right for the colony on the Pacific.

The main caster aboard Jimtee's craft became increasingly agitated as they neared the ground, until her discomfiture finally distracted the captain from his primary goal.

"What in the seven hells has you so worked up, Amarzan?" he asked the caster, an annoyed look in his eye.

"It's the power," the shocked woman replied.

"Yes, it is a powerful Zomoki," Jimtee replied. "But steel your nerves. It is injured, and we are approaching under cover of shimmer."

"No, it's not the Zomoki," she said. "The beast is not here. I sense it departed not long ago at all."

This was news to Jimtee. Very vexing news, at that. "Then what has you so worked up?" he growled, frustration growing.

"It is something else," she said. "Something possibly even more powerful."

"More powerful than the Zomoki that just obliterated an entire ship?" he asked incredulously. "What could possibly possess such magic?"

"Ootaki," Amarzan said, closing her eyes and reaching out with her senses. "It is an Ootaki, Captain. And such a powerful one the likes of which I've never felt."

Jimtee's eyes went wide with shock, but this time of the pleasant variety. If there was truly an Ootaki nearby, he could claim their power and bolster their magic, allowing them to finally recover the portal and bring their entire fleet to conquer this odious galaxy.

"How far?" he asked her.

"Close. Very close. Just below, in fact," she said, staring at the image of the domiciles dotting the bluffs hanging in the air in front of her. "There!" she exclaimed, pointing at the grassy area overlooking the sea, where it seemed a man and woman lay unconscious.

"It could be a trap," Ulus cautioned.

"I am aware of that," Jimtee replied, sliding his most powerful slaap onto his hand. "Take us in."

The cloaked ship touched down silently near the estate, the shimmer-cloaked crew fanning out in a defensive formation while Jimtee led his personal attack squad to recover the Ootaki.

Her hair was visibly glowing even from a distance, he realized as they drew near. There was blood, though. Some of it smeared on her clothing, some on the man at her side. It appeared some sort of violence had taken place between them, but the Ootaki still breathed, and that was all that mattered.

Quickly, Jimtee hoisted the unconscious woman over his shoulder, ignoring the wounded man lying facedown on the ground. He had what he came for, and even a non-powered man like he could still feel the magic this lone Ootaki possessed in her hair. She was a prize the likes of which he'd never expected to stumble upon, and yet, here she was. The key to recovering the portal.

A visceral tug of their connected energy roused Bawb from his stupor long enough to see Hunze's unconscious form being carried off by an invisible abductor. Anger and grief flashed through him, giving his weakened limbs the power to function, albeit in a limited capacity.

Bawb lurched to his feet, attempting to pursue the invisible quarry, when they vanished from sight entirely, having entered their shimmer-cloaked ship and sealed the door. He didn't so much see the ship lift off and fly away as feel it, crying out in rage as it did, unable to stop them from taking his love.

And as the ship gained altitude, deep within its belly Captain Jimtee did something he was confident would change the course of the entire invasion. He fastened a golden control collar around Hunze's slender neck.

CHAPTER SIXTY-FIVE

The battle ebbed and flowed, the advantage shifting sides repeatedly as the rhythm of combat favored both opposing forces on a whim like a fickle lover.

Once the Uroks had overcome the initial shock of the Earth fleet's startling attack, their forces regrouped, and their tactics solidified into a more normal representation of the tactics and skill they were so proud of.

Earth's AI craft and their human and Chithiid wingmen may have lost the initial overwhelming advantage of the early minutes of the battle, but that was to be expected in any battle. They too settled into a more regimented fight, matching the strange new invaders' shot for shot.

But while the space battle was continuing, a deadly shimmer ship and its dozens of cloaked troops was speeding toward the nearest city hub, dropping its ground troops to engage the Zomoki it had tracked there, distracting it and keeping it occupied while their leader prepared to take his new prize of an actual Ootaki out to space. Out to the sun.

Jimtee would complete his task, and once his full fleet passed through the portal, there would be no stopping them.

A dozen Urok ships had also joined the fight on the surface, called in by Captain Jimtee. They beelined to join the Tslavar ship, engaging the fierce space beast before it had the opportunity to recover. Little did they realize, however, their prey was not so hurt as they thought, and they'd be in for far more of a fight than anticipated.

A strange new reading flashed onto Sid's distant sensors in the midst of all of the chaos. Something had arrived, and it was heading straight for the sun. One of the Urok ships immediately peeled off from the battle to join it.

More disconcerting, it appeared it was exerting force on the portal tucked away within. It was slow progress, but it was moving it bit by bit.

"I have a new reading," the AI informed Cal and the others. "There's something new here. Something just arrived at the sun, and it seems to be pulling on the portal tucked away there."

Charlie and Leila shared a look. They knew what that meant.

"The other Tslavar ship," Charlie groaned. "It's back. Dammit, I knew Murphy would go and stick his fingers in things."

"I can go after it," Kip chimed in over comms. "Dookie and me, we're pretty much done here. Cal's got all he needs from us."

"That I do," Cal said. ***"And Captain Pril is providing a great deal of information about the strengths and weaknesses of the Urok fleet,"*** he added. ***"We are attempting to devise a means to disable their vessels without too many fatalities, though it is difficult, to say the least."***

"Admirable, Cal, but not entirely practical in the heat of battle," Charlie said. "And nothing personal, Kip, but you know by now that you don't have the firepower to take on one of those Tslavar ships. We need magic to fight magic."

"Well, I can go after the Urok ships, though."

"Yeah, but I think we can really use your skills to keep these bastards from making landfall."

"I guess," Kip grumbled, a little bummed at not getting to join them in the big fight far above.

But Charlie was right, and he knew it. Magic was needed to fight magic, and while he may have had a konus merged with his frame, providing defense from many magical attacks, he was no match for a fully powered Tslavar ship.

"Ripley is at home," Leila said. "She and Eddie can pick up Bawb and Hunze and meet us here. Shouldn't take more than a few minutes."

"Great," Charlie said. "Call them and get them here ASAP. We've gotta hurry. They're up to something."

Leila had just sent the transmission when the building shook. Moments later the sound of auto-cannon fire erupted outside.

"What was that, Cal?" Leila asked.

"We appear to be targeted by an invisible adversary," he replied.

"Ara, do you smell them?" Charlie asked, reaching out for his Zomoki friend.

"Faint, but yes," she replied. *"However, it seems they have deployed the entirety of their ground forces, including some powerful casters, judging by the level of spells being deployed. Quite a startling tactic, actually, and all are shimmer-cloaked. Worse yet, they are swarming the streets, converging on your location."*

"Can you target them?"

"It's difficult. The ship I can sense, but it has taken off, heading up to join the fight in space, I assume. But these shimmer-cloaked Tslavars are tearing through the ground defenses, and a few Urok ships are now adding their forces to the mix."

Charlie knew it was a decision his friend didn't want to have to make, but the fleet above would have to hold their own for the time being. Cal needed magical defense at the moment, and though they could try, with the other ship's casters deployed on Earth, it didn't seem the newcomer ship at the sun would be getting any help to retrieve the portal anytime soon.

"Okay, everyone, Ara's engaging the cloaked forces outside. Cal, pull your people back and have them lay down suppressing fire. They can't see the Tslavars, but they can target the Uroks. Have them slow them all down."

"I've adjusted my scans to read heat signatures from the cloaked soldiers' footsteps," Cal said, ***"but the sun has heated the pavement to a degree that is making it near impossible to track them."***

"Shit. Well, it was a good idea, anyway," Charlie said, rushing toward the doors to join the fight. "Leila, the Uroks don't have magical shielding against pulse weapons. Grab a pulse rifle and take up an elevated position."

"But do try to wound them rather than kill, if you can," Cal added. ***"The Tslavars, however, show no mercy."***

Leila nodded once, then took off at a run, grabbing up as many pulse packs as she could carry then racing upstairs to aid in the facility's defense. Charlie followed a moment later.

Soon, Eddie would arrive with his Wampeh friend, and between the three of them, he was confident they could hold off the invisible attackers. There were a lot, no doubt, but they'd faced worse odds before and prevailed. Charlie allowed himself a momentary flash of confidence.

A mistake that was soon made apparent.

CHAPTER SIXTY-SIX

"What do you mean there are more of them?" Charlie shouted out over the din of the raging battle. "There were only a few dozen, Ara said so!"

"She appears to have been mistaken," Cal said. ***"Though I believe one of the Urok ships that touched down nearby was the same craft that recently met up with the Tslavar ship orbiting the sun."***

"Shit. You hear that, Ara?"

"Yes. They added to the ground forces. Something big is afoot for them to throw all of their men at Cal like this. And this is an entirely different ship's contingent. I have no way of knowing how many additional cloaked Tslavars have joined the battle."

This was bad. *Really* bad. They were already outnumbered in terms of magic users, but now the degree to which that held true had gone up significantly, and they had no idea by how much. And where the hell was Bawb?

Charlie scanned the sky for the familiar shape of Eddie, but the oddball ship was nowhere to be seen.

"Incoming," Eddie called out, unleashing a salvo of pulse

cannon blasts, the weapons fire appearing out of thin air. Moments later the ground rumbled slightly as an invisible ship touched down nearby.

"What the hell?" Charlie blurted as Ripley and Bawb stepped out from the invisible craft.

"Bawb's work," Ripley said, nodding to the shimmer-cloaked ship. "With an upgrade, courtesy of Hunze," she added.

Charlie was impressed. To have their own shimmer ship was a huge game changer. Then he saw the look on Bawb's face.

"Where is she?" Charlie asked. "What happened?"

"They took her," Bawb growled, his crackling anger almost tangible in the air.

Charlie could only imagine how his friend was feeling. He'd sworn to keep her from becoming a slave ever again, and it seemed he had failed despite his best efforts. The Geist was beside himself, and heaven help the people who had made him so.

Magic blasts impacted Eddie's shielding, but his magic-reinforced protective layers withstood the attack. His shimmer, however, flickered a moment, making him a visible target.

"Get out of here, Eddie!" Ripley shouted. "They can see you!"

The ship lurched into the air, narrowly avoiding a massive spell cast by a cloaked caster. One far more powerful than an ordinary foot soldier could manage.

"They are intensifying the attack," Ara said. *"And they have deployed particularly strong casters."*

"Yeah, we noticed," Charlie replied. *"We're pinned down here. Any idea how many?"*

"No way to tell, but it is requiring all of my efforts to keep these attacks from taking out Cal's research facility."

The Tslavars had effectively removed one of their most powerful pieces from the board, confining the mighty Zomoki to defensive duty on the ground while the battle raged on above.

And worse than that, it looked like they might eventually break through. Keeping them in check was simply not feasible with so many invisible attackers.

"Leila, can you clear us a path out of here? We're pinned down," Charlie said.

"I don't know. The Uroks I can target, but there are too many Tslavars out there. I can't see them to shoot at them."

Charlie looked around, wondering if it was safe enough for Ara to perhaps fly a diversion to give them a window in which to move.

"Another cloaked ship has just torn through the engagement," Sid called down over their comms. "It took out three of my smaller ships on its way."

"Where's it heading, Sid?" Charlie replied as he cast a broad stun spell, hitting none of the cloaked attackers.

"By the path of its destruction, it seems to be heading to join the other craft at the sun," Sid replied.

Bawb looked at Charlie with both rage and understanding in his eyes. "They are attempting to retrieve the portal," he said. "And with Hunze's hair, I fear they will succeed."

"We've got to get up there," his friend replied. "Eddie, can you touch down near us without being seen? We need to stop those ships, and with your shimmer working, you just might be the advantage we need."

"Affirmative," the AI replied. "I'll try to work my way to you, but between the beam weapons and the magic, it's thick as hell down there."

A loud boom rocked the air from high above as a bright orange shape came hurtling toward the ground, growing larger by the second.

"What the hell is that?" Charlie asked, staring skyward.

"It appears to be one of our ships," Cal replied. ***"Though how it is withstanding such a reentry, I have no idea."***

Cal was right, the ship should have been torn to pieces, but somehow it was not.

Ripley hit the deck as a magic blast chipped the wall beside her, a tiny fragment of stone opening a little cut on her chin.

"Rip, are you okay?" Charlie called out to her.

"Fine. Just a nick," she replied. "But these guys are really starting to piss me off."

"Tell me about it," he replied.

Bawb remained silent, casting his deadliest spells with slow precision. The Uroks may have been unwitting adversaries, but in this moment, he simply did not care. To stand against him was to die, plain and simple.

The orange glow above was shrieking toward them at far too great a speed to safely land, Charlie realized. The shockwave of its impact was going to be massive.

"Get to cover!" he called out to the others as he watched the plummeting ship hurtle toward them.

But then something unexpected happened. The ship abruptly decelerated. Decelerated in a way that defied the laws of physics.

"Is that the *Fujin*?" Ripley asked, her eyes wide at the orange-glowing ship's impossible arrival.

"It is," Charlie said as he watched it settle onto the ground.

Magic and beam weapons assailed the little ship, but they seemed unable to find means to damage the craft as its hatch slid open.

Rika stepped out onto the familiar soil of her homeworld, but the woman who had come home was clearly not the one who had left so recently.

"What the..." Charlie gasped. "Rika?"

"Hey, Charlie," she replied, spinning and casting a flurry of disabling spells with a wave of the hand at the end of her newly tattooed wrist, the lines tracing up into her sleeve.

The ink, Charlie noted, was white. Almost translucent.

And it was glowing.

"You didn't think you'd get all the fun, did you?" she asked with an amused smirk.

A powerful magic attack bounced from her defensive spells, but the force nevertheless forced her feet to slide a few feet across the gritty ground.

She spun, and for a split second, Charlie noticed what seemed to be faint, glowing lines inked around her eyes. She raised her pulse rifle and fired off three quick shots, each of them leaving a smear of screaming green Tslavar as they flew true.

"What the hell?" Charlie gawked.

"I'll tell ya later," she said with a grin. "If we survive this, that is."

With that, Rika ran straight into the thick of the battle, the energy crackling along the pale lines peeking out from beneath her clothes. She was casting, and the spells were familiar. But the magic felt odd. Different. Charlie could clearly sense it, but it was unlike any he'd ever encountered before.

"Ara, what is she?"

"I don't know, Charlie. But whatever has happened to her, this is the window you need," she replied. *"Bawb, I know you're hurting, but you and Charlie must get to the sun and stop the Tslavars. This is your chance."*

"You're not coming?"

"I am best equipped to help defend here. But Eddie now possesses a shimmer cloak. Use it to your advantage, and stop them from recovering the portal."

"Eddie, we need you here, *now!*" Charlie barked over comms. "Rika, give us some cover, will ya?"

His friend threw him an amused, glowing grin. "With pleasure," she replied, then upped her game, tearing into the startled Tslavar troops, who suddenly learned they were not so invisible after all. Not to this strange woman with the massive power crackling through her glowing body.

It wasn't a fair fight, the one woman against dozens.

The poor men didn't stand a chance.

CHAPTER SIXTY-SEVEN

Charlie, Bawb, and Ripley were off and blasting into space in an instant, racing toward the pair of Tslavar ships parked near the sun. They were forced to engage several ships as they pulled out of the atmosphere, and as they were in the thick of battle, they were unable to simply effect a short warp to the sun.

They would have to work their way through the fighting until they had a clear shot and could plot the minuscule warp. It was really too close to even attempt in all but the most desperate circumstances, but on this particular day time was of the essence, and every minute could count.

Swooping in to gather them, Eddie had managed to recover his full shimmer functionality just in time to hit the ground near his friends. That was one twist of luck that had finally gone in their favor.

It didn't hurt that the Tslavar forces were *very* preoccupied at that moment, the deadly, glowing woman ripping into their ranks putting quite a damper on their plans.

Combined with the Zomoki that was now able to target the wounded, their blood giving away their location despite their camouflage, the Tslavars found themselves quite unexpectedly on their heels and forced to fall back.

The Urok forces fighting alongside them had been engaging on their leaders' orders, unaware of the invisible soldiers all around them. Seeing the bleeding green men suddenly appear out of thin air on all sides as Rika tore through them caused a reaction unfamiliar to the Urok troops. It made them pause with doubt.

"Sir, we are engaging the red beast as ordered, but there are what appear to be those alien trader people here as well," the leader of the Urok ground teams reported, the sweat of battle beading on his orange skin. "And they are showing up out of nowhere. I mean *literally*, sir."

"Continue your mission," the captain replied, touching his control collar absentmindedly as he directed the ground forces from his low-orbiting ship. "This does not change your objective."

"But, sir, this is not normal," the Urok replied. "And there is a woman fighting alongside the beast."

"A woman?"

"Yes, sir. And, sir, she appears to be *glowing*."

Commander Datano heard the exchange from his flagship, where he kept tabs on all aspects of the engagement underway. This enemy was not what he'd expected. Not only did they seem to be a highly advanced civilization, possibly even more developed than his own, but they apparently possessed some form of power similar to the Tslavar bastards who had subjugated their leaders and seized control of the fleet.

And on top of that, what had originally been described as a mindless, raging beast, now appeared to actually be a sentient creature of great capabilities. One that was allied with this strange race, fighting alongside them, protecting them from the invaders. Not at all what he'd been led to believe was the case.

But, then, most of what he'd originally heard from the

treacherous Jimtee was either a misdirection or outright falsehood.

Datano clenched his jaw in frustration. This was precisely the sort of first contact he had long dreamt of as he ventured out across the galaxy, always hoping to be the one to discover an advanced alien intelligence worthy of an alliance. And now, here they were, served up on a silver platter.

And his forces were fighting on the wrong side.

He cast a glance at Tomak, his right-hand man likewise in servitude, a flash of his golden collar peering out from within his uniform. Tomak shared the same goals as his commander, and one look spoke volumes. They were fighting an unjustified conflict, and the sheer magnitude of the carnage spreading out before them as ships were torn apart, their crews vented into the void of space made their hearts ache.

They were military men, their lives dedicated to the glory and advancement of the Urok people, but they were also men of honor. What was happening right now was anything but honorable, and their blindly following men were paying the ultimate price.

Commander Datano stood tall, casually walking across his command bridge to his number one, surveying the goings-on of all the comms and command crew as he did.

"Tomak, a word," he said, ushering his long-serving friend aside.

"Yes, Commander?"

"You have always been a good man, Tomak. You have served *the Urok people* well. And you will make a great commander, should the *opportunity* present itself."

"Sir?" Tomak replied, a bit confused.

"But one can *do good* in subtle ways as well, you know," Datano added. "Not everything is an overt action. And a wise man, one *bound* for great things, knows the difference," he said, touching his collar lightly for emphasis.

Tomak realized what his commander was saying, locking eyes with a gaze of deep respect and years of friendship. "I will make you proud, sir," he said.

"Of that I have no doubt," Datano replied.

The Urok commander then walked to the chief communications officer's station. There were no Tslavars aboard his ship, but they were close enough, and they were listening. Of that he was certain.

"Yakana, you have had a long shift. Take a moment to refresh yourself," he said, resting his hand on the woman's shoulder.

She too wore a control collar, the pain it could inflict still fresh in her mind. She looked at her commander with uncertainty. His normally hard eyes softened just slightly as he gave her a little nod.

Comms Officer Yakana slowly rose from her seat and walked from the room, the commander taking her place at the console.

Commander Datano's fingers stroked the golden collar affixed around his neck as he stared at the control screen in front of him.

"Fuck it," he growled, his decision made. He quickly switched all frequencies to override, opening a channel to every single ship in their fleet.

"This is Commander Datano," he broadcast. "The Tslavar enemies have invisibility camouflage and have taken control of our flagships, their crews forced to do their bidding. They may be aboard your very ship without you knowing. This is not a justified attack on this world. The Tslavars are our true enemies. Cease your attacks on this world's forces if you are able. Form an alliance for the glory of the Urok people. If you are bound by a control collar, then do what you can to hinder the—"

The distance between their location and the Tslavar ship had caused a slight communications delay. That, and Jimtee's preoccupation with his current task, gave Datano enough time to at least get part of his final message out before the collar around his neck was activated.

The commander cried out in agony, his shriek echoing out across the open channel, then dropped to the deck, dead.

But as he had hoped, his death would not be in vain, and many men and women of both worlds would live another day for his sacrifice.

CHAPTER SIXTY-EIGHT

The utter chaos caused by Commander Datano's final act spread through the fleet like wildfire. Every ship's crew now looked to their leadership, the strange collars many of them wore suddenly making sense.

Something had been wrong. They just didn't think to question beyond their rank. But now, thanks to the commander's sacrifice, the secret was known to all, as was the consequence of disobedience. The resulting standoffs aboard many command centers between free crew and controlled were varied.

Some were violent, the compromised leaders taken down with malice by infuriated crew whose friends and loved ones were dying in this illegal war, while others were merely restrained, their subordinates simply binding them, watching to see if they'd be struck down as Commander Datano had been.

Aboard Datano's flagship, Tomak quickly sent a pulsed message to the other ships. It was a risk, but Datano had given his life willingly to save the lives of thousands, and it would be a disservice to his memory to not at least try, risks be damned.

It was an old system. *Very* old, and only used when conventional communications were damaged beyond use. Or, in this instance, when they were compromised, rendering the transmission of messages in the clear impractical.

The series of tones flashed out to all of the ships in the fleet. A single message, compressed in one blast. Tomak just hoped the comms operators would catch it and relay the message subtly, in case of hidden eyes residing aboard their ships.

The message was a simple one. One that Tomak hoped would save all of their lives, while putting an end to the hostilities. The ships under Tslavar control were to engage their own free ships, leaving the natives alone.

To any Tslavar spies watching, it would appear as if Commander Datano's message had caused a rift to open between controlled and free ships––a battle among the fleet itself. This would allow the collared officers to hopefully avoid the same fate as the commander as they––for all appearances––would be engaging according to Tslavar orders.

However, the message had another hidden directive as well. They were to put on a show of force, but not target any crucial parts of their ships, and only allow the smallest and least damaging of beam blasts to make any contact, their shields absorbing nearly all of the energy.

It couldn't go on indefinitely, but it could at least buy them a little time as they tried to figure out what to do next.

In the meantime, Eddie was suddenly––and rather unexpectedly––free to plot a direct course to engage the Tslavar ships orbiting the sun. Once clear of the fighting, he immediately spooled up his warp drive.

"Hang on," the AI said. "We're gonna warp."

They'd all seen the scans coming from the sun, and they knew the portal was slowly being pulled from within. There was simply no time for chitchat and discussion. Eddie just fired up his systems and warped.

A second later they emerged in the vicinity of the Tslavar ships, their crackling blue warp residue the only sign they had arrived. Eddie's shimmer was fully functional once more, and the strand of hair Hunze had gifted him to help power it was bursting with energy so close to the sun.

The Tslavar ships, however, were surprisingly visible. They were both shimmer-cloaked under normal circumstances, but with all of the fighting going on far away at the blue planet and its moon, the casters usually focusing their energy on maintaining those massive spells had diverted their talents toward recovering the portal deep within the sun.

And it was working.

Even without the Ootaki woman's hair in play, the combined magic users of the two ships were slowly making progress. The extracted essences of the magic-containing plant life the one ship had recovered and brought back to this system was proving difficult, if not outright impossible, for the aliens to command. The power was there in abundance, but something about it simply would not mesh with the Tslavar magic.

"It does not matter," Captain Jimtee messaged the other ship. "We are making progress. The portal will emerge, in time, and then the true invasion shall begin."

It was at that moment the impact from Eddie's rail gun sabots slammed into the shielding of the ship closest to the sun, forcing it to immediately divert all magic to its protective spells. That ship had already been tagged with the tracking round some time before, and as such their shields had adjusted to that type of attack days prior, diminishing the efficacy of the rounds.

Had Eddie shot at Jimtee's ship first, some significant damage might have been incurred, but it was a toss of the coin, and the other ship was fired upon first. Thus the Tslavar captain's craft avoided the initial barrage intact. In any case, Eddie had to be careful. Hunze was aboard one of those craft, so all they could do was disable them, if possible.

"We are under attack!" Ulus blurted. "All casters, divert your power to defenses!"

Jimtee clenched his jaw with frustration. It was a shimmer-cloaked vessel of some sort, but one attacking with the cursed weaponry of this galaxy. "Pull us away while they are engaging the other ship, and have all energy directed to casting a shimmer disabling spell."

"Sir? That will leave us defenseless."

"We must see our enemy to engage properly, and while they are preoccupied with the others, we will have a brief opportunity to target them based on the trajectory of their projectiles. One good hit from our casters and we shall have a visible target, even if their shimmer retains some of its power."

"Of course," Ulus replied, immediately relaying the orders.

Eddie was coming around for another pass while the Tslavar ships shifted their position in response to his initial attack.

"What do we do?" Ripley asked as the ships stacked in a defensive posture. "We can't just shoot them up. Hunze is on board one of them."

"Can we determine which craft?" Bawb asked, the magic in the braid of his love's hair crackling with magical potential so close to the sun. "If so, I will direct all of my power upon the other," he said with grim resolve. "I care not for taking prisoners."

He intended to empty his magical stores if need be. Anything to save Hunze. And there was logic to his reasoning. Two ships put them at a disadvantage, even cloaked. But one on one, they had a chance. And if Ara could somehow break away from the battle on Earth, her powers on top of theirs could turn the tide.

Eddie let off another salvo from his rail gun, but it was met with a near immediate flash of massive magic from the farther ship, rocking him violently from the impact.

"What the hell was that?" Ripley asked, checking Eddie's readouts. "We seem to be okay, but that was huge."

Charlie felt something with his new senses. And it wasn't good.

"Shit, it took down our shimmer," he said.

"It seems to be working," Eddie replied.

"Nope. It's casting all right, but we're visible enough for them to target us now."

"How can you possibly know that?" Ripley asked.

"New stuff is afoot," he replied. "Just trust me, Rip."

The teen knew better than to question Charlie on such matters and refocused her attention on the weapons systems as Eddie tried to compensate for the dual attacks now bombarding his defenses.

They were on their heels in an instant. Not the outcome they'd expected.

"Eddie, get us clear!" she yelled as another series of magical attacks flew true.

"No! We must retrieve Hunze!" Bawb barked.

"Dude, we won't retrieve anything if we're blown to pieces," Ripley shouted back.

"She's right, Bob. We're using all of our power on defense, now. We need to regroup," Charlie agreed. "Get us clear, Eddie."

The AI ship didn't hesitate, firing his drives up on full, violently throwing them clear of the incoming salvo of deadly spells cast by the pair of Tslavar ships.

The deadly assassin stewed in a rage but held his tongue. He knew his friends were right, but his fury was beginning to compromise his objectivity. They would regroup and plan. And then they would get her back, whatever the cost.

CHAPTER SIXTY-NINE

Eddie's now-visible shape quickly shrank into the distance, leaving the Tslavar ships to their own devices, for the time being. But the AI ship remained close enough to monitor the Tslavars, planning how best to retrieve their friend from the enemy's clutches.

"They are running away," Ulus said with a satisfied sneer. "Cowards."

"No, Ulus, they will be back," Jimtee said with certainty. "We have merely bought ourselves some time."

"But we can destroy them, sir. We possess far more power than they do."

"We do, but they have already forced us to divert it from our original task. You forget, we are not here to fight this day, but to retrieve our fleet. *That* is our primary objective. And if we do not hurry, it is only a matter of time before other ships join that one. We simply cannot afford to delay for a hunt. Our casters are already working to their limits."

Ulus realized his enthusiasm for battle had gotten the better of him. "Of course, you are correct, Captain. My apologies."

Jimtee rested his hand on his number one's shoulder.

"Passion for battle is nothing to be ashamed of, Ulus. But sometimes we must forego the glory of combat for less exciting, but equally essential tasks. Have the casters continue their work at once."

The Tslavar captain paced the command chamber as his orders were put into play. They were making progress with the portal, but it was extremely slow going. They'd pulled it close to the surface, but that was nowhere near far enough to be of use to their waiting fleet.

Unfortunately, the sheer amount of power required to pull it from the blazing plasma of this enormous sun--all while keeping the spells preventing their ships from combusting in the process--was simply not going to be enough.

Not if he hoped to complete the task before either the pestering little ship or more of its brethren came to hector them once more. Though he had hoped to save his prize for himself, holding the magic in reserve for his own needs as the spoils of war, he knew what had to be done.

"Fetch the Ootaki," he commanded.

Hunze was resting in one of the vacated officers' quarters, a slave once more, but one afforded the comfort of a private room. This was more for Jimtee's sake than hers, though. The thought of possessing his very own Ootaki, and one with such a massive growth of hair--though the lower half had been shorn by some prior owner--was intoxicating.

He could feel the power she contained in her hair. That which had been untouched was first growth and never shorn. The energy potential of such a find was unheard of for any but the most powerful of individuals, and even then, that required capture and enslavement from birth. Something a man such as himself could never afford.

It was a shame she had lost half of her hair at some point,

but that did not diminish the magic contained in the remaining locks atop her head. Even as a non-magical being, Jimtee had felt the power when he placed the control collar around her neck, her braid brushing against his hand.

She had been injured when they took her, her hand bleeding as she lay unconscious on the grassy knoll overlooking the ocean. Jimtee had bandaged her injury himself, not wishing any other to feel the sheer power she contained. It was selfish and folly, he knew, but a glimmer of hope had ignited within him. Hope that she would be his.

But now things had changed. They simply did not have the time to retrieve their prize at their leisure. It was a blow, to be certain, but keeping her for himself was simply not meant to be. He had a higher loyalty, and it demanded his service. His sacrifice.

This Ootaki would be shorn, and her magical hair used to rip the portal free of its fiery prison, setting in motion an invasion the likes of which this galaxy had never seen.

The golden-haired woman was carried to the command chamber and placed at his feet. She was finally rousing after so long unconscious. Whatever had been done to her had left her dead to the world for a great long while, but now her senses were returning.

Jimtee noted the fine lines of her cheekbones as he watched her lovely eyes flutter open. The disorientation behind them disappeared in a flash, a look of hard panic making her pupils flare as she took in her surroundings.

The Ootaki's hands flashed to her neck, her fingers pulling desperately at the golden collar firmly attached there. Jimtee watched her efforts with a dispassionate gaze. He'd seen many wake to the reality of slavery over his career, and this one would be no different.

Well, perhaps a little different, for she was already a slave before, but one who had apparently tasted the sweetness of freedom, for a time, at least.

"Good, you are awake," the Tslavar captain said. "I hope you rested well."

"Where am I?" Hunze asked, pushing herself up to a seated position. "This is not Earth."

"No, you are aboard my ship," the Tslavar replied. "I am Captain Jimtee. And you are now mine."

"I belong to one man alone, and you are not him," she replied as she rose to her feet, standing tall, sizing him up with a rage in her eyes that he had never before seen in an Ootaki.

This one was indeed different. And so very powerful. He would enjoy breaking her, he decided. It had been some time since he'd had the pleasure of such a task, and this slave would prove an interesting challenge.

"*Nari pa,*" he said, casting a minor shock spell.

Hunze staggered and fell to the deck. A hint of a smile teased the corners of Jimtee's lips. Oh yes, this would be fun, indeed.

The Ootaki woman pushed herself back to her knees, then, to his amazement, rose to her feet once more, staring at her feet as she regained her senses. She *was* powerful, indeed. And it was that power he needed to retrieve the portal.

Jimtee's fun and games would have to wait, he accepted reluctantly. Duty took priority.

He pulled his razor-sharp blade from its sheath and strode casually toward the collared slave. He would take her hair and complete his task. Only then would he have the time to continue breaking her spirit.

Ulus watched the whole exchange. He'd seen Jimtee deal with far more difficult prisoners in the past. This one, while challenging, would undoubtedly fall to his captain's skilled hands.

Jimtee stopped in front of the Ootaki woman, taking her chin in his hand, raising her face so he could see her expression as he cut her hair from her head. It was just as he felt the hand wielding the knife freeze in place that he noted the unnerving golden glow behind the furious woman's eyes.

This was *not* normal.

Ulus realized something was wrong, immediately casting powerful stun spells at the slave. But the magic bounced off of her like water from an oily surface. Hunze turned her attention to him and whispered a spell. A killing spell.

Ulus did not even have the opportunity to cry out as the life was torn from his body, the empty shell of his remains crumbling to the ground.

A sharp flash of something unfamiliar raced through Jimtee's veins. Panic.

"But this is impossible," he blurted, struggling with all his might to move his knife closer, but no matter how hard he tried, his efforts were in vain. "Ootaki cannot use their magic!"

A wicked grin flicked across Hunze's lips. "This one can."

And she knew all the way to her core that it was true. All of the deadly knowledge Bawb had gifted her, fed into her mind via the neuro-stim by her love, was no longer a jumble of unusable spells and arcane wisdom. He had done something to her back on the bluffs. Something impossible.

The bandage fell from her hand, revealing pristine, healed flesh. There was not a trace of her wound.

She felt a warm glow deep in her chest as her new reality became clear. Yes, Bawb *had* done something impossible, and he'd done it for her. She had gifted him all of her hair, and with love. And somehow, he had gifted it back.

Somehow, he had found a way, blending his blood with hers. His magic. Using an ancient spell to bind their gifts and love as one. The hair on her head was more powerful than ever before, and she now possessed full control of it. The first ever magic-wielding Ootaki.

The rest of the crew had been attempting to attack her as she was coming to terms with her new gift, but Bawb's assassin knowledge flowed through her instinctively. Hunze cast defensive spells, stun spells, slaying spells, all without even realizing she'd been doing it.

In seconds, all of the Tslavars in the chamber, save Jimtee, were dead or disabled.

"Something's going on with one of the ships," Ripley said from their observation position in the distance.

"Yeah, the one closer to the sun just fell out of position. The one without the tracker. I think it's the ship Hunze is on. Something appears to have happened to it."

Charlie looked at his friend. Bawb was beside himself with worry.

"Okay, it's not perfect, but we need to take advantage of this opportunity," he said. "Get us in there, Eddie."

The AI ship wasted no time, immediately accelerating toward the wavering ship, ready to engage. But inside the Tslavar craft, a different sort of fight was already underway.

Hunze's hair was aglow with golden fire, the sheer power of the sun so close supercharging her magic to unheard-of levels. Sweat beaded on Jimtee's brow from the effort as he fought to move his knife even a fraction of an inch. But he couldn't. The Tslavar captain was frozen in place.

She smiled at him, the control collar he had once thought so powerful snapping to pieces and falling to the floor, sending an acid flash of fear through the Tslavar's body as he tried to cast with all his might, calling forth the deadliest spell he knew, using every ounce of magic in his konus.

Hunze raised an eyebrow at the killing spell she so easily deflected, locking eyes with Jimtee.

Then the entire Tslavar ship exploded into a million tiny fragments.

Eddie spun into evasive maneuvers, every bit of his AI processing power blazing to action as he plotted a desperate trajectory to avoid the hurtling debris. His passengers held on tight as his directional shifts threw them about, looks of worry in their eyes. All but Bawb.

The Wampeh merely sat quietly, battered by the twists and turns but not noticing as he stared into nothing, not caring what happened to him now.

Hunze was gone.

CHAPTER SEVENTY

The destruction of the Tslavar ship, and subsequent loss of its casters, had snapped the tenuous grip the remaining ship held on the portal. Their magic users strained with all their might, but try as they did, the portal slid back into the sun as they desperately tried every trick they knew to keep a hold of it.

Not far away, a lone AI ship was skimming through the debris field where the other Tslavar ship had once been, searching for any remains of their friend. It was the least they could do for their distraught friend.

Bawb was a Wampeh Ghalian, and assassins of that order did not cry. But the sheer grief flowing off of him was palpable just the same as he sat in his seat with a distant, stony stare.

Charlie felt for his friend. He could imagine just how much this must hurt, but try as he might, there were simply no words he could think of that would be of any comfort. At least, he thought so, until something off the port bow of the ship caught his eye.

"Uh, Bob?" he said.

"Not now, Charlie."

"No, really. You're going to want to see this."

The Wampeh slowly rose and walked to his friend's side. "This is not a good time, Charlie. I simply cannot--"

Words failed him as he saw what had caught Charlie's attention.

"Impossible," he gasped, then sprang into action, latching his helmet in place as he raced for Eddie's airlock.

"Get us over there, Eddie," Charlie commanded.

"Already on it," the ship replied. "But how is that possible?"

"No idea," Charlie replied. "No idea."

The AI ship raced to its port side, but carefully, as it maneuvered through the debris. Bawb was already tied in to a tether in the open outer airlock door, his heart pounding in his chest so hard he wouldn't have been surprised if you could hear it despite the vacuum.

Hunze was there. Alive. Floating in the void, ensconced in a ball of golden magic, the sun's blazing rays absorbing into her hair at such close range like hot water into a thirsty sponge.

She turned her glowing gaze, fixing it on Bawb with a smile that threatened to make his heart burst from his chest. Ignoring his own safety, Bawb pushed off from the ship, drifting straight for the impossible woman floating in the void.

His arms wrapped around her tightly, pulling her to him as the auto-retrieval winch began reeling them both back into the ship. Hunze pressed her head to the visor of his helmet, and despite the barrier, he could feel her flesh against his. Everything was going to be all right.

"What the hell?" Charlie exclaimed when the couple was safely inside the ship. "How is that even possible?"

Bawb couldn't take his hands off Hunze, but he did manage to answer Charlie to the best of his ability given the emotions flooding his body.

"I did not know if it would work," he said. "It was such an arcane spell."

"What spell? What did you do, Bob?"

The assassin kissed his love's head tenderly, then turned to his friend. "I had Cal assist me in creating a neuro-stim connection to help Hunze learn to protect herself," he said. "To share with her my abilities."

"Yeah, we know, Bob. But we all saw how poorly that went. She couldn't cast worth a damn."

Bawb chuckled. "Yes, that is true. But I devised a means for her to overcome that issue. To control her power."

"What did you do, dude?"

"I gave her my heart," he said, plainly. "And with it, my power. You see, she gave her hair to me, out of love. I merely returned the gesture, blending our gifts as one. As a result, she now controls her own magic. It is a part of her forevermore."

And even as he heard the words, Charlie realized that was indeed what had happened. He could smell the new shift in power. Sense it. It was exactly as Bawb had said. They were connected through Hunze's massively powerful magic hair. Only there was something else. Something they hadn't expected.

"Uh, guys," Charlie said, realizing what this meant. "There's something you should know."

A blast interrupted him, shaking the ship and forcing Eddie to quickly dive into evasive maneuvers.

"Tslavars on our six!" Ripley shouted out, trying to target them manually with the rail gun.

"Let me shoot!" Eddie said. "I'm a supercomputer, Rip. Let me aim!"

"I've got this!" the teen replied, firing off another salvo, the shots going wide.

Charlie cracked his neck, his power surging to the surface. "No. *I've* got this."

Without a word, Charlie cast a massive spell, sending it out not just to the Tslavar ship nearby, but through the entirety of the solar system. Moments later, the comms went nuts.

"Uh, Charlie?" Eddie said, confused. "What did you just do?"

The Tslavar ship now floated harmlessly nearby, all aggressions ceased. And from what the AI had just heard over the comms systems, every alien ship had just done the same. The invasion had abruptly ceased, every ship left drifting quietly. The scanners all flashed with the new status update as Earth's forces stood down, shifting to a very unexpected observational footing.

"Charlie?" Bawb said with a very raised brow.

"Yeah, about that," he replied. "You remember how you and me and Ara all kind of merged our power a little while ago?"

"It is not something one would forget," Bawb replied.

"Yeah, well, when that happened, I got looped into your power. The power from Hunze's hair you were using."

"I recall," Bawb said. "But what you just did appears to be excessive even for that bond."

"That's what I'm getting to. You see, whatever you just did with Hunze, well, you and I are already linked. And now it looks like she's tied in as well."

Realization dawned on the Wampeh. "This is a significant development," he finally said.

"I know, right?"

"Uh, guys? A little information, please?" Ripley said.

"Right. Sorry," Charlie replied. "So, the thing is, I can sort of draw from, well, whatever this is, now. A mix, I guess. Ara's power. Hunze's. My own."

"Wait, what? But you just froze an entire fleet from what everyone is saying. Like *all* of them, Charlie. How the hell did you do that?"

"I don't know, exactly. I just did, okay? Look, it means no more dying, all right? And the collars won't do anything while the Tslavars are out of commission. So we can cut the things off without worrying about triggering them."

Bawb nodded, taking the shocking information in remarkable stride, given the magnitude of just what that meant.

"I propose we tow this Tslavar craft back to Dark Side Base, where we can properly remove and imprison the crew. We can leave the other ships to the rest of the fleet. The AI network will better know what to do with them all."

"Works for me, man," Charlie said as they cast a magical tow line to the Tslavar ship and began the trip home. "Freeze 'em all and let Cal sort 'em out," he said with a laugh, the stress of the past weeks finally melting away.

It was all going to be okay. Different, but okay. And that was something he could live with just fine.

CHAPTER SEVENTY-ONE

Several weeks had passed since the abrupt cessation of hostilities in the skies above Earth, and Charlie and his friends had taken advantage of the welcome respite for some much-deserved rest and relaxation.

Leila had insisted that Charlie and she go on a proper vacation this time, and he had agreed. Only it was not exactly what he'd anticipated.

Rather than Bali or some other tropical paradise, his queen had dragged him off into space, their newly tattooed friend flying back with them to visit the Kalamani people who had saved her life.

For Charlie, the opportunity to meet a magic-using people in his own galaxy was an enormous rush. His Zomoki friend had long posited that perhaps if his own kind had long enough to evolve, they too might become a power-wielding culture, one day.

But here, in the far reaches of a distant system, a far more primitive culture was already using magic as part of their daily lives, much as Ara had theorized could be possible. It seemed that in the absence of machinery, and with a native flora that absorbed their sun's magical energy readily, the Kalamani had done precisely what she'd said they might. Namely, learned to use what was all around them.

Ara was thrilled for the opportunity to meet the elders of the tribe, as well as the white-inked shaman who had saved Rika's life. It was only natural she'd want to tag along for the trip, as curious to meet these unusual beings as she was. But she was very understated about it, moving slowly and speaking softly when she first met the tribe's elders, realizing a distant relative of hers had possibly once terrorized worlds in this distant galaxy.

Rika, for her part, came to pay her respects to the village elders, and particularly the shaman who had given her so rare a gift. Only once she'd regained consciousness after her near-mortal injuries had she learned just how little of the pigment that was now an integral part of her body had existed.

He'd used the last of it saving her. Rebuilding her. Creating her in a new form. It would take much time and effort to find the rare plant from which the white material was extracted, and it might be another shaman years down the line who finally replenished the supply. But Rika was a part of the tribe now, and ever more would they welcome her as one of their own. A protector of the Kalamani.

Jo accepted a ceremonial tattoo during the visit, the shaman insisting that the woman who had not slept, eaten, or even moved while her friend lay injured was worthy of the honor. The cyborg had no idea if the magic-laced ink would do anything in conjunction with her mechanical systems, but the design was pleasing to her eye regardless.

Not long after, with their rather unusual vacation behind them, Charlie and Leila flew back to Earth with Ara, leaving Rika to spend some more time with the tribe. To learn how to wield her new power properly. Hers was a magic of an entirely new variety, and it was *strong*. It would take time to get it fully under control, but with the shaman's tutelage, the spellcaster from Earth had high hopes for success.

It was a heady thing, what had been accomplished. A new connection between worlds had been opened, one that would endure and grow. And growth was on Charlie's mind, as he brought back many viable clippings of the Kalamani's prized vegetation on their return to Earth. There was no telling if it would flourish on his planet, or if it would be capable of absorbing the different sun's power, but that was for Cal and the others to figure out.

Regardless, a new existence had begun. One where magic seemed to be very much a part of this galaxy's fabric.

"Hey, you guys miss us?" Leila asked as she and Charlie walked into Bawb and Hunze's place to join them for a welcome back dinner.

The couple had opted to remain at home for their respite. A staycation, as Charlie called it. And they'd certainly earned it.

"Of course we did," Hunze replied, hugging her friend warmly.

"Any news since we've been gone?" Charlie asked his assassin friend as he gave him a massive bear hug. One which the normally stoic man actually returned in kind, for once.

"A new truce, Charlie," Bawb replied. "An alliance has been formed with the Urok people."

"Excellent! So I take it they got all of the collars off without a problem?"

"It was a rather simple affair, without the Tslavars actively trying to use them," Bawb replied.

Charlie grinned at the prospect. "We've just made contact with not one, but two new races, Bob. I mean, I know that's not a big thing, where you're from, but for us Earth folks, this is kinda huge."

"I know it is, Charlie. And there's something else you may find interesting."

"Oh?"

"Yes. You see, when the Uroks were freed, the AIs had to find and uncloak all of the Tslavar forces hidden within the fleet. I helped them, obviously."

"Obviously," his friend replied with a chuckle.

"There were far more of them than expected, really. But once we'd stripped them of their magical tools and weapons, they were simply placed in temporary confinement pending their being sent to more permanent facilities. They are being , overseen by a rather unamused AI, who took their attack on the planet a bit personally."

"Understandable."

"I think so. But what was interesting was the reaction of the Drooks to their newfound freedom. You see, we suddenly possessed the Tslavar ship, but it was a craft that would not fly by your world's means."

"Of course," Charlie said. "So I guess it's just parked somewhere to rot."

"No. That's the amazing thing," Bawb said. "The Drooks were so grateful for their freedom that they volunteered to power the ship. They're going to take it out to explore the galaxy, only not as slave labor, but as full and free members of the crew."

That bit of news actually *was* unexpected, but Charlie guessed it made sense in a way. The Drooks had their entire existence based around flying ships. To suddenly give that up would leave them without purpose. Even for a former slave, that could be maddening.

"So, they're going to become explorers," Charlie said. "Free to see the galaxy. Good for them."

Bawb paused, a long silence in the air.

"What is it, man?" Charlie asked.

"There is still one thing we are going to have to deal with eventually, you know."

"The Tslavar captives?"

"Them too. But what I refer to is the ones who sent them. The ones on the other side of the portal," Bawb replied. "We have won for now, and the planet is safe. But we may not always be here to defend it."

"What are you saying, Bob?"

"What I'm saying is, we may have to actively deal with the aggressors on the other side, and sooner rather than later."

Charlie pinched the bridge of his nose and let out a sigh. "You know what? You're probably right. But for now, at least, let's just have a quiet dinner among friends."

As if on cue, cacophony rang out through the house as Ripley and her family burst through the front door. Baloo was with her, Charlie noted, padding alongside his teenage friend, sniffing the air for treats.

But still more came streaming into the house. Even some of Ripley's metal-limbed extended family had been invited to the homecoming shindig. It seemed Bawb and Hunze had rolled out the welcome mat, and it was going to be quite a bit more than the little affair Charlie had anticipated.

"Sorry, my friend," Bawb said with a warm grin. "It will be dinner among friends, for certain, but I fear it will not be a quiet one by any means."

As the cheerful greetings gave way to excited storytelling and enthusiastic catching up on all that had happened in recent days, Charlie felt himself slowly relax and slip into the groove of the festivities.

Yes, it would be a full evening, he mused as he pulled Leila in close and kissed her forehead before she hurried off to help Hunze and Ripley's madman of a father set to work in the kitchen. But they were home now, and safe. And the portal-- and whatever lay on the other side--could wait another day.

BUT WAIT, THERE'S MORE!

Follow Charlie on his continuing adventures in the fifth book of the Dragon Mage series:
Portal Thief Charlie

ALSO BY SCOTT BARON

Standalone Novels

Living the Good Death

The Clockwork Chimera Series

Daisy's Run

Pushing Daisy

Daisy's Gambit

Chasing Daisy

Daisy's War

The Dragon Mage Series

Bad Luck Charlie

Space Pirate Charlie

Dragon King Charlie

Magic Man Charlie

Star Fighter Charlie

Portal Thief Charlie

Odd and Unusual Short Stories:

The Best Laid Plans of Mice: An Anthology

Snow White's Walk of Shame

The Tin Foil Hat Club

Lawyers vs. Demons

The Queen of the Nutters

Lost & Found

ABOUT THE AUTHOR

A native Californian, Scott Baron was born in Hollywood, which he claims may be the reason for his rather off-kilter sense of humor.

Before taking up residence in Venice Beach, Scott first spent a few years abroad in Florence, Italy before returning home to Los Angeles and settling into the film and television industry, where he has worked as an on-set medic for many years.

Aside from mending boo-boos and owies, and penning books and screenplays, Scott is also involved in indie film and theater scene both in the U.S. and abroad.